"You use your guilt to keep yourself from daring to love anyone else, to keep from taking that risk. I won't be a surrogate woman for your dreams. If . . . if you want us to go anywhere you're going to have to let go of the past."

Carl turned from the window and walked to her then. "You're right," he said, and the tension in him made her reach out instinctively and touch his hand. He grasped hers when she did, and the contact was electric. "But it's easy to say and not so easy to do." Their eyes held, and the air seemed filled with the same current. She felt a helpless ache for him for what he couldn't bring himself to say.

Gently he laid a hand against her cheek, then slid it to the back of her head. Then, slowly, he drew her closer. "I have to kiss you," he whispered raggedly.

Beth lifted parted lips to his and he took them with a heated urgency. He let the kiss deepen until he could hear a muffled moan from deep in her throat . . .

"Engrossing and suspenseful. Will delight connoisseurs of romance."

—*Rave Reviews*

* * *

"A tale of madness and murder . . . passion and love. The tension mounts page by page."

—*Rendezvous*

* * *

"Once you pick it up, you won't be able to put it down!"

—*Affaire de Coeur*

BITTERSWEET

Sylvie

SOMMERFIELD

PARRAGON

This title first published in Great Britain in 1991 by
SEVERN HOUSE PUBLISHERS LTD.

This edition licensed by Severn House Publishers Ltd., by arrangement Warner Books, Inc., produced by Magpie Book Ltd., and published by Parragon Book Service Ltd in 1994

A copy of the British Library CIP data is available from the British Library.

ISBN 0 75250 072 4

Printed and bound in Great Britain

This book is dedicated with sincere thanks
to Fredda Isaacson, editor extraordinaire,
who created the proverbial silk purse.
Without her continued support and her guidance
this work might never have been finished.

* CHAPTER 1 *

She walked the beach, her sandaled feet leaving a light impression in the sand that was quickly wiped away by the coaxing waves.

He stood several feet away, feeling as if he were somehow intruding on her love affair with the wind and the sea.

The honey-gold hair that usually tumbled to her shoulders was lifted by the breeze to blow about her, and her tanned skin turned gold in the light of the sun. She was slim and so very beautiful in her faded jeans and shirt.

Then she saw him and smiled, extending her arms. He could feel the quick pulse of excitement leap within him, and he went to her, taking her hand in his.

Laughter danced in her blue eyes, and love teased a smile about the mouth she raised to meet his kiss.

She tasted slightly of salty sea and a sun-kissed breeze. Her mouth was giving, as always, and he stored this memory of her with the hundreds he cherished.

Had he always loved her? Of course. He couldn't remember the days when he hadn't. The void he had lived in before she had come had vanished as she had danced from room to empty room, lighting the corners of his mind.

Had anything ever really mattered before her? He couldn't remember, for before she had stepped into his life he had never tasted love—not love the way they knew it. He put his arms about her and swung her feet from the ground, listening to the music of her soft, throaty laughter.

"You're warm," he whispered against her throat.

"It's the sun."

"No, it's you."

"Make love to me, Carl," she whispered.

"Here?" He laughed shakily, knowing he wanted that more than his next breath.

"Here . . . in the sun. Make love to me."

Now he swung her up in his arms and carried her to a grassy knoll.

His body hungered to be part of hers. From the first time he had taken her, when he had felt the hardness of him press deep within her, he had been filled with an insatiable passion.

Her skin was smooth beneath his hands. Her mouth—open, hot, and hungry—moved across his flesh until he could have shouted his joy.

He watched her head roll from side to side, her eyes closed. He felt her hands grasp him spasmodically. He felt her slender legs about his thrusting hips. It was an agony of gasping, groaning pleasure, and he reached for the completion only in her power to bestow. But the sun had begun to dim—a gray mist with fingers of its own was tearing them apart. He was trying to love her, yet he could hear her scream. He saw her mouth open in agony. He cried out her name in anguish so deep it tore his soul in two.

She was sliding away from him, carried in a sea of blood, and he struggled to grasp her, only to have her slip from his fingers.

No pain had ever been like this. No agony in his life had ever burned so deep. He screamed her name, over and over and over.

The phone rang insistently, tearing him from the horror of the dream, pulling him to a sitting position. His body was bathed in sweat, and he was trembling.

His teeth were clenched. He knew he had bitten his lips—he could taste the salt of his own blood. He gasped for breath, and tears were hot in his eyes. He stared at the phone with a hatred so violent that he had to restrain himself from ripping it off the wall and heaving it across the room.

He hated the recurring dream, yet for some masochistic reason he held it, because it was his last touch with Sara. Because no matter how good the dream was when it started, it always ended this way.

He wiped the sweat from red-rimmed eyes, cursed softly under his breath, and reached for the intruding phone.

"Hello?" His voice was harsh with sleep.

"Carl?"

"Yeah. Who's this, and what the hell are you calling me so early for?" He was in no mood to be kind.

"Carl? It's me—Joe."

"Marks! What the hell?"

"Carl, for Christ's sake listen before you lose your temper. I'm sorry if the call upset you, but I'm desperate, and I'm scared."

This brought Carl's mind to sudden awareness. He had never known Joe Marks to be afraid of anything.

"Sorry. What's the matter?"

"You heard the news this morning?"

"Hell, no. I was asleep 'til you called."

Joe Marks, who knew more about Carl than anyone, was aware of the memories that haunted him.

"It's been rough?" Joe asked gently.

"Yeah."

"Why don't you—"

"Forget it, Joe, I don't need a shrink, I just need... Forget it. What do you want? You said you were desperate. That doesn't sound like you."

"We've had a murder in Helton."

There was a long pause while Carl reached for a pack of cigarettes and lit one. Then his voice was hoarse and bitter. "Another one?"

"Jesus, Carl, I don't want to dig up anything, but this is a different kind of thing."

"Murder is murder."

"The hell it is."

"Joe—"

"Look, this is a little more than just murder. I need your

help. Now, before you say no, at least listen. I've got people close to panic. I've had twenty-five calls today. You can handle something like this better than I can. You're the expert. I really need help."

"Joe, I can't."

"Christ, Carl, you owe me. I don't want to push you, but you should be the first to understand. Sometimes personal hurts have to be put aside. Phil Greggory has been hot on my trail since the news of this murder broke."

"Good old Phil." Carl chuckled grimly. "He'd like nothing better than to get his hands on me and be able to prove what I'm pretty sure he suspects."

"Your old friends would go down with you, buddy. Phil's a bastard. He never could swallow what happened to you after Sara died. He's pretty sure you lied, and a whole lot of people swore to it. He's still out for my blood and yours."

"He'll never be able to prove anything if I stay out of his hands."

"Carl, I need help. This murder is more than ugly. There's a lot of pressure . . ."

"Not to mention the fact that this is an election year for Helton," Carl replied dryly.

"Sure, that, too," Joe admitted humorously. "But that isn't all. You know damn well we haven't had a murder around here since—well, for a long time. Folks are scared."

"I was supposed to start my vacation tomorrow. This is the first one I've had in three years."

"Carl, you . . ."

"Don't remind me again," Carl replied, disgusted with the sudden turn of events. "I'll be up tomorrow."

"Thanks."

"Don't thank me yet, Joe. I'm stayin' two days—you understand? After that, I'm gone. I worked hard for this vacation."

"Okay, Carl, what time you comin'?"

"I'll be up first thing in the morning. Let me see, that's Wednesday. And I'm leavin' Friday morning, no matter what," he warned.

"That's good. At least maybe you can help us get started in the right direction. And plan on coming out to my house to see Sally. She'd never forgive you if you came to town without seeing her."

"Yeah. Maybe I could finally convince her she picked the wrong guy."

"Maybe she'll call your bluff. What'll you do then?"

"Probably run like hell." Carl laughed.

"I thought so. Besides, after being married to me, Sal could have no doubt that she picked the better man."

"Joe, old times just can't be picked up so easy."

"So, let them lie. Start over. But start here, where you belong, and where people want to help."

Carl sighed. "See you tomorrow."

Joe chuckled lightly. "Okay."

"What's so funny?"

"I know you too well, Carl. You're a bulldog. Once you get your teeth into this, you won't be able to leave until you know who's guilty."

"Don't count on that. I'm leaving Friday, one way or the other."

Carl could still hear the assured sound of Joe's voice as he hung up. There was no way he would try to sleep again. The nightmare would return, and he didn't have the strength to face it again.

He was angry with himself for agreeing so easily just because he owed Joe a few favors—well, actually one large favor. At the age of thirty-five, Carl Forrester had seen too much and felt too much. It showed in the grooves around his firm mouth, in the tiny lines beside his eyes, and in the firm set of his jaw, now blue with the stubble of tomorrow's beard. He lay back on the bed, his arms folded behind his head. But even as he relaxed, the ropelike muscles of his chest and arms suggested latent power. His shoulders were broad, and the balance of his body was lean, tapering into what seemed an endless length of legs. Standing, Carl was four inches over six feet.

His eyes were the deep blue of a bottomless sea, and his hair was thick, often unruly, and a deep gold brown. His smile could be heart-stopping, and had melted more than one woman's resistance, yet he had not smiled much lately.

His penetrating gaze had the ability to look through

people to their thoughts and past deeds. Yet his eyes could be compassionate, gentle, and kind.

His peers among the police regarded him as shrewd, clever, determined, and tenacious. He held stubbornly to a rigid set of rules about right and wrong. Over the years he had carried his personal code of ethics like a shield between him and the profession he had chosen. The gentle man was kept well protected.

Carl slowly maneuvered his car through Helton's early evening traffic. His curiosity had gotten the best of him, and he had reasoned to himself that it was just as easy to come up on Tuesday night as it was to get up early Wednesday morning.

Carl knew Helton well. Although he now worked in Cambridge, seventy miles away, he had been raised here in this once-quiet small town. He knew every street and building, and almost all the people, except for the youngsters who attended the small college just outside of town.

It had been almost three years since he had gone to work in Cambridge. He closed his mind to the grief that had caused him to leave Helton. He had closed up the house he had lived in and tried to put the memories behind him by taking a job in a new town. Although he had visited his old friends on occasion, he had not become deeply involved with the comings and goings here, for even after three years, the memories were too painful.

Helton's two main streets crossed each other in the center of the town at a circular island that boasted a miniature Statue of Liberty presented by the Daughters of the American Revolution after long years of benefit balls, teas, and picnics to raise the money. Helton certainly had a character uniquely its own, he reflected. It seemed finished, complete.

Historic houses and brick sidewalks recalled the quieter, gentler living of the past. Yet Carl couldn't ignore the changes: parking garages, a fast-food place where the old movie house had stood, and a couple of high-rise apartments that gentrified what had been a decaying waterfront. There was a new city hall and federal building that had been built since he had left, along with some private office buildings. But for Carl, the beauty lay in an accumulation of memories nothing could ever replace. He had been a part of this city, had gone to school here in slower-moving, more contented times. It was hard for him to accept the fact that once again, the ugliness of murder had come here.

Finding a vacant parking place at what passed for a combination police station and jail, Carl looked across the street at the courthouse and law offices. He automatically locked his car door, dropped the keys in his pocket, and walked slowly up the four cement steps to the entrance.

Inside he gently closed the door behind him. With a small smile on his lips, he looked around a room that he could have sworn had not changed a bit since he had been here last.

Two huge desks were slid together to form an ell. Behind one sat Sergeant Thomas Grimms, and behind the other sat a young, fresh-faced man who glanced up when he heard the door close, then, unimpressed, looked down at his book again. Thomas Grimms had been born to be a policeman—at least, Carl had always thought so. He was a bear of a man with Irish blue eyes that could twinkle in mirth or grow as cold as ice in the face of problems.

"Hello, Grimms. Still protecting the taxpayers, I see?"

Thomas looked up, then blinked a couple of times to make sure he was really seeing Carl.

"Carl Forrester—I'll be damned. Welcome back."

The younger man looked up again, this time in surprise at the tone of Sergeant Grimms's voice. Carl smiled an even broader smile. He was pleased only because he had purposely cultivated an unremarkable image, and it always gratified him to see it work on strangers.

"Toby," Grimms said, "I want you to meet one of the best policemen it's ever been my privilege to know and to work with—Carl Forrester. Carl is chief of detectives over in Cambridge. Carl, this is Toby Mitchell, my new assistant." Toby rose to his feet, his face flushed with embarrassment. He extended his hand. Carl shook it with much more pressure than he knew was necessary, to show this young upstart not to judge by appearances. It was a dangerous thing to do in their line of work.

"What are you doin' here, Carl?" Grimms inquired.

"Joe called me this morning about the murder case. I've

come for a couple of days to see if there's anything I can do to help."

"Well, we certainly need it. It was a messy murder, and we haven't got much to go on."

"Anything you can fill me in on?"

"Not really. Joe will probably want to tell you all the details. If I think of anything, or if you have any questions, you can ask on your way out. Is Joe expecting you now?"

"Nope," Carl grinned. "I told him I was coming up tomorrow."

Tom gave an answering smile. "You just couldn't rest after he told you what had happened. I'll bet he's expecting you. I'll bet he told you deliberately 'cause he knew you wouldn't be able to stay away."

As if in answer to his words, a voice from the other side of the room replied in an amused tone.

"You're right. I figured Carl would be sniffing around here about now."

Both Carl and Tom smiled at the man who leaned against the door frame, his hands in his pockets and a pleased smile on his face.

Joe had been the first friend Carl had made when his family had moved to Helton. They had been in grade school then. They were as different as day and night. Where Carl tended to muscular, solid bulk, Joe was slender, almost thin. His hair was so blond it was almost white, yet his eyes were deep amber. The crinkles at the corners of his eyes told of a deep sense of humor. The rest of his face was all planes and angles.

Joe held out his hand. "It's good to see you back here. You should be running this office, instead of assisting me."

"I didn't come here for any more lectures. I came because you held a club over my head."

"Do you think I would have brought you here if it wasn't a serious emergency?"

Joe held Carl's eyes a few moments before Carl smiled and walked past him into the office.

Joe closed the door behind them. Carl eased himself slowly down into a soft leather chair with a deep sigh and Joe went around the desk and sat in his chair. He lifted a brown folder from the desk and handed it across. As Carl read, Joe kept his eyes on his friend. The last thing in the folder was an eight-by-ten photo of the victim, Martha Dexter. She was a bright-eyed, smiling girl with shoulder-length brown hair and wide green eyes, and she was very young.

"God," Carl whispered, "she's just a kid. What could she have done to make someone kill her?"

"That's just it, Carl," Joe replied, running his fingers through his hair in a gesture that revealed his frustration. "From all the checking I could do, this girl was popular. Everybody liked her."

"Not everybody. I'd say from the description of the cause of death that whoever it was hated her a lot—he pounded her face to a pulp before he killed her. Almost," Carl mused, "as if it was her looks he was trying to destroy.

"Okay, so fill me in on the details," Carl said as he laid the folder aside.

"It happened sometime between ten-thirty and eleven-thirty. The body was found out in Parma Woods. We've come to the conclusion it had to be pretty well planned."

"Why?"

"Because Martha wouldn't have gone there on her own, and," their eyes met across the desk as Joe said hoarsely, "he left a note with the body. It's a passage from the Bible. It's extremely unlikely that he'd calmly take pen in hand and find a suitable passage *after* the murder."

"A quote from the Bible that justifies murder?"

"I can't believe it, either. I'm telling you, I'm afraid we've got a nut running around who thinks he's the right arm of God or something. Look." Joe handed the note to Carl and watched his friend's lips tighten as he read it.

"Looks as if he planned ahead, doesn't it?"

"Yeah, it sure does. What else do you know? And who do you have for suspects?"

"We figure he had to be a big man. She was methodically beaten."

"Clues?"

"Not a damn one, except that note."

"Was she raped?"

"No. It was like he killed her, then gave her a sort of funeral. She was in a shallow grave, with her arms crossed over her. All her clothes were neatened—like he was being real careful."

"And the suspects?"

"Well, there's Paul Carterson. He's a young artist, reasonably successful, and engaged to a local girl—a teacher at the high school named Amy Realton."

"Why's he suspect?"

"He came back to Helton about a year ago. He left because of a disagreement over a girl. He found out he was being two-timed, lost his temper, and beat the other guy almost to death. Threatened the girl, too. Her parents and the boy's brought charges. When it was all over, Paul thought it wiser to leave town for a while."

"Why does that make him a suspect?"

"The girl was Martha Dexter."

"Who else have you got?"

"We got this one kid—you know, the tough kind who's always acting like Brando in *The Wild One*. He has no alibi for the time of the killing. Name's Michael Brodie."

"Yeah?" Carl prompted. He felt Joe was holding something he was unsure of for last.

"You're not going to like this."

"What?"

"The last person who saw her alive was the young priest at St. Catherine's."

"You're kidding me," Carl laughed. "You don't actually suspect a priest?"

"Well, I wouldn't, but when I sent for some information on him, I found out some things that he'd rather not have known."

"Like what?"

"The last parish this priest was in, he lost his temper over something and beat up the son of one of his wealthy parishioners." Joe laughed. "I think he was transferred here as some sort of punishment. St. Catherine's isn't exactly the ultimate goal for an up-and-coming young priest, now, is it? He could be angry, bitter, or even off the edge, couldn't he? Besides that, who could quote the Bible any better?"

"Yes, I guess. I think I'll talk to those three tomorrow. Maybe a new approach by a new face might turn up a clue."

"Good. I'll pick you up in the morning and we'll . . ."

"No, don't bother. There's no sense in our both following the same trails. I need to get a fresh slant on this. Maybe, if I'm not seeing things through your eyes, I can pick up some new details. I think I'll mosey around alone for a while, if you don't mind."

"I don't mind. Maybe you're right. You always were a lone wolf, anyway. Sara always used to say . . ."

Carl's face closed to a rigid coldness that Joe had never seen before. He cursed himself for his stupid slip of the tongue. Sara's name hung between them. Joe could not find the words to apologize, and Carl could not seem to find the words to bridge the silence.

Carl rose and walked to the door. "I'll see you in the morning." His voice was crisp with bitterness.

Joe spoke gently. "I'm sorry."

Carl turned to face him, and said with a desperate stiff smile, "It's all right."

"You've got a place to stay?"

"Yeah, I called ahead. I'll be at the El Rio."

"Why don't you come and stay with Sally and me? We'd be pleased to have you."

"Well, like you say, Joe, I work better as a lone wolf. Explain to Sal for me, will you?"

"Sure. Good night—and thanks."

With a half wave of his hand, he left the room, closing the door behind him. For several minutes, Joe looked at the door, then suddenly slammed his fist on the desk.

"Damn!" he muttered. "He should have taken a punch at me for being so stupid."

When Carl stepped outside, he stood for a few minutes looking down the main street. The cool evening air brushed piles of leaves in tiny swirls across the now almost vacant street. The streetlights made puddles of light at their feet and tiny areas of dark shadows in between. Slowly he walked to his car, his heels clicking sharply on the cold cement. He unlocked the car door and slid under the wheel. Just outside of town he found the El Rio and checked in. He drank a beer from the six-pack he had bought on the way to the motel, then lay down on the bed for some much-needed sleep.

* * *

As Joe walked up the path to his house, the door flew open. Sally Marks had been waiting all afternoon for word from her husband. She was a petite woman of thirty-two, although she looked much younger. She had her black hair twisted in a knot on top of her head and a worried look in her brown eyes.

"Joe?"

"Hi, honey," he said as he slid his arm about her waist and walked in the house with her.

"Did you call him?"

"Yes."

"Will he come?"

"He already has."

"Where is he?"

"At the El Rio. I think he wanted to be alone tonight."

"Can't I at least call him? I'd like to hear his voice, to know that he's really all right."

"It's hard for him, Sal, coming back here like this. Leave him alone—he'll come around."

"Joe, what are friends for? Carl has taken the first step. Can't we try to reach him?"

"Give him time, honey. He'll be here. You know Carl. He has to work things out at his own pace."

"It's been three years."

"I know, but I don't want to push him. If he needs us, we'll be here. Until then, let's just let him play things his way. Okay, hon?"

"Sure, Joe." She smiled and kissed him on the cheek. "Sit down and get comfortable. Dinner will be ready in a few minutes."

Joe stood at the window and watched the shadows lengthen into night. He hoped that Carl's visit would do two things: help find the person who was guilty of this terrible murder, and somehow free him from what was keeping him from coming home.

Deep in thought, Joe ignored the insistent ringing of the phone. Finally, Sally came from the kitchen to answer it.

"Hello. Yes, he is. Just a minute, please." Sally put her

hand over the mouthpiece as Joe turned to her. "It's our charming district attorney," she whispered.

Joe grimaced. "Phil Greggory. What the hell does he want?"

"He sounds very formal."

"He always sounds formal. He's an ass."

Sally laughed softly. "Well, the ass wants to talk to you."

Joe took the receiver from her hand, and his voice was heavy with his annoyance.

"Yeah, Phil, what can I do for you?"

"Joe, I hear we have an out-of-town visitor."

Joe's annoyance was slowly growing into anger. "You sure as hell get your news fast. You got spies in my office?"

"Don't worry about how I get my information. Is it true Forrester's back?"

"Carl came at my request."

"He has no authority in this town. You better remember that."

"I remember a lot of things. One is what a great cop Carl always was, and that your jealousy was always getting in his way. I've asked for Carl's help, and I intend to make use of it."

"You're asking for trouble, Joe."

"Is this some kind of a threat, Phil? If it is, you can shove it."

"It's not so much a threat as a word of caution. You and I both know the reason Carl ran away from here. His coming back can mean trouble for everybody. I'd hate to have to use my office to go digging into something he and his friends don't want circulated."

Joe's grip on the receiver tightened. "I'll tell you what you can do with your office. I'm going to solve this murder, and I'm going to use all the help I can get from Carl. I'll put him on in an official capacity, and if you get in my way, I'll kick you and your office both in the teeth. Get off my back! I'll give you a piece of advice: leave Carl alone."

"Either you're a fool, Joe, or you're covering up something we all should know. Take my advice . . ."

"You and your advice can both go to hell!" Joe slammed down the receiver, his face white with anger and his hands shaking. He turned to look at Sally, and they both realized the tendrils of the past were entangling them in a new nightmare.

* CHAPTER 2 *

Carl couldn't stand the confinement of the motel room. He would not admit to himself that it was fear of the dreams that kept him from bed. Despite the fact that he wasn't really very hungry, and it was already past ten, he left the room and drove toward town. There seemed to be more action than he remembered, and he realized that the college kids had brought new activity with them. Old memories served him well as he gave thought to the few restaurants that might be open late.

He walked into Valentino's, which was a combination restaurant and bar with a latticework wall separating the two sections. He sat at the bar for a while and slowly drank two beers, then he ordered a third and gave instructions for it to be brought to his table.

He walked around the lattice wall and found a seat at one of the few small tables. His beer was set before him, and he was handed a menu by a pert, young waitress who promptly disappeared. He had already decided what he wanted, so he laid the menu aside and looked about him.

He was sitting across the room from the only other customers. The two of them sat together at a table, one facing him, and the other with her back to him. The one facing him was an attractive woman somewhere in her early thirties. She was laughing at something the second woman had just said. Even with her back to him he could tell she was slim. Her hair was dark—almost midnight black—and her skin was a golden tan. She obviously enjoyed the sun.

He had not seen her face yet, and was shaken by an almost urgent desire to do so. Memory brushed him with familiar fingers, and he lit a cigarette, realizing his hands were shaking.

He couldn't take his eyes from her. He realized then that his intent gaze had caught the attention of the woman facing him. She bent forward slightly and spoke rapidly. No matter how it looked, he could not bring himself to avert his eyes—he had to see the dark-haired woman's face.

In a town as small as Helton, everyone knows everyone else. He counted on their knowing Joe as he rose and walked toward their table. As he moved toward them, the woman started to turn around. He was shocked when he realized he was holding his breath. This reaction was beyond his understanding, and he felt a tug of impatient anger at himself. He was like a schoolboy approaching the homecoming queen to ask for a date. If he hadn't felt the strange touch of fear, the situation would have been laughable, yet he had no inclination to laugh at all. By the time he reached their table, she had turned fully to face him.

"I thought I'd best explain that I'm a policeman, before you two ladies decided to call one. I'm Carl Forrester, from Cambridge. I'm a friend of Joe Marks."

"We hadn't reached a state of panic yet," she replied, with a touch of amusement. Her voice had the feel of velvet, yet it scraped his nerves like sandpaper. Somehow it sounded familiar.

Her eyes were blue—the kind of blue that could sometimes hover near purple—and she was very pretty. He was close enough to smell her perfume. It was an elegant wisp of scent that teased and spoke of silk and satin. She had the kind of slim figure that carried well the heavy, oversized white knit sweater she wore atop a dark blue skirt. Several gold chains circled her neck. She wore gold earrings, a fine gold bracelet glittered on one wrist, and a rather expensive gold watch on the other. She also wore one ring, a diamond, but not on her wedding ring finger. Altogether, she was somewhat breathtaking.

"Well, I wanted to nip any anxiety in the bud before you did," he said with a laugh.

"You do not strike me as a man who incites panic in women," she said, laughing with him. Her laugh was throaty and deep, filled with a sensuality she seemed to be unaware of. "My name is Beth Raleigh and this is Eve Pierce. I'm the librarian here in Helton. Please sit down." She motioned to the seat next to her, and Carl slid into it. "Do I know you from somewhere, Mr. Forrester? Your face seems rather familiar."

He wanted to say that her face was more than familiar, that it was somehow part of something special, and that he didn't have the damnedest idea what, but he didn't.

"I don't think we've met." He offered his most charming grin, feeling as if it were frozen on his face. "I would certainly have remembered you."

"You're here because of that murder, aren't you?" Beth said. "It was awful. Martha was such a nice girl."

"You knew her?" Carl asked.

"Yes, we both did. In fact, I've already had to give a statement to Joe. You see, I was at a party where Martha was a guest."

Carl listened to Beth as she continued to talk, but he hardly heard what she said. Her eyes held his as she talked, and a puzzled frown touched her brow, as if she could see within him to the damaged place he had guarded so long and pitied him—a response he couldn't handle.

He could feel his pulse begin to race and his palms sweat. Confusion held him. Why was he suddenly afraid she would see beyond the face he showed to the world? He realized he had to leave before he said or did something he would regret. To keep from losing his grip on himself he had to keep distance between his emotions and all the things the town, and this woman's gaze, seemed to evoke.

"That is very interesting," he said. Not all she had said had penetrated, for most of his concentration had been on Beth herself, but he had cornered some details he'd think about. He rose, "Well, I have a few more things to do before I call it a night. It was nice meeting you both."

If the women were surprised at his abrupt departure, it was nothing compared to Carl's response; he was seized by a panic he could not understand or fight. He made himself a silent promise to keep some distance between himself and

Beth Raleigh. He was entirely too vulnerable, and she was entirely too astute.

He bought another six-pack of beer, then left the restaurant. He drove back to the El Rio thoughtfully, trying to dissect what had happened, but he found no answers. There was a quality about Beth Raleigh that had touched and disturbed him. He couldn't identify it, but he couldn't face it, either.

He parked the car and went to his motel room. He had not eaten, but he had no appetite. He took four aspirins and then stood in a hot shower to ease the tension that pulled every muscle.

As always, the evening hours were the worst. He had to face sleep, and in sleep he had to face dreams. He turned on the television and sipped one beer after another, hoping to blunt his senses until he could sleep one dreamless night. Finally, he drifted into sleep without turning off the television.

Her dress was soft and white and flowed about her suntanned legs to her ankles. Her feet were bare, and the gentle surf caressed them with lacy bubbles. Her hair tumbled about her, and moonlight played through the web of spun gold.

She laughed, and the night air was warmer to him. Her hand held his, and his world was complete.

The sound of soft music came from the portable radio they had brought to the beach house with them, and they danced on the warm sand and drank champagne from paper cups.

Then they lay on the blanket beneath a moon that he was sure had never seen anything as beautiful as she was. They made love slowly, gently, rejoicing in the unique oneness they possessed.

Afterward, very reluctantly, they gathered up the blankets, the basket that held the remains of food and the empty bottles, and walked back down the beach. Then it came again—the terror he could not fight, the blood and weeping, the emptiness and loneliness, and the rage.

Carl Forrester groaned aloud in the empty room. His body was sweat-slicked and his huge hands were closed into fists. He writhed on the tangled sheets. Only the empty television screen was witness to his anguish as he struggled within the torturous grip of his nightmare.

* * *

"Why," Eve said as she and Beth watched Carl leave the restaurant, "he didn't even order any food. That's funny."

"Yes," Beth said softly. Her brow furrowed in a frown of concentration. "I don't know why, but I feel I've seen him someplace before."

"He's rather handsome, in a rough kind of way."

"Eve," Beth said, "don't start matchmaking. Having dinner with you is like playing a role in *Fiddler on the Roof*! Don't you think I'm a little old to be mothered?"

"He seemed rather upset when he saw you."

"Oh, yes," Beth said in a dramatic voice, "I am so beautiful that he was speechless. Come on, Eve, be realistic—and for God's sake, stop trying to find a man for me. I am single by choice, not by chance, and," she held up a hand as Eve started to speak again, "I'll hear no more about it."

Eve surrendered and the conversation turned to other subjects.

Tuesday-night dinners had become a habit for Beth and Eve, who had been close friends since Beth had come to Helton a few years before.

Eve had been a widow for several years, and she and Beth found they had much in common. Their freedom to confide in each other without reservation was unique, and both women valued their relationship.

They usually met at Valentino's to share the ups and downs of the week. Eve laughingly referred to their dinners as confession without penance.

Usually Beth left their meetings feeling buoyant and relaxed, but not tonight. As she moved about her small cottage, she remembered the look in Carl Forrester's eyes as he walked toward her. She had seen him someplace. She was not one to forget people and places. She was also a logical, self-possessed woman not usually given to fantasies, yet she could not deny the feeling that something had been left unfinished between them. From that moment, until she fell asleep two hours later, Carl Forrester did not leave her mind.

* * *

Coffee was all Beth usually had for breakfast. She stood near her sink and sipped the last of her second cup. Then she rinsed it and set the cup and saucer in the sink.

She left the cottage a few minutes later and drove to the center of town, where she parked behind the new library. The old library, which had been dilapidated and dangerous, had been torn down three years before. With the new building had come modern equipment, including microfiche. It was this she planned to use, for it had finally come to her where she had seen Carl before—in a newspaper article. Now all she had to do was find it.

By noon she had searched through at least a year and a half of papers with no luck. She promised herself that she would enlist some help after lunch.

She had just returned from a quick lunch when she was called to the phone.

"Hi, Beth, this is Sally."

"Oh, hi, Sal. I haven't seen you in ages. Did you need something from the library?"

"No, not really," Sally replied. "It's been so long since Joe and I saw you last, we wanted to invite you over for dinner Saturday. You're not busy, are you?"

"Saturday night, no, I'm not busy. What time?"

"Oh, around six-thirty. Is that all right with you?"

"Fine. I'll see you then. 'Bye."

Beth went back to her search, giving no more thought to the engagement she had just made.

—

Sally Marks sat across the breakfast table from Joe, who had been silent for some time, which was very unusual for him.

"Joe? What's wrong?"

"Just about everything, I guess. Why would anyone have wanted to murder Martha?"

"Could the murderer have been a stranger—someone who was just passing through, and is gone now?"

"I thought of that, and even Carl suggested the possibility. But it's unlikely that Martha would have gone out there with someone she didn't know. No, Sal, it was someone from town—someone we know and most likely trust."

"How frightening."

"Yes. What worries me is, will he kill somebody else before I can stop him?"

"What has Carl been doing?"

"I gave him a rundown on everything and a list of everyone I could think of who might be even remotely connected. You know how Carl is. He'll move slow and easy." Joe laughed softly. "He says he's only staying until Friday."

"You find that funny?"

"Don't you? Carl couldn't walk away from this."

"I guess you're right. Devotion was always one of his strong points—or maybe one of his faults. He always puts so much of himself into things that when something happens, it seems to tear a part of him away. How is he really, Joe?"

"I don't know. Maybe I made a mistake in forcing him to come back."

"I wish I could talk to him."

"You know he won't leave without paying you a visit. He was pretty close to you, Sal."

"Maybe that's why he won't. Oh, Joe, I'd hate to believe he was still . . ."

"Look, I'll do my best to get him to stay a little longer. I could invite him over again, but I can't guarantee he'll come. He does things when he's damn good and ready."

"You invite him anyhow, and tell him I won't take no for an answer."

"I'll do that," Joe chuckled.

He rose from the table and helped Sally clean up the dishes. Then he slipped into his jacket, gave her a kiss, and left.

Sally stood by the window and watched Joe back out of the drive. She had been as close a friend to Carl as it was possible for a woman to be. She had been the recipient of his enthusiasm when he was happy, and had supplied the understanding shoulder when tears threatened.

Maybe, she thought, that was why he hadn't come to see her. The pain he held so close now, guarded so fiercely, was too much to share even with her. It scared her to think that Carl would never again be whole, that he would continue to run away until it was too late to retrieve any normal life. That he would always be lonely was a fear she could not push aside.

* * *

Beth was exhausted. After finishing her work, she had spent hours at the microfiche viewer. At five o'clock, when the part-time evening employees arrived, she had decided to work another hour or so. It surprised her when she looked at the clock again and found it was past closing time.

She couldn't believe herself. Carl Forrester had touched her life for only a few minutes, and anything she could learn about him now was truly none of her business. She felt guilty, as if she were peering into a keyhole, yet she could not seem to quit searching.

How far back had she gone? She checked the date on the last paper. Two years! Maybe it was a useless exercise. She must have seen his face somewhere else. Why, then, did she feel it was so important that she keep going.

Beth, old girl, she thought to herself, *you're getting compulsive. One more year, and if you don't find anything, you chuck this idea and forget about him. He's just a ship passing in the night.*

She sighed and stretched to relieve her cramped muscles, then reached for the last card. She flashed the papers by, rapidly scanning headlines and watching for pictures. January, April, May . . . August!

There it was—a large picture of Carl beside one of the most beautiful women she had ever seen. Eagerly she read—first the headlines, then the entire story.

After a while Beth shut off the machine and replaced the microfiche. Tears stung her eyes and she felt guiltier than ever. Probing his past was wrong. She had uncovered a story that was too personal and too painful. Almost absentmindedly, she switched off the lights and locked the library doors. The street where the library sat was nearly deserted, and her heels echoed as she walked to her car.

She wasn't hungry, so she didn't make her usual stop at the grocery store. When she arrived home, she mixed a very strong drink and sipped from it as she ran a bath, then finished it as she soaked in the hot tub.

She could not erase Carl from her mind, and she was surprised at herself. She had had her share of teenage boyfriends, had graduated to college affairs, and once, had even believed she had found what she truly wanted. But that love had died from lack of nourishment. He had wanted so many things that she hadn't. When she looked back now, she knew their relationship had never been what she needed, but the experience had solidified her ideas and ideals. She would know when she had found the right man, and she would settle only for total commitment.

She began to wonder about Carl and why he affected her. He had looked afraid—as if he carried ghosts that terrified him. She understood now that she knew something of him and his love.

She wondered why he had come back to Helton. If she had been in his shoes, she would never have come back. She wondered too about his guilt. The papers, with the exception of one, had crucified him. She remembered the description of the trial.

". . . Carl Forrester showed no sign of remorse or guilt. In fact, his face was a frozen mask. . . ."

She rose from the now-tepid water, dried herself, and slipped into a comfortable robe. She was not a television watcher, so she sat down to write some letters. An hour later she gave up. Thoughts of Carl had broken her concentration, so she decided to go to bed early.

* CHAPTER 3 *

Carl pushed himself away from the table after eating a huge breakfast in the motel's dining room. Despite the aspirins he had taken and the six-pack of beer he had drunk the night before, he still had not slept well. He had known the dreams would come—they always did. Now he felt drained and extremely tired as he paid his bill and headed for his car. He drove to the nearest gas station and asked the way to Paul Carterson's home.

"Go out to the end of Main Street and make a left at the last light. You go on about eight miles and you come to a crossroads. Take a right immediately; there's a dirt road that turns off. You take it about three miles, and you run into a building that looks like an old barn. That's Carterson's place."

"That's the old mill," Carl said with a smile of fond remembrance.

"Yes, sir. Paul bought it about a year ago. You wait until you see what he's done with it, you won't believe it."

"You know Carterson?"

"Yeah," the young man grinned. "Paul and I are what you might call drinkin' buddies."

"I see. Has he been to town recently?"

The young man's eyes narrowed as he looked through the half-closed window at Carl.

"You a friend of Paul's?"

"I'm Carl Forrester—I'm a detective."

"Lieutenant Marks got you to come down on Paul? Well, he's wrong. Paul never would have killed anyone."

"You sure of that?" Carl asked softly.

"Yes, sir," the young man said firmly. "Paul would rather stay away from people than have any trouble with them. He's not the kind to nurse an old grudge, let alone kill anybody. When he came back to town, he and Martha talked to each other a couple of times. I tell you, everything between them was gone and forgotten, especially after Paul met Amy."

"Amy Realton?"

"Yeah."

"Maybe the girl caused a problem between Paul and Amy, and he felt it was best to get rid of her."

"No way. First off, I don't think any other woman could cause a problem between Paul and Amy. Things are too good between them; she would have understood."

"You kind of like the two of them?" Carl grinned.

"Yeah, they're a great couple. I'll tell you, you go on out and talk to Paul, and after that, take a look at some of his paintings. They'll tell you all about him."

"I think I'll do just that." Carl smiled now in a disarming way, and the young man smiled back.

The young man watched the car pull out onto the main highway. A deep frown lined his face. When he could see

Carl's car no more, he walked back into the station, slid a coin into the pay phone, and dialed.

Carl held the speed at fifty-five and whistled lightly as he watched the familiar landscape flash by. He reached into his pocket and withdrew a copy of the note Joe had given him—the one that had been found with Martha's body. He read it again.

Lamentations

Mind not the deceit of women, for the lips of the harlot are like honeycomb droppings and her throat is smoother than oil.

All her beauty and her majesty have gone.

She thinks of all the precious joys she had before her mocking enemy struck her down. And there was no one to give her aid.

An artist might have written it, with the reference to beauty and the physical description.

Carl turned down the dirt road that led to the mill. It had been in active use until twenty years before, when the owner had died, and had remained unoccupied for several years after that. It sat between two hills and beside a rapidly moving stream. The area was deeply wooded and one of remarkable beauty.

As he rounded the last bend in the road, he could see the old mill itself, but he was pleasantly surprised. The new owner had renovated the place, but with obvious consideration for the beauty that surrounded it. The mill had been painted a deep wine color. It was a large, two-story building with the giant paddle wheel still intact. Shutters had been added to the windows that could be closed against the heavy snows and cold winds that raged often in the winter. Stone walks had been added, and a three-foot-high stone wall bordered the stream on both sides of the house. Carl could see that the windows had been altered at one end of the house. The one facing the rising sun was at least ten feet high and, he guessed, twelve feet long, replacing most of the wall. His estimation of Paul Carterson jumped a notch.

He walked up the walk to the door. There was no sign of a doorbell, so he knocked. After several moments passed, he knocked again. There was still no answer. He tried the door, but it was locked. He put his hands in his pockets and began to walk around the house.

As he neared the stone wall and looked over, he saw a man seated on a flat rock beside the stream. He had a sketch-book braced against his knee and was sketching rapidly. All his attention was riveted on something, and Carl followed his gaze upstream. There on the bank stood a magnificent buck. Carl watched as the young man finished his sketch. Then he laid the pad slowly down on the rock beside him and sat quite still, savoring the view. Suddenly the buck, startled by Carl's movement, lifted his head, and in two quick bounds was gone. The young man looked back toward the wall with obvious annoyance on his face.

"Paul Carterson?" Carl called.

"Yeah, what do you want? I'm not buying anything and you're trespassing on private property."

"I'm Carl Forrester. I'm a detective. I've come out to have a few words with you."

Paul sat for a moment watching Carl, then got to his feet.

Christ, Carl thought, *he's big enough to have killed Martha, and he looks strong enough, as well.*

When Paul effortlessly climbed the small hill, swung over the wall, and landed on both feet beside him, Carl could see that he was two inches taller than Paul.

He judged that Paul Carterson must weigh about a hundred and eighty pounds, not one of which was fat. He was an extremely handsome man, about twenty-seven. His hair, thick and blond, was just a few shades lighter than the brows over his deep blue eyes. His mouth was broad and sensitive, and when he smiled, which he did as he extended his hand to Carl, he showed strong, white, even teeth. His face was tan, and his square jaw was bristled with at least two days' growth of beard. He wore snug-fitting jeans that complimented his long, muscular body. The plaid shirt, open at the neck, was covered partially by an unbuttoned jeans jacket that had obviously seen much wear. He was at home in these clothes and in this atmosphere. Carl smiled in return, gripping his hand firmly.

"I'm sorry, I didn't mean to be so abrupt. I get a little upset sometimes at trespassers who come out to see a painter paint," Paul said with a laugh.

"It's all right. If this is an inconvenient time, I can come later."

"No. The sketches I was working on were for my own pleasure. I can't even honestly say I was working. Sitting down there," he gestured to the rocks below, "I can shut the rest of the world away and pretend I'm Adam, alone with Mother Nature."

"Is she the only woman in your life?" Carl grinned to ease the nature of the question.

"No, there's another, much more human one, but just as pretty. Amy Realton."

"Is she here now?"

"No, she isn't, but she should be soon. Come on in. I'll make some coffee, and you can meet her."

"I'd like some coffee, thanks," Carl replied as they began to walk slowly to the back of the house.

"Mr. Carterson . . ."

"Paul."

"Paul, I'm afraid I have to ask you some questions about the death of Martha Dexter."

"I can sum it all up for you, Mr. Forrester," Paul began.

"Carl."

Paul smiled. "I knew Martha a long time ago, before I went to college. At that time, I was an impressionable kid, and I thought I was in love. I also had a pretty good temper, which I think I've learned to control, with time and a few extra years. Anyway, when I found out she was seeing someone else, I lost my temper and beat him up, then threatened to do the same to her. I thought she had just ruined my life." He laughed cynically. "It brought everyone, including the law, down on my head. I ran away to school with my tail between my legs, certain that I would never be able to live again without Martha. I not only discovered that I could, but that I thoroughly enjoyed my new life. I guess you might say I grew up. Anyway, I finished college and went to

France to put a little experience under my belt. I studied for four years and began to paint seriously, but nothing ever sold. Then a friend of mine told me that sometimes it's better to paint the things you know and love.

"So I came home. Martha was one of the first people I met after I arrived. We talked, and both of us realized what had been between us was dead, or maybe had never really been what we thought it was. Contrary to popular belief, there were no hard feelings. We talked, parted friends, and that is all I know about anything."

"Who would want to kill a girl like Martha in such a brutal manner? What kind of person was she that she could have made such an enemy?"

"That's what is so impossible about this whole mess. Martha was a sweet girl. I don't know of a soul who could have had a reason. Not in this town—not the people who knew her well."

"Maybe it was someone who didn't know her that well," Carl mused. "Are there any newcomers around that she might have impressed the wrong way?"

"I know most of the people Martha knew, and I know all the men she dated."

"Who were they?"

"For the past eight or nine months, it's been mostly Michael Brodie. Before him, she dated a few others, but nobody steady or serious."

"Serious . . . like Michael?"

"Yeah, he was pretty serious, I guess."

"Was Martha?" Carl asked quietly.

"Yeah, she was." Paul sounded annoyed. "No one I know would have done such a thing, and that includes Michael."

"You're sure."

"Hell, I'm not sure of anything. Couldn't this have been some transient—someone who just grabbed a girl at random?"

Carl shook his head. "Whoever murdered Martha left a note that showed premeditation."

They had moved inside the mill now, and Carl looked about him in open-mouthed admiration at the transformation Paul had worked.

"Make yourself comfortable. I'll go and brew us some coffee," Paul said. Then he disappeared through an archway, and Carl could hear him moving about the kitchen.

Carl walked about the room slowly, admiring the rustic way it had been decorated. Large, heavy wood pieces were randomly placed about the room. The polished wood floor reflected the sunlight streaming through the huge window. In front of the window, its back facing him, stood a large easel, upon which sat a canvas about thirty inches wide and forty-eight inches high. He walked around to look at it and found a half-finished portrait of a very beautiful girl.

She smiled out at him from the canvas, and Carl sensed immediately that this must be Amy Realton. What struck him was that she bore such a resemblance to the dead girl. She had the same deep auburn hair, though she wore it quite a bit longer. Her green eyes, slightly slanted at the corners, shone with bright intelligence. Paul had caught every detail of her beauty, including the tiny freckles sprinkled across her nose.

Carl was looking at the portrait when he noticed a small table in a shadowed corner of the room that held another canvas, covered with a white cloth. When he walked over and lifted the cover, he felt a prickly tremor of shock. It was a finished portrait of Martha Dexter, and it had been slashed—an angry crisscross of destruction. He wondered at that moment if Paul had lied to him about his feelings for Martha, and if he had savaged the portrait in a fit of rage. Could he have been angry enough to destroy the girl herself? Carl dropped the cloth when he heard Paul's approaching footsteps. By the time Paul entered the room, Carl stood again in front of Amy's portrait.

"Is this Amy?"

Paul nodded as he bent down to set the two cups on the coffee table.

"Yes. I don't think I caught just how pretty she is. There's something about her that's kind of elusive, but," he grinned, "I'm going to marry her. Then maybe I can pinpoint what it is and capture her on canvas. That portrait would be a beaut."

Carl sat down opposite Paul and looked at him levelly

across the table. "And the portrait of Martha in the corner?" he asked, "Who tried to destroy it—you or Amy?"

Paul's face grayed a little, but his eyes never left Carl's. "You won't believe me if I tell you what happened to that portrait," he replied as he raked long, sensitive fingers through his hair.

"Try me."

Paul sighed deeply, rose from the couch, and paced the floor for a minute. Then he stood by the window looking out.

"It's your property, Paul," Carl said. "You don't have to tell me anything about it."

Paul sighed again. "No, I can't just let you go from here with your imagination working overtime."

Carl shrugged as Paul turned to face him, but he said nothing. For a moment their eyes held. Paul chewed on the corner of his lip for a second, then spoke rapidly, as if now that he had decided, he couldn't wait to get the words out.

"I didn't do that to the portrait. It was one of my better works, and I wanted to show it in New York, with my next collection. I originally had hung it in my den. One night I had a small party here. The next day I found the portrait as you see it now, completely destroyed."

"Could Amy have done it in a jealous fit?"

Paul laughed. "Amy would never do such a thing. She is absolutely secure in the knowledge that I worship the ground she walks on. She doesn't have a jealous bone in her body. In fact, when she saw the portrait damaged, she was angry. She also considered it one of my better efforts."

"Can you tell me who was at the party?"

"Sure. Not that many people were invited. There was . . ."

"Just a minute," Carl interrupted, as he reached into his jacket pocket and withdrew a notepad and pencil. "Okay, shoot."

"Amy, Leslie Gabriel, Jake Magee, Paula Craig, Larry Jackson, Beth Raleigh, Michael Brodie, Father McAllen, David Mondale and his girlfriend, Ellen Knight, Jim Frasier and his wife, and Joe and Sally Marks. And, of course, Martha came with Michael."

"Did you notice if Martha was having trouble with Michael, or problems with any of the others?"

"No," Paul said thoughtfully, "not really. She seemed to be having a good time."

"Then, who among them do you think could have slashed the canvas?"

"Not one of them."

"Well, one of them must have."

"I know, but I can't imagine any of them could, or would."

"Paul," Carl said seriously, "somebody in this town is mentally disturbed—disturbed enough to brutally kill a girl. We'll find him, but he may kill again first."

"I've got a world filled with beauty here—this place, Amy? Do you think I'd jeopardize all that?"

"No," Carl answered, his eyes holding Paul's, "but would you try to stop someone else who would jeopardize it?"

Paul returned his gaze, his blue eyes clouded with anger. "I did not kill Martha. She couldn't and wouldn't harm me. I did that portrait of her after I came home from Europe. Does that picture show a girl afraid of me or angry at me? No matter what you think, I did not kill her."

Carl was about to reply, when someone turned the key in the front door and entered. He watched Paul's face as Amy walked toward him, and it was obvious how deeply in love he was.

"Paul?" she said softly as she stood beside him and slipped her hand in his. He could have laughed aloud at the picture she made. The top of her head came just to Paul's shoulder. She had pulled her long auburn hair from her face and braided it in one long braid that hung to her waist. She was slender, and yet had soft curves and a natural grace when she moved. Her wide green eyes were not smiling, as they had been when she had posed for her portrait; they blazed with the anger of a mother bear protecting her cub. Paul smiled with amusement as he put his arm about her waist and hugged her gently to him.

"Paul," she repeated, "Davy called me from the station when he couldn't get hold of you. Is there anything wrong?"

"No, Amy, this is Carl Forrester. He's a detective, and he just came to ask a few questions about Martha."

Amy gave Carl a half smile of acknowledgment, but her eyes were wary and mistrustful.

"It's nice to meet you in the flesh, Miss Realton. I've just been admiring the portrait of you that Paul is doing."

Carl could see Amy visibly relax at his reference to Paul on what seemed to be a friendly, first-name basis.

"Carl, your coffee is cold by now. Why don't you join Amy and me in some lunch and a fresh cup?"

"I'm sorry. I have a few stops to make, and I'd like to get back down to headquarters before Joe leaves. I'll take a rain check, though." Carl grinned and watched as with obvious relief, they returned his smile.

"Any time. Come on out some evening and we'll have a drink together and discuss how the painter paints."

As Carl walked slowly to his car, several questions nagged at the back of his mind. One was, why had Amy and the station attendant felt the need to protect Paul? The other was, who among the party guests had damaged the portrait of Martha? He needed to talk with Amy alone. He slid behind the wheel of his car and drove slowly away from the mill, enjoying the beauty of the surroundings and remembering his youth.

After the door closed behind Carl, Paul took Amy in his arms and held her trembling body in silence for a few minutes, then moved her a little away from him and looked deeply into her green eyes.

"Everything's all right, Amy. Don't worry so. I didn't have anything to do with Martha's death."

"I know that, Paul. It's just . . . I don't like the implications they make—about you and Martha, I mean."

Paul smiled down at her. "Does that mean the green-eyed monster is sitting on your lovely shoulders?"

She laughed and stepped closer to him, sliding her arms about his waist. "Of course. I can't bear the thought of you with anyone else. You, my tall, handsome friend, belong to me, and I would make your life unbearable if you so much as looked at another woman."

"The only way you could make my life unbearable is by leaving it," he answered seriously. "I couldn't stand it if anyone or anything took you from me."

His arm tightened about her fiercely, and he kissed her with possessive passion until she was breathless.

"Now, why don't you go make us lunch. If you play your cards right, I'll let you pose for me for a couple of hours."

"Oh," she said in mock anger, "you always lure me out here with suggestive promises, then put me to work like a slave."

"Well," he replied softly, with an evil twinkle in his eyes, "I figure if we eat, then paint as quickly as possible, there'll be a lot of time later for me to keep all those suggestive promises."

She laughed, then moved away from him toward the kitchen. He watched the sway of her slender hips in the tight-fitting jeans she wore. After she had closed the kitchen door behind her, he looked unseeing at it for a few minutes. His eyes narrowed and became cold and hard as he walked to the table that held the damaged portrait of Martha. He looked at the portrait several minutes, then slowly and viciously ripped it to shreds. He removed a few logs from a firewood holder that sat against the wall, dropped the remains of the painting inside the chest, and replaced the logs on top. Then he left the room and went to the kitchen.

"It's about time you came to join me," Amy teased him. "What were you doing?"

"Throwing out some garbage," he replied in a quiet voice. They sat for a while together and ate their lunch. As soon as they were finished, Paul rose to his feet. He didn't want to waste the light.

He turned to Amy and smiled. "Come on, let's get some work done, or that painting will never be finished."

"All right, slave driver." She tried to smile, to help him forget Carl's visit.

He posed her on a tall stool, picked up his palette and brush, and began to paint. After a while he forgot everything but the miracle he was trying to catch on the canvas.

The light shining through the large window brushed Amy's face with its sunny glow. It was exactly the look Paul wanted to catch, and it held his complete attention. Amy smiled, realizing Paul hardly knew she was alive as he worked to catch what he kept referring to as her "hide-and-seek" look.

Three hours later she stirred. She was tired of sitting, but she remained still until Paul dropped his brush on a small table near him and made a sound of disgust.

"Paul?"

"I don't know, Amy," he chuckled. "I have you for a minute, then you just . . ."

"May I move?"

He looked at her as if he just realized how long she had sat so very still. Then he looked at his watch and groaned.

"Good God, Amy, why didn't you say something? I'll bet you're exhausted."

"I am," she admitted. Her eyes sparkled with laughter. "But you've made such extravagant promises of great rewards if I was good, that I just couldn't bring myself to move."

Paul walked to her and lifted her from the high stool on which she sat. She looped her arms about his neck and watched with pleasure the way his eyes warmed when he was close.

He kissed her lightly several times, then carried her to the large couch and bounced down on it, still holding her close. Their laughter mingled minutes before their lips followed, tasting slowly and sensuously with a lazy, languorous touch.

"Ummm, you taste good," Paul said softly, as his lips moved from hers and brushed against her throat.

"That reminds me," she said in a silky whisper.

"Of what?" he asked hopefully.

"I'm hungry." She giggled when he lifted his head and gave her a mock distressed look.

"Woman, how can you think of food when I am offering you my handsome, masculine charms to do with as you will?" he complained.

"My will is to fill my stomach first."

"Let me remind you that woman does not live by bread alone. You did say *first*—that means before?"

"That's *man*," she corrected as she tried to rise, "and yes, I did say first, or before, or previous to, or . . ."

"Man?"

"It's the man who doesn't live by bread alone. Woman needs to be fed."

"Trust me to get involved with a teacher who gives

lessons on quotations, and makes me feed her before she relents and gives me what I really need to live on."

"And what's that, my primitive painter?" she laughed.

"You, Amy," he said, his eyes growing serious. "You know that, don't you? That you're every breath I take or thought I think. Sometimes I want to hold you so tight that I get scared. It's like I want to pull you inside me."

"I know, Paul," she whispered. "I love you very much." She held his face between her hands and kissed him, her lips parting and her tongue caressing his hard mouth until, with a groan of sweet passion, his hungry mouth responded, claiming hers in a breathless demand.

They kissed hungrily, wildly, fueling the passion until both were aflame. When their lips parted, both were breathless.

"So," he whispered huskily. "Are you still hungry?"

"Oh, yes," she murmured. She pressed both hands against his chest and rose slowly. Standing erect, she unbuttoned her shirt slowly, then shrugged it from her shoulders, revealing the fact that she wore nothing beneath it.

Her eyes held his as she unzipped the jeans and slid them down over her hips, taking the scant wisp of silk panties with them. She kicked off her sandals, and then stepped from her jeans.

Paul could not take his eyes from the vision before him. She stood in the glow of the sun, and he found his breath constricted.

He had always referred to her as the only true work of art he knew, and each time they were together made him more sure of it. She was slender, and her breasts were small but firm—enough, he had assured her, to fill his hand, which was the sign of her absolute perfection. And absolute perfection was the only way he would ever be able to describe what she brought to him with the simple touch of her hand.

He wanted to keep looking at her, as if he could absorb her beauty, but he wanted to hold her too—to taste the texture of her skin, to breathe in the scent of her hair that he already knew would smell like a warm summer day.

Slowly she came to him and began to work the buttons of his shirt. With trembling fingers, he helped and hastened the removal of his clothes.

Amy's hands moved over his hard, muscled body, stimulating the fire that coursed through his veins. She was possessive in her need for him. He closed his eyes as he let his hands memorize more fully her sleek beauty.

"I love you so very much, Amy," he whispered raggedly.

He watched her face as he joined with her, spellbound by the emotions that played across it. Then he lost track of time and place and knew only the miracle of loving her.

They lay together for a long time, totally together, for he did not leave her body, but remained linked to her in the most primary way. Amy held him, soft now, but knowing the hard strength would return. She wanted to feel him grow within her. She knew he absorbed that strength from her, and that gave her the greatest of all pleasure.

Later, as moonlight replaced the sun's glow, they sat before the warmth of the fireplace and drank red wine and laughed together, a lover's custom they firmly believed was their own invention.

Paul bent to kiss Amy just as the phone rang.

"Ahh," he groaned as he rose and walked across the room to answer it. He talked for a few minutes, then returned to drop down on the rug beside Amy.

"Who was it, Paul?"

"My agent, asking about the pieces for the show."

Before Amy could question any further, he kissed her again and eventually took her mind from the phone call.

Much later Amy slept beside him, but Paul lay awake. This was the second time Father McAllen had called him, and it took all Paul's control to fight the sudden feeling of panic. He held Amy closer and determined that he would let nothing destroy what he had found with her—nothing, and no one.

* CHAPTER 4 *

"Hi, Carl."

"Tom. How are things going?" Carl asked as he entered police headquarters.

"Nothing new. It looks like we've run up against a brick wall. Every clue we've got just seems to peter out and leave us hanging."

Carl sighed, clapped Tom on the shoulder, and walked past him to open the door to Joe's office.

"Hey," Joe said as he rested back in his chair, "you're a welcome sight. Sit down. I need an excuse to take a break."

He watched Carl expectantly as he eased down into a chair. "You talked to Carterson?"

"Yeah, I talked to him."

"What do you think?"

"You mean is he guilty or not?"

"Is he?" Joe questioned softly.

"I'd hate to think so."

Joe laughed bitterly. "I'd hate to think anyone I know could be guilty of this. Where do you go from here?"

"Paul gave me a list of people who were invited to a party he had. You and Sal were there, too. I'd like to know about the rest of the guests—except for the priest. I'm going over there to see him, after I take you to lunch."

"Let me see."

Carl passed the notepad to Joe, who studied it. "I told you about Brodie. Mondale is a teacher at the Catholic school and coach for Father McAllen's football team. Beth Raleigh is the librarian here." Joe continued with the balance of the names. He was engrossed in the list and didn't see Carl's reaction to Beth's name, or he might have been curious at the fleeting look that Carl struggled to control. "You might just drop by and talk to her, too. She's an observant lady—she might recall something. And you remember Jim Frasier. He runs the local paper, and a friend of Jim's owns the restaurant where," he grinned, "you are about to take me to lunch."

"If you're laughing, I'm sure it's expensive."

"Too expensive for this policeman's salary, but you come from the big city, so c'mon, big spender. Let's go."

They left the building and walked toward Carl's car.

"Carl, do you feel that there's something significant about this party?"

"I'm not sure just how important it is." Carl went on to explain the destruction of the painting of Martha.

"So, you think Paul cut it?"

"He or one of the guests. Why don't you try to think back over what happened that night. Maybe you saw something that you didn't know you saw."

"I'll give it some thought. Why don't you come to my place for dinner tonight? I have a feeling that if you don't, Sal's going to come and get you."

"I was supposed to leave here Friday on a fishing trip, remember?"

"You're not going to let me down, are you?" Joe smiled, then his face grew serious. "Carl, I don't want to take advantage, but stay for a few days."

"For your benefit, Joe—or do you think it's for mine? If that's in your mind, let it go."

"I guess that might have been part of it. I'm sorry, but no matter what, you'd better pick a night, or else."

Carl chuckled as he reached to open the restaurant door. "Sounds as if I'd better," he replied as he studied the restaurant. It was a subtly decorated room, and he had a feeling the food would be exceptional.

They found a table, ordered, and waited until their food was brought. Before they could resume their discussion about the murder, someone stopped at their table, and both men looked up to see Jim Frasier. Joe smiled, and Carl rose and extended his hand.

"Jim."

"Carl? Carl Forrester. I'll be damned. I never thought I'd see you around these parts again. How've you been? It's been—what two, three years?"

"Three years," Carl agreed. "I've been fine. How about yourself?"

"Great, except for what's going on now. I can't believe it."

"Join us, Jim. I'd like to talk to you."

"You mean, question me?" Jim smiled, but his eyes were solemn. He was about thirty-eight—a tall, broad-shouldered man with sandy brown hair. Carl remembered him as being very serious in school, sometimes even intense.

"Well, not exactly, but as a newspaperman, you understand that you always have to make sure you have the facts."

Jim laughed as he slid a chair up to the table. "You were always slick, Carl. You haven't changed."

"So, where were you?"

"The night of the murder, I was covering a story halfway across the state. I have two senators and about sixty other people to verify it. Is that good enough?"

"Depends," Carl chuckled. "Were they Democrats or Republicans?"

Now all three men laughed, and it did a great deal to ease the situation. The conversation mellowed into football, and after a while, Jim rose and said he had to go.

"I really hate to, but I have a deadline. Stop over at the paper, Carl. I'd like to see you again—and welcome back. I hope you're entertaining the idea of staying."

"I doubt it, but I'll drop by."

"Fine. See you two later." He walked away and Carl turned back to Joe.

"Now, give me a rundown on the people on the list. I'll need their addresses, too."

"I'll get the information for you."

"We know for sure it wasn't a woman, so we can eliminate them."

They discussed in length all the information Joe had at the moment, which didn't amount to much.

After lunch, Joe went back to his office and Carl drove in the direction of the church to talk to the priest, still amazed that Joe actually suspected him.

Joe and Carl had both been raised as Catholics. Yet Carl had a hard time remembering the last time he had entered the small church he was driving toward. It must have been just before Sara had died. He allowed the bitter memories to touch him for one moment, then ruthlessly thrust them away. It hurt to remember.

When he arrived at the church, he was surprised to see the parish had built a school close by. He walked around the church to the rectory, and smiled his warmest, most disarming smile at the plump matron who answered his knock.

"I would like to speak to Father McAllen, please," he said.

"I'm sorry, Father isn't here at the moment."

"Can you tell me where he is?"

"Yes, he's over at the school." She smiled. "You must be a stranger here."

"Kind of," Carl admitted with a grin. "How can you tell?"

"Most everybody knows where to find Father McAllen in October—on the football field. His boys are champs, and he likes watching the practice. Confidentially," she laughed, "I think he'd like to be playing with them."

Carl smiled and thanked her. He walked toward the school and soon heard the voices of the football team. He stood on the edge of the field and watched for a while, trying to decide which of the three men in sweat suits and jackets was the priest.

All three were very big men. Carl groaned. Why couldn't he find some suspects that were small and weak? It would make the process of elimination much easier.

After a few minutes his presence was noticed. The three men stood talking for a minute, then one started in his direction. He stopped close to Carl, appraising him for a few seconds before he spoke.

"Good afternoon."

"Afternoon," Carl replied. "Are you Father McAllen?"

"No," the man said with a boyish grin. He was tall and very muscular, with close-cropped blond hair, and his crystal-green eyes were alert. Carl was aware that he missed little.

"I'm David Mondale. I teach here and I'm Father's assistant coach. Is there something I can do for you?"

"I'm Carl Forrester; I'm a detective. I've come to ask a few questions about the murder of Martha Dexter."

Carl watched as the green eyes darkened and the lips formed a hard line.

"There isn't much Father can tell you."

"Why don't you let him speak for himself. He might have some answers I need."

Carl could see anger glisten in Mondale's eyes and watched him struggle to control it.

"The police have already asked him questions. Why does he have to answer more? This is ridiculous. He's a priest, for God's sake. What could he know about a murder?"

"I only want to talk to him. He doesn't need protection, does he?" Carl asked gently.

"I'll get him for you," David said, and turned away before Carl could answer. He walked across half the field and spoke to a tall, dark man whose eyes lifted from the football he was holding to flash in Carl's direction. He nodded and spoke rapidly to David, who seemed to be arguing with him. Then he clapped David on the shoulder and moved toward Carl.

When the priest offered his hand and smiled, Carl was struck by McAllen's unaffected warmth and the fact that his gray eyes looked tired and older than the man. He was tall, with an athletic build, and probably had played football himself. His hair was ebony black and his smile was wide and friendly. Had he not known the nature of man, Carl would have found it not remotely possible that this man had killed anyone. But Carl did know—he had seen the wide and innocent smile of killers before. He reserved any judgment.

"I'm Father Patric McAllen. David said you wanted to speak to me. You're a detective?"

"Yes, Carl Forrester, a friend of Joe Marks."

"I've known Joe ever since I came to Helton. I don't think I've seen you about before."

"No, I'm from Cambridge. Joe called me in for a little help."

"With solving the murder of Martha? I can't believe anyone would want to kill a nice young girl like her."

"You knew her well?"

"Yes, pretty well. She had done some work at the rectory for me, off and on."

"For how long?"

"Oh, I guess about a year and a half. Let me see. I've been here over two years, and she came to work about six months after I got here."

"Have any kind of trouble with her?"

Father McAllen's eyes narrowed as he gazed at Carl. The smile remained, but it was forced. "Mr. Forrester. . ."

"Father," Carl's voice was quiet. "This child was killed in a violent and most brutal way."

"What is it you want from me?" he asked gently as his eyes softened.

"The truth. That's all I want to find. This was once my town, and I don't want to see something evil fester here."

"Why don't you walk with me to my office. We can discuss the truth over some coffee. Mrs. Martin makes a delicious coffee cake."

"My weakness," Carl admitted. But as he and Patric walked away together, Carl sensed the intensity in the eyes of David Mondale, watching them leave.

"So, you're been here two years?" Carl asked as they headed toward the rectory.

"Give or take a month or so," Patric replied.

"You know just about everybody in town?" It was much more a statement of fact than a question.

"In a town this size, it's hard not to."

"I take it you came from a much larger one."

"I came from St. Louis, Missouri, which is many times larger than this one. Have you ever been to St. Louis?"

"As a tourist," Carl grinned. "You know, up in the arch and down to the river."

"That's about as good a description of what most tourists see as any I've heard."

When they were settled in Father McAllen's office, Mrs. Martin brought the tray. She poured two cups of coffee, and Carl was amused to see she added sugar and cream to Father McAllen's without asking. It was quite obvious that he had a staunch supporter in Mrs. Martin. When she was gone and they had sat in silence for several minutes, he asked, "Tell me, Carl, do you have some suspicions as to who murdered Martha?"

"It's too soon for me to have solid ideas. I'm just trying to talk to everyone who knew her. There's a motive somewhere, and I'd like to find it."

"How can I help you?"

"I'll be honest with you," Carl said firmly. He watched the priest's face closely. "You were the last person known to have seen Martha alive."

Father McAllen's face remained still and quiet, and Carl began to wonder if it were not a severely controlled quiet.

"You are right about one thing," he spoke in a saddened voice. "I'm the last 'known' person. The killer was the last one. I have the feeling you have added me to your list of suspects."

"I have no choice until I find out who killed her. I suspect everyone and anyone. You and I both know well the deranged mind is not restricted to the few—occupation is not an indicator."

Father McAllen's face had paled a little, and his mouth was a grim line as he bent forward to place his half full cup on the table.

"What is it you want from me?"

"I want honest answers and information about your parishioners. Can you supply it?"

"As long as it doesn't breach the confidence of the confessional, I'll tell you whatever you want to know. Where shall we start?"

"With you," Carl said softly. If possible, Father McAllen's face grew grayer and his mouth firmer.

"I see," he said softly. "So, you already have a lot of information about me."

"I have words written on paper. They're black and white. No one knows better than I that there are a lot of gray areas. You're the only one who can tell me all of the truth."

"What do you know?"

"That a man, who just happened to be a priest, lost his temper and did something he regretted."

Father McAllen sighed. "Thanks, Carl. I had begun to believe that you, like so many others, would see only the priest and forget there's a man inside who can get terribly angry at injustice. I made a mistake, but I know I would do it again."

"Just what did you do?"

He sat back in his chair and began to speak slowly, allowing his mind access to thoughts he had hoped to put away forever.

"It happened over two years ago. I was assistant pastor at St. Mark's, a very wealthy parish. One particular family there had a son to whom they had given everything, except a sense of decency and honor. The boy was a distasteful, arrogant, and very stupid young man who thought there was nothing his father's money could not buy. He liked the ladies—he liked girls, of any age.

"He was twenty-five when he seduced the fourteen-year-old daughter of a couple in the parish. She became pregnant. When he was told about it, he laughed. First, he said he had nothing to do with it. Then he got to her somehow and talked her into an abortion—not the legal kind, but a bloody butchered job.

"The next day the girl died. She was an only child, and the parents were grief-stricken. I was with her when she died. I had been with her parents through the burial, and I was tired, which is no excuse. But he came to them, in their poor little home, and offered them money.

"I think I could have held my temper, but they refused the money and told him to get out. He became abusive. Then he said that their daughter was a cheap tramp and wasn't even worth the money he had paid her to sleep with him. I am afraid something snapped. I saw their pain and grief and I'm afraid I used a little force to eject him."

"A little force?"

"To be accurate, I beat him until he was unconscious and threw him out into the street. It is part of my creed to forgive. I failed, and I have had to ask God's mercy for that. But," for the first time he smiled, "even the good Lord lost his temper a time or two."

"So, it wasn't just black and white?"

"I'm afraid, for my vocation, it was black."

"So now, I have to ask you. What was Martha doing with you the night she was killed?"

"I can't tell you that."

"Did she say where she was going? Who she was going to meet?"

"I can't tell you that, either."

"Do you know if she was mixed up with some man?"

"I can tell you she was popular, had a lot of friends, and she dated a few boys who seemed all right. But there's nothing I can tell you about that night. She came to me in confession."

"Then, you can't even defend yourself. You can't even reveal what you said or did."

"I'm afraid not."

"It looks as if you could take the blame for something more serious than before."

"I'll just have to have faith that you'll find out who killed Martha and vindicate me."

"And if I don't?"

"That's a chance I have to take."

"It's a big chance. You have a lot to lose."

"I'd have a lot more to lose if I violated the confessional. Just where would I be then?"

Carl nodded. "Good point. Tell me—this loss of temper, has it ever happened again?"

"I'm trying to control it," he replied with an infectious smile. "Of course, on the football field, it's touch and go. David sort of takes the edge off it."

"You played before?"

"All through college."

"Were you good?" Carl grinned.

"You're tempting my vanity. Let's say I was adequate."

"Can you give me names of people you felt were acquaintances of Martha's? I have one, but you might be able to add a name or two."

"I'll give you as many as I can."

Carl removed the battered notebook from his pocket and recorded the new names.

"Well, that's all for now. I'll probably be talking to you again."

Both men rose, and again Father McAllen extended his hand to Carl.

"You said you weren't from Helton?"

"I live in Cambridge now, but I lived in Helton originally."

"Oh, really?"

"Joe and I are old friends. It's the reason I came back."

The tone of his voice told the astute listener that there was much more behind the words. His gaze held Carl's, who suddenly felt the distinct urge to run. He hid his discomfort by tearing his eyes away and walking to the door.

"Carl?"

He turned. "Yes?"

"I'm never too busy to talk—to anyone."

The words were gentle and profoundly affecting. But Carl had clung to his dreams too long. He knew that sometimes pain was a crutch to hold on to when the only alternative was nothing at all.

"Thank you. I'll remember that."

Father McAllen watched Carl go with a frown between his brows. Then he reached for the phone. He dialed and waited, then a voice replied on the other end.

"This is Father McAllen. I have to talk to you—as soon as possible."

* CHAPTER 5 *

It was Thursday morning, and Carl reminded himself, somewhat angrily, that he would have to decide by evening if he was going on the fishing trip he had planned for months, or staying to find the answers to the questions that knotted within him.

This had been his town, and he was torn with the urge to stay and the fear that if he stayed, he was going to come face-to-face with a past he was not prepared to deal with.

Confusion made his mood less than friendly. That, combined with the fact that he had had too many beers the night before, had given him a fuzzy head, taut nerves, and an uneasy stomach that called for food—preferably accompanied by hot black coffee.

He was just finishing his third cup of coffee when he saw Joe enter the restaurant. Carl saw his lined and worried face crease in a smile as he found him, and Carl realized he would stick around as long as Joe needed him.

Joe slid into the seat across from him.

"Coffee?" Carl asked.

"Yeah, I've only had a gallon or so since six this morning."

"Well, then," Carl laughed, "one more cup is not likely to tear any more holes in your stomach than you've already got." He waved at the waitress, who came with the pot and filled both cups. "I'd like to go over to your office and read through the information you have on the suspects again. I'd like to see if there's anything I might have missed."

"Sure, come on over. I'll call Paula, Leslie, and Ellen. All three can come in tomorrow morning. I'll throw a few questions at them. I'll save Jake and Larry for later in the afternoon. They might have some insight into this party. Maybe one of them has an idea who might have destroyed that painting of Martha."

"Why don't I talk to Leslie, Jake, and Larry, and you can call Ellen and Paula in?"

"Yeah—and how about your dropping around to see Mrs. Lowrey? She's David Mondale's alibi."

"That ought be as strong as iron." Carl laughed, then sobered. "Mrs. Lowrey," he repeated quietly. She was one of his finer memories; still, she was a thread that led to others he just didn't want to face.

"Beth Raleigh is on your list, too," Joe said amiably, "so talk to her."

"Yeah, all right. But I'll see Mrs. Lowrey first."

"She might have a few questions for you." Joe laughed.

"I haven't seen the old girl since I left. Before I go there, though, I'm going out to see your Brando-type character, and then later, I'd like to just scout around and talk to people in general. Someone might have seen something or know something that doesn't seem important to them, but might mean a lot to us."

"And then what, Carl? Do you still intend to go?"

"Don't sweat it, Joe. I'll stick around until everything gets cleared up."

"Great!" Joe beamed at him. "I was hoping you'd change your mind."

"I think you knew I'd stay, right from the beginning. You were always a shrewd operator, my friend."

"That calls for a few cold beers in celebration. Carl, Sal's been dying to see you. Why don't you come for dinner—say, Saturday night?"

"Knowing Sal like I do, I expect to see her camped on my doorstep pretty soon. I guess I'd better."

Joe chuckled. "I used to be jealous of you two once. That was before she showed me the difference between love and friendship."

"Next to you, Sal was probably the best friend I ever had."

"Then you'll come?"

"Yeah, I'll come. But tell her not to go to any trouble." He grinned. "One of her seven-course gourmet meals will do."

Joe laughed with him, realizing Carl must know how relieved he was.

They left the restaurant and returned to Joe's office, where Carl sat for nearly two hours, reviewing the case again, hunting for avenues Joe had not explored. He had to admit that Joe was painstakingly thorough. He could not shake the worrisome thought that this was a psychological murder, and if that were true, it might happen again. He was scared that if he and Joe couldn't find him soon, the killer might just have a field day and terrorize the town—the town he still loved.

Just as Carl was about to leave, Tom entered with a plastic bag that held a white envelope. Joe looked at him, then groaned. "Another one? What the hell is he trying to tell us?"

"Did it come in the mail? To the police department?"

"Yeah."

"Let's see it." Carl rose and took the note from Tom. "Has it been dusted?"

"Yeah, for all the good that will do. It had been handled a lot. Not much left in the way of prints."

Carl tore the note open and read.

Lamentations: 2

She sobs through the night; tears run down her cheeks. Among all her lovers there is none to help her. All her friends are now her enemies.

My hand will punish yet another until they learn. Why don't you listen?!

Joe read over his shoulder. "Christ," he muttered. " 'All her lovers'. That sure could mean Michael Brodie, from what I've been told."

Carl breathed an exasperated sigh. The notes could have been written by anyone who knew Martha. And now the murderer was threatening to kill again.

After lunch, Carl drove out the highway toward the address he had for Michael Brodie.

His was a small, white, wood-frame house that sat nestled in a wooded area. Carl had some difficulty finding it. He tried to keep his mind clear of any preconception of the man's guilt or innocence until he spoke to him, but he observed that the location of his home made it easy for Michael Brodie to come and go as he pleased, without anyone seeing him.

He pulled his car to a stop and examined the area carefully. The house was not well maintained, and two junk cars sat nearby. There was also a large, magnificently chromed and adorned motorcycle that a loving hand had polished to perfection. Carl was examining it when a rough voice spoke from the house. "Keep your hands off that. You're trespassing on private property."

Carl turned. The man stood just within the doorway, his form vague and shadowed.

Carl explained quickly who he was and why he was there. For a while the man made no move to speak or step from the shadows. After long, impatient minutes, when Carl stood rock firm and determined, the man stepped out onto the porch. He was also a big man. Didn't Helton grow any small ones?

"So," Michael said with a scowl, "why did you come

out to see me? Can't you hang the blame on any of the upright citizens of Helton?"

"I've already questioned a lot of them, and I'm not hanging blame. I'm just trying to get some answers."

"Why me?"

"Because you knew Martha. Are you afraid to talk?"

"There ain't been a man born I'm afraid of. I can tell you for certain you're lookin' at the wrong man. I would never have hurt Martha."

"Oh?" Carl replied softly. "There was something between you and Martha?"

"You bastard," Michael grated. "Don't make it sound like something dirty. Martha wasn't that kind of girl. Sleepin' around wasn't her style." He walked closer to Carl, who was familiar enough with grief to recognize it when he saw it.

Michael's eyes were deadened with red-rimmed, heavy lids, as if he still wept internally after all outward weeping was exhausted. As Carl approached, Michael's hand trembled and he lit the cigarette that had hung between his lips. His clothes were rumpled, and Carl was quite sure he had slept in them.

"Take it easy, Michael. I'm not here to accuse you or to sling mud. I'm here to find out who killed Martha and why."

Michael studied Carl, realizing his voice had gentled and his attitude was not hostile. He walked down the steps and stood closer to Carl. It was as though Michael was cold and was seeking any source of warmth that might help him ease his misery. Carl took these few minutes to study him closely.

He was quite handsome, in a rough-cut way. He had a lantern jaw that had not been shaved in three or four days, brown eyes, and thick black hair that needed cutting.

"There wasn't no reason for anyone to kill Martha. She was fine—real fine. Only a nut would do a thing like that to her."

"You have some suspicions?" Carl asked softly.

"I ain't pointing the finger, but you should go ask her painter friend. She saw him a few times, and they was fighting about something. Last time I seen Martha she was mad as hell at him for some reason. She wouldn't tell me."

"Why not?"

" 'Cause she knew I had a yen to go and beat the shit out of him anyhow. He was mixed up with her somehow, and she knew for damn sure I would have tried to put a stop to it."

"You were in love with Martha?" Carl asked.

Michael's red-rimmed eyes blinked twice, as if to resist any threat of tears.

"Yeah, I was in love with her. I would have done anything she wanted me to do, and she knew it."

"Tell me," Carl said. "Were you jealous of her connection to Paul Carterson?"

"No. I knew she didn't love him, but I ain't too sure he wasn't tryin' to pick up some old ties. He's the kind who could have more than one thing going at the same time. We almost had a fight about it that time at his house."

"You were an invited guest?"

Michael laughed harshly. "Only because he wanted to know what Martha had told me."

"What did you tell him?"

"I told him whatever Martha said to me was none of his damn business."

"You weren't mad at Martha for any reason?"

"Me? Hell, no."

"And you didn't see the portrait of her that Paul was painting?"

Michael's eyes gazed out over the wooded area, and he seemed to withdraw into himself. "Yeah, I seen it."

"Did you destroy it, Michael? Did you get mad and slice it?"

"No."

"Did you get angry with Martha for posing for it?" Carl asked.

"No." Michael's anger was growing.

"Did you lose your temper, slice the portrait, then do the same to Martha because you thought she was betraying you?"

"No! Dammit, no! I wouldn't have hurt her."

"Michael," Carl said quietly. "Can you tell me where you were the night she was killed?"

"Christ," Michael whispered, "I was alone out here. Martha was supposed to come out that night. We were going to talk." He shook slightly. "I figured she was coming out to me, and that damn bastard offered her a ride. Then he killed her because she was gonna dump him and come to me. I'd like to see him dead."

Carl saw the gleam of violence in Michael's eyes, and it worried him. Yet he had no way of proving any guilt or innocence. He had to do some more probing before he pushed Michael any further.

"If you don't mind, I'd like to talk to you again in a day or so."

"After you've checked out my story?"

"That's my job," Carl said firmly. He opened his car door.

"Mr. Forrester?"

"Yes?"

"I didn't do it," Michael said softly. "I loved her."

Carl nodded, then got in the car and drove away, leaving Michael standing in the center of the drive, as if he didn't know or care that Carl was gone.

Carl wanted to believe him, but he, of all people, knew that murder was often done in the name of love.

Next on Carl's agenda was Jake Magee. Driving to his address, Carl had the irksome feeling he was about to find another big man, and he did. Jake told him he sold insurance, and that he had paid for his education with a football scholarship. He was a man used to dealing with pressure, and he took the interrogation well, yet he didn't seem to have any answers.

Carl noted everything he said, including the times and places he had been the night of the murder, and made a special note that at the exact time of the murder, he had been home alone.

His luck with Larry Jackson was not much better. He would have felt better if either man had produced an alibi he could rip apart. They cooperated, answered the questions, and in Carl's eyes looked as possibly guilty as any of the others.

He knew he had to interview Beth Raleigh, yet he sought ways to postpone their meeting. He wasn't sure why, and he didn't want to dissect his feelings when it came to her. What he wanted was a way out of seeing her again. He found a fast-food place and put down three cheeseburgers, fries, and a cherry pie. Then he began a canvass of the town, stopping randomly to question people, just in case someone had seen Martha the night of her death, after Father McAllen had seen her. He discovered his witness in a florist shop. He walked in and found the woman behind the desk quickly susceptible to his warm smile and friendly attitude. They chatted for a while about the weather, the flowers, and assorted other things before he eased into who he was and why he was there. She was fascinated.

"My heavens, a policeman from Cambridge."

"Yes, ma'am," he said. "Joe Marks and I are very old friends. I just thought I'd see if I could be of any help."

"Oh, that was so terrible about poor, dear little Martha."

"Did you know her?"

"I'd seen quite a lot of her. She used to come over to order the church flowers."

"Mrs.—"

"Mrs. Graham," she said.

"Mrs. Graham, I'd like to ask you something very important."

"Of course."

"Think carefully now. By any chance, did you see Martha the night she died?"

"Yes, I did—late that evening. I didn't close the shop until very late, and she came just before closing time to order some special flowers. It was after nine."

"I see. Did she say where she was going when she left here?"

"Why, yes. She did."

"Where?"

"Back to the church. She was going to do something for Father McAllen. She said he was waiting for her."

"I see," Carl replied, trying to keep his voice from registering his tension. Martha Dexter had died between ten-thirty and eleven-thirty.

"Thank you, Mrs. Graham. You've been very helpful."

"Oh, you're very welcome, Mr. Forrester. I do hope you and Joe Marks catch that terrible person."

"Don't worry, Mrs. Graham. We'll catch him. I promise you that."

He left the florist shop and walked slowly back to his car again. He slid behind the wheel and sat for a while, trying to think.

Finally, unable to delay any longer, Carl left the parking lot and drove to the library. He found Beth at the front desk. She was busy helping a small boy and didn't notice him. It gave him a moment to study her.

She wore a soft white blouse that was supposed to look businesslike. On her, it looked like shimmering silk as it cascaded from her shoulders to her very trim waist. Her skirt was a kind of woodsy green.

There was something disquieting about Beth Raleigh, and it took him a minute to realize what it was. She seemed so stable, so secure—and yet innocent. Serenity was the word he found among his thoughts, and he fit it to her easily.

He waited, taking a deep breath and releasing it slowly while he gathered his own shield closer, uneasy with the effect she had on him. At last, he caught her attention and she turned quickly to face him. She smiled a professional smile, but her eyes were full of questions.

"Mr. Forrester, can I help you?"

"Yes. Miss Raleigh, I'd like to ask you a few questions, if I may."

"Of course. Follow me."

She stopped for a second to get someone to take over the desk, then led him toward the back of the library. The free and easy way she walked struck a chord of memory that made him uneasy. He would have preferred to have questioned her in the safer atmosphere of the library, and not in some small, private room. She had remembered his name from their chance meeting, and even this annoyed him.

In her small office, she motioned him to a seat.

"No, I'll stand."

She could read his discomfort, and was puzzled by it. "You wanted to ask me some questions?"

"Yes. You attended a party at the home of Paul Carterson before Martha Dexter was killed."

"Yes. There was . . ."

"I know who was there," he interrupted. "What I'd like to know is if you saw anything unusual, or sensed anything out of the ordinary."

Her brow furrowed in a frown, as much annoyance at him as in her thoughts about the party. Somehow he seemed antagonistic and almost defensive. When she replied, there was a chill to her voice.

"No, it was just a group of friends getting together to celebrate a very fine talent."

"You stayed the whole evening?"

Beth hesitated. She didn't want to tell him that she had left early because her aloneness had eaten at her. She had seen happy couples like Paul and Amy, and their togetherness had threatened something fragile within her. How could she tell him that she had very nearly run to the sanctuary of her empty, and that night very lonely, home. Carl could see the defenses rise in her eyes and wondered what kind of nerve he had struck.

"No, I'm afraid I didn't. I had some work to finish up and wanted to get home early."

"The party was on a Saturday night," he reminded mildly.

"So?" Now she was stiffly resentful of his breach of her defenses.

"So, you had all day Sunday to work."

"I preferred to do it Saturday night. What has my preference to do with this murder? I have no real information for you."

Confined in the room, they were standing much too close to suit him. He could almost feel the warmth of her body. The texture of her skin looked soft, and her bones seemed delicate. As he watched, a faint pink touched her cheeks. He knew he was staring, and she was growing as tense as a bird being pursued by a cat. Everything about him unnerved her, from the almost breathtaking breadth of his shoulders, to the height that drew her eyes up only to meet his. The man was overpoweringly sensual, and her nerves screeched in protest. There was a mystery about him, and his firm-set, shadowed jaw only made it more pronounced. She didn't want to solve his mystery—she had enough to deal with herself.

"Mr. Forrester, if you will excuse me, I'm very busy. I really don't have much information that would be of any help."

"No, I suppose not. If you think of anything unusual that happened that night, will you please call?"

"I'll call Joe," she interrupted, and the message was clear.

"Yeah, you do that." He'd gotten the message, and

though he was satisfied, he was somehow angered. "Thanks for your cooperation."

For a pulsing, breathless moment, their eyes held, but then Carl fled the tense atmosphere. He put the small notebook and pencil back into his pocket to occupy his hands, which actually shook with the desire to touch her.

"You're quite welcome," she replied. She watched him leave, as puzzled with the reaction she felt, as with the obvious reaction she saw reflected in his eyes. Carl Forrester was somehow dangerous, and it would be better if she stayed as far away from him as she could.

It was late enough for a dinner he wasn't hungry enough to eat, and too late to catch Joe at the office. The last thing he wanted was to return to his room. He knew the location of the murder and quickly decided to look it over to see if he could come up with anything.

He arrived at the scene half an hour later and parked his car by the side of the road. He locked it, slipped the keys into his pocket, and with a flashlight, trudged into the woods. He stayed out of the cordoned-off areas, to avoid destroying any clues. Instead, he circled and surveyed it several times. The rough, hollowed grave was still a ghastly reminder. Wondering if the girl had been killed at the grave site or had been carried there, he circled the squared-off area again, more slowly. There was no sign of anything.

He was empty of reasons not to go back and face the quiet room and empty bed. Dejected, he started to walk back toward his car. When the light from his flashlight reflected off something that glittered in the grass and leaves, he stopped and flashed the light around until he found the shiny object. He picked it up and held it in the palm of his hand, then cursed to himself. It was a crucifix and a chain of several black beads—part of a broken rosary. He slipped it into his pocket. He didn't even want to think about it tonight. He'd decide just how to explain its presence tomorrow. Now he was emotionally drained and knew he had yet to face the worst part of the day.

Once within the city limits, he stopped to pick up a couple of six-packs, then started back to the motel.

He showered, turned on the television just for the sound, then sat down to concentrate on his beer and the piece of rosary he had laid on the table beside the bed.

There were too many players—too many people who could be guilty. Had the killer planned it that way, or had it just happened? He had no answers—none at all.

The beer did little more than blunt his senses. It was too early to sleep. Of course for him, just about any hour was too early to go to bed. Feeling suddenly like a caged animal, he decided that a long walk might relieve his tension and tire him enough to sleep.

The motel sat just at the edge of town, so everything was pretty much within walking distance. The night was crisp, but not cold enough to be uncomfortable.

He walked slowly, looking into store windows and refusing to settle his mind on anything. The monster of loneliness ate at his vitals and for the hundredth time, he cursed himself for listening to Joe—for responding to the pull of friendship that had brought him here.

Carl paid very little attention to where he was going until he discovered he was standing in front of an apartment building, across the street from the library. He gazed at the library, which, to his surprise, still had lights burning within.

Suddenly he knew why he was here and self-defense alarms tingled through him. He didn't want to see her again! He didn't want those deep, knowing eyes to pierce the fragile defenses he had built around himself, but nevertheless, he waited.

Beth was the last person to leave the library Thursday night because it was the one night of the week the part-time help was off. She did a last-minute check of everything, snapped out the lights, pulled the doors tight, and turned the key in the locks.

Beth was a fall person—she left her car at home on autumn days and enjoyed the walk to work.

Thoughts of Carl had been scurrying around in her mind most of the day. She had even reread the newspaper article, and had found its terse, cold report unsatisfactory. What scars he must be carrying! More than once she had told herself all this was none of her affair, but the way he had looked at her had stirred an emotion. Was it pity? If so, it was probably the last emotion a man like Carl Forrester would welcome.

"Oh, well," she sighed, "he's not very likely to come interview me again."

As she started to walk, she felt the sensation that she was being watched. Since the murder of Martha Dexter, everyone in Helton was nervous. Beth looked about and saw no one whose attention was on her. She shook her head, laughing at her own fear. Here she was, in the center of town, with people everywhere—she should have no reason to be afraid. She walked slowly away. Carl stood within the shadows of the apartment doorway across the street and watched her go.

He was amazed at himself. For God's sake, why didn't he just cross the street and talk to her? He sighed. Why should he make the effort; Beth Raleigh had no answers for him. He returned to the motel and went to bed.

* CHAPTER 6 *

Carl knew he should have mentioned the rosary to Joe first thing on Friday, but when he arrived, Joe was out, and Carl followed his own agenda. He circulated through the town again, trying to find out if anyone had seen Martha Dexter in someone else's company after she had left Father McAllen.

While he was doing this, he renewed some old acquaintances, expertly dodged the questions of people who were curious, and found a small drop of satisfactory warmth in the eyes of a few who'd believed in him in the past and wanted him to know it. He still had Mrs. Lowrey on his list. Maybe tomorrow. . . .

Because it had taken him so long to get to sleep, Carl slept much later on Saturday than he had planned. When he rolled over and looked at the bedside clock, he was surprised to find it was nearly eleven.

He reached for the phone and dialed Joe's office number. He got a gruff-voiced Joe on the second ring.

"Joe?"

"Yeah. Carl?"

"Sorry if I sound foggy—I just woke up."

"You coming in?"

"Yeah, I've got a few things to talk over, and something to show you. I was out at the murder scene."

"I thought it had been checked over pretty thoroughly."

"What I picked up wasn't right at the spot where the body was found. Are you sure she was killed where you found the body?"

"You think she wasn't?"

"No. I think it happened some distance away and the body was carried to the scene. Anyway, I'll be in in a little while."

"In time for lunch?" Joe chuckled.

"If you're buying this time. I'm going to have you put me on the city payroll."

"You help me solve this and you can name your price."

"Careful, Joe." Carl laughed.

"You won't be forgetting dinner tonight?"

"Nope, I'll be there."

"Seven, sharp."

"Seven, it is. See you in a little while."

Joe looked at the phone for a few minutes after he hung up. He was worried about Carl. He hoped contact with Sally might at least open the door between them, so someone could see inside. Carl had always been self-possessed and one to keep his problems to himself. Sally was one of the few people in whom he had ever confided. It had been difficult, but Joe was pleased he'd gotten Carl to agree to come. Oh, hell, he'd forgotten to tell Sal. He picked up the phone and dialed home. He let it ring ten times before he hung up. Sally wasn't home, and she had forgotten to turn on the answering machine.

He was sure she wouldn't care, but he promised himself he'd call her back later. Then he dug into the massive amount of work he still had piled on his desk.

Joe didn't notice the passage of time, and looked up in surprise when Carl walked in.

"Ready?" Carl asked.

"Is it lunchtime already?"

"It's after one."

"Good. I'll tie this up Monday. I'm going to call it a day."

They left the office and walked to the restaurant. Over their meal they discussed the rosary. He lifted it from his pocket as though it were weighted and reluctantly placed it in Joe's cupped hand. Joe's eyes widened in surprise.

"You know how this looks?" Joe said.

"I know. But I'd like you to keep quiet about this—at least for a couple of days."

"That's withholding evidence. I could have my head chopped off for doing that. Christ," Joe said softly, "wouldn't Phil Greggory like to prove something like that?"

"Especially since he's tried before," Carl said.

"You sure he's innocent, Carl?"

"No. I'm not sure of anything. But we're going to do our damnedest to find out."

"All right. I'll keep quiet about it until Wednesday. That's three working days. It's the best I can do, Carl. It could mean my job."

"So, go out and do some honest work for a change." They both laughed.

"That's against my principles," Joe retorted. "I need a week or so of good fishing and no work."

"We'll have to see to your rest and recreation when this is over."

"I'm going home," Joe said. "I'll see you tonight."

"Okay."

When Carl and Joe separated, Carl returned to the florist shop and had a bouquet of yellow roses sent to Sally. He remembered how well she liked them.

Joe's coming home early was a delightful surprise for Sally. He found her in the kitchen preparing a very elaborate meal. Joe bent to kiss her flushed cheek.

"Open the wine so it can breathe," she said. "How does prime rib sound?"

"Terrific," Joe replied, puzzled. "Sal, am I getting forgetful? Did you know we were having someone special for dinner?"

"Of course I knew," Sal laughed. "I invited her, didn't I?"

"Her who?"

"Why, Beth, of course."

For a few minutes, Joe just looked at her.

"Joe." Sal laughed again. "Beth has been here dozens of times. Why are you so surprised tonight?"

"God, I should have called you."

"What for?"

Before Joe could answer, the doorbell rang and Sally went to answer it while Joe sat down, wondering just how he was going to get around this.

Sally returned, pale of face and carrying a beautiful bouquet of yellow roses. The card trembled in her hand. "They're from Carl," she said. "He said he's looking forward to dinner tonight. Oh, Joe."

"Now, it's nothing to get upset about."

"Joe—he'll think we're trying to fix him up with someone. He'll be hurt and angry. We might drive him away again."

"I'll explain to him, Sal."

"What if he thinks we're interfering in his life?"

"Sal, I'll explain to him. We just got our signals crossed."

"Well, anyway, he's never met Beth, so he just might be polite and understanding."

"I meant to call you, but I got busy, and Carl has taken pot luck with us a lot of times, so I didn't think it would matter."

"I wish you had called."

"Now, come on, hon, don't make such a production out of this. Can't we have more than one friend for dinner without it being a major affair?"

"If it were anybody else but Carl." She sighed. "Well, there's not much we can do about it now. Beth will be here at six-thirty."

"And Carl will be here at seven." He grinned. "And they might just decide they like each other."

"Then, tie on an apron, my friend, and let's make this the best meal they've ever had. Maybe a lot of wine will mellow them both, and they'll forget about thinking this was a setup."

"A setup." Joe laughed as he put his arms around her and kissed her soundly. "You sound like some of the shady characters we drag in who accuse us of setting them up. Where'd you'd pick that up?"

"From all the junk you mumble in your sleep."

"I don't talk in my sleep."

"You don't? Hmmm, then I must have been sleeping with someone else. Let's see, it must have been yesterday afternoon. Ouch, Joe!"

"Sleeping with someone else, huh." He chuckled. "Don't I keep you busy enough, woman?"

"Well, last night was the football game; the night before, you fell asleep in your chair; and the night before that . . ."

"I get your point, lady," he said as he took her in his arms again and kissed her very differently. "Maybe we can get our guests to go home early."

"Maybe we'll be lucky, and they'll take a liking to each other and go out together."

She laughed as Joe looked at her suspiciously. "If I didn't know for certain you didn't know that Carl was coming, I'd swear you did set this up."

"Start cutting up salad, handsome, and we'll just let everybody be on their own tonight."

Beth arrived a few minutes before six-thirty and was welcomed enthusiastically.

"Hi, Beth," Joe said as he closed the door and turned to take her coat. "It's been too darn long since you've shared a meal with us."

"Would you like a drink, Beth?" Sally offered, coming in from the kitchen.

"Not right now."

"Well, you and Joe talk a few minutes. I have to set the table."

"I'll help you."

"You don't have to do that."

"Sal," Beth said, laughing, "since when am I such a formal guest that I can't help set the table?" She walked to the kitchen with Sally and began to get dishes from the cupboard.

"Ah, we'll need four dishes, Beth. We've invited someone else to dinner, too."

"Oh, great. Is it someone I know?"

"No. It's an old friend of Joe's from Cambridge—Carl Forrester."

Beth became very still, and neither Joe nor Sally missed the sudden change.

"I'm sorry, Beth," Sally said quickly. "This whole thing was just a mistake in communications between Joe and me. I invited you, and Joe invited Carl, but we forgot to tell each other. Joe tried to call and tell me today, but I was out. It wasn't planned this way."

"I believe you. It's just that . . . well, Mr. Forrester might be the one who is upset. You see, we've already met, and he might just believe the three of us were sort of maneuvering." Beth smiled. "If he didn't mention our meeting to Joe, well, maybe he just didn't think it was important." She went on to explain how they had met.

It wasn't too hard to piece together the puzzle of why Carl had left so abruptly. Joe and Sally exchanged quick, silent glances. Neither was too sure now that Carl's homecoming dinner was going to be a very pleasant affair after all. Nobody felt comfortable when the doorbell rang, and Carl came in with several gaily wrapped packages.

"Hey! Anybody home? I smell food, and I'm so hungry I could eat burnt buffalo!"

Joe and Sally stood in silence, with Beth close behind them. All three watched Carl struggle to retain his smile as his eyes met Beth's.

"I . . . ah . . . didn't know you had company," he said lamely, unable to find anything more appropriate. Sally tried her best to relieve the situation. She came to Carl and took his face between her hands. The packages made it impossible for him to do anything other than submit. She kissed him and smiled nonchalantly.

"Beth isn't company, she's almost family. Joe and I just got our wires crossed. He forgot to tell me you finally decided to come and see this lonely old lady. I've missed you, you big lout."

Carl had only one choice, outside of turning around and

running, which was what his first inclination had been. He smiled and dragged his eyes from Beth to Sally.

"Old lady!" he teased. "It's just living with that old man over there. Why don't you give up and run away with me to Tahiti or some place?"

"I can't get into my bikini," she said, giggling.

"You look pretty good to me."

"Keep your grubby, big-city paws off my wife," Joe said, laughing.

"Haven't got 'em on her," Carl responded. He handed the packages to Sally. "Would have, though, if they hadn't been full."

"Beware of Greeks bearing gifts, Sal. He's trying to corrupt you."

"Candy, flowers, perfume." Sal looked distressed. "I'm afraid I'm lost, Joe."

Beth watched the interaction between what were obviously the closest of friends. She saw Carl's face seem suddenly young as he laughed with them. Then his attention was drawn back to her, and she saw his eyes grow shuttered and wary. It angered her. Why should he be so upset just to see another woman present? She certainly had no designs on him, and the sooner he understood that, the better it would be for both of them.

"Hello, again." He smiled, but it never reached his eyes.

"Hello. I'm sorry for this mix-up. Really, I have a lot of things to do. I think I'll just go and . . ."

"No . . . no," Carl said quickly. "I'm sorry if I made you feel uncomfortable. I was just a little surprised."

Uncomfortable, she thought with growing irritation. *Why should I feel uncomfortable? He's the one who seems to have a problem with the situation.*

Carl felt several swift and very conflicting emotions. He knew she was angry, and he wondered why that made him feel safe. She also had a disturbing presence that strummed his nerves like guitar strings. As far as he was concerned, it was going to be a long and tedious night.

Anxious to relieve the tension, Joe and Sally played off each other with a kind of laid-back finesse. At first it brought laughter.

"And so Joe and I, who had saved every dime we could, spent our vacation snowed in in a ski lodge." Sally laughed as she finished her story.

"How awful," Beth replied.

"Oh, I wouldn't say that." Joe chuckled, with a glitter in his eyes that made even Carl laugh.

"Joe!" Sally actually blushed.

"Well, honey, what can I say? I remember that vacation as one of the best we've ever taken."

"We've only taken two," Sally shot back.

"That's right. But, honey, vacations like that are so . . . ultimate, that two is enough for a lifetime."

"Is this your way of telling me we don't get a vacation again next spring?" Sally raised an eyebrow and looked at Joe with a ferocious scowl.

"Now, dear, violence at the dinner table will alarm our guests."

"I'll give you 'dear,' " she threatened.

"Don't worry about us, Sal." Carl chuckled. "If Joe's got it coming . . ."

"My buddy," Joe said in a martyred voice.

"You mean, you've only had two vacations since you've been married?" Beth asked Sally.

"Now's my chance to be clever. Let me tell you, Beth, every day with Sally is like an exotic vacation," Joe said smoothly.

"Ohhh!" Carl and Sally groaned together while Joe looked very satisfied with himself. Beth had to smile, but inside she felt hollow, remembering her own failed marriage. She had wanted it to be like Joe and Sally's.

Carl's face revealed nothing of his thoughts, but he was nearly desperate for the evening to end. Every moment of laughter, every teasing joke, ripped open the sealed memories he held of another time—four people together, one of whom was gone.

The repartee between Joe and Sally seemed to be drawing them closer. Carl and Beth could see the warm exchanged glances, the light touch of hands, and both could feel the sensual emotions building.

It was frustrating for Carl, because he felt Beth's presence even when he wasn't looking at her. It set every nerve he had on edge, but he held his control with grim resolution. Soon the meal would be over, and she would be gone from his life. As time went by, however, things didn't work out as Carl had predicted.

Beth was intelligent; Carl found himself listening when she talked. As she drew him to her, he kept raising his mental barrier higher, until he was fighting a battle with every breath and word.

Beth was sensitive to this, and her growing antagonism chilled the air.

Only Sally's sense of humor and Joe's grim cooperation kept things going, despite the fact that she would like to have murdered both Carl and Beth for being so blind. She had already decided that they might be good for each other if they could lower the barbed-wire fence for a minute.

To Beth's relief, the magical hour of eleven finally came, and she could legitimately say she had to leave.

"Beth, it's only eleven," Sally complained. "You don't have to work tomorrow."

"I know, but I promised Eve we'd go to the museum. I'll call you, Sal."

Beth rose, said a quick good night to Carl, and a much pleasanter one to Joe. Sally walked her to the door.

"Beth, I'm sorry," Sally said quietly.

"For what?"

"I just don't want you to think . . ."

"Sal, I've been friends with you and Joe too long. If you say it was bad communications, then that's what it was. Don't give it another thought."

"Thanks, Beth. Carl is a very fine person. Tonight was not the best night to judge him, really. He's had a lot of problems."

"I know."

"You do?"

"Yes." Beth was suddenly embarrassed. "I guess I was prying. I looked back in the files and read the whole story. I'm sorry for him."

"Carl doesn't take well to pity."

"I'm sure he doesn't," Beth said gently but firmly. "But

he certainly didn't give any indication that we could even be friends. Why don't we just forget the whole thing? Good night, Sal. Call me."

"I will. Good night, Beth."

Sally closed the door and smiled to herself. Beth was more attracted to Carl than she would admit. Why else would she take the trouble to look into his past, after meeting him for only a minute? She returned to the living room, where Joe and Carl lounged comfortably.

"Come sit by me, Sal," Carl said, "and let me tell you how much I missed you."

"From the way you ate tonight, I think it was my cooking you missed."

"Living in an apartment and doing my own cooking leaves a lot to be desired."

Sally sat down beside Carl. "I have really missed you, Carl. I wish . . ."

"C'mon," Carl said gently, "don't waste your wishes. You never know how many your guardian angel has left to give you."

She sighed, then reached out to touch Carl's hand. "I loved the flowers. It seemed like old times."

Sally's sentence was interrupted by a knock on the door. Joe opened it and was surprised to find Beth standing there.

"My car won't start!"

"Come on in and sit with Sal, I'll go take a look."

Carl went out to see if he could help Joe, but no matter what they tried nothing worked. Carl tried to jump start the battery, but couldn't.

Both men returned to the living room.

"I think you need a mechanic, Beth," Joe said.

"You'll never get anybody tonight," Sally said.

Only Joe recognized the devilish look in Sal's eyes.

"I think the best idea is for Carl to take you home. It's only a little out of his way." She looked so angelically innocent that Joe very nearly laughed.

Carl had little choice but to agree, as graciously as he could. He said a quick good night, then told them he would be going back to the motel from Beth's. When he left with

Beth, Sally leaned against the closed door and smiled impishly at Joe, who threw back his head and laughed.

"If he doesn't come back and throttle you, I'll be surprised."

"What did I do?"

"I think," Joe put his arms about her, "that that was about the best setup I've ever seen done."

"I just took advantage of an opportunity," Sally replied as she slid her arms about his waist and moved to fit her body against his. It was a comfortable, pleasurable movement, done with a smoothness that spoke of years of sweet intimacy. "Wouldn't it be wonderful if Carl could find someone who..."

"Sal, that's dangerous. You could tell as well as I that he was a little tense."

"I guess you're right." Sally looked up at him with a mischievous grin. "And, at the moment, you feel a little tense."

"Sweetheart," Joe said, grinning, "that is not tense, it's downright rigid."

Sally could feel his warmth, and she needed it. She always needed it, but tonight, in the face of the emptiness she knew surrounded her snug little world, she was extra grateful for the arms that held her, the eyes that looked into hers and promised so much.

"Oh, Joe, I do love you so much."

He understood her need and mirrored it in his own heart. He tipped her chin up to take her willing mouth in a deep and sensual kiss that seemed to drug her. By the time the kiss ended, his hands were already moving on her body, slipping beneath her blouse to caress her. She let out a tiny moan as his hands slid down to trace the curve of her hips, then to grip her bottom and urge her hard against him.

Without another word he swung her up in his arms and carried her to the couch, with its scattering of soft cushions. They sank down on it together. Each knew the other so well, knew what brought pleasure. One kiss led to another, each deeper and more passionate. Their breathing deepened as hurried fingers worked buttons and zippers.

Sally met him halfway, craving the hardness of him, panting as the heat within began to grow to uncontrolled fierceness. He stroked her in slow, even thrusts until he could feel the love of her drawing him. With every move he loved her more. He closed his eyes for a moment as they reached for the climax together. When it struck, he opened his eyes to look into hers. With a groan of pleasure so deep it was very nearly pain, they reached a prolonged and powerful climax.

For a long moment they held each other, with ragged panting the only sound.

Joe's gentle hand lifted Sally's face. Her eyes were filled with tears.

"Sal?"

"Oh, Joe, I feel so sorry for them. I have you, and all they have is loneliness." Words were unnecessary. Instead, he kissed her deeply and with fervent thanks.

Carl drove for several minutes in what to Beth was a maddening silence. Both were held by thoughts they didn't want to face, measuring their loneliness by what they had left behind.

"Carl, I'm really sorry to take you out of your way like this."

"It's no trouble. As Sal said, it's practically on my way."

"But you certainly weren't ready to leave."

He gave her a quick glance. "I can see Sally and Joe again soon."

The more he protested, the more she felt his subconscious anger.

"Carl," she began firmly, "I'd like to get one thing straight."

"What's that?"

"This dinner tonight. I had no idea you would be there. It was certainly not prearranged."

"Yeah, I kind of thought it must have been Sal's idea, but it sure was an untimely one."

"I don't know what it is about me that antagonizes you so much, but I want to make my position extremely clear." She was now slowly losing the fragile hold she had on her temper. "I have no desire to have an arranged relationship with anyone. I make my own choices as to whom I care to see. At this time in my life, I have complete control, and I don't intend to have it interfered with. I'm sorry if you got the wrong impression, but I'm not out to take anyone's place. I . . ." She stopped abruptly, regretting the reference to his past.

"You seem to have heard about me. Was that Sal's contribution, too? Did she tell you all about Carl Forrester's sordid past? Tell me, was it interesting?"

"You underestimate your friends. Neither of them planned this, and neither of them told me one thing about you."

"Then," he added, "you must have been listening to gossip."

"Wrong again. I read about you in the old newspapers. Remember the night we met, and I told you I thought you looked familiar. Well, I'm sorry again, but I was curious."

"Curious?" he repeated, and the intonation was an indictment.

When they reached her home, he stopped the car and reached across her to open the door.

Beth got out of the car and turned to look at Carl's uncompromising face.

"You," she said with cold fury, "are completely content in your shadowed little world of self-pity. Well, I wouldn't disturb it, even if I could. Some people are worth reaching for and saving from their own faults. In my opinion, you are not."

She slammed the door before he could reply and walked rapidly into her house, where she satisfied her emotional outburst by slamming the door again.

As quickly as her temper came, it was gone, and she reluctantly admitted to herself that part of her anger stemmed from self-defense, and the other half from guilt for probing into his life.

She began to enlarge on her own illogical reaction. He was right in assuming tonight had been prearranged. She had thought the same thing, at first. And his cold response to her might have been her own, had anyone done the same thing to her. After a few minutes, her remorse got the best of her. She went to the phone and called for a taxi.

Carl was boiling with emotions, ranging from rage at her intrusion of his privacy, to renewed guilt at what she must think.

He had struck out at her because he recognized a sensitivity and understanding he could not accept. He had nursed his dreams too long. They were companions to his guilt, and they were the only reasons he could find for not facing the past.

Beth Raleigh was a source of light that might illuminate the dark cobweb-filled corner of his mind. Like a wounded beast, he was thrashing about mentally, willing to destroy any remote touch that might take away the self-inflicted punishment of his dreams and leave him no place to hide.

He paced his room in a murderous mood. No matter what situation Joe was in, he was going to leave Helton as soon as he possibly could.

Sleep was a complete impossibility, so he decided to go for a walk.

The beach was less than a mile away, and he felt it might be the best place to walk alone.

He put on a pair of jeans, a sweatshirt, and tennis shoes. Before he could turn out the light, there was a timid knock on the door.

At first he thought it might be Sally or Joe. Most likely Sally, he thought. He walked to the door and opened it. He was taken totally by surprise to see Beth there. She spoke first.

"I feel like an utter fool. Could you please spare a minute to let a lady apologize?"

* CHAPTER 7 *

His habitual policeman's observation took in her slim body in slacks and sweater. The fact that she had taken a taxi left him no recourse but to invite her in or take her home.

"There's nothing to apologize for," he said in a voice he hoped would end any further discussion.

"I don't usually lose my temper and say such stupid things. I had no right to pry into your life."

"Consider it forgotten." He grinned as amiably as he could manage, again wondering at his own gnawing fear.

"Can't I at least buy you a drink to seal my apology and my promise that I'll not make such a stupid mistake again?"

He didn't want to go anywhere, especially with her. But short of tossing her out, he had no other options. He sighed and shrugged.

"Why not," he replied. "There's a little bar down the road."

"Angelo's?"

"Yes. You know it?"

"I do. Angelo makes the best Bloody Marys in the world."

"Then, let's go." He moved inside to take his keys and wallet from the dresser, and she followed.

When he turned to look at her again, she stood close enough to touch, and he was thoroughly shaken by the desire to do just that.

Their eyes met and held for what seemed to be interminable minutes. She had the most remarkable blue eyes, he thought, even as he tore his gaze from hers.

"I don't usually carry much when I walk on the beach—just in case," he said aloud, realizing he was grasping for any words that came to mind.

"Well, you could always call a policeman if you ran into problems." She laughed.

"Yeah, I guess I could." He chuckled. He was grateful when they stepped back outside and he pulled the door closed behind them. "My car's right over there." He pointed across the lot. She nodded and walked beside him toward the car.

He started to move toward her side of the car, intending to open the door for her.

"Don't bother, I can manage," she said, a smile softening the abruptness of her words.

"My chauvinism showing?" He grinned.

"I'll bet your mother was from the old school."

He laughed aloud now. "My mother could have outrun O. J. Simpson, outboxed Ali, and most likely, outmaneuvered Kissinger."

She laughed openly and enthusiastically, and he was surprised that he not only enjoyed it, but laughed, too.

At the table at Angelo's, Beth raised her drink to him. "Here's to appropriate apologies."

He touched her glass with his. "To unnecessary apologies."

She sipped her drink, then set it down.

"Carl, this terrible murder—do you and Joe have any idea who could have done it?"

"Not yet."

"Not even a suspicion?"

"A whole lot of suspicions, but it's like having a truckload of pieces to a puzzle. You have to sort them first, then see what fits together."

"Joe seemed upset tonight."

"You must know him pretty well."

"Why?"

"He's pretty good at hiding his feelings."

"I've known Joe and Sally a little over two years."

"Ah, I see. I still think you're pretty astute to see through him."

"Remember, I'm Sally's friend. Women talk about such things. I was watching her, and when she kept watching Joe, I knew with reasonable certainty that he was upset."

"Yeah," he said, chuckling, "Sal is a pretty good barometer for Joe's emotions. She's a little fond of him."

"My, my." Her eyes sparkled mischievously. "I kind of got the feeling when you arrived tonight that she was a little fond of you, too."

"Sally and I go way back. Even before . . ."

The words hung in the air like a thick, unbreathable cloud.

"Well, anyway, for a long time," he finished. "Joe and I were boyhood friends."

"I see. I was lucky enough to meet Sally just a few months after I arrived here."

"Oh, you weren't a Helton native?"

"No, I was born in Boston."

"What in God's name brought you from a great city like Boston to a little town like Helton?"

"Running away, I guess."

"Running? You don't look like the running type."

"Thank you. I'd like to think I'm not now, but a few years ago I was." She took another sip of her drink and set it down slowly, as if she were contemplating her words. "I made a very bad mistake. I married a man who," she shrugged slightly, "wasn't what I thought he was."

"Not very many of us are what people think we are."

"No, I imagine that is one of the things that makes your job so difficult—all the faces people present to you. How can you look behind the masks people wear to find someone who kills?"

"Sometimes you look inside yourself, see behind your own mask. Sometimes you can even understand why some kill."

"I can't believe there is any reason to kill."

He looked at her for several moments, and she could almost feel a subtle withdrawal in him. "No," he said quietly, "I imagine you wouldn't."

She realized she had touched a vulnerable spot. She regretted her words and her inability to recall them.

"So," he added quickly, "you just decided to move to Helton?"

"I had an aunt who lived here. She died since then and left me a bit of money—nothing monumental—and the small house I live in. I'm quite comfortable, and quite happy."

"No outside interests?"

"Another man?" She laughed. "I have some friends I go out with, but nothing serious. I don't need that in my life now."

"It seems you have your life neatly tied in a gift-wrapped box, ribbon and all."

"You make that sound almost wrong."

"No, that wasn't said condemningly. I guess I envy you."

"Why?"

"To have everything decided—not to have any doubts."

"Did I say I didn't have any doubts? Everyone has doubts."

"So, what do you do with them?" he questioned quietly.

"Learn to live despite them," she replied firmly.

He sighed and took the last of his drink in one long swallow. "Well, I'll take you home. Joe has no mercy. Even if tomorrow is Sunday, he'll most likely be on the phone before I can even open my eyes."

Beth said nothing. She rose without putting words to the thoughts in her mind. She wanted to fight the unseen force, to do something to tear away the shuttered look in his eyes, and she had no idea how. She was certain of one thing—he had no intention of letting her near enough to try.

Carl pulled his car into the short drive to Beth's small house. It was completely dark, and his brows furrowed as he turned to look at her.

"You don't leave a night-light on when you go out?"

"I've never been afraid before."

"I think it's more a matter of caution than fear. But you should get in the habit."

"Yes, Mr. Policeman." Beth laughed.

"I sound like an overprotective father, but this murder—well, it's strange."

"What do you mean?"

"Usually when people commit murder, they have some kind of definite motive. In this case, there doesn't seem to be one. A girl everybody liked . . ." He left the thought unfinished.

"I'll be more careful in the future. Carl, thanks for being so understanding, and accepting my apology."

"How could I resist?" he grinned. "You plied me with liquor and good company—a sure way to get what you want from me."

"Well, at least we're friends. Good night."

"Not yet," he replied as he reached for the door handle. "I'm going to see that you're safely locked in."

"Chauvinism again. Your mother would be chuckling, I presume."

"Probably." He met her at the front of the car, and his hand lightly touched her elbow as they walked to the long, dark porch.

Beth fumbled in her purse for a moment, then Carl flicked his lighter so she could see. "I told you, you should leave a light on."

She unlocked the door, swung it open, moved quietly across the room to turn on the light. Then she returned to Carl to hold her hand out.

"Thanks again, Carl. I hope you catch this person, and I will be more careful in the future—I promise."

"Good . . . and thanks for the drink."

"Sure, good night."

It seemed to Beth that for a moment, there was something more Carl wanted to say. She waited expectantly, but the moment passed.

"Good night, Beth. Go on in and lock the door."

She did as he said, and he was satisfied to hear the solid click of the lock.

Beth leaned against the door for a moment and heard him walk back to the car, slam the door, then, after several moments, start the engine. The silence that followed was surprising in its oppressiveness. It was as though his departure had created a physical void. She shook her head as if she couldn't quite believe the almost uncomfortable effect his consideration had on her.

Carl walked down the three porch steps and the path that led to the drive. He slid behind the wheel and slammed the door, but he didn't reach for his keys at once. He sat in the dark car and gazed at the small house. There was a sheen of light perspiration on his forehead, and the hands that gripped the wheel shook. He looked at them in complete and profound amazement.

He had looked into the depths of Beth's perceptive blue eyes and he had wanted her! He had wanted to kiss her mindless, to tear the clothes from her and satisfy an almost animal ferocity that rattled his mind.

It was the last thing in the world he needed. She had come too close; she had found cracks in his wall of defense that he was unprepared for.

Almost angrily, he thrust the key into the ignition. He backed rapidly from the drive and started for the motel, deliberately pushing all thoughts of Beth and her damned penetrating blue eyes from his mind.

The motel room had never looked emptier or felt lonelier. He realized suddenly that there was a tremendous difference between being alone and being lonely. The intruder in his self-enforced loneliness was Beth, and for a startling moment, he hated her.

He was angry for not bringing something back from the bar with him to blunt the conflict within.

He clicked on the television and watched a small portion of the news while he took off his jacket. Then he braced the two pillows against the head of the bed and sat down to try to watch the rest of it, but he wasn't interested.

Finally, he rose and shut if off, then grabbed his jacket and left the room. He walked the distance to the beach, and despite the cold touch of the wind, he stood for a while and listened to the surf crash against the shore. Then he walked some more until he was tired enough to sleep.

The dreams were worse than they had ever been. He awoke with an anguished cry in the small hours of the morning. The sheets were wet with his sweat, and he was panting as if he had run for miles. There would be no more sleep.

While Beth, Carl, Joe, and Sally had been at dinner, another drama was being played out that would make Carl's nightmares tame in comparison.

It was just dark. Streetlights cast a mellow light, and most of Helton's inhabitants were eating their dinner. The street in front of St. Catherine's was deserted. The church itself was empty, except for the two people who were standing outside the doors.

"I appreciate your offer to help, Paula," Father McAllen said. "Since this terrible thing with Martha, I'm afraid everything in the office has been in a jumble."

Paula Craig was a slim, vivacious girl who smiled often. Her hair was a deep auburn, and her green eyes were filled with the excitement and challenge found in the young.

"I don't mind helping, Father. Since my dad died, you've really been great to Mother and me. I'm just glad I could find a way to give you a hand."

"Well, I appreciate it, even if you won't take credit for it."

"I'd better get home. I'm twenty years old, but my mom still gets anxious when I'm roaming around late." She reached out to touch his arm, then spontaneously kissed his cheek. "I am grateful, Father, and I'll do a good job, I promise." Her eyes sparkled and she laughed softly. "Don't think you're fooling anyone. We both know there are a lot of girls who would do this for you. I know you chose me because of Dad, and you know Mom and I need help."

"You're a clever lady," he said, grinning, "but then,

that's why I hired you. Wait until you try to cope with the mess that office is in. You won't be so grateful."

"I'll be grateful 'til the day I die," she said, laughing.

"Well, you've got a lot of good years left yet, despite your rapid descent into old age. So I guess I can hope for some way to get this tangled mess worked out."

"I'll do my best."

"That's good enough for me."

"Good night."

" 'Night, Paula." He watched her leave with a serious look and a slight frown on his face.

She ran down the eight or nine steps and walked around the corner of the church toward the parking lot, where she had parked her blue Mustang. She hummed lightly as she approached her car and began to fumble in her purse for her keys. She did not hear the footsteps of the person who followed until they were close behind her. Then the sound caused her to spin about with a gasp. Martha Dexter's violent death had unnerved everyone, but Paula's eyes brightened in recognition of the large man who stood close to her.

"Oh—did I forget something?" she asked.

"No," he replied with a responding smile. "I've just found myself in a bit of a jam. I'm going your way, and I need a ride."

"Well, no sooner said than done. Get in."

"Thanks." He walked to the passenger side of the car and got in while she got in the other side. She looked across to him and smiled.

"Buckle up. I'm a stickler for seatbelts."

"You believe in precautions, do you?"

"Most certainly. I'm a very careful lady."

"It's wise," he said quietly. "You just can't be too careful."

They pulled out of the parking lot and drove toward the outskirts of town.

Anyone seeing her car who knew her usual route would have been surprised when the car suddenly veered from its normal path and drove in a direction it had not traveled before. They would have seen the speed suddenly increase. But they would not have understood the terror that drove it.

* * *

A pale moon sent thin beams of light through the barren trees. A bed of autumn leaves muffled the sounds of the two people who struggled together. Paula Craig fought valiantly for her life, but the battle was doomed from the start, for she was half the size of the man. It was impossible for her to cry out again after her first scream for help; her attacker had beaten her brutally about her face until she could utter only soft whimpers of fear. A terror, black and deep, filled her, taking what little breath she had. It welled up in her in a bubbling, soundless scream. Her eyes were wide and blurred by hot tears of pain and fear. She knew death was near and she was too weak to hold it off.

The uneven battle ended in a few short minutes as the man's hands closed about her throat and silenced any sounds. Slowly her body sagged, held up only by his grip about her throat. When he loosened his hold, her body drifted down to the leaf-covered ground and lay still. Wide, unseeing green eyes looked at the cold, uninterested moon.

He stood over her for a few minutes, panting heavily. He inhaled deeply, and the scent of her perfume came to him. It brought with it visions, shadows of black memories, and a low feral growl came from deep in his throat. The visions had whispering voices that urged him on, consoling him with the sure knowledge that he was the hand of God, being used to rid the world of an evil. After a short time his breathing slowed to an even pace, but still he looked down at the body of the girl that lay at his feet.

"Whore," he whispered softly. "Whore to tempt as you did. For such a sin, all like you should die."

The man was extraordinarily strong. He lifted the young woman's lifeless body effortlessly from the ground and carried it to the base of a tree. Without care, he dropped it to the ground, then slowly and rhythmically piled leaves upon it. It took some time until he was completely satisfied that there was no evidence that any crime had been committed here.

He wiped the perspiration from his face and hands with a white handkerchief, then shoved it back in his pocket. He stood looking intently at the leafy grave. For a moment his eyes glowed with the fire of extreme passion; then, they cooled again to a contemplative look. Afterward came remorse . . . and compassion.

Slowly, as though a huge hand were pressing on him, he dropped to his knees beside the grave, murmuring with pain. Then, with a hand that trembled, he made the sign of the cross: forehead, heart, shoulder to shoulder. For quite a while he remained kneeling, eyes closed and head bowed, deep in prayer.

Then slowly he rose and began to whistle lightly through his teeth, as if he had completely forgotten the woman from whom he had taken the gift of life a short time before.

It was almost a half-hour walk from the depths of the woods to the narrow dirt road, and he traveled the distance in a ground-eating trot. About a quarter of a mile down the dirt road he reached the place where he had forced Paula to park her car. He drove it a short distance to the edge of a small lake, put the car in gear, and pushed it from behind until it started to roll. He watched it sink below the surface. Then, at the same rapid trot, he returned to the car he had parked nearby less than four hours before. He was humming a strange tune to himself when he pulled onto the main road a few miles later.

* CHAPTER 8 *

Carl woke early Sunday, and decided he would take advantage of the day to do some checking before the call from Joe came, as he was sure it would. He finished his shower and shave, then headed for the restaurant where he and Joe had eaten before.

Just as he slid into a seat, he heard a voice behind him.

"Good morning, Mr. Forrester."

Carl turned and looked up into David Mondale's eyes. They

were smiling now, but he remembered their glare of condemnation when he had forced the interview with Father McAllen.

"Good morning. David, isn't it?"

"Right. David Mondale."

"Care for a cup of coffee?"

"Yes," David said, laughing. "I don't seem to have the ability to get my motor started without a pot of it in the morning."

"You're up really early."

"Always am. Been an early riser since I was a boy. I usually go to six o'clock mass and talk afterward with Father to get instructions for the day's practice." David grinned. "I may be the coach, but Father is the iron hand behind me."

While they ordered their coffee, Carl watched David. The phrase "All-American boy" again leapt into his mind. David was extremely handsome, and was powerfully built. Carl wondered again why he had been so protective of Father McAllen, and why he had been angry at Carl's questioning of the priest.

"So, David," Carl asked with a smile, "you've lived in Helton all your life?"

"No, I came here only a few years ago, when I got a teaching position at St. Catherine's."

"I see. Where are you from?"

"Up near Bridgefield. My family had a house near the lake. I lived there until my parents died, then I moved a few miles away to live with my Aunt Caroline and my Uncle Robert. He's my mother's brother."

"What brought you to Helton?"

"Is this a friendly question, or police work?"

"Can't it be both?"

"I found a teaching position here—an opportunity. That's what brought me to Helton."

"You live alone here, David?" Carl asked quietly.

"Yes," he replied in the same level voice as Carl's. "Yes, I live alone, but I can tell you where I was when Martha was killed. At ten-thirty—that's the time the newspaper says she was killed—I was having a cup of hot tea with Emma Lowrey, my landlady. She's really a warm old soul. She can tell you herself." He took a piece of paper and a pen from his pocket and wrote down the address. "I had no reason to kill a girl I hardly knew. The few times I did meet her were in Father's office while she was working for him." David laughed softly. "She was almost like his shadow—trailed him around like a homeless kitten."

"Father McAllen didn't like that?"

"Father!" David laughed again. "He is the most tolerant man I've ever met. He always has time for everyone and their problems. Sometimes I see him so exhausted he can hardly think, but if someone calls for him, he'll run to take care of it."

"Martha had problems?"

"I didn't know enough about her to be able to say. I know she came over to talk to Father a lot. I went over to see him late one night and found her there—long after working hours. She left as soon as I got there."

"You sound like you admire Father McAllen."

"Admire him? Yeah, I do. But I'm only one of a whole town that does. He's a special kind of man. He has a quality that makes him so damn . . . I don't know. *Special* is not a strong enough word. He's a gentle man with those who need strength, and he's understanding with those who need understanding."

"Sounds almost perfect."

"Nobody's perfect, but if you want someone close to it, then Father McAllen's it."

"Sometimes," Carl replied gently, "one finds the gods have feet of clay."

Carl watched a spark of anger light David's eyes and sensed his antagonism, just as he had at their first meeting. Carl cautioned himself not to push until he had some concrete evidence, but the investigation had slipped into a higher gear, and he was shaken by the fact that the evidence seemed to be pointing more and more toward Father McAllen.

David rose and looked down at Carl.

"Father McAllen is the best thing that ever happened to this town. He's a fine and honorable man, and a more than excellent priest. I don't think there are many in town who would say a word against him, and I don't believe there's anyone who would believe him capable of murder. You'll have to look somewhere else for your killer. But not in my direction. If you talk to Mrs. Lowrey, you'll find I was with her the night Martha died."

He turned and walked away. Carl watched until he left the restaurant. If David did have Mrs. Lowrey to testify that he was with her when Martha died, his alibi would be airtight. Carl had known Mrs. Lowrey from the second day his family had moved to Helton. He'd been meaning to talk with her anyway. He'd do it as soon as possible.

Carl was surprised to find Joe at his office.

"They found Martha Dexter's car last night," Joe told him. "We've been looking for it since the body was found. We don't know if the killer rode with her or ran her off the road, but there might be something in the car to give us a lead. And I wanted to go over a couple of things that were bothering me last night. We'll have the autopsy report pretty soon. Maybe that will tell us something."

"You have some suspicions?"

"We have a chance of finding she was pregnant. It would sure put a finger on Brodie."

"Why?"

"She was pretty close to him."

"Could be a better motive for someone else, who didn't want to have it spilled."

"Like Paul?"

"Like Paul," Carl agreed. Joe sighed and leaned back in his chair to brace his feet on his desk. Carl slouched in the comfortable leather chair across from him. He was well aware of the tense look in Joe's eyes.

"I was given instructions by Sally this morning," Joe grinned. "She's a little uncomfortable about last night."

"Serves her right," Carl said, laughing. "Teach her not to meddle. Because she's so damn happily married, she's not past pushing her friends into it. I imagine Beth—Miss Raleigh—thinks the same way."

"Beth?" Joe grinned. Carl shrugged, then both men laughed.

"Seriously, Carl, have you turned up anything?"

"Very little."

"If we don't dig up something real soon, I'm going to have to bring Father McAllen in for questioning. I don't want to do that, but that broken rosary is evidence, and I can't hold it too long."

"I was just butting heads with someone else on the same subject."

"Who?"

"David Mondale. I met him in the restaurant this morning. He's a staunch supporter of Father McAllen. In fact, he just told me to stay away from him."

"David Mondale?"

"Yeah. What do you have on him?"

Joe scanned a paper from the pile on his desk. He read for a moment in silence, then slid it across the desk to Carl.

"Nothing. The man's clean. He's never even had a parking ticket, and he has the best alibi. He lives with Mrs. Lowrey. She swears that he was sitting at her table at ten-thirty the night Martha was killed, and she was positive about the time, so...." Joe shrugged. "Stickin' around for lunch?"

"No, I think I'll nose around some more. I'll talk to Amy Realton, if I can. I want to see just how far she might go to protect Paul. She teaches at St. Catherine High School, doesn't she?"

"Yeah. You'll probably be able to find her home."

"Or maybe at Paul's?"

"Maybe. He's doing a real fine painting of her." They were silent for several minutes. "God, I hope he's not guilty, Carl. They're nice people. I'd hate to see them messed up. I'd hate to pull 'em in for a thing like this."

"We have to do a whole lot of things we don't like. But think of Martha. No matter who's guilty, we have to find him."

"Well," Joe said gently, "maybe I've been a policeman too long."

"I was thinking along those lines myself a while ago, but a friend of mine wouldn't let it stand that way. He twisted my arm into remembering a debt. Now, old friend, you got me into this, so let's find a way out. Let's find our killer, Joe," he added softly.

* * *

Amy had risen early because she intended to pose for Paul in the early morning sun. She laughed softly at his humorous disgust at not being able to recreate her on canvas the way he wanted.

She slipped into her jeans and sweater, took her jacket from the closet, and was just reaching for the doorknob when a knock made her jump back reflexively. She opened the door. Carl smiled pleasantly, and was troubled by a look he could only describe as fear that leapt into Amy's eyes.

"Carl."

"Hello again. May I come in? I'd like to talk for a few minutes."

"I was just going out to Paul's. Would you like to come with me?"

"Not right now," he said gently. "I'd like to talk with you alone."

"Come in," she said. She stepped aside to let Carl pass her, then closed the door and followed him into her living room.

Carl watched her approach, reading uncertainty in her face and in the nervous clenching of her hands.

"So, how is Paul's portrait coming along?"

"It's a fine piece—one of Paul's best. Of course," she said, "he doesn't think it's going well, but he's such a perfectionist, especially with his work."

"I thought it was nearly perfect when I saw it. You are an excellent subject."

"Thank you, but you didn't come here to tell me that."

"No—not exactly. I came to ask you a few questions."

"What could I possibly tell you that you don't already know?"

"From what the police have been told, Paul was with you most of the night of the murder."

"Most—no. Not most—all of that night."

"From what time to what time?"

"I've told the police that."

"So, tell me again."

"From a little past eight at night until after six in the morning."

"He never left you?"

"Not for a minute."

"Amy," he said softly, "what would you say if I told you there's a witness who saw Paul alone, after ten-thirty that night?"

Amy licked suddenly dry lips, and her eyes moved from his. "That's not true. He was with me."

"I know you love Paul, but a lie never helps. It just clouds up the waters. Then it's hard to find the real truth. Now, I'd like to ask you one more time. Was Paul with you all night?"

Amy looked close to tears, but her chin was defiantly lifted, and now her eyes held his.

"Whoever your witness is, he's lying. Paul was with me all night, and I'll testify in court if I have to."

There was no witness to nullify Amy's word, but Carl could tell she was lying. He wondered why she felt she had to lie to protect Paul, if she thought there was nothing between Paul and Martha?

"Did you know Martha before you were involved with Paul?"

"Slightly—mostly by sight."

"You knew about the incident between Martha and Paul?"

"Of course. Paul was a kid. Kids make mistakes. He made his peace with Martha a long time before she was killed."

"How?"

"What?"

"How did he make his peace? By meeting her?"

"Yes, he met her to talk."

"Often?"

"No!"

"Did it bother you?" he prodded.

"No!"

"Were you jealous?" he snapped quickly.

"No!"

"They're doing a complete autopsy on Martha," he said bluntly, watching her face go gray. "Will it turn up anything surprising?" he added mildly.

Amy again moistened her dry lips, and Carl had to admire her control. She meant to stick by Paul, no matter what the consequences.

"How would I know? Look, Paul is innocent. He wouldn't kill—not for any reason."

"Even for you?"

"Even for me. Paul knows a life could never be built on such a tragedy."

Carl smiled at her, part of him wishing she was right, and the other wishing he did not have the certainty she was lying to him. He had to find out just where Paul Carterson really was that night, and why.

"Well, it's a nice Sunday, and the sun's bright, even if it is cold out there. I expect Paul will want to be painting. I'll let you go. Tell Paul there are a few more questions I have to find the answers to."

"Let him be, Carl," Amy almost whispered.

"I can't do that, and you know it. Unless I have all the truth, we'll never know who killed Martha. If Paul is innocent, the truth won't hurt him."

"Whose truth? Sometimes the truth gets twisted. People believe what they want to believe."

"Not a policeman, Amy. It's not my job to nail Paul; it's my job to find out who committed murder. If the truth will catch the guilty, it will also free the innocent."

"I hope you're right."

"Well, I can't be Batman for all the Robins of the world, and I'll be the first to admit the system's fallible, but it usually works, and I intend to see that it does in this case. Tell Paul that unless there is guilt somewhere, or something to hide, the truth is always the better weapon."

"I'll tell him that," Amy replied. Carl was not sure he read relief in her eyes, but she seemed to lose some of her tenseness.

"Good girl."

Amy closed the door after Carl, and he walked to his car and slid behind the wheel. Before he could turn the key in the ignition, his attention was drawn back to the house.

He watched Amy walk across the lawn to her car. She intended to go straight to Paul.

Carl sighed as he watched her small sports car disappear. He knew a big piece of his puzzle was tied up in Amy and Paul, and that he would eventually find the answer. He only hoped Paul wasn't guilty and Amy made just as guilty by protecting him.

It was Sunday, and he felt displaced—an alien in his own town. It irritated him, yet he knew he was the one who had raised the barriers and opened the gulf.

He drove aimlessly for a while. He wasn't hungry, and it was too early to satisfy his urge for a drink. Something very close to panic suddenly seemed to constrict his breath. It was as if he had to have a destination or he would lose control.

When he pulled up in front of the house, he sat for a while in the car and looked at it. It was a white, two-story Cape Cod. The windows were boarded securely, and the lack of human presence could be felt more than seen.

Carl walked up the path and the four steps to the porch. At the door, he reached a tentative hand to the knob, as if he expected it to open. It was securely locked.

He took his key ring from his pocket, picked out the key, and slipped it into the lock. The door swung open and he stood for several minutes on the threshold before he stepped inside and closed the door behind him.

All the furniture that remained was covered with huge white drop cloths, and the room Carl stepped into echoed softly with his footfall on the hardwood floor. He walked from room to room, searching for something that flitted before him, ghostlike, just out of reach.

He climbed the steps, walked to a bedroom door, and swung it open. The room had not changed, except for the loss of the vital life that the woman who had decorated it had given it.

What crushed Carl was that no matter how he strained, he could not reach the sense of peace he sought. He felt hot tears in his eyes, and his hands shook. He wanted to walk into the bedroom, and would never understand the force that restrained him. He stepped back and closed the door with a sharp click that echoed down the hall.

A numbing, breathless fear held him now, and he had to slide his hands along the wall to find his way to the stairs. He took them two at a time, and by the time he reached the front door, he was running. He very nearly slammed the door behind him, and had to try several times before he could fit the key into the lock.

Back in the car, he sat until he could breathe freely again. "Dammit," he muttered, angry at himself for running from a fear he could not even name. He was grimly determined that somehow, he had to come to grips with it, but he couldn't find a way.

With a clenched jaw he started the car and drove toward the other barrier that could not be surmounted.

St. Catherine's Cemetery was only a mile and a half from the city limits. He drove the distance single-mindedly, refusing to harbor any thoughts except those required for driving the car. He turned into the drive that divided the cemetery, then curved into an elongated figure eight. He drove unerringly. One does not forget that path once walked. He stopped the car and moved across the neatly manicured grass, passing stone after ornate stone, until he came to a large tree, beneath which a gray-white oblong stone stood. The gravestone was simple. It said only, "Sara Forrester," and gave the dates of her birth and death.

Suddenly, his mind was whipped by the black rage he had never been able to bring under control—the rage that had driven him to do the unthinkable.

"God, couldn't three years set me free?" he grated. "I never should have come back here, Sara, I never should have listened to Joe. He could have taken care of this murder without me. Sara, Sara—I've tried. For God's sake, I've tried. It's no use."

He turned from the grave and walked back to his car. Now he drove slowly, not really wanting to go anywhere. He debated telling Joe he was leaving Monday morning, but he knew he would be persuaded to remain. In any case, he was in no mood to talk to or be with anyone.

He returned to his motel room and changed into more comfortable clothes. Then he sat at the desk and pored over the papers Joe had given him, until he knew every word nearly by heart, but no answers came to mind. By the time he finished it was nearly six o'clock, and he realized he had not had any lunch.

He was still not fit mentally to share any part of the day

with anyone. There were no words he wanted to say that anyone else would understand, and he was not prepared to conform his thoughts to what anyone wanted to hear.

He decided to walk rather than ride to a restaurant, mostly to be less noticeable. He went into the semidark room and found a corner table that would keep him out of the main flow of diners.

He ordered a drink, intending to have quite a few—at least enough to blunt his senses until the remote chance of sleeping might be more feasible. He had finished the third drink before he ordered his meal, and had just begun to feel the tension in him ease, when a voice from behind him shattered his meditation—the very last voice in the world he needed to hear. He turned and looked up into the wide blue eyes of Beth Raleigh.

* CHAPTER 9 *

"Beth." He was surprised for a moment, then rose quickly to his feet. She was alone, which surprised him even more.

She laughed softly. "I didn't mean to interrupt your meal. I just saw some rather broad shoulders that looked familiar, so I thought I'd make certain."

"You're not interrupting anything important. Would you like to join me?"

"Oh, no. I didn't intend—good heavens."

"Of course you didn't." He grinned. "So sit down and have a drink with me. Have you eaten yet?"

"No. I had just decided to take a walk, and when I got hungry I ended up here. I'm a friend of John Troutman. He owns the line of Troutman's restaurants, including these Village Inns. It makes it easy to just drop by for a snack. I can always get a table."

"Pays to have friends in high places."

"Oh, I agree." She laughed again. "If you have any problems, I have a couple of friends who are policemen, too."

"Well, if you want to keep one as a friend, you'd better sit down and have a drink. I wouldn't want to have to place you under arrest."

"I doubt that the food in jail is as good as it is here, and drinks would be hard to come by, so I'll surrender peacefully."

She sat opposite him, and he sat back down slowly, amazed at himself. One moment he was deep in a despairing mood, and the next he was inviting to dinner the biggest threat to his peace of mind he had met in three years.

"You walked here?" he asked, his brows furrowed in a dark frown. "It's after dark."

"It wasn't dark when I started out. Don't worry, I intended to take a taxi home. I like to walk. If it were still daylight, I'd walk out to the beach. On nights like this, the ocean's beautiful."

"Nights like this are dangerous for a woman alone when there's been a murder already."

"You don't believe this murder was just an indiscriminate attack?"

"Do you?"

She laughed again, a sound he was beginning to like. "Does a policeman ever answer a question with anything but another question?"

He had to grin in response. "I suppose not. It's kind of automatic. But you sound like you have an opinion."

"Not really. I just can't believe that any of the people I know could have had a thing to do with it—especially Paul Carterson."

"How long have you known him?"

"Just for a couple of years. I know Amy much better. She's the one who led us to Paul when the library wanted the mural painted. He did a fine job. He's a very sensitive man."

"And that excludes him from being able to commit a crime?" Carl chuckled. "You sound like a romantic."

"Maybe I am a little, still."

"Still?"

"I thought I had my romanticizing cured a long time ago."

"I don't think it's a curable disease. I think it's once a romantic always a romantic."

"Well, then, I guess I'd better quit fighting it."

Carl was about to answer, when a man stopped by the table. Beth looked up and smiled. Carl was caught by the warmth in her eyes. It was a moment or two before he looked up at the man standing near the table.

"John," Beth said.

"Nice to see you again, Beth. It's been much too long."

Quick to read people's eyes, Carl was intensely aware that John was more than just pleased to see Beth. Carl ignored the fact that it irritated him. Beth's friends were none of his business, and he had no intention of getting involved enough to care.

"It has been a long time, John, but I've been exceptionally busy. John, this is Carl Forrester. Carl, this is John Troutman, owner of one of the best restaurants Helton has to offer."

"Thank you, Beth." John chuckled. He held his hand out to Carl, who rose to take it. "It's nice to meet you, Mr. Forrester. You're new in Helton. I thought I knew just about everybody."

"I live in Cambridge," Carl replied, well aware of Beth's eyes on him.

"Carl is a police officer. He's here to help Joe solve Martha Dexter's murder."

"Terrible thing," John replied. "I hope they find whoever's guilty soon. In a town as small as this, panic spreads easily." John returned his attention to Beth. "I tried to call you last week."

"I went up to the lake for a couple of days," Beth replied.

"Oh. Well, I'll call you again. Have a good dinner—both of you."

"Thanks, John." Beth smiled. "It's hard to have anything else here."

John chuckled and moved away. He was almost immediately replaced by a waiter, who took their order.

Both ordered a salad, and Carl, soup and a sandwich. Beth asked for coffee, and Carl signaled he wanted another drink.

"You don't eat much," he observed as he sipped his drink.

"I'm usually a good eater. Don't let tonight fool you. I'm a sucker for pizza."

"I'll remember that," he smiled.

"What's your favorite food?" she asked. "Just in case I want to invite you to dinner."

"Would you believe spaghetti?" He laughed.

"I'll remember that." She repeated his words as solemnly as he had said them, and he laughed again. They finished the meal with only casual conversation.

"Well, I guess I had better be on my way," Beth said.

"You're really taking a taxi?"

"Well . . ."

"Tell me the truth."

"I suppose I could get a taxi easily," she began.

"But you really didn't intend to."

"You're quite a prosecutor."

"That doesn't answer my question." He grinned. "And you're right. You can't get out of a direct answer, so tell me what you were going to do."

She sighed and shook her head. "All right, I was going to walk home."

"Since you've been so good about it," his eyes sparkled with laughter, "I'll tell ya what I'm gonna do," he said, mimicking the old comic line.

"Just what are you going to do?"

"I'm going to let you walk me home."

"Really," she replied in mock excitement.

"Yep. Then I'm going to get my car and drive you home. Then I'm going to repeat my lecture on beautiful women walking alone at night, and I'm going to do it policeman style."

"Thank you." She chuckled.

"For the ride or the lecture?"

"For saying I'm beautiful. I'd argue the fact with you, but my ego enjoys it too much."

"Are you taking me seriously?"

"About telling me I'm beautiful?" she said with wide, innocent eyes. "I've never taken anyone more seriously in my life."

"I think," he said with a pretend frown, "that if I need a lawyer, I'm going to call on you."

They both laughed and rose from the table. Carl reached for his wallet.

"Oh, no you don't," Beth said immediately. "I did not have an invitation to dinner. It's Dutch."

Carl threw some money on the table and reached to grasp Beth's wrist. "Now, I'm taking no more sass from you. My male chauvinism has suffered enough at your hands. Let's go or I'll have to use force. Then, you'll be crying police brutality."

"I'll come meekly, sir." She smiled, and Carl laughed as he took her elbow, and they left the restaurant.

The night was October crisp with the hint of frost in the air, yet it was pleasant to both Carl and Beth as they walked slowly.

"I can smell winter coming," Beth said as she inhaled deeply.

"You like winter?"

"Next to fall, yes."

"What else do you like, Beth Raleigh?"

"Me? Oh, I like the ocean, fireplaces, Christmas—and pizza." She laughed.

Carl was stung to momentary silence as a sudden memory crashed against his thoughts. What had Sara said when he had first met her? "I like warm fireplaces and blue oceans." He could feel a lump that sat in the center of his chest like a core of iron. He looked down to find Beth's eyes on him.

"I'm sorry," she said softly.

"Sorry for what?"

"I don't know."

"It's nothing—old memories. Sometimes they're hard to get rid of."

"Why get rid of them?"

"What?"

"The only memories we should want to get rid of are the ones that didn't give us any pleasure. If they're good memories, we should hold on to them as long as we can. There are too few things worth holding on to."

"What have you done with your bad memories?"

"Put them away in a dark closet to handle when I'm ready."

"Sounds easy."

"I didn't say it was easy."

"What did you say?"

She stopped and looked up into his eyes. "I said maybe you should let go of the bad ones. Maybe you're finding some kind of perverse pleasure in clinging to them. Maybe," her voice grew softer, "you use them to punish yourself."

For one blank instant he felt a surge of hatred for her, coupled with a sudden sense of vulnerability that left him momentarily wordless.

"Let's get going. It's still quite a ways," he said finally. She fell in beside him. They walked for several minutes in silence, then Beth spoke again.

"I'm sorry, Carl. I guess I keep saying that, but it's true. Can you just forget what I said?"

"Sure," he replied. "Consider it forgotten."

In the car, they kept the conversation light, carefully avoiding sensitive subjects.

When Carl pulled into Beth's driveway, she asked him to come in for a drink.

"I don't think . . ."

"You're angry with me."

"I'm not angry with you, Beth." Carl had to smile.

"And I'd really like you to come in for a drink."

His eyes held hers in the dim light from a nearby streetlight.

"You're sure about that?"

"Yes, I'm very sure."

He switched off the motor, and they walked to the lighted porch. She dipped into her bag and easily found her key.

"You see, I took your advice and left a light on."

"Yeah," he said with a chuckle. "Then you decided to walk home. Very comforting."

Beth laughed as she opened the door. He walked in behind her and stood while she moved across the room to switch on the light.

Carl looked about him and knew immediately that Beth had spent a lot of time and love on her home. It was warm and inviting—the kind of place that spoke of roots and permanence.

"Very nice."

"Thank you. What do you want to drink?"

"To tell you the truth," he said, "I'd like a beer. But if you don't have any, I'll take coffee."

"Sorry. I've almost everything but beer. I'll go put the coffee on. Make yourself comfortable."

Beth took off her jacket and tossed it on a chair as she walked toward the kitchen. Carl removed his jacket and laid it across hers. Then he followed her as far as the kitchen door, where he leaned a shoulder against the frame and watched her.

He thought of his earlier reference to her as beautiful, and realized that even though he had said it casually, he had meant it. She was beautiful.

In minutes she had prepared the pot and plugged it in to perk. Then she returned to Carl's side. "It should only take a few minutes. Besides, I thought you were going to make yourself comfortable."

"I'm not a trusting man. I had to make sure you really knew how to make coffee."

"I'll have you know I make the best coffee in town. The question is, do you know a good cup of coffee when you taste it?"

He laughed. "I'm an expert."

"Expert, huh? Well, we'll see."

As she passed him and he turned to follow her he was aware of the subtle scent she wore.

Beth kicked off her shoes, then curled her legs beneath her on the corner of the couch and waved her hand toward the seat near her. "Sit down."

He sat close enough to touch her. He found it hard to read the look in her eyes, and would have been as surprised as she was at the thoughts that existed there. He looked so strong, she mused, and so capable of lending that strength. Suddenly she was a little afraid. Borrowing someone else's strength was not part of her plans, and the desire to do so now was unsettling. He looked almost mysterious as he continued to study her with a brooding gaze.

Carl was feeling his way, as unprepared to expose any of himself as she was. His eyes held hers, and he saw much in her that he could not reach to touch. She would bring sunlight to dark corners, and he was incapable of letting the dark corners be so exposed. There was a rawness, a ragged scar, that couldn't be let go of so easily. Pain had been his companion, and his consolation, for too long.

"Are you planning on staying in Helton for a while?" she asked.

"As long as it takes to catch our man."

"Will you go back to Cambridge when all this is over?"

"I suppose so."

"Do you really want to?"

"Have you been talking to Sally?" He grinned.

"No," she said, "I've just got the feeling you belong here more than there. Is there something—someone special—that draws you back to Cambridge?"

"Someone special?" he repeated. "There's really not a whole lot of time or room for anybody special." He reached the short distance and touched her hand with his fingertips. The caress was light, and he found a kind of gentle joy in the softness of her skin. Then, without meeting her eyes, he took her hand in both of his, letting the almost sensuous pleasure wash through him. She did not draw her hand away. For a second they were silent. Then he looked up at her again, as if suddenly aware of her.

"What about you, Beth? How much room is there in your life for something special?"

"I don't really want someone special in my life now. I guess I was hurt enough the first time to be a little scared. Well, maybe not scared but wary."

"Must have been a bad time," he said gently, his fingers tightening on hers just a little.

"It was a foolish mistake—a marriage between two people who didn't know each other and thought that passion would bridge all the gaps. When it didn't, everything seemed to fall apart. I guess the only thing I'm grateful for is that we were smart enough not to have children."

"You don't blame him, do you?" he asked, slightly surprised.

"No, not completely. Toward the end, when I knew he was seeing someone else, I didn't try anymore. I refused to let him touch me, to attempt to stop what was happening. I began to think there was something wrong with me." Her voice shook. "That maybe I was less of a woman than . . ."

"Beth," he said gently. She raised her eyes to his. He reached out and cupped her chin in one huge hand. "Don't doubt yourself for a minute. I'll bet I could speak for a lot of the male population in Helton. You're beautiful, and you're a desirable woman."

She could see the warmth lying deep behind his eyes—a warmth that could change into something more volatile and destructive. At that moment she wanted to run. Old memories bubbled up from the depths in which she had buried them—of how she had always fallen victim to the overwhelming desire that Todd had brought to life. She was on the fringe of this force again, caught in a swirl of emotions. She wanted Carl's touch, was very nearly desperate for the kind of emotion she was sure he could draw from her. Yet she had never been more aware of the possibility that she might be repeating the disaster she had managed to survive before.

Carl Forrester was a man who could fill her needs. She wanted to touch him, to let her fingers slide into his hair. She needed someone to tell her that it would be all right, that this time she would find fulfillment. But she knew he couldn't tell her that lie, and she could not accept it. Touching him could be more than dangerous—it could be destructive.

"You know, that's the second time you've called me beautiful." She laughed to cover her fears, and withdrew her hand from his.

"I meant it," he said softly. Carl had become so aware of her—of the softness of her skin, the depth of her blue eyes, and the physical response of his own body. His heart was pounding and sparks were swirling within him as he felt himself slipping beyond control.

"I want to touch you, Beth—I want to kiss you." His eyes were filled with heat now, and she drew back from it, knowing its force would damage them both.

"No," she whispered.

He tried to fight the need for this intimacy with her, knowing it was wrong—the timing was lousy, and both of them would probably suffer for it. But his yearning was stronger than the voice of caution; he stood and drew her up beside him. Then he took her face between his hands and heard the whimper of resistance. His parted lips met her half-parted ones and he felt the shocked intake of her breath.

Beth felt as if she was losing herself, caught in something she must resist. Determinedly, she summoned up memories of being victimized by her own sensuality and the disastrous toll it had taken. She couldn't let go or she would fall too easily into what might be the same trap again.

It was then Carl realized that what he was doing could only be a beginning. Reality ripped the curtain of desire and let him see. This same desire had cost the life of another he had cared for. His passion was all he could offer, and hers was all he could take, and that would not be enough for either of them.

They stood, almost touching, and he could see the tears pool in her eyes.

"Please, Carl. Please, just go."

"You're right. I'm sorry, Beth."

"No, I don't want you to be sorry, but I guess neither of us can handle this right now."

Carl mentally cursed her husband and then himself. Beth had already been hurt enough, yet he wanted desperately to make love to her.

Very slowly, he stepped back from her. There was so much to read in her eyes that for a moment, he wanted to take her into his arms again. But he knew that he had deliberately let something go, and she was not going to let him touch that vulnerable spot again. Not now, not tonight; the moment had passed. Silently he turned, picked up his coat, and left. Beth stood immobile until she heard the door close behind him.

If anything, the terrors of Carl's dreams were worse that night than they had ever been. He was jolted awake at three in the morning, and sat in the dark room, refusing to sleep and to face the dreams again. Against his will, his mind created fantasies about Beth. He could feel the smooth texture of her body against his. He knew how she would feel and how she would taste. He lay with her in his mind until the pain was too great. Then he forced away the contemplation of her gentleness and sweetness and concentrated on trying to probe the circuitous working of a deranged mind, to find the motive that drove the murderer. Maybe it was the only way to keep his own sanity.

* CHAPTER 10 *

Thunder rumbled in the distance, and a slow and steady rain began to fall.

Beth, who had been preparing for bed, was caught by the sound of the storm. She rose and walked to the window. Outside, it began to grow. But that was not the storm that frightened her—it was the one raging within her.

She was thinking of the paradox of Carl Forrester and the unique experience of her contact with him. She had almost invited him to her bed, and was still rather shaken by it. She had not reached out for any man since her divorce from Todd. It was difficult even to find a reason, except that the depth of his sadness, his loneliness, had drawn her to him, had struck a responsive chord in her.

They had touched briefly but deeply, but she knew she couldn't allow it to mean anything, because he was still lost in something she did not understand. She would not make herself a victim again—she could not survive it.

She thought of asking Sally for the complete truth, but she was certain Carl would feel betrayed by that. And what if she learned something so unpleasant that it would ruin any relationship she and Carl might have begun? Whatever his secret was, it was like a cancer eating him from within. She tore her thoughts from him only to find them replaced by the specter of Todd, whom she had loved so intensely and who was a vital danger. She knew that he could still touch something within her that she had never had the ability to kill. These two men could fill her life with disaster if she weren't careful. She must keep her distance—from both of them.

* * *

Carl had paid no attention to the car that had passed him as he was leaving Beth's house, which was unusual, for he was cautious and an expert at observation. But his mind was on the look in Beth's eyes when he had left. It was as if she could see right to the center of his mind.

After Carl left, the car pulled slowly into the drive and a man got out, walked to the door, and knocked.

Beth was surprised, but she assumed Carl had returned for some reason. She opened the door and blinked in surprise.

"Todd?"

"Hi, Beth," Todd Palmer said softly. "I have to talk to you. Will you invite me in?"

Beth stood stunned for several minutes before she regained her voice.

"What are you doing here? Anything we had to say to each other was said a long time ago."

"God, Beth, you make it sound like it all was bad. Can't you at least talk to me?"

"What do we have to talk about?"

"I want to tell you something important. Can't you just listen?"

"Important to whom? You, as usual?"

"Don't be so quick to jump to conclusions. Let me come in and tell you about it . . . please."

Todd Palmer was a man of great charm, but had little in the way of character to match it. Beth had discovered this fact after their marriage.

Todd had been the handsomest and most enviable catch. He had had money to spend, the nicest car, and enough sex appeal to win any girl.

For a long time after their storybook wedding, Beth had devoted a hundred percent of her time to making Todd happy in every way. That lasted until she realized he was devoting just as much time to the same thing.

Beth's only problem now was a memory that clung to the good as well as the bad. Todd still exerted a sensual hold over her, despite her attempts to ignore it, and it threatened the peace of mind she had fought so long and painfully to acquire.

He was still almost breathtakingly handsome, with thick black hair and a deep tan. Despite his liking of luxury, his tall, lean body had retained its sleek muscular look. His brown eyes were still lit with liquid gold, and his almost-too-perfect face wore a practiced smile. His 'little boy pleading for a candy treat' act had caught many an unwary girl—including Beth. Her nerves tightened and she felt a tingle of warning against the danger she might still be susceptible to.

Reluctantly, she moved aside and let Todd precede her into the living room. She closed the door, hesitated for a minute, then followed him. She stood for a moment in silence, just looking at him.

"So, what is it you want?" she said.

"Do I have to want something? I hated the way you left, Beth. I never saw you during the whole divorce. We never had the chance to even try to talk it out."

"There really didn't seem to be much left to talk about. If you're interested in conversation, why don't you go back and talk to Janet? You two seemed to be hitting it off pretty well the last time I saw you—together, in my bed, in my house."

"That was a terrible mistake. I was stupid."

"One mistake among many."

"That's not true, Beth. There weren't many. You just believed what you heard."

"I believed what I saw."

"You never gave me a chance to even try to explain."

"Todd, for God's sake. It's been too long to rehash that."

"That's not why I came."

"Why did you come?"

"Because I can't get over you." He was beside her before she could react, catching her in his arms. "I've tried, Beth. I've tried to wash you away with others, with drinking. I can't. I came back to ask you to let me into your life again. I know you must be able to remember how good it was between us. We were fantastic, and I want a chance to make up for my mistakes—to love you again. I swear, this time it will be different. This time I'll be smart enough not to do anything to lose you."

"You're insane." Beth choked on her fury. "I gave you that opportunity once!"

It had been before Beth had really decided on a divorce. She wanted to give their marriage another chance; and when

Todd had pleaded and begged, she had weakened and decided to try again. But the reunion had only lasted a few months. In that time she had tried—and he had accepted her attempts, as if they were owed him. But he had strayed again, and Beth had been the last to know. In the end she had been forced to see the truth, and finally divorced him. She came to Heiton and leaned on Eve, Sally, and Joe, who helped her over the hard places. She had wanted to try to put the pieces of her life back together. It took another year for her to begin to feel that life was worth living.

"I know, Beth, I know. But I've changed. I've tried to build a life without you, and it just doesn't work. Can't you at least let me come and see you? Let me show you how different I am?"

"I don't want to see differences, Todd. I don't want your apologies or your promises. I just want to be left alone. I've made some sense of my life." She pushed him from her. "Do you truly think you can walk in and out of my life as if it has a revolving door? Well, you can't."

"I know you're surprised and angry now, but in time you'll see. I'm not the same man, and I realize now what I was foolish enough to lose. Give me one more chance to prove it, Beth. Let me come to see you. In time you'll see."

"No, Todd. I don't need any time or any convincing. I just want you to leave now. I won't let you move in and spoil my life again."

"I'm not asking you to let me move in with you, for God's sake. I'm just asking you to let me see you again—let me prove to you how much I've changed."

"Did it ever occur to you that I really don't care if you've changed or not? I just don't want to get involved with you again. We've been through this twice, and I don't intend to go through it a third time. I want you out of here, Todd—fast—and I don't want you to ever come back. Go back to Boston."

"I'm not living in Boston anymore. I'm planning on staying in Helton, as soon as I find a place."

She wanted to hit him hard enough to shatter the satisfied look she saw in his eyes.

Todd had been her weakness. He was a scoundrel able to

reach inside any shields she had raised and touch a vulnerability she tried to protect. She knew now that Todd had always thought of her as a quality acquisition, like a piece of fine art or a rare piece of jewelry. He had been pleased to know he had control over her, and she wondered if her departure had been more of a challenge to him than a finality. He wanted her more to prove he was still her weakness than to commit himself to loving her.

She felt suddenly tired and wanted him to leave her alone so she could gather herself together.

"When are you going to understand, Todd, that I don't want to ever see you again? Of all the towns in Massachusetts, why did you choose Helton—just to make me miserable? I have a life that doesn't include you, and I don't intend to make room for you to walk back into it. Now, please get out of here before I call the police and have you thrown out."

"Does your stubbornness have anything to do with the guy I saw leaving when I drove up?"

"That is none of your damn business!"

"You are my concern," he said in a level, cold voice that suddenly choked off her reply. There was something in the tone of his voice that actually frightened her. His eyes had darkened to near black, and his mouth was a grim line. "No matter what you think, I still love you, so I intend to keep you my concern."

"I will not have you interfering in my life! Your concern for me is just a little too late. You gave up any right to be concerned about me the day you took another woman to my bed." She walked close to him. "Now, I'm going to repeat this just once, then I'm going to the phone and call the police and have you thrown out. Get out of here!"

"All right, Beth. I'll go, for now. But I'm not going to give up that easily. I want us to get over what never should have happened. Our breakup was a mistake. You'll see," he said in a velvet voice. "One day, you'll see."

He walked to the door, and in minutes she heard it click shut behind him. She was frightened and didn't know why. There was a threat in his eyes she had never seen before. Without a doubt, she knew he meant every word he said.

Suddenly she felt helpless—a feeling she had thought she had overcome forever.

She had picked up the pieces of her life and rebuilt them into something she could live comfortably with. Now, suddenly, two men had stepped into her life, and she found the walls being shaken. It was impossible not to compare them. Todd made too many sweet promises, and Carl gave none at all. Angrily, she decided that she was not going to allow herself to sit and dwell on either of them.

"What I need is a change of scene," she muttered.

Without giving it much more thought, she put her coat on, grabbed her purse and keys, and went to the door.

She smiled to herself as she returned to the room to switch on the lamp and turn on the porch light before she left. Carl had at least made her more cautious.

She slid behind the wheel of her loaner car. It was practically new, much better than her own. She smiled. Maybe it would be all right if they didn't repair hers too quickly. She pulled out of the driveway, unaware that the phone had begun to ring. It rang at least ten times before it quit.

The hours passed. Sometime near midnight, it began to ring again. This time the ringing continued for several minutes before it ceased. Then, half an hour later, it began to ring again.

* CHAPTER 11 *

Joe looked up from some papers on his desk when Carl walked in the next morning.

"Where the hell have you been?" Joe asked. "I've been calling your room for over two hours."

"Early breakfast. Got something interesting?"

"Real interesting."

"What?"

"Martha Dexter was a little over three months pregnant."

"And she never told a soul who the father was?" Carl asked quickly.

"We don't even know if she told anyone she was pregnant."

"Well, somebody knew."

"You think it was the motive for her death?"

"Don't you?"

"I'm not sure," Joe replied.

"Well, that's two of us. I'm not sure, either."

"I can see a guy getting scared. I can even see him getting a little violent. But to kill a girl because she's pregnant? That's not a big deal anymore, not such a scandal."

"Unless her being pregnant was going to ruin the killer's life completely. Maybe interfere with a well-planned future . . . or a marriage."

"Carterson?"

"Maybe. I think I'll go out to see him right now."

"Stop back as soon as you do."

"Okay," Carl said as he turned to leave.

"Carl."

Carl turned. "What?"

"I just wanted to tell you I'm glad you're finally really back."

"And what's that supposed to mean, old friend?"

"That I and a whole lot of other people wish you would think about staying. For the record, your old job is here if and when you ever want it."

Carl shook his head as he closed the door behind him. Joe sat back in his chair and looked at the door for a long time.

When Carl got out of his car at Paul's, he noticed a second car parked in the drive. He was reasonably sure he would find Amy inside.

"Carl—good morning." Amy answered his knock. She tried to camouflage her nervousness at seeing him again.

"Good morning, Amy. I'd like to talk to Paul, if I might."

"I'm glad you're here. He's been painting me since dawn, and I could use the break. Come in."

He passed her and she closed the door.

"Carl, is there something new about—"

"Not a whole lot. I have just a few more questions."

Without another word, he followed her. He hadn't lied to her, but he hadn't wanted to prepare her for what was to be said. He wanted to see both their reactions.

Paul stood before the easel in faded jeans and a worn shirt with sleeves rolled to his elbows. He was frowning at the portrait, as if sheer will would make it develop as he wanted.

Carl was quick to see wariness in his narrowed eyes as he walked toward him.

" 'Morning, Carl. What brings you out here so early?"

"Couple of questions."

"Shoot."

"You said there was nothing between you and Martha Dexter?"

"Right."

"But you did say you saw her several times after you got home, even painted her?"

"Yes," Paul answered, but he had laid his brushes down, and his full attention was on Carl now.

"And," Carl's voice lowered, "you and Amy were together the night Martha was killed?"

"What are you getting at? We've gone through all this before, with Joe and with you. Is there something new?"

Amy had walked close to Paul, and Carl was again subtly reminded of what he was already very sure. Amy would do anything she could to protect Paul.

"Yes, there's something new."

"What?"

"Martha Dexter was pregnant."

He said the words without any gentleness to ease the blow, and he watched both faces closely. Amy's face turned pale, but she said nothing. Paul's lips grew taut and white, and Carl watched his hands clench into fists. Then Amy reached to touch his hand, as if somehow to control the anger they implied.

"So, what does Martha being pregnant have to do with me?"

"I just wondered what you knew about it," Carl asked quietly. "Do you think it was Michael Brodie's child?"

Amy sucked in her breath and Paul clenched his teeth and kept control.

"I told you there was nothing between Martha and me. Are you accusing me? It's most likely Brodie's."

"I'm not accusing you. I'm just asking you," Carl said calmly.

Amy had turned to look at Paul, her face paler still, but she said nothing. Maybe I was right, Carl thought. Maybe Paul wasn't with Amy the night of Martha's murder.

Carl read Amy's face easily before she could regain her composure, and he was sure Paul could read it just as well. The suspicion crowding her mind that Paul could be the father of Martha's child scared her.

Paul looked frightened, too, as if his world was falling apart, and he had no way to gather the pieces together.

"No," Paul insisted. "I am not the father of Martha's child, and I didn't kill her!"

"Let him alone!" Amy said, gathering her anger now. "Unless you can prove something and arrest him, stop harassing him!"

"Amy, I'm not harassing him. I could yank him in and book him on suspicion, but I want to have all the proof I need before I do that. When and if I do, I'll arrest him. Until then, I have to ask questions."

"It's all right, Amy," Paul said. He took her hand and brought her close to him. "I'm sorry I got so angry, Carl. I know you have a job to do."

"Brodie could certainly be the father." Amy said with desperation cracking her voice. "He should be suspected before Paul. Just because Paul knew her before isn't enough to convince you that they had an affair, or that he killed her. What's truly in your mind, Carl?"

Amy was trembling as Paul put his arm about her. Carl was sure now that Amy was afraid, and he knew what she was afraid of. In the back of Amy's mind was the thought that Paul just might be guilty.

"We're not accusing anyone yet, Amy, but there might be some more questions Joe will want to ask. If there are, he might call you in. He wants to find whoever it is as badly as I do, but he wouldn't question a friend if he didn't feel it was necessary."

"Necessary?"

"Maybe more a necessity to prove you're innocent than to prove you're guilty."

Paul breathed deeply. "I guess you're right. I'm sorry. It's just that being accused of murder kind of shakes you up. Tell Joe I'm willing to cooperate any way I can. We both are, aren't we, Amy?"

"Of course we are," Amy replied quietly.

Carl wanted to break the tension that still clung to the air. "May I see your progress on the painting?"

"Sure." Paul stepped back and motioned toward the painting. "Take a look."

Carl stepped in front of the portrait. It had taken a surprising change since he had last seen it. To him it looked like the vision on the canvas might begin to breathe at any moment. Love was obvious in every brush stroke.

"It's beautiful," he said quietly.

"Thank you. I think I've finally got her."

Carl turned to look at Paul and his words were gentle, but very clear.

"You're a lucky man. Make sure you don't do anything to lose her."

Before Amy or Paul could speak again, Carl walked to the door and left.

There was a long poignant silence in the room after Carl closed the door behind him. Paul broke it with one softly whispered word.

"Amy?"

She turned to look up into Paul's eyes. "I never asked before, Paul, but now I have to know."

"You already know. Are a few words from a stranger going to change your mind? You know I love you. Isn't that enough?"

"I know you love me, Paul. I never asked why, when you needed me, but I'm asking now."

"Just what are you asking?" His voice lost some of its vitality and became flat and uncertain.

"I'm not sure," Amy said quietly. Her eyes had widened, as if she could somehow read past his immobile face. "Could you be . . . were you . . . ?"

"What bothers you most, Amy? The fact that you're not

sure whether I killed her, or whether I'm the father of her baby?'' He laughed bitterly.

''Dammit, Paul, I don't find any of this funny!''

''Neither do I. I thought we had some trust between us.''

''You've asked for all the trust. How about trusting me? Tell me the truth.''

''I already have. I didn't kill her.''

''I believe you,'' she whispered raggedly, but he knew the real question still needed to be answered. It hung in the air like a lead weight.

''But that's not what you're afraid of?''

''Do I have a reason to be afraid?''

''Amy, you know you've been the only woman in my life for a long time.''

''And that doesn't give me an answer at all!''

''Now, come on,'' he said soothingly.

''Don't patronize me! Answer me!''

''No, dammit, no! I'm not the father of anybody's child. The only woman I've ever wanted to have a child with has been you!''

They were both silent and breathing heavily, as if they were suddenly aware that they were forming a breach they might not be able to bridge. Paul went to her and took hold of her shoulders.

''Amy, for God's sake, don't let this rotten thing come between us. We have something too good to let it go.''

Amy shook with the realization of what was happening. She moved into his arms, and for a long time he just held her.

''I'm sorry, I didn't mean to yell at you. I can take anybody pointing the finger at me, except you.''

''I guess it's my stupid jealousy. I can't stand the thought of you having been with her—of your being the father of her child. I want that for us. I don't want to share you.''

''Don't let anything make you forget that,'' he whispered. ''You don't know how good it is to know you care so much, and that you're here.''

''I'm here.'' Her voice softened and her arms tightened about him as he bent his head to kiss her. It was a new kind of kiss, tentative and searching, as if he were afraid that she still doubted him.

He sought a warmth from somewhere deep inside, and little by little he sank deeper into tasting the life force of her.

Slowly they surrendered themselves, became aware and completely immersed in that awareness.

Amy arched her body against his until he could feel himself flow around her like a warm, deep-currented river.

She guided his hands down her body, urging him, needing him. She touched him, making of her soft, almost fragile sensitiveness a strength he couldn't believe but couldn't let go.

She wanted him with no doubts and no reservations. Barriers were broken. He drank her in like the breath of life and the wine of survival.

There were no questions in her surrender as they exploded into passion. He closed his eyes and savored the feel of her skin, cupping her breasts in his hands, tasting the pink-tipped nipples, moving down to the skin across the soft flesh of her belly. He was moving with deliberate leisure, wanting most of all to ease her anxieties and erase her doubts.

He teased her earlobes and his tongue traced her lips lightly before taking them again. With tantalizing slowness he aroused her senses, until he knew she stood with him on the brink.

Then he took her hand and walked to the bedroom. She threw the rest of her clothes aside and watched with renewed pleasure as he undressed. She would never cease to enjoy the firm, hard body that gave her such pleasure. Even the first time they had been together, when she had been unsure of where their relationship might go, she had watched him in fascination. He had an athlete's body despite his size, and she had to control the urge to run her hands over his firm muscles and feel them tighten and quiver in response.

They reached for each other, and fell to the bed together.

From the very first time they were together, Amy had been pleased at Paul's expertise. He was a considerate lover who carefully saw to her enjoyment as he heightened his. He was strong, yet tender, and for a blinding moment the vision crossed her mind of Martha and Paul together. It was a nightmare she pushed aside. She would not allow doubt to intrude—not now.

His mouth was like fire on her skin. She threw her head back and allowed him full freedom to find the deep hollows and warm wetness of the deepest shallows and swells of her womanhood.

He heard and enjoyed the soft, inarticulate sounds she made and the urgency with which her hands touched him.

For a while she was the possessor, drawing sounds of pleasure from him with soft hands and mouth. Her lips skimmed his flesh, and her hands moved over him. She would never allow his love to belong to anyone else if she could prevent it.

He lay on his back and she threw her leg across him, in one swift movement taking him inside her. She moved slowly, sensually, until she felt him arch beneath her. His hands were like hot flames against her body as she increased her tempo. She was smiling and watching the heat of his desire light his eyes. Their gazes held while she moved faster and faster.

For the moment of climax, she had to grit her teeth to hold on to her trembling nerves. But they met the climax together, and she fell against him in total exhaustion.

He was capable, for several minutes, of just holding her until they could bring their breathing under control.

"I think," Paul said softly, "that you just told me something pretty special."

"So, you got my message?" Amy laughed softly.

"Like getting hit on the head with a club." Paul chuckled. "I don't think I'll forget too easily."

"You better not," she threatened.

"Maybe you should plan on reminding me—often."

Amy laughed again and pushed herself up on her elbows to look into his eyes. "I plan on it." Her face grew serious. "Paul, I'm sorry I even thought what I did. I know there couldn't have been anything like that between you and Martha. I want to just forget the terrible questions and concentrate on us."

"There has been nobody else, and I don't think there ever will be." His voice became serious, and he turned to look into her eyes. "Don't think about Martha—she's a past I'd like to forget. I'm not a fool. I wouldn't jeopardize what we have for any other woman. I won't let anything spoil this." His voice had grown vehement with the last words, and his arms had tightened.

"We'll forget her, Paul, and we'll just hold on to each other, no matter what Carl Forrester thinks."

"What do you think he thinks?"

"Well, he knows for certain that Martha was pregnant. I'm sure he's going to find out who the father was."

"With Martha dead, how could he do that?"

"I don't know. I suppose there are blood tests or something. With forensics the way they are today, I expect they can find out just about anything in the laboratory."

Paul had to exert every ounce of control he had over his body and mind not to react to this. It was something he had never thought about, and it scared him.

They left the bed and showered together, which extended into an interlude of laughter and kisses. After they dressed, Paul said he was hungry, and Amy decided to drive to the market to buy what she needed to fix a meal.

When Paul heard her car leave the drive, he sat on the couch and buried his face in his hands. He was caught in a dilemma that was bound to bring him grief.

For the first and only time in his relationship with Amy, he had lied to her. Now he was trapped, knowing the truth could destroy the love she had for him. He wondered how long it would be before Carl Forrester knocked on his door with some irrefutable facts.

"Martha—damn you."

* CHAPTER 12 *

Carl turned the car onto the highway and drove toward Michael Brodie's home. Michael was at the top of the list of the men who could have been the father of Martha's child.

When he stopped in front of the house, it looked deserted. He went to the door and knocked. After several minutes of waiting he knocked again, but still no one answered.

He walked around the side into a large backyard and looked across its well-littered length to see Brodie kneeling before a dismantled motorcycle, thoroughly engrossed in working on it.

"Brodie," Carl called, and watched as he jerked in surprise, then closed all expression from his face. He rose and walked toward Carl. As he passed the porch, he bent to pick up a can of beer and carry it with him. He stopped by Carl, his face a mask, his eyes shuttered and unreadable.

"Yeah?"

"I'd like to talk to you, if you're not too busy."

"Would it really make a difference if I was?"

"This is a lot easier than Joe dragging you in."

Michael heard the subtle threat in this, and his eyes grew colder.

"Can't you people dig up anyone else?"

"You're not the only one being questioned."

"I'll just bet. Does our resident artist get the same treatment?"

"Get the chip off your shoulder, Michael. If Carterson is guilty, he'll pay for it. In the meantime, you'd make it a hell of a lot easier on us all if you'd quit pushing your grudge and just answer questions."

"He's guilty as hell, and you people are busy trying to pin it on me."

"Nobody's trying to pin anything on you. If we had proof against you, you'd already be in jail. Now you said you and Martha were going to get married?"

"Yeah. I'd been asking her over and over, and she wasn't sure. Then . . ." He shrugged. "One night she just said she would, and she thought it would be best to do it right away."

"Did you ask her why she changed her mind?"

"No. What are you getting at? Do you think I'm lying?"

"No. But I do think you might not be telling me everything."

"What the hell else is there to tell you?" Michael snarled angrily.

"You could tell me that the reason for your quick marriage was because Martha was already three months pregnant."

He had hit Michael with it as coldly and deliberately as

he could. Michael's face paled and his hand clenched around the beer can. It was a long moment before he spoke, and when he did, his voice was ragged and shaken.

"That's a lie."

"No, it's the truth."

Michael's breathing seemed to stop.

Carl watched as he struggled to regain some hold on his belligerence and failed. The struggle was wrenching, and Carl could almost feel the pain and anger in it.

"The bastard." Michael groaned through gritted teeth. "The dirty, fuckin' bastard. Is that why he killed her? God," he whispered, "he didn't have to kill her!"

"The baby wasn't yours?" Carl asked quietly.

Michael turned his blazing eyes on Carl. "Do you think I would have killed her if she was carrying my baby?"

"Maybe you found out it wasn't, and were as mad then as you are now."

"I'll tell you something," Michael said. "I would have married her, not killed her."

"Even if you thought the baby was Paul's?"

"Even then. You wouldn't understand."

"Were there any other men in Martha's life who could have been the father?"

"You make her sound like a whore. She wasn't."

"I'm not calling her names—I'm just trying to find a good motive. Did it ever occur to you that if she was going to marry you, Paul had no reason to kill her?"

Michael was silent, but Carl knew he was never going to accept this logic. In Michael's mind, Paul was guilty, and Carl was beginning to worry about whether he might try to find his own kind of revenge.

"No," he muttered, "no."

"The baby might not have been the motive at all. It's not really a good reason for a man to kill."

"The son of a bitch thinks the whole world should go the way he wants it. He thinks he can do a thing like this and get off free. Well, I'll see to it he doesn't get away with it."

"It's not your job to see to anything."

"You think the cops around Helton are going to take my word for anything?"

"When it comes to something like this, it's only the truth that counts. Just because you think Paul did something doesn't make it so. We have other suspects."

"Meaning me?"

"You have no alibi for the night Martha died."

"That doesn't make me guilty. If I was guilty, don't you think I would have gotten myself an alibi?"

"It could be a clever move."

"Forget it, cop. You'll find out I didn't do it."

Carl sighed and remained silent for a while. He was sure he had pushed Michael as far as he could, for now. He didn't want him exploding and doing some irreparable harm.

"Michael," he said quietly.

"What?"

"I'll find who killed her."

"You're sure about that?"

"As sure as you're here."

"Well, maybe I'm not so sure."

"That doesn't matter," Carl said. "Don't interfere with me, or I'll see to it that you're put in a safe place until it's over."

"You can't arrest me for no reason!"

"Try me," Carl said quietly. Their eyes met and held. It was several long seconds before Michael turned away.

"Okay, cop—okay. Only, don't let him get away."

"Don't worry," Carl replied in the same granite voice, "I won't." He started to walk away, then paused and turned to him again. He looked into Michael's intense eyes. "No matter who it turns out to be, he won't get away."

Michael watched him until he turned the corner of the house, then his eyes grew meditative and introverted. "No," he whispered, "he won't get away."

Carl drove until he saw a phone booth. Even in the midst of his work, he couldn't get Beth out of his mind. He slid some coins into the phone and dialed, but before the one ring could be answered, he snapped his finger down on the cradle.

What was he going to say to her? Why had he even memorized her phone number? He looked at the coins in his hand before he shoved them back into his pocket. It was no good. He had nothing to say to her except that he was sorry, and he was reasonably certain it was the last thing she might want to hear.

He climbed back behind the wheel and drove back into town. He would check with Joe to see if there were any new leads.

The door to Joe's office stood open, and voices that sounded nervous filtered through. He walked to the open door unobserved and leaned against the frame.

"It's the same M.O.," Tom was saying.

"Christ," Joe groaned, "we've got to stop this guy."

"He's some kind of nut," Tom replied angrily.

"What's going on?" Carl inquired quietly.

Both men turned to look at him, then Joe answered with contained anxiety.

"He's killed again. Whoever the hell this screwball is. And he left another note." Joe handed the white paper to Carl.

> Lamentation: 8
> She's indulged herself in immorality, and refused to face the fact that punishment was sure to come. Now she lies in the gutter with no one left to lift her out.
> Proverbs: 16:17
> Only wisdom from the Lord can save a man from the flattery of prostitutes. These girls have abandoned their families and flouted the laws of God.

"He sounds like a religious nut," Joe said angrily.

"Or a deranged priest." Carl's heart began to pound, hoping he was wrong. "Good God, this man is insane. How did it come down?" Carl asked quickly.

"Bunch of boys in the woods. They fell across another body. A girl—Paula Craig. Killed the same way. Whoever this guy is," Joe said softly, "he's crazy. He's killing for no logical reason. None of this makes any sense, and I'll be the first to admit, I'm damn scared."

Tom's face was pale. "You think we got a serial killer here?"

"Well, we have somebody who's mentally unbalanced," Carl said.

"Carl, you're not going to like this," Joe said. "The last place she was seen . . . was going into St. Catherine's, and the last person to see her alive was Father McAllen."

"When was she killed?"

"Coroner says sometime late Saturday night."

"Does Father McAllen have an alibi?" Carl asked.

"I don't know," Joe said. "He looks a hell of a lot like a prime suspect, only I'm stuck for a motive."

"Well, it has to tie together somewhere."

"Yeah, but where? Other than these crazy notes, we don't have a thing to go on. There are no prints on the notes, and although they're all on the same kind of paper, it can be bought in any discount store. The ink is from a cheap pen, bought probably in the same place. Dead end, not one lead."

"What about a handwriting expert?" Carl asked quickly.

"I called one in."

"And?"

"Seems our note maker is careful and tricky. He must know about it."

"Each note was different?"

"Carefully and deliberately so."

"We'll just have to keep digging."

"You going to stay until I get it solved?" Joe asked quietly.

"I'll take leave—I'll make the time."

"Thanks, Carl."

"Tom, get me the statements all the people involved have made. There has to be a common denominator. Maybe, if we dig hard enough, we'll run across something."

"Okay, Carl." Tom left quickly, pulling the door closed behind him.

Joe sighed and sat back in his chair. "Where have you been?"

"I went to see Paul, and then Michael."

"They act any different? Nervous, maybe?"

"No, more angry than nervous."

"I wish I could get a handle on this thing—one grain of reason or motive."

"Paula was at Paul's party. Was she a friend of Martha's?"

"Yes, why?"

"Maybe that's your motive. Girls talk. Maybe Martha told her things she didn't realize were deadly."

"Yes," Joe said thoughtfully. "It would sure give the killer a reason, if he knew the girls were close."

"It has to be somebody close to both of them."

"Man, that narrows the field," Joe said bitterly. "It doesn't eliminate one suspect."

"We just have to keep looking. He'll make a slip."

"I hope he does it pretty quick."

Before Carl could answer, Tom stuck his head in the door. "Joe," he said quietly.

"What now, Tom?"

"We've got a little problem with the newspaper."

"Jim Frasier's here?"

"I'd forgotten about Jim's nose for news," Carl said.

"Tell him to come in, Tom."

Joe rose to his feet, and Carl stood facing the door when Jim walked in.

"Joe," Jim began. Then he stopped talking and looked with narrowed, curious eyes at Carl. "No luck yet?"

"Not much."

"And now there's another killing to investigate. What do you have to say about Paula Craig's death, Joe?" Jim took a small notebook from his pocket as he spoke. "Does this look like the work of the same killer? We've got to have something to print."

"I don't have anything."

"Joe, come on."

"Truth, Jim. I don't have a lead, and I'll break your head if you print that."

"Well, what the hell can I print? The people in this town have a right to know what's going on."

"They have a right," Carl said smoothly, "but do you want a panic on your hands?"

"I don't want a panic. I want the truth."

"The truth is just what Joe said. There is some mentally twisted person who's killing. We don't know the motive, but we've got some suspects. Give us a little time, Jim. Don't get people riled up until we have something concrete to work on."

"Just what do you want me to do, Joe—suppress the truth?"

"Hell, no, but I want you to print only the truth. You don't need to embellish it. Keep it under control. We need all the help we can get."

Jim looked from Joe to Carl, then slowly put the notebook and pen away. "All right, suppose you tell me all about this new case, and I'll tell you what I'll print."

Carl and Joe exchanged glances, then Carl shrugged. They didn't have many choices.

"You talk to him, Joe. I'm going to church."

Carl stopped his car in front of St. Catherine's. He didn't want to question Father McAllen. Nor did he want to look into those eyes that had penetrated his thoughts or hear the voice that had questioned him gently, and conclude that this man could have done what had been done.

Reluctantly, he walked to the rectory door and knocked. The housekeeper opened it again and smiled as she recognized him.

"Hello, are you looking for Father again?"

"Yes, I am. Will you tell him I'd like to talk to him?"

"Oh, I'm afraid I can't—he's not here. But Father Spencer is right here if you need a priest."

"Father Spencer? Where's Father McAllen?"

"I can't say."

"Can't say?" Carl said in surprise. "I'm afraid you will have to."

"If you need a priest, sir," she said coldly, "Father Spencer is here. I don't have to tell you anything about Father McAllen at all."

Carl reached for his wallet and flipped it open to show the gold badge. He smiled again and spoke quietly. "I'm afraid you have to do just that. Now, where is Father McAllen?"

"He had some personal business. He's just not here."

"How long has he been gone?" Carl demanded.

"Since late Saturday afternoon," she said in an awestruck whisper. Carl felt a pang of utter dismay. It was certain that Father McAllen had no alibi for the second murder.

Carl left the rectory and walked slowly to his car.

The day was beginning to drift away into a red and gold sunset, and he took a minute to enjoy it. Then his sense of contentment faded. The close of the day meant night, sleep, and dreams.

In reflex his mind leapt to Beth, but he knew he was

prompted only by a need to use her for temporary release. He didn't want to do that to her. Asking himself why was beyond his ability to handle.

He drove back to his motel and got out of his car, locking the door. He decided not to go out again because he knew with certainty where he would go.

Inside his room he threw his keys on the dresser and removed his coat. He went to the small refrigerator and took a beer. He had put a couple of six packs in it so he wouldn't have to go out. He snapped the cap and drank half the can in one long gulp, set it down and began to remove his clothes as he walked into the bathroom and started the shower. Showered and dried, he put on his pants. Then he returned to his beer, drank the balance, and threw the can away.

He looked at the bed for a minute, then turned on the television.

It was no good, and he knew it. He went to the phone and dialed. He listened to the ring over and over, then slowly replaced the phone in the cradle.

The bed loomed like some grotesque four-legged monster, beckoning him to remember.

Grimly he sat on the edge and reached for the phone again. He dialed and waited impatiently, refusing to break the connection.

Slowly, he replaced the phone again. He sat, aware that he could keep the dreams at bay if he didn't sleep.

Sometime after midnight he tried the phone again, but it was useless. It was just as useless to face the prospect of bed.

He rose and dressed and left the room. Even though his mind denied it, he knew exactly where he was going.

There was one light on in the house and the porch light was on. He smiled at the fact that she had taken his advice. He settled himself to wait.

It was past one o'clock when her car pulled into the drive. He watched her walk from the car to the porch, then left his car. She was fumbling for her key when his voice, from behind her, made her gasp in fright and spin about.

"Beth?"

"Oh! Oh, God, Carl—you scared me."

"I'm sorry. I thought you heard me coming."

"No, I didn't. What are you doing here?"

"I thought I might interest you in some pizza," he said with a smile that told her it was a very flimsy reason to be there, and he knew it.

"Pizza—at one o'clock in the morning?"

"Seemed like a good idea at the time." He shrugged innocently. "Nice-looking car you're driving."

"It's a loaner," she said, laughing. "It's better than mine. I don't know if I want to give it back. Well, it's a little late for pizza," she said quietly, "but if you'd like some coffee, I'll make some."

"Sounds good," he replied. "Sounds real good."

* CHAPTER 13 *

Leslie Gabriel had made her novena for nine consecutive Mondays. She looked at her watch—seven forty-five. She had fifteen minutes to get to St. Catherine's, but she would make it in plenty of time.

She parked the car in the lot across the street from the church, got out, and pushed the door closed.

She half ran across the street and up the steps to the church door. Inside, the soft lights and the glow of candlelight eased her impatience. She dipped her fingers in the bowl of holy water, made the sign of the cross, and tiptoed down the main aisle. She genuflected beside the front pew, slid in, then pulled down the kneeler.

Very few worshipers were present, and those were scattered randomly, as if seeking a form of solitude even here. Leslie's thoughts had wandered from her purpose. Father McAllen, she sighed to herself. How very handsome he was. What a shame that he was a priest. She was supposed to feel guilty about such thoughts, but she found that difficult. He had always been so kind to her, and really, she rationalized, she had never been forward, or given him any idea that she admired and respected him so much. Well, at least she could show him some gratitude. He had gone out on a limb to get her the position she had at the bank. He had given his good word so that she could buy her car, and he had counseled her when her brief marriage had ended in her young husband's untimely death. She had never felt closer to any other human being. She came to see him often, urging him to find some way she could repay him. She had also kept her emotions and her affection to herself.

He watched her through narrowed eyes when his attention was drawn by the attempt she made to silence her footsteps. He sucked in his breath with outrage. *Damn her! Look how she displays herself. Doesn't she realize this is a house of God? She cannot be allowed to act like a harlot here.* His eyes swept over her. She was tall, slim, lushly curved, with those long slender legs. *She has no pride, no self-respect. Her dress is too short, too tight. Look how it clings to her wanton body—it's an open enticement to any man. Whore of Babylon! Look at her hair, so loose and free. It's a temptation! She should be taught a lesson.*

The candlelight cast a mellow glow over Leslie's face. Her lips were slightly parted, and her eyes were wide with her intense concentration. Her hands were folded on the pew before her, and her whole body throbbed in response to her mental involvement. After a while she rose and made her way forward to receive communion.

He was enraged! His mind swirled with a red mist of fury. *How she flaunts herself! She dares to go to communion when her mind, heart, and soul are so befouled by her degenerate thoughts. She walks so slowly—she wants to be admired, to deceive and mislead a soul that is pure. Someone must stop her. Surely she must be stopped. She is an abomination! She is a whore . . . a whore . . . a whore!*

Leslie moved back to her seat for the last of the service. She felt the warmth inside her as she always did when she received the host.

Even when the mass was over and Father McAllen had left the altar, she remained. The vigil candles flickered in dancing shadows, and she stayed to enjoy the peace. Her life was filled with struggle, and these quiet moments of self-renewal gave her the energy and strength to face them.

She knew it would be quite late by the time she left the church, but she grasped the last few minutes. Then she slid out of the pew and walked back down the aisle toward the door. With no one else in the church, she need not worry about the sound her high heels made as she moved.

The dark shadows concealed the man dressed in black as he moved parallel to her. He did not rush and kept out of her line of view. He did not hurry—he knew he could reach her before she found safety in her car.

Since the church stood on the edge of town, the area was probably deserted. He paused as she reached the huge doors. Then, as they swung shut behind her, he moved toward them. *It is my duty to chastise her! To make her understand her sinfulness. I must explain to her why she is so evil, so soiled. I must explain before I punish her . . . but I must punish her. It is my duty—my calling. I must rid the world of her presence so the house of God will never be degraded by her again. It is my duty!*

He pushed the door open as Leslie reached the bottom of the steps. *Now*, he thought. But before he could step out, a voice called to her.

"Hey, Leslie!" a man called, and she turned to face him as he approached from some distance down the street.

"Hi, Larry," Leslie replied, when he came close enough to be seen. "What are you doing here?"

"I stopped by your house, and your mother told me where you were. I thought you might be interested in stopping somewhere for a drink."

"I'd love to. Where's your car?"

"Just over there." He pointed back down the street. "You know, it's pretty deserted around here. A pretty girl like you shouldn't be walking around alone."

"I'm just going from the church to my car. Who in heaven's name is going to hang around a church to cause trouble? And no one is likely to be looking just for me."

"My sister was robbed on the steps of this very church one night. It was so traumatic, she won't go alone again. I wouldn't want something like that to happen to you. I'll walk you to your car, then I'll follow you. Do you want to go home first?"

"You're a worrier, Larry." Leslie laughed. "I've been coming and going from St. Catherine's at night for years."

"Yes, but there have been two murders in Helton. Aren't you scared?"

"I don't know who would want to kill Martha Dexter or Paula Craig, but I don't have any enemies. I don't intend to live my life in fear, and I don't think I'm in any danger at all—unless you get out of hand."

Larry laughed. "I'll be good as gold. Get in your car and I'll follow you. What about Delmonico's?"

"Sounds fine to me."

"Okay, get going. I'll meet you there. Then afterward, I'll follow you all the way home, so don't give me any arguments."

Leslie laughed again and started across the street to her car. Larry watched until she was safely inside and the motor turned over, then jogged to his car. In a few minutes the area was deserted.

His entire body quivered with a burning hatred. *She leaves our house and flaunts her wares in the streets, seducing men and bringing them down to her level. I must put an end to her brazen ways. How she laughed with him, how she inflamed his desire. She is wicked! Wicked! I will stop you, harlot! I will bring down the wrath of God on your head. You must pay. And I am the hand that will be used to end your wanton ways.*

Beth unlocked the door and preceded Carl into the house. Mutual uncertainty crowded the room with silence.

She hung her coat in the closet, then turned to take his. Their hands brushed as she did, and suddenly, the moment was filled with a sense of intimacy that made her breath catch. She turned away and hung the coat up. Carl followed her into the kitchen and leaned against the door frame with his hands in his pockets as he watched her move about, preparing the coffee. HIs well-honed instincts told him she was running from him as determinedly as he had from her.

"I called earlier, thought I might catch you in time for dinner," Carl began. Beth turned to look at him, but supplied no answers. "To tell you the truth," Carl said, laughing, "I've been calling all night. I got worried, so I thought I might come over just to make sure you were all right."

Beth grew exasperated with him. "Is that really why you called, Carl? If you can't be honest with me, at least try to be honest with yourself. Aren't you tired of hiding behind your shadows and secrets?"

"Beth!" Carl seemed momentarily shocked. "What's eating you? If you don't want me here, why the hell did you invite me in? I can leave if you're not up to it."

"Go ahead," Beth snapped. "Leave, go and drink, or do whatever else you do to keep from facing your problems. Run away one more time. It seems to be a habit for you."

"Has my coming here bothered you that much, Beth?"

"I'm just so tired of deceptions. It seems to be everyone's stock-in-trade today—use everybody to get rid of your own self-deceit."

"Do you think I'm using you?"

"Aren't you?"

"I live in a world where it's hard to make promises."

"Did you hear anyone ask you for promises? That's a rather egotistical assumption on your part, isn't it?"

Carl stood silently watching her for a moment. There were a lot of things boiling inside Beth. He wasn't sure what had directed her anger at him, and finding out might require more commitment and involvement than he could give. Yet, even while these thoughts were occupying his mind, he found himself moving across the kitchen to stand close to her.

"I'm sorry, Beth."

"For what?"

"Whatever it is that's bugging you. What happened today?"

"The eternal policeman, always asking questions." She half turned from him, and he put his hand on her arm to keep her from moving away.

"This is not a policeman's question, Beth—it's a friend's question," Carl said gently.

"Well, don't worry about me." She looked up into his eyes. "I've been taking care of myself for a long time—

long before you came into my life—and I will be long after..."

"After you shut someone else out of it? C'mon, Beth," he added gently but firmly, "has someone or something been getting to you?"

Beth caught her lip between her teeth, and for a moment she closed her eyes. How was he able to touch the most sensitive spots, to understand when she hurt, and still keep such a distance between them?

"Last night, after you left, Todd came here," she said in a half whisper.

"Your ex-husband? Why?"

"He wants to put the past away and try again."

Her face was again turned from him, and he couldn't see her eyes.

"And how do you feel about that?"

"I don't know."

"You mean you still don't know?"

She spun to face him. "Nothing is so simple, Carl. We spent a lot of years together. There were good things as well as bad."

"I never said it was simple. I'm just reminding you to keep in mind how he left you. I don't want to see you torn up like that again. I think you're just beginning to get yourself back together. Maybe I admire that because I can't seem to do it. I just think maybe you're stronger now than you were before."

"God, you confuse me."

"I don't mean to. What I do mean is, whatever is between us shouldn't have any bearing on this. Even if I weren't around, and no one else was here for you to reach out to, you'd be strong enough to stand on your own. You don't change a leopard's spots, Beth. Sure, you remember the good things, too. But you paid a price for them. I guess what you have to decide is if the good times were worth the price. I don't think they were. In fact, I don't think there's anything worth one ounce of pain for you."

They looked at each other for several minutes, then Beth smiled. "That's a long lecture for such a laconic policeman."

"It's the longest I've made since high school," Carl said, grinning, "it deserves that coffee you were about to serve."

Beth nodded and turned away to take the cups from the cupboard.

Carl moved through the kitchen doorway to the small living room. *Good lecture*, he thought. *Why the hell can't you take your own advice?*

Beth came in, carrying a tray with two steaming cups and containers with cream and sugar. She prepared his and handed it to him.

"How'd you know how I liked my coffee?"

"That's not too difficult. I heard you tell Sally the night we were there for dinner. Sweet as honey and black as sin, right?"

"That's right."

"How's the investigation coming along?" Beth asked as she took her cup and sat back comfortably on the couch.

"There are still too many loose ends, too many possibilities, no clear motives, and too many suspects that had an opportunity."

"Sounds terrible."

"It's worse than terrible when the suspects are mostly people you've found you like."

"I never realized how hard and demanding your job must be."

"Yeah, I suppose it must look that way."

"But you don't feel like that?"

"I suppose that's why I became a cop. There's something about injustice that sticks in me. I guess I'm a man who likes everything to come out even."

"For everyone, or just for your friends? I thought I was the romantic."

"Maybe I think you're a little more than a friend," he said quietly as he replaced his cup on the table. He looked at her for a long moment. "I don't suppose this is the kind of night I should be hanging around."

"If you give me a shoulder to cry on I probably will, but after your advice, I guess it's time I did some thinking."

"That'll teach me to give advice." He laughed as he rose. Beth walked to the door with him. As he shrugged into his coat, he looked down into her eyes. "Beth, I'm as close as the phone, if you want."

She laid a hand on his arm and spoke quietly. "I know Carl. But I won't lean on you, because I won't let you lean on me. I guess maybe we both have some thinking to do. If I can face my shadows, maybe you can, too."

"'Night, Beth."

"Good night."

Beth closed the door behind him, half wishing she had asked him to stay. It would have been a temporary comfort, but most likely would have made both their problems worse. She went back into the living room, gathered the coffee cups, and prepared for bed. But her tangled thoughts were a barrier to sleep for a long while.

Carl walked from Beth's house to his car and drove back to the motel as slowly as the traffic would allow. Maybe he could have convinced Beth to let him stay; maybe she could have driven the dreams away for another night. But she was right, and he knew it. It was time for him to quit running—face whatever he had to and bring a little peace to his life.

Back in his room Carl drank his beer, scrunched the empty can in his fist, then tossed it across the room into the wastebasket. "Two points," he muttered as he rose to get the last beer. He finished it and returned to his bed, where he lay with his hands behind his head and gazed in unseeing silence at the ceiling while his mind spun cobwebs of possibilities. He was calling on all the experience he had with killers during his time as a policeman. He also wondered just what the killer might be doing at this same moment.

He, too, lay with his hands folded behind his head, and it would have surprised Carl to know he was thinking about him. They were adversaries, he and Carl. But that, he thought, was only because Carl didn't understand. The note he had given them should have explained the need for what he was doing. Maybe, he thought, he should write directly to Carl the next time. After all, they could be friends. They were both dedicated to the same thing—ridding the world of those who had no right to live because of their evil ways. The world needed guardians like him and Carl.

He rose from his narrow bed and walked to a windowless wall. A rather large chest of drawers stood against it. It was almost his height, yet he was strong enough to move it aside with little effort. Behind it the pale moonlight caught the glossy reflection of the three pictures pinned to the wall. One was of a smiling Martha Dexter with a black X marked across it from corner to corner. Another picture was of Paula Craig. It, too, carried a black X. The third was a recent picture of Leslie Gabriel, still unmarked.

He brushed his hand lightly over Leslie's picture and smiled almost fondly. A wave of peaceful contentment filled him. He knew he was only an instrument, a means to do what needed to be done. He breathed deeply, savoring the few moments of peace before he had to prove his worth again. Then he walked across the room to the small stand by the bed where a Bible lay. He sat down and began to search through it. Then he smiled and reached for a pad and pencil.

* CHAPTER 14 *

When the doorbell rang Leslie was surprised, but she continued to get ready for work. She could hear the murmur of her mother's voice and the deeper voice of a man.

When her mother came to the bedroom door, her face was pale and her hands were shaking. Her mother was easily excitable.

"Leslie, there's a man here. He says he's a policeman and that he wants to talk to you."

"To me? What for?"

"He wouldn't tell me. He said he had to talk to you." Her eyes were moist with tears that she was prepared to shed at any moment. "Leslie, you aren't in any kind of trouble, are you?"

"Oh, Mother, don't get excited. I'm in no trouble. Did you ask him in?"

"Yes, he's in the living room." Her mother, a habitual pessimist, wrung her hands, knowing that something had to be wrong to bring the police to her door.

Carl rose and smiled as Leslie walked in. *What a beautiful girl she is*, he thought immediately. *She's pretty enough to attract a psychopath.*

"I'm Leslie Gabriel. What can I do for you?"

"I'm Carl Forrester." He liked her at once. She looked him straight in the eye and seemed unworried about his visit, which was surprising, for most people had some sense of alarm when a policeman came calling. "I'm working with Joe Marks on the murders of Martha Dexter and Paula Craig."

"That was a terrible thing. I knew both of them. Paula and I were friends."

"Were you close?"

"No." She gulped and fought the tears. "But we were friends."

"How well did you know Martha?"

"We met socially quite a few times."

"I was told by Paul Carterson that you were one of the guests at a party he gave a short while ago."

"Yes, I was."

"Can you tell me if anything happened at the party that seemed out of the ordinary? Were there any altercations between the guests, or anything else you might have noticed that was odd in any way?"

"No," she said thoughtfully, "not really. I don't think Martha was in an exceptionally good mood, but then, Martha had been moody a lot lately. I had a suspicion she had man trouble. Paula didn't have any problems that I knew of. At the party, she seemed to be enjoying herself."

"Did Martha or Paula have anything going with any of the men at the party?"

"Martha had been seeing Michael for a few months. Paula wasn't serious about anyone."

"They were pretty close, Martha and Michael?"

"Yes, but that night I got the feeling he was hassling her about something. A couple of times she came down on him, and he was drinking some."

"What about Paula and Michael?"

"No way. He wasn't her type at all. Paula was class and Michael is . . ." She shrugged.

"Different?" he supplied.

"Yes, different."

"Leslie, did you know Martha was pregnant?"

"No." The surprise was evident in her voice.

"If you had known, is it most likely you would all have believed the baby to be Michael's?"

"Sure. Maybe that's what the hassle was the night of the party."

Carl didn't want to tell her that Michael had been just as surprised, maybe more, than she was. It was a point he kept to himself. "Who had Paula been seeing?"

"I know she dated Larry Jackson and a couple of others, but none of the relationships was serious."

"Do you have any idea who the others were?"

"Not all of them. Is it important?"

"I don't know yet. Is there anything else you can remember?"

"No, it was just sort of an average party."

"Miss Gabriel, do you have any idea who might have wanted to hurt Martha or Paula?"

"Absolutely not. Martha was, well, sort of the girl-next-door type. She was probably a Girl Scout or a cheerleader at one time or another." Leslie laughed. "It's hard to imagine her attracting someone vicious enough to commit murder. And as far as Paula was concerned, like I told you, she was class, and she attracted class." Again Carl kept the knowledge to himself that the psychotic was always the last one to be suspected—often described as one with class.

He would have to ask Larry Jackson about his relationship with Paula, and if it went back to any relationship with Martha.

"This is the reaction I get everywhere, but obviously the killer was drawn to both the girls. I would take it as a personal favor if you would call me if any kind of an idea came to you that might give us a lead."

"I certainly will. But I doubt if I'll be very helpful."

"Well, you never know. Sometimes we see or hear things and forget them, only to have them surface later. Oh, by the way, did you see a painting that night that Paul had done of Martha?"

"Yes. When we first got there he was showing it off, but Martha began to get embarrassed at everybody fussing over it, so she had Paul put it in the next room."

"Did you see it after Paul moved it?"

"No. The last I saw of it, Paul was carrying it into the next room. Once he closed the door, that was it."

"Well, thank you for talking to me."

"I'm sorry I couldn't be of more help."

"But you will call me if something comes to mind?"

"Yes, I will."

Leslie walked Carl to the door. When she closed the door behind him, she turned to look at her mother. She realized again that her mother had seemed to be afraid of something all her life. "It's all right, Mother. None of this has anything to do with me at all." Her mother nodded and watched Leslie walk back to her room, but the fear never left her face.

Ellen Knight sat in Joe Marks's office with her hands folded in her lap. Joe watched her and realized she was not a bit shaken by his request to come in and talk to him. Joe smiled to himself. The younger generation certainly had guts.

"Ellen, I'm afraid I have to ask you some questions about Martha's murder—and a few about Paula, too."

"I've been expecting questions. I knew both of them."

"Were you good friends with them?"

"Reasonably."

"Close enough that they would confide in you if they felt they were in some kind of danger?"

"Yes, I think so."

"Did they?"

"Tell me they were in danger? No. In fact, Paula seemed to be pretty high lately, and Martha—well, she was quieter than usual but nothing seemed to be wrong."

"High? About what?"

"I don't know. She never told me."

"Can you tell me about Paul Carterson's party after Sally and I left? You did stay quite a bit longer, didn't you?"

"Yes, I did. But there's nothing to tell you about it. We all had a great time. It was just a fun party."

"Did you see the portrait Paul did of Martha?"

"Yes, just before Paul put it away."

"And after that?"

"No, I never saw it again. But it was really good. Everybody there thought it was one of the best things Paul had ever done."

"Do you know what happened to it?"

"No, I suppose he was going to display it in one of those art shows or something."

"Did you know most of Martha's and Paula's friends?"

"Most of them, I guess."

"Can you give me their names?"

"I don't want to get anyone in trouble."

"Why should it cause anyone trouble?"

She shrugged, but he could sense her tension as she recited a slow litany of names and addresses.

"Thank you, Ellen. If you can think of anything else, please call me."

"I will."

She seemed quite pleased to be leaving, and Joe gazed at the closed door of his office, wondering what he'd overlooked.

Carl drove toward the next address on his list as reluctantly as he had returned to Helton. It was a quirk of fate that David Mondale boarded in the home of a woman who knew Carl nearly as well as Joe did. He had mowed her lawn as a teenager, and she had been an honored guest at his wedding.

It was going to be difficult to interrogate her and keep her from asking him personal questions. But David Mondale had told the police that he was having tea with her at her kitchen table at the time of Martha's murder.

Knowing Emma Lowrey's impeccable reputation, Carl felt her corroboration of David's statement would effectively take him off his list of suspects.

He drove to the two-story, wood-frame house and sat for

a moment looking at it. This house held such warm memories. Emma Lowrey had always had time to talk to him, and had always had some freshly baked treat for his ever-empty stomach. He climbed out of the car and walked slowly up the crumbling sidewalk. The steps were beginning to rot, and the porch itself seemed badly in need of a coat of paint. In fact, the whole house needed work.

He rapped on the door and was amazed to find he was nervous. When the door opened, a thousand memories struck him at once. Old polished wood and kitchen aromas mingled, evoking a sense of warmth and homecoming in him. A tall, slender, gray-haired woman stood in the entry. Her blue eyes narrowed a bit to study Carl, then lit with memory. Though she was nearing seventy, Emma Lowrey was in total command of her faculties. Her gray hair was clipped in a short style, waved back from a face surprisingly unlined for a woman her age, and her eyes were alert and intelligent.

"Carl," she crowed, "how nice it is to see you again." Her mellow voice strummed its fingers through his memory. "Come in." She swung the door wide.

"Mrs. Lowrey, you look well."

"I'm fit as a fiddle, thank you. And Carl, dear, I do think you're old enough now to call me Emma. It's been a long time since you've visited here. I'm just sorry about the reason."

"You know why I'm here . . . Emma?" Carl grinned.

"Well, not exactly why you're visiting me, but I've read about the deaths of those poor girls in the paper. I was hoping your visit was just so we could chat again over tea as we used to."

Carl grinned. "A chat over a cup of tea would be great."

"Fine, come in the kitchen."

"My pleasure. Something smells too good to pass up, and if my nose doesn't deceive me, you've just baked those caramel rolls with all the nuts and goo on them."

"Right you are; they're fresh out of the oven."

"My timing's still perfect. I used to smell them clear across town when I was a kid. Didn't you ever get suspicious that I always showed up at your house about the same time you closed your oven door?"

"Oh, I was wise to you." Her eyes twinkled. "Why do you think I always made an extra dozen?"

Carl laughed. Inside the kitchen he sat at the large, square wooden table, while she put a kettle of water on the stove and set out cups, saucers, and a dish of rolls. Then she sat down opposite Carl.

"Well, Carl," she said gently, "I really am happy to see you. I've been worried about you for a long time."

"Worried? You shouldn't worry about me."

"You were as near a son to me as a boy could get. I know how hurt you were after what happened, but you left before I got a chance to talk to you. Are you home to stay? It's where you belong, you know—here, with people who care about you."

"I can't stay. I have a job in Cambridge to get back to. I was supposed to be on a fishing trip, until I got the call from Joe."

"And he conned you into coming here and giving him a hand." She chuckled. "Joe's been around to visit pretty often. He sends a boy to mow my grass." She bent toward him conspiratorially. "But he doesn't do nearly as good a job as you did. I could offer you employment if you want to come back and live here with me."

Before he could answer the kettle whistled, and she set about preparing the tea. When she again sat beside him, he spoke first to keep her train of thought from the destination he knew it was headed.

"Emma, you've taken in a boarder?"

"Makes ends meet a little better. I supply him with room and one good meal a day. In return, I have the safety of a man in the house and a little extra cash." Again she laughed wickedly. "You don't suppose it will ruin my reputation, do you?"

"I think you'd whip anybody who cast aspersions on your character," Carl replied. "Your boarder is David Mondale?"

"Yes. Nice boy. He's been boarding with me since he moved to Helton. The police asked me about where he was that night already."

"Yes, I know. But I'd rather you told me. The murder occurred around ten-thirty."

"And at ten-thirty David was sitting where you are now."

"You're positive of the time?"

"I certainly am. I have a clock in every room. At my age time is important, and I don't want to lose or waste any."

"So you checked the time?"

"Yes. When I put the kettle on, it was exactly ten-fifteen. He sat with me 'til past midnight, then went to bed. I bolted the door and went to bed, too."

"Well, that takes him off the hook."

"Did you really suspect him?"

"Everyone is under suspicion when it comes to murder."

"Who are your suspects?"

"That's privileged information." He grinned teasingly.

"No names, no rolls," she replied.

"Well, you've got me." He ticked off the list of names quickly, then hesitated before the last one. She caught his hesitation quickly.

"And there's one more?"

He felt like a boy being reprimanded by a teacher. "Yeah."

"And I'm not going to be happy about it?"

"Father McAllen," he stated bluntly.

Her eyes grew wide with shock, and she sat back abruptly in her chair. He found it difficult and somewhat funny that he felt as guilty as a child with his hands in a cookie jar. "Father McAllen! That is a joke, isn't it?"

"Murder is no joke."

"He's a priest—and a fine, devoted one! I think there are very few in this town who have ever been in need who have not felt the touch of his hand. Carl, I don't believe you." She looked totally shaken.

"I didn't say I thought he was guilty of anything, and besides, he was on the list before I got here. The only reason for that is because he was the last one to see Martha alive—and the last to see Paula, too."

"What's gotten into Joe?" she demanded. "Such fine Catholic boys as you two were, and you're suspecting a priest!" She was indignant.

"I didn't say I was suspecting a priest," he protested,

"but there are a lot of questions about Martha's last visit to him that he won't answer."

"Won't, or can't?"

He sighed. "Emma, in an investigation into murder, we have to have answers."

"Find them elsewhere. I have all the confidence in the world in both you and Joe. Besides, I remember you both as altar boys, and I'm just sure you won't arrest a priest."

"I hope not," was all he could reply, hoping he could change the subject soon. But she did it for him in a way he least expected.

"What about you, Carl?" The question was so quick and so gentle that he almost replied without thinking.

"Me?" was all he could manage. He took a roll from the plate and concentrated on it. "There's not much new with me. It's the same old grind."

"I thought we were old friends?"

"We are."

"Then why have you not mentioned Sara since you walked in my door?"

"Because it's a closed subject, and I'd rather not talk about it."

"You'd rather not," her voice was too gentle for him to bear, "or you still can't?"

"Have Joe and Sally been talking to you?"

"They're your two best friends, next to me, and we loved Sara almost as much as you. Why, I remember . . ."

"Don't!" Carl said the word sharper then he had planned to, but he couldn't face her recollections when he was so busy trying to face his own. "I'm sorry, Emma, but . . ."

"Memories can be healing, as well as destructive. Lock them up and put them away, and you'll really have nothing left."

"I know you mean well, Emma, but you don't understand." He rose to his feet.

"Maybe I understand more than you think. I lost my Daniel many years ago. It's hard to get over, but life shouldn't stand still."

He had to stop her. He couldn't let her open doors he'd

nailed shut. "Let it be, Emma." His voice was chill, and she knew she'd met a barrier bigger than she could understand.

"Forget what I said. I'm an old busybody. Sit down and finish your tea. There are two more rolls left. You're not going to leave here without eating them."

"Good thing I don't live with you. You'd have me as fat as a pig in no time. It's a wonder David isn't bigger than he is, and he's big enough."

"Well, David runs it off. He runs every morning and every night. That was where he came from the night of Martha's murder. He'd been out running. Got home at exactly ten after ten. I remember the time as if it were yesterday."

"Well, I don't run," Carl laughed, "so I'm going to leave those two rolls on the plate. I'll stop by to see you again soon. I've got a lot to do today."

"You see that you do get back here," she admonished. "And, Carl . . ."

"What?"

"I'm sorry if I said things I shouldn't. It won't happen again. I don't want anything to damage our friendship."

"Nothing could damage our friendship." He smiled at her.

She walked him to the door, and he bent to kiss her cheek as he left. When she closed the door behind him, she stood in thoughtful silence, then walked to the phone and punched numbers rapidly.

"Hello."

"Sally, this is Emma Lowrey. If you're not very busy, I'd be really pleased if you'd come over and have a cup of tea with me."

Carl slid behind the wheel of his car feeling strangely tired. He planned on going back to the station to see what progress Joe had made, and to tell him he agreed that David's alibi was airtight.

He pulled the car into the parking lot across from the station and got out without paying much attention to what was going on about him, so he didn't notice the silver-haired man who had just come out of the station. But the man had spotted Carl immediately. He stood motionless, watching Carl walk toward him. Carl was nearly to the steps when recognition came to him. He paused only for a moment, then continued to approach.

"Hello, Phil," Carl said. "What are you doing here—giving Joe a little lesson in push and shove?"

"Ah, Carl," Phillip Greggory chuckled mirthlessly, "still the same smart mouth. You never could learn to keep it under control, could you—at least, until the judge started asking you a few questions."

Carl's face froze. "And you're still the same bastard you always were, aren't you, Phil?"

"You should have stayed away. Coming back here might open up a can of worms."

Phillip Greggory was extraordinarily handsome. His silver hair glistened in contrast to his well-tanned skin. His smile was as white as a toothpaste ad. Tall, and with a slimness carefully maintained at a health spa, he exuded the confidence of a successful politician. He was the D.A. now, but he had loftier aspirations.

Carl was aware that Phil would use every case he could to advance his career. Media coverage always found Phillip Greggory preening and ready for comment.

Carl knew one more thing for a certainty—Phil would give his soul for Carl's head.

"Stay out of my way. There's a murderer loose in your town, and Joe and I just want to put a stop to him."

"Oh, I agree with that. Anyone who commits murder ought to pay for it. But there's some who do it who think they can't be caught because they have a lot of friends . . . or because they wear a badge."

"I still wear a badge, and I'm out of your jurisdiction. Joe called me in for a little help. Stay off my back, and off Joe's. I might . . ."

"Might what? Kill somebody?"

Carl's look was murderous, but he remained silent as he pushed past Phil and into the station. Then he stopped, not wanting to appear in Joe's office while he was still shaking with rage. It took him several minutes to get himself under control—or, at least, he thought he was, until he walked into Joe's office. Joe looked up from his desk and smiled.

"Well, I see you ran into our old and dear friend."

"Good old Phil," Carl said bitterly. "He never lets go, does he? The man's still an arrogant bastard."

"Yeah. He was trying to get me to get you out of town. He wants to pick old bones, Carl. Keep your distance from him."

"I will, only because he could put the pressure on you."

"He can't do a thing, if you don't let him push you into saying or doing something stupid."

"Don't worry. Let's just get down to what we've found out today."

"Pull up a chair," Joe replied as he leaned back in his. "You saw Leslie and Mrs. Lowrey?"

"Yeah."

"Get anything?"

"Nothing new."

"Well, I got nothing new from Ellen, either."

"Joe, you questioned Paula before . . . ?"

"Yeah, I did, but she had the same story. The party was fun, and she didn't notice anything unusual."

"Then maybe we're sniffing the wrong trail. Maybe the connection between these murders has nothing to do with the party."

"What are you thinking?"

"I don't have a handle on it. I just get the feeling we're coming at this the wrong way—that maybe there's something that started a long time ago."

"I don't understand."

"Neither do I." Carl laughed. "Let me think about it for a while. So far, we've struck out on all the girls who were at the party."

"Yeah," Joe said softly, "and two of them are dead."

Carl nodded, and both were temporarily silent. Then Joe sat back in his chair and added, "I've checked out Jake Magee, Larry Jackson, and David Mondale's alibis for the time of Paula's death. Larry claims to have been home watching television, but there's no one to verify that. I asked about programs and such, but that's too easy to get around. We have nothing to take him in on, except that he has no alibi. He has a damn good one for Martha's death though—he was in the hospital."

"And Jake?"

"Jake was at a late dinner party with his parents to celebrate their anniversary."

"That leaves David."

"David was with Father McAllen. It seems Father had some personal business out of the city. David drove him to his sister's home in Brighton and dropped him off so he could run some errands. He picked him up again Sunday morning."

"So, they both had the opportunity to get back and do the job and . . . Would Father McAllen's sister give him an alibi?"

"Most likely. It's being checked. Except for Martha's death, David has an airtight alibi."

"Yeah," Carl agreed."

"So," Joe said quietly, "it seems we're back to square one."

"Joe, whoever killed Martha also killed Paula, and most likely is going to keep on. So, first things first. We go back over Martha's death until we find something. There has to be something."

"We solve Martha's murder and we solve Paula's as well."

"Right."

"Yeah . . . right."

After this both men were silent.

* CHAPTER 15 *

Beth decided against going out for lunch. She was in no mood for the hassle and the noise. Besides that, she really wasn't hungry, so she went to the small back room of the library, where the makings for coffee and tea were kept. The room had a small couch and a couple of mismatched chairs.

She finished her tea and set the cup aside, then laid her head back and closed her eyes. Carl leapt to her mind almost at once, plodding through it with his heavy feet and dark secrets. But his advice had been sound—sound for her but not for him, she thought angrily. "Remember," he had said, "how

Todd left you before." Don't just react—think, she told herself.. Her thoughts were interrupted when the door opened and Sandy, a young part-time worker, stuck her head around it.

"Miss Raleigh, there's a man out here to see you." She grinned. "He's a hunk."

"A hunk?" Beth chuckled as she rose. "Most likely, it's someone who wants to borrow a book nobody ever heard of."

"No, this dude looks to me like he always knows what he's looking for."

"Okay, let's go see."

It was Todd. He leaned nonchalantly against the front desk, his arms folded before him and a warm smile on his face. She paused only for a moment, then walked briskly toward him. That he had practiced his charm on Sandy was quite obvious; she couldn't take her eyes off him. Beth was sure that if she hadn't been around, he would have had few compunctions in pressing his charm a little further.

"Hello, Todd. What are you doing here?"

"I came to talk to you, Beth."

"What do we have to talk about? I thought you'd put this quiet little town behind you by now."

"I have no intention of leaving Helton—at least, not until you've given me a chance to talk to you. I've found a really nice restaurant. Let's go to dinner and talk—that's all I want. Is it so much to ask, considering what we were to each other?"

"I'm not one for digging up a past that's dead and buried."

"Are you so sure the past is dead, Beth? If you are, then why are you afraid to be with me?"

"I'm hardly afraid of you, Todd," she said dryly.

"Then, what's the harm in our having a drink and some dinner together? If it has to be final, at least we can part as friends."

He had pushed her into a corner, and she began to wonder if she really was afraid that he still had the power to make her forget all that she'd been through. Carl would have all the answers to this, but why should she care about his answers? She had to find her own. Once and for all, she had to wipe the slate clean. She had to prove, as much to Todd as to herself, that his clever manipulations were wasted and that whatever had been between them could not be resurrected.

"All right, Todd."

"Pick you up around seven-thirty?"

"That will be fine."

Before she could react, he bent toward her and kissed her lips lightly. Oh, God, but he was good at this, she thought. He'll never be convinced one touch doesn't bring me to my knees until I prove it to him. Well, girl, here goes.

"See you later." He smiled again and was gone.

Beth watched him stop just outside the door for a minute, then walk across the street. She wasn't aware of Sandy standing next to her until she spoke again.

"I don't know where he came from, but you're sure lucky. He's really something. He looks like a cross between George Hamilton and Pierce Brosnan."

"Yes," Beth replied gently. "He's movie star material, all right, but don't be so certain about the lucky part."

As Beth turned away to return to the back room, Sandy sighed. She knew what she would do if a man like Todd Palmer walked into her life.

The doorbell chimed, and Beth took a deep breath. When she swung the door open, she could actually feel Todd's eyes move over her in warm appreciation.

"I can't remember you looking prettier," he said in a mellow, velvet tone, "except when we celebrated our first anniversary."

It was a compliment meant to revive the most pleasant memories, and she knew it for the ploy it was. She wasn't about to let him start off their evening by getting away with it and putting her at a disadvantage.

"I think we'd better get one thing straight before we leave. This is not a night meant for the revival of old memories. They're past, Todd, and I don't intend to hash them over again—neither the good nor the bad."

"Okay, Beth, no resurrected memories."

He looked at his watch. "We have a reservation at seven forty-five. That doesn't give us much time."

"All right." She was amused by the fact that Todd hadn't changed. He might casually commit adultery, but he'd be damned if he would be late for an appointment.

"It's getting pretty nippy outside, so you better wear a heavy coat. What about that fur I gave you? Sorry."

"I got rid of it—sold it," she said bluntly. If he wanted to reminisce, she would make it as painful as possible. "I needed the money."

"That was a mistake; I won't mention the past again. I don't want to fight with you, Beth. I have too much to say to you for us to begin the evening by arguing."

"Fair enough. I'll get my coat."

She slipped into the coat at the closet, knowing Todd's smooth chivalry would only make her uncomfortable. Leaving a lamp on in the living room, Beth switched on the porch light as they left.

"Scared of the dark?" Todd laughed.

"No," she said quietly, "just being cautious." But his words brought Carl to mind vividly.

They walked off the porch and down the walk to the car. And drove away not knowing the phone was ringing.

Carl was completely drained of energy, as well as defenses, by the time he left Joe's office. Emma Lowrey had opened doors and let ghosts out, and they had been haunting him all day. Worse yet, Phil Greggory had stirred up a thick black mist that was swirling in his mind.

He took the longest route back to the motel. After he had turned off the car's ignition, he sat and looked at the door of his room. All the doors were the same color—forest green with gold numbers. All the little cubicles were the same—carbon copies of one another. Once, Carl had taken pleasure in mowing his own grass and pruning bushes and trees. There had been flowers all around his house. Sara had had a green thumb and everything seemed to grow when she touched it. Now he hated the blank emptiness of this room, and the prospects on his return to Cambridge were no more exciting. He climbed out of the car, but found he just couldn't walk to that green door. Instead, he walked to the phone booth at the corner of the parking lot, and reached into his pocket for the required coins.

He had no right to call Beth every time he felt like this, but he picked up the phone and slid the coins in. He wouldn't blame her if she told him to go to hell. He dialed. What the hell was he going to say to her—that he was lonely and the ghosts were having a field day with his mind? The phone rang, and he found himself growing tense and gripping the receiver with a sweaty palm. The phone rang again, and again, and again. He hung up in the midst of the tenth ring. It was early yet; maybe she had worked late. She could be anywhere, doing anything. "Damn," he muttered.

He walked away from the phone a lot more slowly than he had walked toward it. The green door loomed like a monster with glittering gold teeth. There was no way he was going near it. He went back to his car and slid in behind the wheel again.

He drove aimlessly for a while, then pulled into a bar. There were few people inside, and the bartender wiped the bar aimlessly while he watched the news on T.V. Carl climbed up on a stool and ordered, maintaining his silence when the bartender cast him a curious and surprised look. Then he placed the glass in front of Carl, whose hostile glance told him he needed no polite conversation and wasn't about to answer any questions.

Carl tossed the first drink down rapidly, sipped his second one for a while, and then ordered a third. Besides the drink, he was nursing an unbelievable anger at himself. In Cambridge he had had only the dreams to face, but here he felt as if he were losing control of something vital that had held him together for a long time.

He recognized the fact that he had begun to think of Beth as a sanctuary—a place to hide when things became difficult. He had no right to do this, either, and he knew it. But it didn't stop him from leaving the stool and heading for the phone again. He dialed and listened to the phone ring until he'd lost count. Who had told him to let it ring ten times to be sure no one was home?

He returned to the bar, told the bartender to bring him another drink, and found a table in the corner.

After the fifth drink he gave no notice to the fact that there was a new bartender. He served Carl for quite some time without saying anything, but he knew he'd seen him before. Then, the name suddenly came to him.

"Carl—Carl Forrester?"

Carl narrowed his eyes and scowled. He made it soundlessly clear he wanted no company and that he didn't recognize him.

"I'm Robert Duvall. A few years back I was hustlin' cars, and you yanked me in. Then, after I got sprung from that one, I tried again and you kicked my butt, got me a job, and straightened me out."

"What's all this leading to?"

"I just kinda thought you looked . . ."

"As if I needed help? Well, I don't. I'm just fine, so let me be. I've got some serious work to accomplish here tonight. Bring me another drink, and—what's your name again?"

"Robert Duvall."

"Well, Robert, my friend. You keep the drinks coming as long as this lasts." He threw several bills on the table.

Carl drank methodically and Robert watched closely. It seemed as if he was pacing himself. He would take the drink in his hand, look at it for a few minutes as if he really didn't want to drink it, sip it slowly until empty, then sit back in his chair and glare at the empty glass as if it were his worst enemy.

Three hours later, Robert could have sworn Carl was stone sober. That was when he decided Carl was in some kind of trouble. Remembering that Carl and Joe Marks were close friends, he made a decision he hoped Carl wasn't going to kill him for. As he walked to the phone he looked at his watch. *Christ,* he thought, *one-fifteen in the morning—almost closing time—and I'm calling people on the phone to help someone I'm not too sure needs it.*

Joe had come home late, suffered through guests, and collapsed in bed just after midnight. Sally couldn't sleep, so she pulled the bedroom door closed quietly and sat in the living room watching TV with the volume low so she wouldn't disturb Joe.

When the phone rang, she was startled. She grabbed it from the cradle to keep from waking Joe. A ringing phone in the middle of the night always made her think the worst. Her heart pounded, and she answered hesitantly.

"Hello?"

"Mrs. Marks?"

"Yes."

"This is Robert Duvall. You don't know me, but I'm the bartender down at the Arcade on Wyck Street. I have to talk to Mr. Marks. I know it's really late, but this is important. It's about a friend of his. I think he needs help."

"Who?"

"Carl Forrester."

"What's wrong? Is he hurt?" Her voice must have registered her panic.

"No. It's just—well, he's been here for hours. He's finished off a bottle, and he looks like a bomb that's ready to explode."

Oh, God, she thought frantically. "Okay, Robert, I'll be right down. Don't let him leave."

"*Let* him! Mrs. Marks, if he wants to leave, there ain't anybody big enough to stop him."

"All right, all right. I'll be there in less than twenty minutes." She hung up before Robert could answer.

Sally started for the bedroom to wake Joe, then stopped. Maybe it would be better if she went alone.

She drove as fast as she could, but it was still a little over twenty minutes before she pulled to a stop before the Arcade.

"Robert Duvall?"

"Yes, who are you?"

"Mrs. Marks. Where's Carl?"

Robert pointed, and Sally turned to look across the room, then walked toward Carl's table.

"Hey, sailor," she said quietly when she stood beside him. Her hand rested lightly on his shoulder. "How about buying a lady a drink?"

Carl raised his head slowly and tried to focus on the woman who was disturbing his thoughtful obliteration. It took a few minutes to get her wavering parts to come together. He had to laugh at the process.

"Sally, Sally. What's a nice girl like you doing in a place like this?" He chuckled, enjoying his own humor.

Sally slid into the seat opposite him. It registered in his mind that she was there, and Joe wasn't.

"What're you doin' runnin' around loose?" He grinned a trifle foolishly.

"I've come to take you home."

For a fleeting moment, she saw a look of sheer panic flicker behind his eyes. "Home," he muttered. "Sally, girl, din' nobody tell you there ain't no home?"

"There's always been my home, Carl. Come on. Let me take you."

"I doan think . . . I think maybe I better stay here. Ya see, Sal, I've got to stop this. I got to find out how deep I can go, so's I can push off the bottom. You remember when we were kids, and we used to swim down at Sutter's hole. Well, I used to go all the way to the bottom, until I could feel like my heart was goin' to stop. Then I used to push off the bottom as hard as I could to see if I could beat dyin'. Well, it's like that now. I got to push off the bottom . . . or . . . ya see, Sal?"

Sally brushed a tear off her cheek then reached out to take one of his hands in hers.

"Yes, I see. But you and I are special, Carl, and if I can't push off the bottom with you, who can? Come on, come home with me. You can bunk on my couch, and we can talk. You know we haven't had a talk since you came back. You owe me."

"Where's Joe?"

"He's sleeping."

"That's where you oughta be."

"Not until you come home."

"You're stubborn—always were."

"When it's really important, and you're important. Come on." She stood up.

"Can't." He chuckled again. "Ain't got no legs."

Sally walked around the table and helped Carl heave his weight up from the chair. He staggered, and her knees almost buckled under his weight.

Robert and Sally worked together, and finally, Carl was safely deposited in the car. Sally took the largest bill she had out of her purse and handed it to Robert.

"Thank you. This was really important."

"No, that's all right, Mrs. Marks. I owed him more than this. Take care."

* CHAPTER 16 *

The car moved slowly and smoothly through the sparse traffic of early morning. The first thing Carl did was to turn on the radio. Sally smiled; it was his way of saying he was not interested in conversation. She reached over and turned it off. Carl gave a ragged groan and slouched down in the seat, resting his head on the headrest and closing his eyes.

"So, what happened today?" she asked. He remained silent. "Carl?"

"Sal, you're a nosy broad."

"Yeah, always was. You've told me that a million times or so."

The cold night air had taken some of the edge off Carl's inebriated state—just enough to let the unwelcome thoughts back in.

"I went to see an old friend today," Sally said.

"I'll bet you had a nice cup of tea and some sweet rolls," Carl offered. Again he chuckled, feeling terribly humorous.

"Well, we had the tea." Sally laughed.

"Two nosy broads." He paused to inhale a ragged breath. "I never should have come back here. It can only bring a lot of trouble. You know as well as I do that Joe could get his ass in a sling for this, too."

"Phil Greggory's crossed your path?"

"Yeah—I ran into him outside Joe's office."

"He's a bag of wind who likes to make threats. Joe's glad you're here. These murders are giving him a lot of stress. So why worry about Phil—or is it Phil?"

"I don't know, Sal. I was doing fine until I came back here."

"You were like hell doing fine." Sally's patience was ready to snap. It was so obvious that Carl had to chuckle.

Even with his eyes closed, he could see the set of Sally's chin and the flinty look in her eyes. He remained silent.

"You didn't come back here for Joe," Sally said. "You came back because you've always had a policeman's mind, and you don't like loose ends. You came back because you left something here, and you've got to find it before you can go on living."

They were close to home, but there Carl could evade her. Sally pulled the car into a side street, switched off the engine, and shut off the lights. Then she turned to face Carl, seeing only the blur of his profile in the dark.

"So we talk about Sara—about what happened—and about Beth."

There was a paralyzing silence in the car.

"Maybe you wouldn't be so eager to talk if you knew what you were talking about."

"I don't understand. Besides you, who knows any better than me? Carl, I was there when you met Sara, when you fell in love with her, when you married, and when . . ."

"When I killed her," he added bluntly.

In four words Sally heard the acid drip of guilt and felt the pain of it.

"That's not true." Her voice quivered with the shock. Carl gave a snort of derision. "Carl, that's not true. She was killed by a couple of maniacs."

"A couple of maniacs who were after me. Dammit, Sally, let it go!"

"Why should I? You can't!" she stormed. "You're wallowing around in a puddle of self-pity."

Carl remained silent for a long time. It was an iron-hard, stubborn silence—one filled with the hope that she wasn't going to pursue what he adamantly refused to respond to. But he should have known Sally better. She wasn't about to let go.

"I didn't mean that, Carl, but you're so damn reticent. You sit there in your bulldog-stubborn silence and take the blame for something you couldn't have prevented. I know how hurt you were—Joe and I were there. But it's grief, not guilt you've got to get rid of. It's eating you alive. Sara would never want this, and you know it."

"Maybe, if Sara knew . . ."

"Knew what?" She was puzzled, and suddenly aware that there was something much more than Sara's loss tormenting Carl.

"Sal, I'm drunk, and I'm damn tired. I just don't want to talk about it anymore. Now, if you want to start the car I'd be grateful. I'm not feeling too good, and it's sure as hell getting cold in here."

"Well, you just freeze your butt off. If you don't unload whatever it is you're carrying around, you can grow icicles on your balls."

Carl gave a short, harsh laugh and shook his head. "You never change, Sally. When you're mad, you have an imagination that rolls around in the gutter."

"And I'm mad as hell. What are you doing, Carl—shutting us out of your life?"

"Christ, woman, don't you ever give up!"

"No!"

"Sara's dead," he said. The anger in his voice was sharp enough to bite through steel. "Now, let it alone. My grief is my own damn business."

"Maybe that's the trouble. You're holding onto it with both hands. Where does that leave all the rest of us who'd like to help?"

"Meaning Beth?" Again he laughed dryly. "Beth is tied up in a few little strings of her own that she can't break. Besides, I'm not too sure I want her to break them—especially not for me."

"I don't understand. I thought you and Beth . . ."

"Were a social item?" he retorted. "Well, she's out tonight being romanced by her charming ex, I think."

For the first time since she picked Carl up, a half smile touched Sally's lips. "You're rather green-looking. Are you sick or jealous?"

"Right now," he grumbled, "I'm sick—sick and tired of talking about things I can't do anything about. I need another drink."

"You need to go to bed," Sally replied briskly as she turned the key in the ignition.

Again, the thought of the motel, with its gold-toothed

green door, sent a paralyzing fear through him. Not drunk enough to handle it, he had only one other choice.

"I'll take the couch," he muttered. Sally smiled to herself as she pulled away from the curb. Neither of them spoke again until she drove into the driveway.

Sally climbed out of the car, but Carl remained motionless, so she walked around and opened his door. She reached in and shook his shoulder gently. "Carl, come on."

"Huh?" Carl sat up abruptly. After he oriented himself, he slowly withdrew one leg and swung it out of the car, then maneuvered the other, catching it on the edge of the door frame and struggling until both feet were planted. He sat that way for a minute before he heaved himself up, holding on to the door. He grinned at Sally. "Don't worry, I'll be fine." He swung the door shut, weaving slightly but quite proud of the fact that he could still stand up.

Sally chuckled. "You're gonna hate yourself tomorrow, and you'll deserve it."

"I've drunk more than this on a Sunday outing," Carl protested. Sally slid her arm about him, and they stumbled to the door. He leaned against it as she turned the key. She switched on the light while Carl shrugged out of his overcoat, letting it drop on the floor.

Sally's smiled faded quickly when she watched Carl move slowly across the room to the small bar and remove a bottle of whiskey. She moved quickly to his side and made an attempt to take the bottle. "I'll pour you a drink."

"Don't get cute, Sal. Go keep Joe warm. I can handle pouring a drink." He pushed past her and sat on the couch. "Toss me a blanket on your way to bed."

The look in his eyes made it clear that this was the last of their conversation. He wanted to be alone, and there was nothing else she could do. She turned without saying good night, her anger leaving a smile on his lips. She might have gotten in some licks, he thought, but he'd had the last word. In his whiskey haze, that pleased him.

When Sally slid beneath the covers, Joe stirred and turned. She smiled as his arms went about her. It was an automatic gesture they'd developed over the years, and she curled close to him.

"Where ya been, honey? God, you're cold." His voice was sluggish and thick with sleep.

"I've been down to the Arcade, having a drink." She giggled.

"Ummm," he muttered as he drew her closer. For a long minute there was silence, then Joe's voice broke the stillness. "Where did you say you were?"

"Oh, we're awake now, are we?"

"I could have sworn . . ."

"What?" she asked innocently.

"You're cold."

"So, warm me up."

"You were out?"

"Right."

"Alone! At God knows what time!"

"Right again. You're a sleeping wizard."

"My wife was running to bars at weird hours?"

"Give the man a cigar."

Joe sat up and switched on the lamp by the bed, his hair tousled and his brows drawn together in a deep frown. "Let's back up a few minutes."

"A few minutes ago you were asleep."

"Sal, what's going on?"

"You went to bed, and I stayed up for a while. About one-thirty a bartender from the Arcade called." She explained what had happened. "So, I've dumped him on our couch. I think he didn't want to go back to the motel."

"So he tied one on. He has a right."

"He's having a lot of trouble with this, but I've got a good feeling about it."

"You've got a good feeling about him having a hard time? We both better get some sleep."

"Joe, it's Beth. He got so damn touchy when I brought her name up, and he turned seven shades of green when he told me she was out—how did he say it?—'being romanced by her ex.' "

"Well, well," Joe said, grinning, "that's about the best news I've had since Carl agreed to come here."

Sally looped her arms about his neck and smiled up at him. "Just how good does it make you feel?"

Joe smiled, put his arms around her, and growled deep in his throat as he fell back against the pillow, taking her with him. Sally's soft, satisfied laugh filled the room.

Carl clumsily removed his shoes and his belt, tossing them on a chair with his jacket. He loosened his tie and sat on the edge of the couch and picked up the bottle. Then he looked around for a glass and found none, so he returned to the bar, retrieved one and returned to the couch where he sat to pour a liberal drink. He was drunk, but not drunk enough. A few more drinks and he'd have a pleasant sleep, with no dreams to jerk him awake and no guilt to rub his nerves like sand paper. He looked at the glass for a minute then gulped the amber liquid down.

The evening had been much more pleasant than Beth had expected it to be. Seated across from him at a candlelit table, she reflected that Todd was still the handsomest man she had ever seen. Certain that all her self-protective shields were in place, she allowed herself to respond a little. If she were going to be fair and listen to what he had to say, she couldn't do it in a frigid silence.

"So, you're practically running the library now?"

"Not really," she laughed, "but I've got a reasonably good job I like to do, and I've never felt better about myself or my future." She sipped her wine. "What about you, Todd?"

"Well, you know—no, you don't know. I was made a vice president in the Stafford Organization a few months ago."

"Congratulations," she replied. "I'm sure it's a well-deserved promotion."

"That's why I'm here in Helton. I'm opening a brand new branch of the corporation here."

"So, your stay could be permanent," she responded.

"It was their idea, not mine. The company does the expanding, not me."

Beth laughed softly. "Remember me, Todd—I've been around for a bunch of those promotions."

"I remember a whole lot of good things you were around for. In fact, the best things that ever happened in my life, you were around for." He watched the suspicion and animosity leap into her eyes. *Mistake, Todd,* he cautioned himself. *Don't move so fast.* "You know, just before I left Boston, I ran across a mutual friend of ours."

"We had a lot of mutual friends," she replied warily.

"I think, if you try hard, you can remember the very first friend we ever made. We'd just gotten married and were looking for someplace to settle in. We found this dingy old three-room apartment, and above us . . ."

"Old Mr. Tucker." Beth laughed. He liked the sparkle and warmth in her eyes as she reached back for a memory that would tie them together. If he played his cards right, he could renew those ties.

"Old Noah Tucker," he agreed.

"Why, I'll bet he's past eighty now."

"He is, but he's as sharp as ever. Remember how he conned us into his place without stepping on our pride when he realized we were too broke sometimes to even buy pizza."

"Yes, he used to say he'd cooked too much food for one person, and it was a sin to waste it when people were starving."

"Yeah, and how about the time he was painting his apartment? He said he had two or three cans of paint left over that he couldn't return, so would we please take them off his hands."

"Yes." She laughed again. "And then he wouldn't let us pay for them. Said it would be a favor if we just took them."

"And we found out six months later that he'd never painted his place at all."

They laughed together.

"That was a great little place by the time he got finished with us. We went from sitting on the floor in an empty room eating warmed-over pizza and beer, to total comfort."

"Even when we built the house, I kind of hated to leave there," Beth said softly. "Noah Tucker—what a wonderful friend he was."

"He asked about you. You were pretty close to his heart. I think he felt you were almost his daughter."

"Maybe I'll drop him a line," Beth replied. It was much too dangerous to go on with the remembrance.

"He'll be pleased." Todd sat back in his chair and set the menu aside as the waiter approached their table.

"You are ready to order, sir?"

Beth watched Todd perform as he had so many hundreds of times. He ordered for both of them, and what annoyed her the most was that he ordered all her favorite things, done the way she liked them. He knew exactly what wines to order, and he did it with a brilliant smoothness that set her teeth on edge. She had the urge to countermand his order, but she knew he would sense that he'd touched a vulnerable spot. She also knew he would react with little-boy surprise and ask her what she would like to have, and he would know she had done it out of reaction and uncertainty. Beth wasn't about to give him that satisfaction.

When the waiter left, Todd turned his smile back on Beth, and she steeled herself for more walks down memory lane. It shook her control when Todd brought up a different subject altogether.

"I think I've found a place to stay, but I'd like some advice, if you don't mind. I've been looking at an apartment in the Grosvenor Arms complex. What do you know about it?"

"Only that it's the most modern, most expensive, and probably the most beautiful place in a hundred-mile radius. You've got the top of the world in Helton if you get an apartment there. It's only been open for about six months, and I hear the apartments are very elegant."

"You've seen them?"

"Hardly. Eve and I tried to get to the grand opening, but it was done by invitation, and we weren't exactly on the top of the list."

"Would you like to see it?" Before she could reply with the absolute no he saw coming, he laughed. "Let me finish. You and your friend Eve come to the moving-in party I plan to have. It will be safer then."

Again she was annoyed with the subtle innuendo that she was afraid to come alone. She bit back an answer, not wanting to rise to his bait.

"I'd love to, and I'm sure Eve would, too."

"Great. I'll make some plans."

Then again he swung to another topic of conversation, and she was caught off guard with the quick leap. Every time she began to build a wall, he moved away, leaving her uncertain and shaky.

"After dinner I've made some reservations at the Breakers Club for some drinks. I've been told they have some great dancing."

The cool night air and the ride to the Breakers was enough to lull Beth into the confident feeling that she was again under control.

The Breakers was one of the best places that Helton could boast of. Decorated like a Hawaiian beach, it was relaxing, and the subtle lighting created a romantic atmosphere.

Todd waited until they'd had their second drink before he asked her to dance. As she rose, the band broke into a piece of music Todd and Beth had danced to in a happier time. Beth resisted looking into Todd's eyes as he put his arm about her, but she could feel the tingle of warm memories, and it unsettled her. Damn, he could still stir her senses. With determination, she fought for control. This was the emotion she had to defeat once and for all.

Beth was suddenly frightened by the tingle of excitement she felt when he held her close and their bodies moved together. Damn him, was he doing this deliberately? She looked up into his eyes, and for a startling moment, their eyes locked in a surge of mutual response.

Before she could speak, Todd bent his head and kissed her—a soft and pressureless kiss that left her shaken.

They continued to dance without speaking, and he didn't kiss her again or say anything.

Todd knew he'd done a lot of damage to the wall between them. He also knew exactly when to stop, to leave her precariously on the edge, unsteady and vulnerable to his next attack. One way or the other he wanted Beth back, and he meant to have her.

Beth expected Todd to ask if he could come in for a nightcap, and she was ready to end the night by making him understand the futility of it. But Todd was too clever. He didn't even try to kiss her. He waited until she unlocked the door, then wished her a good night and pleasant dreams.

He left her, knowing he had made a dent in her resolve and already planning the next.

For Beth, it was a night of confusion mingled with a fear that she might be a victim again—and worse, a willing one.

* CHAPTER 17 *

The sound of whispering voices wakened Carl, and within minutes he was wishing fervently that he hadn't. The throbbing in his temples and the upheaval in his stomach made him wisely keep his eyes shut. But the wisdom didn't protect him too long, for he had stirred and raised his arm to cover his eyes. The movement had been seen by Joe, who was standing in the kitchen doorway watching.

Joe walked into the room carrying a steaming cup of coffee, which he set on the coffee table close to Carl. Then he walked across the room and made himself comfortable. He remained silent, waiting for Carl to decide if he was going to survive or not.

Carl was seriously debating the fact. His mouth felt as if a platoon of soldiers had walked through it with shoes fresh from a cow pasture. He couldn't decide if he had enough courage to try and sit up. When he did, he groaned and buried his face in his hands, resting his elbows on his knees.

"You alive?" Joe questioned mildly.

"God, I hope not."

"You owe me a bottle of whiskey."

Carl dropped his arm and looked in surprise at the empty bottle that lay on the floor beside the couch—he didn't remember finishing it. He moved and a jolt of pain surged through his head. With hands that shook he reached for the steaming cup of coffee. He took a deep gulp and cursed as the hot liquid burned its way down to his stomach.

Sally came down the hall from the bedroom, walked to the couch, and bounced down beside Carl, who groaned again and closed his eyes.

"I've turned on the shower," she said brightly. "Want me to carry you in, or hold your hand or something?"

Carl slowly reached out and set the cup down. Then, just as slowly, he rose to his feet. "You are a sadist, Sally—a sadist," he muttered. "You haven't an ounce of humanity."

Sally's soft laugh followed him as he walked toward the bathroom as if he were treading on eggshells. He had to use his hand to feel his way down the hall.

In the steaming bathroom he went to the toilet and raised the lid. For a moment he had to decide which was going to come first, the relief of a quakingly full bladder or an even quakier stomach. The bladder won, but only by minutes.

He stripped off his clothes, stepped into the shower, and stood with his eyes closed while the hot water slowly began to wash some of the ache away. But even the shower was not enough, and when he toweled himself dry, his head was still pounding. He hated to look down, for fear his eyes might fall out.

Carl knew from past experience that there was always an extra toothbrush in a container in the cabinet, but he was certain that brushing his teeth would set his stomach off again. He rinsed his mouth with mouthwash, spat, then braced his hands on the side of the sink to prepare himself for his first look in the mirror.

The whites of his eyes had red spiderweb lines, and his face still carried a pasty gray color.

"You stupid bastard, you look like hell." The reflection agreed.

When he walked into the kitchen, Sally and Joe were both seated at the table having breakfast. He slid into a chair, propped one elbow on the table, and rested his throbbing head in the cup of his hand.

Without another word, Sally placed another steaming cup of coffee before him. This one was laced with whiskey.

"A little hair of the dog might pull you together," she offered at his questioning look. "Want me to rustle you up something to eat?"

"You have to be kidding," he replied, speaking softly so the lightning in his head wouldn't strike again. Carl glared at Joe, who was eating with obvious pleasure. "I need a lift to my car, and I've got to go back to the motel and change clothes."

"Yeah," Joe agreed, "you smell like a brewery, but don't worry. I'll take you to the motel and wait until you change, then drop you off at your car. You can follow me into the office. We've got an idea."

"What?"

"I'd better tell you when you can pay more attention. You need some air. We'll talk at the office. C'mon, let's get going. I'll get the wheels out of the garage and be out front."

"Okay."

When Joe left, Sally and Carl sat in a minute of silence.

"Thanks, Sal."

"For what?"

"The ride home, I guess. Probably for a whole lot more, but I'll be damned if I can remember. I didn't say anything . . . out of the way last night?"

Sally knew he meant had he talked about Beth. She shook her head. "All you had to say was gobbledygook anyway."

He knew she was giving him some space, but he also knew he must have said a whole lot.

He rose and walked to the kitchen door, but as he opened it and started out, Sally called to him. "Carl?"

"Yeah?" He turned to look at her.

"Give Beth a call," she said softly.

Their eyes held for a minute, then, without a word, Carl pulled the door shut, and she heard his footsteps fade away.

"Darn you, Carl Forrester, you ran from a problem once in your life, I hope you're smart enough and lucky enough not to run again."

"Pull up by the drugstore," Carl said as Joe entered the main street of town. Joe did and waited in the car while Carl went inside.

He bought a bottle of aspirin, opened it, and tossed two of them into his mouth, swallowing quickly and grimacing at the bitter taste. He put the bottle in his pocket.

He climbed back into the car and relaxed against the seat as Joe once more pulled into traffic.

"You've got a line on something, Joe?"

"A long shot."

"Like what?"

"Well, when we found Martha, I had a boyfriend in mind, so I got a court order from Judge McKenna."

"To do what?"

"You know when you do an autopsy on a murder victim who's pregnant, you can't touch the fetus. Well, I wanted a blood type, so I went around the law a little."

"What good is it going to do you? We both know blood tests don't tell who the father of a baby is."

"No," Joe said quietly, "but it might tell who isn't—at least, that's what the pathologist told me. Maybe we can eliminate a couple." He shrugged. "Especially if the suspects don't know enough about the test to know how little it can tell us."

"How can we connect the two murders this way?"

"Paula and Martha knew each other. Maybe the killer either suspected Martha had said something to Paula, or maybe Paula was wise enough to guess and tried a little blackmail."

"So he killed Martha, and Paula knew him," Carl said. "Why didn't she say something as soon as she found out Martha was dead?"

"Like I said, maybe she liked him, or maybe she wanted something from him. Either way, she remained silent a little too long."

"You could be right, Joe."

"But you don't quite agree?"

"I've just got this hunch."

"Your hunches were pretty good before. What is it?"

"I don't think Martha and Paula were as close as that, and I don't think he killed Paula because of Martha."

"Then what do you think?"

"I think," Carl said seriously, "that he just kills for some reason buried in a sick mind. Those notes are crazy! And I'm scared that we haven't seen the last of it."

"So the baby idea is nothing?"

"No, let's play it out. You see Michael, Larry, and Jake—David, too, since he was at Paul's party—and I'll see Paul."

There was a long moment of thunderous silence. Neither man wanted to voice the next thought.

"And?" Joe asked.

"I'll go see Father McAllen, too."

It was against everything either knew or believed, yet as men of the law, they had no choice. They had to treat the priest they respected and admired first as a man, and second, as a suspect.

They reached the motel, and Joe waited in contemplative silence while Carl changed clothes. The heavy silence clung all the way to Carl's car.

Carl got out of Joe's car and came around to the driver's side. He braced a hand on the window Joe had just opened, and bent toward him.

"I'll go out and see Paul, then I'll run on over to the church. See you sometime this afternoon."

"Good enough," Joe agreed. He wound up the window as Carl walked away.

When Carl drove into Paul's driveway he saw Amy's car parked in it. That suited his plan perfectly. He'd told them both that Martha was pregnant, and he was sure they had talked about it, maybe argued about it. Just as he was sure Amy was lying for Paul, he was as sure that Paul could not afford to refuse a blood test with Amy there.

He walked to the door and knocked, and it took so little time for Paul to open it that Carl suspected his arrival had been observed.

"Carl?" Paul's voice held a faint tinge of wariness.

"Mind if I come in? I've got something to say that's important."

Paul stood aside and motioned Carl into the main room. He was not in the least surprised to see Amy seated on the high stool before the huge window.

"No work today, Amy?" he asked.

"No, I'm on a leave of absence. It gives me time to pose for Paul so he can get this portrait done for his next show. Besides, the wedding plans are getting rather frantic, and I've been doing the house, too. I just needed the time."

"When's the show?"

"Just before Easter," Paul explained, but his eyes hadn't left Carl. "That's not why you're here, is it?"

"No, not exactly."

"Why are you here—on official duty?"

"Yes."

"I'm under arrest." Paul said it as if it were definite, and Amy looked at him in surprise.

"No, I've come to get your cooperation."

"My cooperation?" Paul laughed mirthlessly. "When haven't I cooperated?"

"I didn't mean that you hadn't—I meant that we need a little volunteering from you."

"For what?"

"Joe wants all the men involved with Martha Dexter or with this case in any way to come in on a volunteer basis so blood tests can be taken."

"Blood tests! Why—to find who the father of Martha's baby was? Well, you can just go to hell. If you think you have a reason for leaning on me, then do something about it. But I sure as hell am not taking a blood test."

Carl remained still. Then he said softly, "Why not?"

"I thought a man had rights in this country. I thought you were innocent until proven guilty."

"You are," Carl replied. "It's just a technicality."

"The hell it is. Forget it. No blood test."

Carl shrugged as if it were beyond his control, but he'd watched Amy, and he was sure a new seed of doubt had been sown.

"Well, I came to tell you. If you don't want to take the test, I guess it's your right." Carl turned away and walked to the door. When it clicked shut behind him, the air in the room was filled with the electrical current of doubt.

Paul walked to the huge window, shoving his hands in his pockets. For a long while he stood looking out at his domain. He remained still, hoping Amy would say something to reassure him. But when she spoke, the sound of his name hurt as badly as if she had struck him.

"Paul?" He couldn't answer. "Paul?"

"Let it go, Amy," he whispered.

"I can't." Her voice was thick with both doubt and fear. He spun from the window to face her.

"Why won't you take the blood test? What difference could it make?"

"Why should I?"

"So there'd be no doubt in anybody's mind."

"Meaning yours?"

Amy went to him and put her arms around him. He held her, and they stood for a long time. Amy laid her head against his chest and closed her eyes, trying to keep her mind from the abyss of doubt, but it was useless for them both.

"Paul, take that test." It was a plea for both herself and him. She stepped back and looked up at him. She could see refusal in his eyes. With effort, she controlled her trembling and backed away another step.

"I'm going home."

"Are you going to let a stupid thing like this spoil what we have?"

"What do we have? Trust? Truth? If you weren't afraid to take that test, you'd have gone with Carl. Is there a chance that the baby she was carrying was yours?"

"Amy, for God's sake!" He took a step toward her, but again she backed away.

"Is there?" she demanded.

It was the voice of finality, and Paul knew it. The lie had to end. Only now, would Amy believe the truth when she heard it?

"Yes," he said hoarsely.

Amy gasped and looked as if he had struck her.

"Are you going to let me tell you the truth?"

"What have you been telling me all along?"

"Everything is not the way you think it is. At least sit down and let me talk to you."

Amy sucked in her breath. She refused both tears and anger. She was too hurt to let either touch her.

"I'm going home, Paul. I think we both have a lot to think about. If you want to call me, make it after you take the test. I don't know how I'll feel—I have to think."

"Don't go." His voice held the pleading of the near hopeless. He knew he couldn't stop her. Paul closed his eyes for a moment after Amy left. Then he walked to the portrait and stood before it, seeing the morning light glisten on Amy's smile. So beautiful! He reached out and touched her face on the canvas, then turned away and walked back to the window. How little beauty would be left in his life if Amy were never to return.

Carl drove slowly. This was one stop he hated to make. It went against everything his upbringing had taught him. The dedication the priesthood required had inspired him, but it could be a mental drain far beyond what most people would ever understand. Was it possible for a priest to be psychotic without anyone recognizing it? Without even the priest himself recognizing it? He just didn't know enough psychology to have an answer.

He wasn't too sure where he would find Father McAllen, so he went first to the church. He was met at the door by the housekeeper. When she folded her hands before her and stood firmly enough in the doorway to prevent his entry, he was reasonably sure some form of gossip had reached her. He just wondered who had talked.

"I'd like to speak to Father McAllen."

"I'm afraid Father isn't here."

"Can you tell me where he is, please? I'm afraid it's very important."

"The man's run ragged today. He's at the hospital, and from there he's got other stops."

"I've got to catch him somewhere along the way." Carl persisted. "Now, why don't you tell me where my best bet will be?"

"I expect he'll be going over to the school around three-thirty or so. He doesn't miss practice with his boys."

He looked at his watch. "That's over five hours from now. There's no way to catch him before that?"

"I don't know what else to say."

"Well, then, I'm afraid you are going to have to give him a message."

"Sure. What is it?"

"If he's back before lunch tell him to call me, Carl Forrester, at Joe Marks's office in the police department. If he comes back after noon, then it would be better if he just came down to the police department."

"Whatever for? Surely you can't mean . . ."

"I don't mean a thing, except that it's important that I talk to him today."

"All right. I'll give him your message."

She nodded with her lips pressed firmly together. Much as Carl would have liked to have convinced her otherwise, he had to let her negative opinion of him persist. "Thank you very much."

When Carl entered the office, he was met by a glum-faced Joe.

"Did you see Michael Brodie?"

"Yeah. He was beside himself with pleasure. He can't wait. That boy wants two things. He wants that baby to have been his, and if it's not, he wants to know whose it was."

"So he can commit some murder and mayhem of his own?"

"I'd guess. What about you?" Joe asked wearily.

"Struck out." Carl described Paul's reaction and Father McAllen's absence.

"Paul doesn't sound so squeaky clean anymore, does he?"

"Hell, nobody does. That isn't all that's got you down, though, is it?"

"No. We found Paula's car, and it doesn't give us any new clues."

"Don't give up yet. I have a feeling all five of these guys are going to show up for that blood test."

"I've already told Jake Magee and Larry Jackson."

"They'll be there?"

"Yes."

"Good."

"But you said Paul . . ."

"He might have been reluctant, but Amy was there, and I think I left him with the little problem of explaining to her why he doesn't want to take it. As far as Father McAllen is concerned, he has too much at stake not to take it."

* CHAPTER 18 *

When Carl and Joe walked back into the station after lunch, the first person they saw was Michael Brodie.

"I told you he was eager," Joe said.

Michael rose from a straight-back chair against the wall and walked over to them. "So, where do I go to get this blood test?" he asked gruffly.

"The lab, two doors down," Joe supplied. "It will only take a few minutes, then you can come back here. They'll call us as soon as the results are in."

Michael nodded and walked away.

Joe turned to look at Carl, who shrugged. They started toward Joe's office again, when the outer door opened and a pale but grim-faced Paul walked in. He crossed immediately to Joe and Carl.

"You made your point with Amy, just as you planned," he said to Carl. "I'm here to take that test. What do I do next?"

Carl was reasonably certain no amount of effort on his part was going to make Paul any friendlier. He remained quiet while Joe gave him the same instructions he had given Michael. When he walked away, Carl and Joe exchanged looks. "Those two could make quite an explosion if they bump into each other," Joe observed.

"Which is what they're going to do," Carl replied, "but I think Michael will keep his cool—until he gets the results."

When Michael and Paul returned, they sat across the room from each other in stony silence, waiting as impatiently as Joe and Carl for the answer.

Fifteen minutes later, Father McAllen and David walked into the station, followed five minutes later by Jake, then

Larry. When Tom opened the door and stuck his head inside, Carl was reasonably sure why.

"Father McAllen's here to see you. Says you asked him to come down."

"Good afternoon, gentlemen." Father McAllen smiled pleasantly. "Mrs. Martin said you wanted to see me. Is it important?"

"I'm afraid so, Father," Joe replied. Carl could hear the uncertainty in Joe's voice and knew he was uncomfortable, but Joe was not the kind of policeman to let anything interfere with the truth. "I have to ask you to do something for us."

"If I can be of help, just let me know."

"I want you to volunteer for a blood test."

"A blood test? I don't understand."

Joe cleared his throat and cast a desperate look at Carl, who remained defensively silent. With no more preliminaries, Joe explained, watching Father McAllen's face go grayer with each word. With some difficulty, he regained his composure.

"I can tell you my blood type, if that's all that's required. I'm B positive."

"I'm afraid, Father, that it's a legal technicality. I have to have our lab type you. I'm sorry."

"If this is necessary to prove I'm not involved, then I see no reason not to go through with it. Where do I go?" he added quietly. He left without another word, and Joe was relieved. He couldn't have handled protestations. He was grateful for Father McAllen's understanding.

"If news about this slips out," Joe said, "the media is going to have a field day. I can see the headlines now. The way people around here care for this man, we'll have them at the door howling for our blood."

"I hate to think any one of those six could be guilty of something like this. If I could only wrap myself around some kind of motive."

"The baby's not enough?"

"Well, look at it. Michael would like to be the father. All Martha would have had to do was let him believe he was. There goes the motive."

"Unless she had a conscience. She had a fine reputation, so the chances of her lying like that are zilch."

"Right back to square one again. I wish I knew what was in that killer's mind."

"Yeah. He's sitting out there in my office as calm as can be, maybe even laughing at us."

"You know what scares me more?" Carl said. "If he is as psychotic as I think he is, then any ordinary motives can be tossed out the window. It's something in his own mind—a figment of a demented mentality. How does logic trace that?"

"We ought to call on Dr. Reuger at the university. He might be able to give us some kind of handle on it. He's been teaching psychology for several years."

"Let's run up and see him after the tests are over."

"Fine—we need something to sink our teeth into." Joe sighed as he ran his hand through his hair and leaned back in his chair. He eyed the telephone as if he could make it ring.

He sat very still, the blackness welling up in him. *These cold men of the law! How dare they reach out to touch a man of God? I'll pray for them—of course I'll pray for them. They don't understand what has to be done. I'm only a messenger—the hand that wields the sword of Armageddon. Someone had to stop those women, with their teasing eyes and wanton bodies—those tempting, vile women. And it was my duty. I knew them, I recognized them as no others did. Others looked at them with the eyes of lust. The whores deserved the punishment they got. This town has to be cleansed of such creatures. It's my town—I have responsibility.*

The outer office was unusually quiet. Tom and Toby worked on the forms before them. Neither wanted to acknowledge the men gathering there. One by one they had come in, had their blood drawn, and had returned to sit quietly, each with an invisible wall about him and each caught up in his own thoughts.

The atmosphere was electrically charged, and in the inner office, even Carl and Joe had not spoken for several minutes. When the phone rang, Joe grabbed it.

"Yeah, Carmichael? Doc, you have some answers for me?"

"Joe, what I got is results, not answers. I told you when you got started on this idéa that there was no way to tell who the father of this girl's baby was." Dr. James Carmichael's voice sounded somewhat exasperated.

"But you did say you could tell me who wasn't."

"Sure."

"Then tell me what you've found out."

"Genetics are kind of complicated, old buddy."

"Give it to me in English, if you can." Joe laughed.

"Okay, I'll give you what I've got and a wild guess to go with it. But something like this will never stand up in court. A good lawyer will rip it to shreds."

"I know. Just give me something I can get started with."

"Okay, here goes. Your priest, Jackson, and Mondale are B positive. Michael Brodie and the Magee kid are AB positive. I can hazard a pretty good guess that none of them was responsible. The mother was O positive and the baby was B negative."

"So?"

"Paul Carterson is B negative, too. If I had to go out on a limb—way, way out—I'd say the kid's father was Carterson. Usually, the Rh positive pulls stronger because positives are more dominant. But this time, if it's a choice among the six (and I'm sure there are a lot of men right here in this town who could fill the bill, too), then I'd say Paul Carterson was your man."

"How good is your guess?"

"Come on, Joe, give me a break. I can't nail him down for you. The only thing I can say with certainty is that the others were not."

"Good enough. I owe you."

"I'll collect. See ya."

"This is going to be hard to explain to you," Joe said as he put the phone back in its cradle.

"I'll listen while you tell the others. How do you plan to do this?"

"One at a time. I don't want any trouble in here."

"Who's first?"

"Father McAllen." Joe's answer was prompt and relieved.

"I take it there's no way?"

"You're right. No way." Joe buzzed Sergeant Grimms. "Tom, tell Father McAllen to come in."

He looked around at the other concerned faces. Inside, behind his mask, he smiled. Could they really have believed he would even touch those harlots? It was forbidden, but even if it were not, he would not have soiled himself. But he must forgive them because they didn't understand. Still, he must carry out his duty. Look at the others—frightened, frightened little men, afraid to listen to the voice that tells them of truth. He listened, and he carried out the commands to cleanse the wicked from the earth—those who would tempt and mislead. He listened . . . and he obeyed.

When Father McAllen walked into the room, both Carl and Joe were aware of his lack of concern. He seemed assured of their finding.

"Father," Joe began, "I believe Carl and I both owe you an abject apology. I hope you understand our position."

"Don't worry about it, Joe. You have your job, the same as I. Knowing you're not guilty is a fine shield. My vows are my life. I've listened to the heartbreaking guilt of others, and I have enough difficulties in my life without trying to live with that one."

Carl's eyes narrowed, then he drew a deep breath. "Confession," he murmured. Joe and the priest looked at him—Joe with curiosity and Father McAllen with a sad smile on his face.

"What did you say, Carl?" Joe's brows were drawn together in a questioning frown.

"Confession," he repeated. He smiled at Father McAllen, who remained silent. "You're locked into someone's confession again." Still the priest did not answer. "And it was Martha?" Carl asked, then quickly added, "Sure it was. Martha came to you in confession and told you who the father of her baby was." Carl's voice grew harder. "What else did she tell you?"

"Carl!" Joe exclaimed.

"You know I can't tell you that," Father McAllen replied.

"Even if he could have killed her?"

"I'm not the judge," Father McAllen said quietly, "and I can't condemn. All I could do was console and advise her."

"So, you might have advised her to face the man and tell him of her situation. You might have suggested that he would have conscience enough to do something about it, and you just might have set her up to be killed."

Carl realized all at once that he had lost control. He was the one who didn't believe the baby was the reason for Martha's death, yet he was openly accusing of destroying her the one man Martha had chosen to go to for help. Carl's pounding head was growing rapidly worse, heightened by the sympathy and understanding in the priest's eyes.

"I'm sorry, Father, I didn't mean that," he added in a helpless whisper. Not only had he not meant it—he couldn't understand why he had struck out at the priest.

But Father McAllen understood and would remain silent until the day Carl chose to speak to him of the obvious grief and even more obvious guilt that plagued him.

"I've got a busy schedule, so if you don't mind . . ."

"No, of course not," Joe said quickly. He was still struggling with the urge to hit Carl over the head with a club.

Father McAllen left, closing the door quietly behind him, and Joe turned a baleful eye on Carl. "If I thought it would make your headache worse I'd belt you. Maybe you'd better take a couple more aspirin."

"Sorry," Carl said, "you're right. That was a mistake."

"It must be hard enough on him to know some answers and not be able to say the words that might make things easier for us."

"Yeah." Carl sighed again. "So that lets him off. Now we have Paul and Michael. Who's next?"

Michael sat with his elbows resting on his knees and his hands hanging limply between his spread legs. His head was bowed, and he was caught in his own bitter thoughts. He was unaware of any movement in the room until David's voice came from beside him.

"Michael?"

He looked up, surprised to find David there. The surprise quickly turned to suspicion. Michael Brodie was not used to the hand of friendship being extended without a hidden barb that would draw blood.

"What do you want?"

"Nothing. You just looked—I'm sorry about Martha. I know how you felt about her. It's a hell of a thing to happen."

"All this about the baby makes Martha look bad. Martha wasn't like that."

"You want it to be your baby, Michael?"

Michael licked his dry lips, and his hands clasped convulsively before him. "I hope so," he whispered.

"After all this is over, why don't you come around and talk to Father McAllen? Maybe he can help you over the rough spots."

"Help me! He had to take the blood test, too, and he was the last one to see Martha alive."

"You don't believe he had anything to do with this, do you?" David said in a rough whisper. "He knows how you feel. He understands. You might be surprised. I just hate to see you eating at yourself like this when you just need someone to talk to."

Before Michael could answer, the door between the offices opened, and Father McAllen came out. David rose and went to his side.

"Come on, David. We have a lot to do today."

"Father . . . ah, let's wait a few minutes."

"Why?"

David jerked his head, and Father McAllen's eyes shifted to Michael, who had already returned to his meditation.

"He's on the edge, and I'm afraid he's gonna break."

"You think the baby was his?"

"No, what I think is, maybe it wasn't. If it turns out to be Paul Carterson's, I think he might need us."

Father McAllen nodded quietly, and he and David sat down. Grimms looked up from his work. "Brodie, go on in."

Michael rose from his chair as if he found it difficult, and walked to Joe's door like a man condemned. When the door clicked shut behind him, there was total silence.

Michael stood near the door and looked across the room at Carl and Joe.

"Come on in, Brodie, and sit down," Joe said.

"Just tell me," Michael said hoarsely. "Was the baby mine?"

"These tests aren't conclusive. They . . ."

"Don't feed me none of this shit. Just tell me straight."

"It wasn't your baby."

Michael stood for a minute as if he actually hadn't heard. Then a low growl bubbled up from deep inside him, and he spun around, tearing the door open.

Everyone seemed temporarily frozen, then Michael launched himself across the room toward Paul who was just rising from his chair.

Paul was halfway erect when Michael's huge bulk collided with his, and he tumbled backward, crushing the chair beneath him and carrying Michael with him as he fell.

Before Paul could gather enough wits to realize the cause behind the attack, Michael's fist found his jaw with a resounding blow that set stars sparkling before his eyes. Paul raised both hands to try to defend himself, but Michael had too much advantage. Paul could already taste the salty blood in his mouth, and the next blow rattled his senses as it caught his right cheek, splitting it and sending droplets of blood flying.

"Bastard! Rotten, fucking bastard!" Michael was half groaning, half crying as he rained punishing blows on Paul's already semiconscious form.

By this time, the others realized what was happening and why. Joe and Carl burst from the office, and it took both of them to pull Michael, panting and sobbing, away from Paul.

"I'm gonna kill you!" Michael cried, his anguish tearing through Carl, who had heard these words before in a situation nearly the same. "I'm gonna kill you like you killed her!"

David and Father McAllen rushed to Michael's side and held him back as Carl bent to check Paul's condition.

Paul struggled to rise. Blood dripped from the corner of his mouth and the cut on his cheek. One eye was already beginning to swell. He got to his feet, clinging to Carl until he got his balance. He looked into Michael's face and saw the gleam of hatred, then looked at Carl and saw the truth. This blow was the worst.

"God," he groaned, and his knees nearly buckled again.

"You don't understand," he panted as he spoke to Michael. "It's not like you think it was."

Michael's struggles increased, but David and Father McAllen held him.

"I'll take him out of here," Father McAllen said to Carl, who nodded. But the struggle was almost too much for him and David.

Michael kept shouting back at Paul, "I'll kill you! I'll kill you!"

When his voice faded, Carl and Joe led Paul to a chair. "Let go of me. I can manage." He took a handkerchief from his back pocket and wiped some of the blood from his eye. His face seemed suddenly gaunt and haunted as his eyes moved from Carl to Joe, then back again to Carl.

"It's true, then." His voice cracked with the weight of having his own suspicion verified. "Amy," he said in a whisper so low it carried only to Carl.

"You tell us," Carl replied in the same quiet voice.

Paul nodded slowly. "It's not like you think. I didn't kill her."

"This is not conclusive evidence, Paul. It means nothing, except that you had an affair with Martha Dexter," Carl said.

"No, it doesn't even mean that! Look, are you arresting me?"

"No. We can't arrest you on this kind of evidence. But you should have told us the truth to begin with," Joe said.

"Then, I'm free to go?"

"Yes, for now. But don't get any ideas about leaving Helton," Joe answered.

"Don't worry. I did that oncc. I'm not going to run from something I didn't do." Paul bent and grabbed up his fallen jacket. He started for the door, but before he left, he turned to face them again. He used his index finger to point and punctuate each word. "I didn't kill Martha Dexter, and I had nothing to do with Paula's murder. I'm not running— not from you, and not from Brodie. If he comes for me again, I'm going to make him wish he hadn't."

Paul slammed the door, and Carl and Joe stood breathing heavily, feeling reasonably sure they were going to have to keep an even closer eye on Michael Brodie and Paul Carterson.

Joe turned to Carl. "I could use a couple of those aspirins."

"Me, too," Carl muttered. "I have a feeling I'm going to need the whole bottle."

* CHAPTER 19 *

"So, maybe you ought to give your professor friend a call," Carl suggested.

"Yeah. Why can't it just be cut and dried?" Joe sighed. "Find a victim pregnant, find the father, find the killer—simple."

"You weren't cut out for the simple life. I guess before we started this we knew it wouldn't prove enough."

"Just what were you hoping for, Carl?"

"I thought that Amy might decide the truth was better than lying for someone who was sleeping with another woman behind her back."

"And you got stung by your own sting."

"Yeah," Carl replied thoughtfully. "Joe, you call your professor and make a meet. I'll run over and see Amy."

"You don't think she'll be waiting for Paul at his home?"

"No, I don't think so—not this time."

"Okay, get on your horse. I'll make the call and see if we can see him sometime today."

"Good enough." Carl rose and left. He knew that he had hurt Amy terribly and felt he had to help her somehow, because she was only another victim in this ugly thing.

Amy opened her door when he knocked, and he could tell she had been crying.

"Go away, Carl," she spoke softly, but he could hear a touch of panic in her voice. She didn't want to hear what he was going to say.

"I'd like to talk to you."

"I don't have anything to say, and I don't want to hear what you have to say, either."

"You're being real tough, lady," he said softly, "but I know you'd feel better if there were no lies."

She turned away, leaving the door open. He walked in and closed it behind him, then followed her into the living room. "You really don't have to tell me—I know," she said frigidly as she sat down and pulled her jeans-clad legs beneath her.

"Someone called? Paul?" he inquired.

"No."

"How did you know?"

"Paul told me there was a chance, so I told him he had to take that test. I did exactly what you forced me to do, didn't I? Are you satisfied, Carl?" Her voice was brittle with condemnation and a controlled fury that was threatening to surface.

"Amy, I didn't do this to hurt you. But we need to know all the truth if we want to find out who killed Martha and Paula."

She looked at him with a puzzled frown. "All the truth? Then you don't believe this test is conclusive? You set me up! I have to admit you did a pretty good job, but it was a shitty thing to do, don't you think? You set out to prove that Paul was shacking up with Martha while I stood around like a fool with egg on my face."

"This proves that there was a possibility that Martha Dexter was pregnant with Paul's child. There are some circumstances about that situation that you should ask Paul about."

"Was the child the reason for her death?"

"If there had been only one murder, I might believe it, but after Paula," he tried to smile in the face of her growing anger, "I'm not so easy to convince."

"Do you believe he's innocent?"

"Not completely."

"Then what do you want?"

"The truth, Amy, I want the truth."

She turned away from him with her hands clasped before her. "I don't know what you're talking about."

"Yes, you do. Paul lied to you and it hurt. But there are a lot of other lies that could hurt Paul worse."

"And not hurting Paul is the most important thing in the world now, isn't it?" she snapped.

"No, not Paul—you."

"Don't hand me that!" She swung her legs from the couch and stood up again. "Don't be the sweet-talking cop coming in here to play sympathy scenes with me. You don't give a damn one way or the other what happens to me as long as you nail your man!"

"It's my business to nail him!"

"But my life is none of your business!" Her voice rose as her anger began to reach its bound.

"It's my business when you lie!" He was not so cool by this time either.

"You say I'm lying—well, if you can prove it, then arrest me. If you can't, get the hell out of my house and leave me alone!" She took a step toward him, and her smile was bitter and cold. "What's in this for you, Carl—a promotion? Some kind of perverted publicity that will make you hero for the day?"

"If it is any of your business, I'm getting nothing but the satisfaction of bringing down a cold-blooded killer who took the lives of two women."

"It's none of my business, just like my life is none of yours," she retorted furiously.

"Look, Amy, I'm sorry for you if this . . ."

"Sorry for me! Well, don't be. I don't need your sympathy or your interference. In fact, I'd like you to leave!"

"I'll find who killed Martha Dexter and Paula Craig with or without your help. But if you keep throwing me roadblocks, and I find a way to prove you and your friend are lying, I'll yank you in so fast your head will spin."

"You do that—when you can prove it."

"So you're going to roll over for Paul and hang on to your lie until it explodes in your face."

"I don't roll over for anyone, and as far as I'm concerned, you and Paul can both go to the devil. I just want to be left alone. Are you too dense to understand that? Just leave me alone!" The last word ended on an angry sob.

"Okay, I'll leave you alone," Carl said, clinging to his

own temper by a thread. He held his voice even. "I just hope your conscience can."

He turned and walked out, and Amy remained immobile until she heard the door slam. Shaking with rage, she reached for the first thing she could touch, which was a vase of flowers. Water, china, and flowers hit the wall and slid down it. She grabbed her purse from the table and ran for the door.

Paul closed the car door and leaned against it for a minute. "Christ," he muttered. In little over a week, his entire life had come apart at the seams.

He felt rotten, and he was pretty sure he looked just as bad. Blood had dried on his cheek and on his lips. He could feel it crack and flake. Inhaling deeply, he pushed himself away from the car and walked to the front door, fumbled for the right key, and slid it into the lock. Inside, he began to strip off his dirty clothes as he walked to the bathroom. He turned on both spigots and cupped his hands beneath them, then bent to rinse his face.

Making his way to the bedroom, he changed into jeans and a sweatshirt, then returned to the main room to pour a much-needed drink. He lifted the glass to his mouth and took a sip. The sting of the whiskey on his cut lip was no worse than the jolt that struck him when his eyes caught the painting of Amy.

Carrying the drink, he walked to it and stood staring at it. She smiled at him from the canvas, and he reached to draw his fingers across her face as if he could actually feel her flesh beneath his hand. He took a drink. Only one question filled his mind, and he dodged the answer. Amy knew by now, he was sure of it. The only question now was, how much damage had he done her?

He tossed off the rest of the drink and walked to the couch to toss himself down on it. He couldn't paint because he couldn't look into Amy's eyes while he tried to finish the portrait.

He heard the car in the drive, the slam of the door, and the rapid tattoo of footsteps. The key turned in the lock, and Amy stood in the doorway.

"You are a rotten bastard," she said coldly.

"Is that all you came to say? If it is, that isn't news anymore." He swung his feet to the floor and sat up. "Would it do any good to say I'm sorry?"

"Sorry for what—because the baby was yours, because you lied to me, or because I lied for you?"

"I'm sorry for the whole damn mess. Considering everything, you might give me a chance to explain."

"God, your ego is overwhelming! What do you want to explain—how you were screwing a friend while you were making a fool out of me?" Her voice was like shards of ice, and they cut deep enough that he could feel the emotional blood.

"I didn't have anything to do with Martha's death."

"But you sure had a lot to do with the baby she was carrying."

"When you say it like that, it sounds like an ugly, sordid thing. It just wasn't that way."

"Of course not," Amy replied scathingly. "It was moonlight and roses and probably a lot of 'scene of the passion' promises."

"Dammit, Amy, it wasn't like that, either!"

"It was rape?" she asked derisively. "Did you rape her, or did she rape you?"

"It was a one-time thing! An accident—one that Martha regretted as much as I did. I was never with her again."

"Of course," she laughed angrily, "and I'm supposed to believe that. Just like I believed you when you said there was nothing between you and Martha at all."

"It was too hard to tell you. I was afraid I would lose you. Don't you think I wanted it to be different?"

"Paul, the night Martha died, you weren't here all evening. I called a million times. You were with her that night, weren't you?"

"We had to settle the problem."

"You mean you knew? You actually knew?"

"Not really. I was suspicious." He knew every word he said dug the hole deeper, but he couldn't stop the truth now—it was like a force tearing him open to get out. "Martha was in love with Michael. She was afraid he wouldn't love her if he knew. She came to me that night and said she wanted to marry him, but she was scared and confused." He stopped talking, seeing the distrust in her eyes. "You don't even believe the truth," he said quietly.

"And just how am I supposed to know what's true and what isn't? I know you were with Martha sometime that night, and I know it's likely the baby she was carrying was yours. I don't know if you were scared enough or mad enough to kill her."

"Amy!"

"So many things are possible. You were mad because she wouldn't lie about your baby. You were mad because she was stupid enough to get pregnant. I know your black moods, too, Paul, and your temper. You said you had to settle the problem. Just how did you settle it?"

Paul sagged to the couch and cradled his head in his hands. "I didn't kill Martha, Amy," he whispered. "I didn't kill her."

Amy turned and walked to the door. As she reached for the knob, Paul spoke again. "Amy." She turned and their eyes met. "What are you going to do?"

"You're afraid I'm going to tell Carl and Joe I lied. Well, don't worry, I'm not. You're in your sinking boat all by yourself, and your lies are weighing you down."

"That's not what I mean."

"You mean us." She said the words wearily. "I don't know."

"I love you." It was spoken with a sad finality, as if there was nothing else left to say.

"I'm just not sure I can survive your brand of love."

"Stay and talk. We can work this out. Please . . . stay."

"Not now. I have to think about it." She left, closing the door so quietly behind her that he couldn't believe she was really gone, maybe for the last time.

He felt as if a huge hand had crumpled him like a used sheet of paper tossed in a wastebasket. He was in a tunnel, and there was no sign of light ahead.

He rose again and walked to the window, keeping his eyes away from the portrait. He stood, hands deep in his pockets, without seeing anything before him.

* * *

Joe's first question when Carl reached headquarters was about Amy. Carl told him about her anger.

"Sounds like guilt," Joe offered.

"It is. She's lying her head off, but she's right. Unless I can prove he was elsewhere, I haven't got a prayer. He was somewhere else and with someone else. If it was Martha, then Father McAllen . . ." He paused thoughtfully, then snapped his fingers. "Hell, it could be that Martha was so distraught about the baby and her association with Michael that she went to Father McAllen, either for confession or advice. Or both."

"And Paul just might have been with her."

"Do you know if he's Catholic?"

"No, but I could find out."

"That might be why Father McAllen was the last to see her alive. If she had gone to confession, he couldn't tell us anything she said. The questions are: Did she leave with Paul? Did he leave before or after her? Or did she go with someone else who came along?"

"Michael?" Joe said quickly.

"Maybe, but he doesn't strike me as a churchgoer."

"But, maybe she asked him to come. Maybe she needed Father's help to tell him her situation," Joe suggested.

"No, won't work."

"Why not?"

"Because Michael didn't know. That was no act he put on; he meant to kill Paul—maybe he still does."

"But, maybe it was *just* that, an act."

"Damn good one."

"Yeah. One brick wall after another."

"Did you get hold of your professor friend? I'd like to get a psychological slant on this killer. One of our suspects is as nutty as a fruitcake, but they look like such nice, uncomplicated, ordinary men."

"I called him. We can ride out to the college and see him in his office tomorrow. He said he didn't know what kind of help he could give, but he was willing to brainstorm with us."

"What time?"

"Nine-thirty or so."

"Okay, I'll be here."

"Where you going now?" Joe asked.

"For some well-deserved dinner. Then I might take a ride out to see Paul—maybe even Michael. He's hurting pretty bad, and this might just be the time to question him some more."

"Then, I'll see you in the morning—unless you want to stop by the house later. You can fill me in on what you find out, then we can relax for a while, maybe have a drink." Joe added the last with a wink.

Carl shot his friend a painful look, his color paling a little at the mention of alcohol. "If I come by, I'll pass on the drink. As near as I can recall, I pretty well drained your stock last night."

"Well, if you're sure . . ." Joe was chuckling as Carl left the office.

"Later, Joe," was Carl's only reply as he closed the door.

Carl found himself back behind the wheel of his car. He meant to go to Paul's, but found himself heading for Beth's house without thinking. He just wanted to see her.

Beth was so intent on her own problems when she got home from work that at first, she didn't notice the car parked in front of her house. When she saw it, she recognized it, and looked for its driver. The car was empty, but she could see him after a few minutes on her porch, his back resting against the door frame and his arms folded as if he had enough patience to wait a long time.

She got out of her car and walked slowly toward him.

"Hello, Carl."

"Hi. I was on my way out to see Paul and thought I'd stop by. If you haven't any other plans, would you like to have dinner with me?"

She wanted to say she did have other plans, and that she couldn't go with him, and was somewhat surprised when she found herself agreeing.

"I'll come by and pick you up around seven."

"All right."

"I called you last night."

"Oh?"

"Couple of times, as a matter of fact."

"I'm sorry I wasn't here." Beth was determined not to tell him where she'd been. "How's the case coming along?"

she asked as she unlocked the door and Carl followed her inside.

"Confusing."

"You mean our special investigator from the big town is baffled?" She smiled to blunt the edge of her words. "Sherlock Holmes would turn in his grave."

"Bull. Sherlock Holmes would be baffled, too. Whoever we're dealing with doesn't have both his oars in the water."

"He's insane?"

"Has to be. Who else would send quotes from the Bible after he commits murder?"

"I didn't know that. It's frightening. But he must be some transient or . . ."

"You mean none of your fine, upstanding friends is capable of murder? I wish you would stop thinking like that, Beth—it's dangerous."

"Dangerous?"

"You're too trusting that way."

"But I know most of the people here in Helton. No one looks or acts like . . ."

"Like a murderer? What does one look like, Beth?"

"I don't know. I never thought . . ."

"You should read the story of Lizzie Borden."

"I've read it. 'Lizzie Borden took an ax and gave her father forty whacks. When she saw what she had done, she gave her mother forty-one.' "

"Seen her picture?"

"In books."

"What does she look like?"

"Like . . ." Beth paused.

"Yes, like some nice, sweet girl from next door. And that is what I'm trying to tell you. This guy is nuts—A nice, all-American, small-town, guy-next-door kind of nut. But I'm going to get him if it takes my last breath—before he kills someone else."

"I didn't mean to be so flippant."

"So," he said, "you can convince me over dinner."

"Was there something special you wanted?" she asked.

"What?"

"Last night, when you called."

Beth had moved to the end of the couch as she spoke; now she sat down. She was slightly startled when Carl sat close—too close.

"I was thinking about you. In fact, you've been on my mind a lot."

She wanted to say something clever—something amusing that would change the warmth she saw in his eyes—but she couldn't think of a witty word. "Why?" was all she could muster. He was much too close and his presence was something she could feel.

He felt something vital leap between them and knew she felt it, too. He could read it on her face.

Beth was not used to deception, and that pleased him, too.

"I don't know," he said in matching confusion. "It seems as if you're always there."

Beth was aware, much too aware, but she was not prepared for him to cover one of her hands with his, bend forward, and lightly touch her half-parted lips in a kiss that was both gentle and excruciatingly sensual.

Beth grabbed in mental desperation for the control she needed. This man had a power that was almost overwhelming.

"Don't," she breathed.

"Why not?" His voice was a whisper as he hovered close. "Beth . . ."

"Stop it, Carl." She deliberately made her voice cold. "I don't think, with everything else you have to concentrate on, that this is the time to play games."

"Play games?" He moved back so he could look down into her eyes. She could see he was prepared to battle, and she took the only way she knew to stop it.

"Isn't that what you're doing? Or have you made decisions I don't know about?"

The reference to his own secrets and shadows was instantly effective. She could see the look in his eyes, and for a minute, she had some regret, but not enough to allow her to be any more vulnerable than she already was.

"Touché," he said. "I'm sorry." He chuckled. "So I believe in chemistry, and I find you irresistible." He rose and moved away.

Beth smiled, too. It was better to let laughter maintain the distance. "Suppose we just forget it."

"I meant what I said. You have been on my mind a lot, but I didn't mean the sloppy move. You really are special, Beth. Don't doubt it for a minute."

She smiled and he returned it, pleased not to see anger. "Is our dinner date still good?"

She could have said no, but she didn't want him to believe his slip had such an effect on her. She nodded.

"Good. I'll get out of here. See you at seven." He grinned. "No hands and no passes—just good food and conversation."

"Agreed." She laughed. "Since you promise to be so good, I'll promise to be good, too."

"Thanks," he said with a frown, "but I'm not sure for what."

"Why," she said innocently, "for keeping you from compromising yourself."

"Lady," he chuckled, "I'm glad I met you. I'll see you later."

He walked to the door, and when Beth closed it behind him, she inhaled deeply. Carl Forrester was a man who could stir the senses of any woman, and she could still feel his touch.

* CHAPTER 20 *

Leslie tossed her purse onto the seat and slid behind the wheel of her car. She was tired; the day had been the kind that stretched energy and patience beyond normal. But she was in the car and she felt good now. Her car was her greatest pleasure. She had worked and saved for a long time to get it, and she babied it.

Tonight she would stop for gas. She did it every Wednesday because Jerry Marshall at the gas station had extra help on that day and could give her a little special care.

She spun the little car out into traffic, unaware of the large black car that followed. When she pulled into the gas station, the black car drew to a halt across the street.

He watched her as she got out of the car. She stood with the breeze whipping her hair about her face, clutching her coat closed.

He could feel his blood pound in his head as the fury rose in his throat. He was outraged that she had escaped him. *But you won't again, harlot! You won't tout your wares in the street*. Look at her, with her pretty hair all free to tempt a man. *You walked in my house that last time, and the evil saved you. But not the next time. The next time, I will punish you.*

Leslie laughed, tossing her head with the exuberance of the young.

"No, Jerry, you can't buy my car for a hundred bucks. Just fill her up, will you."

"So, if you won't sell me your car, how about goin' to that concert with me Saturday night?"

"You've got tickets to it?"

"My brother-in-law got two, and he can't go. Said he'd sell 'em to me. How about it, Leslie?"

"Sounds like fun."

"Great." He laughed. "You want to drive?"

"Nope. We'll go in your junker."

"Oh, well, I tried. Pick you up right after I get off work Saturday."

"Fine."

Jerry moved to the next car and began to pump gas. Leslie turned and reached for the door handle, when her eye caught the car and the man watching her. She waved and smiled, and he waved back. Then he pulled his car into traffic and vanished. Leslie got into her car and drove from the gas station.

Carl stood before Paul's door. He had knocked several times, but there was no sign of life from within. Paul's garage was entirely windowless, so Carl had no way of knowing if his car was inside or not. He knocked again, waited, and pounded harder. He finally walked back to his car.

As he drove back toward town, he decided to make a quick stop at the church rectory. He wanted to apologize again for his outburst in Joe's office. To have expected a priest to tell him what someone had said in confession was unrealistic. But maybe there was something he remembered about that night that hadn't been part of confession. At this moment he would grasp any clue, no matter how small it might be.

Carl was met again by the housekeeper. He was informed that Father McAllen had gotten a call and had gone out, telling her he would be back in an hour or so.

Well, he had tried. He'd make another effort tomorrow. Right now he wanted to go back to his motel, shower, shave, change, and get to Beth's.

When he thought of Beth, he realized how evasive she'd been when he had spoken to her earlier. What she did, whom she saw, and where she went was none of his business, yet he was irritated all the same. He didn't want her hurt. The more he thought about that idea, the more surprised he was.

Beth was ready and waiting at seven. As she took out her coat and laid it over the back of the chair, she thought of Todd and his mention of the beautiful fur he had once bought her. She ran her hand across the soft brushed wool and smiled. It was a symbol of her independence, and she wasn't about to surrender that independence to anyone.

When Carl knocked on the door, Beth answered almost at once. As she slipped on her coat, she told him that Sally had called and invited them for drinks after dinner.

"What did you tell her?"

"I said it was up to you."

"I don't mind. Do you want to go?"

"Sure. I'll call her back right now."

Carl had made reservations at the restaurant where he had first met Beth, and she wondered if he hadn't done it to nudge her memory. But the dinner was pleasant. Of course, the murder came up for discussion.

"Aren't there any new clues at all?" Beth asked.

"I have a funny suspicion there are a whole lot, and I'm

dancing around them without seeing them. It's the strangest feeling to think you have answers in the palm of your hand—without the questions to go with them."

"You'll find them, Carl."

"Hmmm . . . I'm not so sure. There are so many things I can't figure out."

"Like what?"

"Like you, for one."

"Me?" she laughed. "I'm not hard to figure out. I'm a small-town librarian who wants a quiet, peaceful life with no problems."

"Nice, if you can get it. I don't think the world works that way. Unless, of course, you're never a participant, just a bystander."

"You think that's what I am—just a bystander?"

"Are you?"

"Are you?" she countered.

"Who could be a bigger participant than a cop?"

"I think you wear two kinds of shields."

"Two shields? What are you saying?"

"One is a nice gold badge that gives you the privilege to ask a lot of questions, to get involved in everybody's life."

"And the other?"

"The other is the one that keeps everybody else out of yours."

"I guess," he said quietly, "I deserve that. Sorry, I've been prying. Maybe I've been on this side of this badge too long. Suppose we call a truce. No more third degrees."

"Sounds fine to me. Oh, by the way, what did you call me about last night? Was it something important?"

"Seemed important at the time," he grinned, "but now that we've made an agreement and a fresh start, I'm sure not going to be the one to break the rules first. I'm a law-abiding man."

"I went to dinner with Todd."

"I see."

"You've no right to ask questions."

"I didn't ask any."

Her cheeks flushed at her jump to conclusions and she felt relieved when the waiter returned to see if they wanted dessert.

"How about you, Beth?"

"No, thank you. I don't care for any. But you go ahead."

"What do you have?"

The waiter named several rich concoctions, and Carl listened.

"Tell you what. Get one of those pies and wrap it up. We'll take it with us." He grinned at Beth again. "Think Sally and Joe would be in the mood for dessert?"

"That would be nice."

Carl paid, and he and Beth left with the pie in hand. Beth held it on her lap, and they drove to Joe's house.

They were met by Sally. "Joe just called."

"You mean he's still working?" Carl said in surprise.

"He said something came up. I told him you were on your way and he said good, stay put. He has something to show you."

"A break! What's he found?"

"How would I know? I could hardly understand him. He was either damn mad, or really excited."

"Mad or excited—or maybe both."

"Maybe. He'll be here pretty soon, anyhow, so you two come on in and have a drink."

"We brought a treat," Beth said as she handed the pie to Sally.

"Good, that's the way to Joe's heart. I'll put it in the kitchen. Make yourselves comfortable," she called over her shoulder as she walked away.

Sally had not returned from the kitchen when they heard the car in the driveway. Joe came in, and one look at his face told everyone present he was exceptionally worked up about something.

"Carl, I'm glad you're here."

"What's come down that's got you all excited?"

"Excited hell—I'd like to get my hands on this guy. He's written to say he's going to do it again!"

"Write to you? What are you talking about?"

Joe reached in his pocket and took out a crumpled paper. "Don't worry, it's only a copy."

Carl took the crumpled paper, smoothed it out, and read:

Proverbs 29

For you closed your eyes to the facts and did not choose to reverence and trust the Lord. You turned your back on me, spurning my advice. That is why you must eat the bitter fruit of having your own way and experience the terrors of the pathway you have chosen. For you turned away from me—to death; Your own complacency will kill you . . . fools!

Another will be punished.

"Sure looks like he's announcing the fact. But there's no clue to who or where." He handed the note back to Joe. "It goes with the others you got. Either he's real clever, or he's getting scared."

"I'm getting scared, too," Joe said angrily as he shoved the note back in his pocket.

"You must be to be dragging this stuff home."

"I wanted you to see it."

"That lunatic is actually blaming someone else because he's committing murder. From the looks of the other notes, he seems to have a misconception about the women in question. He keeps referring to them as ladies of the night."

"I've brought copies of all the notes with me. I want to show them to Professor Reuger. Maybe he can tell us something about the guy who wrote them."

"Carl, I'm going to pull all three of our suspects in tomorrow. If this note is supposed to be a warning, then I'm going to take it."

"We're going to have a circus when we do."

"Better a circus than another funeral."

"God," Beth whispered, and both men became aware that they had been so intensely involved with the notes and their problems that they'd forgotten where they were.

"C'mon, Joe, let's eat that pie." Carl recuperated quickly.

"What pie?" Joe's interest was piqued. "And here I thought you came over to try some of my better whiskey," he added innocently.

Carl's jaw twitched as he clenched his teeth and tried to smile. But the smile was lost in Sally's soft, muffled laugh. Beth was aware at once that something had passed between the three that amused Carl much less than it seemed to amuse Joe and Sally.

"We brought dessert home with us." Carl spoke in a voice devoid of humor, making it clear he wanted the subject dropped.

"Okay." Joe laughed. "Let's eat it."

They sat around the dining room table and enjoyed pie and coffee. Joe and Carl smiled and laughed, while they prayed silently that whoever was responsible for the note didn't plan to act on his threat this night.

You're an evil boy—an evil boy. You must stay on your knees until you repent. You are wicked to look at girls like that. I found you out. You must get down on your knees and pray for repentance. They are whores—whores—and they will tempt you. I must teach you, it's my duty. Down on your knees—repent. You were meant for God, not for these women. They are bad, and you are evil.

He had been careful this time. He would not let her escape him as she had before. He had been sure. He would not have to be punished this time. He would punish her.

Leslie left the store and walked across the street to her car. It had been parked as close to the light as she could get, but still, it was half in shadow. She opened the door, pushed her seat forward, and put the bag of groceries on the backseat. Flipping her seat back, she slid behind the wheel and snapped the door locks. Then she breathed a sigh of relief. She slid her key into the ignition and turned it. It ground, whined softly, and died. She tried again and got the same result. She knew nothing about cars, but at least she felt she knew someone she could call. Jerry would come and give her a hand. She wasn't worried half as much about herself as she was her car. She fished about in her purse for coins and reached for the door handle, when a dark form appeared by the window. For a moment she was frightened, then the man knelt down so his face was by the window, and smiled.

Leslie opened the door and stepped out. "Hey, it's great to see a friendly face around here."

"What's the matter—car trouble?"

"I don't understand. It was working fine this afternoon."

"Well, it's probably something minor. Why don't we ride on down to the gas station and give Jerry the word. He can come and fix it."

"I could just wait here, if you wanted to tell Jerry."

"Well, it's getting kind of late, and I hate to leave you here alone. Why not just ride with me? I'll bring you both back, and then you can drop Jerry off."

"Are you worried about me?" She laughed.

"Yes, I am. This town's been too dangerous of late. Now, come on, lock your car up and jump in mine. In a little while, the problems will all be taken care of."

"Always lending a helping hand, aren't you? I'll bet you were a Boy Scout when you were young."

"You know," he laughed, "I hate to tell you, but I was."

"I should have known."

"Come on, let me do my good deed for today."

"All right."

She locked her car door and walked into the darker shadows with him, where the black car was parked and waiting.

At midnight, the last clerk left the small market. He noticed the small sports car still parked outside, and he walked to it and looked inside. The bag of groceries still sat in the backseat. Something was drastically wrong. He debated only for a moment, then went back to the store and let himself in. He walked to the phone and dialed the police.

Beth and Carl said good night to Joe and Sally just after one o'clock in the morning. The ride home was a comfortable one, for after the pie, as the hour grew later, they had broken open some wine. Now, both of them felt pretty good.

When he pulled up in front of Beth's house, she reached for the door handle, only to have him reach across to stop her. She looked at him in surprise.

"I want to talk to you, Beth. Will you invite me in?"

"Do you think that's wise?"

"If you think you need protection, call a cop."

"All right, you can come in for a while."

They walked up the path, and Beth unlocked the door and

preceded him in, turning on lights as she did. They removed their coats in silence.

"Can I get you something?"

"No, nothing."

Beth kicked off her shoes and curled on the end of the couch with her legs tucked under her. "There was something you wanted to say to me?"

"There's a whole lot I want to say to you, Beth. I feel like a heel. I called you last night, then went out and got stoned. I've been thinking about it all day, and I realized something. I'm worried about your ex using you, when I was planning on using you, too. It's a lousy way to have a relationship."

"Is that what we have, Carl—a relationship?"

He went to her and sat down close. "I thought it might get to that."

"Are we doing a balancing act again?"

"No. If I'm asking you questions, it's because I intend to answer some, as well."

"What questions?"

"Are you still in love with him?"

"Does that matter?"

"For some reason, it matters a great deal. You're someone special, and probably neither one of us deserves a thought from you. But I want to start somewhere."

"Maybe," she said softly, "we could start as friends."

"Friends?"

"It's a beginning."

"Yeah, I guess it is."

"Carl, do you want to tell me what really happened the night your wife was murdered?"

"I'm not sure I can do that, or if I did, I could make you understand. How could you understand, when in three years, I haven't been able to?"

"As a friend, I could at least try."

Carl stood up and walked a few steps away, only to return and sit beside her again. She could see the doubts and a kind of uncertain misery, but he was struggling. She waited.

The phone jarred them both. Beth answered. "Hello—yes, he's here." Carl looked up in surprise as she extended the phone to him. "It's Joe."

"Joe? What's up?"

Beth watched as Carl's face sobered and his shoulders sagged. He listened for a few more minutes. "All right, I'll come over and pick you up." He hung up.

"What is it?"

"A girl—Leslie Gabriel—her car's been found. Joe and I are going out to the same place we found the bodies of those other girls. Joe's got a feeling—I'm afraid I do, too. Our Bible-quoting maniac has found another victim."

"How can Joe be so sure?"

"She's a good, honest, hard-working girl. She is not the kind to run off and leave her car parked in front of a small, isolated market."

Carl grabbed up his coat and started for the door.

"Call me," Beth called after him.

"I will. Lock these doors."

* CHAPTER 21 *

Carl drove rapidly. The spot where the first two bodies had been found was being patrolled, but it was in a heavily wooded area difficult to cover. Three dirt roads cut off the main highway into the area, and scouting them every two hours was the best the small police force could manage.

Just as Carl turned off the main highway, he saw the police car parked and hit his brakes. He and Joe got out of the car.

"Seen anything out here tonight, Brady?" Joe asked the man on duty.

"No, sir. I've been up and down the road about three times tonight."

"Are there any side roads off these?"

"Couple of cow paths, but I don't think you could drive a car down one. What is it, Joe?"

"We've got a feeling he's been here again. We're calling

for help. Get your light and let's go—we'll cover ground on foot. Get on the horn and tell Andrews and Tyler to come in from the other side."

A gray haze heralding dawn made the woods a vague, shadow-filled place. Police flashlights cast yellowish-white beams through the mist, and the soft thudding of rapidly moving feet echoed through the stillness. Each man could feel his heart pound with the expectancy of seeing someone in the woods, or worse yet, not seeing him and finding his handiwork instead.

Carl stopped dead in his tracks. The fringe of light from his flashlight had caught something. He moved the light slowly forward. The body of a girl lay at the foot of the tree, half covered with leaves. He walked slowly forward, muttering angry curses. He knelt beside her and reached to touch her neck where there should have been a pulse—where warm blood should have flowed. It was cold and still. Her hands were clenched, and when he brushed strands of hair from her face he could see the blood where she had been struck, more than once, by someone much stronger than she.

He heard a sound behind him and his reflexes made him spin about as his light caught Joe full in the face. "Joe!"

"Yeah. Get that light out of my face!" Carl knelt beside the body. "Christ, Carl, she's just a kid. What could this crazy bastard have against her?"

"Who knows what's in his mind? Maybe your professor can tell us. We need answers—we're sure as hell doing something wrong. This guy came in and out of here as if he owned the world."

"He must know the place like the back of his hand."

"And he must have a pretty good idea what we're doing."

Joe's attention was drawn back to the body. He didn't want to disturb anything, but he carefully reached for what had caught his eye—the piece of paper that was stuck just under the lapel of the coat she wore. He lifted it out by the edge, grateful he had chosen to wear his gloves. Trying not to touch any more of it than necessary, he unfolded it and read:

Ecclesiastes 27

And I have found a woman more bitter than death, who is the hunter's snare, and her heart is a net and her hands are bands. He that pleaseth God shall escape from her. But he that is a sinner shall be caught by her.

My hand will punish another until they learn. Why don't you listen?

Joe held the note out so Carl could read it as well.

"I'll stay with her, Carl. Find the men and have them send for the coroner. And tell them to cordon off this area. It's almost daylight, and we'll sure as hell have the media down on us when they hear about this."

Carl nodded, his eyes still on the girl. Joe looked up at him again. "Carl?"

"Yeah, I'm going." He walked away slowly, and Joe looked at her again. He shone his light all around, trying to spot one sign that could help him name the man who had done this.

It was daylight when Joe climbed into the car, exhausted. Carl turned the key in the ignition, and they drove back to the station in thoughtful silence. Carl wondered if Joe was feeling the same kind of guilt he was—as if he could have, or should have, done something.

"Want to stop somewhere for breakfast? I want to call Sal."

"I could use some coffee. Maybe I should give Beth a call, too. Better still, I'll go down with you and fill out the reports, then stop by Beth's on the way home."

"Good idea."

Carl pulled into an all-night diner, and they went in and found an empty booth. They sipped their coffee without much conversation, then Joe went to the pay phone and called Sally.

Carl sat holding the hot cup in both hands. He'd never felt colder. The girl was so young. At this thought, the anger began to boil inside. If he could have put his hands around the killer's throat, he would gladly have put an end to his life.

Joe returned. "Sally's going to call Beth. I told her to tell Beth you'd stop by the first chance you got. She'll probably be going to work around nine. Let's go. I want to get to the office. We have a date with Dr. Reuger, remember?"

"Yeah. After tonight, I can't wait to hear what he has to say. God, I hope he can give us a fresh slant on this."

"Or any kind of slant. We have three dead, and God knows what the nut we're after has planned."

Curt Reuger had an Albert Einstein face, and an unruly crop of white hair. His eyes were a penetrating blue. Carl had the distinct and uncomfortable feeling that he was looking inside him, and an even worse one that he didn't quite like what he saw.

"Come into my office where we can talk more comfortably," Dr. Reuger invited after Joe had explained why Carl had come along. "So, what can you tell me, Joe?" Curt inquired.

Joe explained what they were up against, and when he was finished he took a manila envelope from his breast pocket and handed it to Dr. Reuger. "These are the notes he left for us."

Curt pored over the notes so long and so carefully that Carl's nerves were on edge by the time he finished. "A terrible thing," he muttered. "Such a terrible thing."

"What can you tell us about the killer?" Carl asked.

"You said there was some time between the first death and the second?"

"Yes, but less between the second and third," Joe urged.

"And," Curt said softly, looking at the men intently, "there will be less time until the next one."

"You think he'll murder again and again?"

"Unless you stop him. Whoever this person is, he's hopelessly insane."

"Great. Give us some description, some explanation."

"The psychotic mind . . ." Curt began.

"Do it in English, will you, Doc," Carl smiled for the first time. "I'm afraid we won't be able to follow any psychological mumbo jumbo."

"Mumbo jumbo," Curt chuckled, "you make me sound like a witch doctor."

"Doctor, if I thought a witch doctor could give him to me, I'd get one."

"I'll do my very best to tell you . . . in English . . . without any witch doctor spells. This man," Dr. Reuger began, "seems to kill for a reason logical only to him. So, you must try to walk into his mind. To do that, you must first find him."

"Great. I'd like to do that," Carl interjected.

"I didn't mean find him physically. You must find him mentally. He must have had a horrible childhood." Now Carl bent toward him. "He is a damaged soul, Mr. Forrester."

"Am I supposed to go down to the morgue, look at that pretty, young girl, and tell myself I should feel sorry for him?"

"Murder is an extremely serious human act, yet the motive for committing it may appear to the sane person to be downright trivial."

"Go on, Curt," Joe urged.

"Divide us into parts, gentlemen. Call one part our id and the other our superego. They are always at war with each other. You see, the id wants to satisfy all kinds of fantasies, and our superego may say no."

"The conscience," Carl said almost to himself.

"You might say so. Fortunately, the rational part of our mind, the ego, serves as a sort of mediator. If the ego fails, unhappiness or guilt can overwhelm an individual, and he can become mentally ill."

"So we have a balancing act. Just what is it that tips the balance?" Joe asked.

"The ego has another problem to cope with. In Freud's view, we are born with not only a life instinct, but a death instinct, as well. Part of this death instinct is an aggressive drive directed at other people, rather than ourselves. But, again, our superego demands that this be suppressed. For example, our aggressive drive may want us to cut up another person's body or defeat him by taking his life. Our superego stops this."

"You've read these notes. You think we have a guy here who's lost the battle. Where and how do we look for him? What kind of sign are we looking for?"

Curt Reuger sighed and leaned back in his chair, tenting his hands before him, giving Carl's questions considerable thought. "Sometimes, if we are deprived of love or subjected to brutal attacks during our childhood, our aggressive drive can become too irrational for our ego to cope with, and too powerful for our superego to subdue. Consequently, we could engage in an extremely violent and bizarre murder. I'll tell you of a case. Edmund Emil Kemper III, as a child, bitterly resented his parents' separation and hated living with his quarrelsome mother. At the age of twenty-one, Kemper murdered eight young women by shooting, stabbing, and strangulation, then cut off their heads and hands, had sexual intercourse with the corpses, and ate flesh from some of them. Finally, he went home and killed his mother. He chopped off her head, then cut out her larynx. He said later that he did it because of the way she bitched, screamed, and yelled at him over the years."

"Jesus," Carl murmured. "If that's what we're dealing with, we're in for a real time."

"I would say you are."

"But, how can he look so sane?"

"Sometimes, parents try too hard to transform us into 'good' boys and girls by severe punishment. This is the kind that usually turns into the 'very nice' person and suddenly commits murder to the great shock and disbelief of family, friends, and neighbors. There was a boy, Anthony Barbaro, who was seventeen years old. He was the kind of son parents brag about. He was quiet, considerate—a Little Leaguer, altar boy, and Boy Scout. He studied hard, worked twenty hours a week as a busboy, and managed to be in the top two percent of his high school class. He didn't drink, smoke, or do drugs, and came from an excellent family. During the Christmas holidays in 1974, this 'nice boy' took a shotgun and rifle to the top floor of the high school building and opened fire. In two hours, three were dead and eleven injured."

"So, there is a key somewhere in this guy's past," Joe said meditatively.

"Yes, I would say so. Besides that, I might hazard a guess and say that in his mind he is killing the same person over and over again. You must remember, as you search out his past, that he is quite different from the usual delinquent or criminal. He comes from a family background where conformity to the rules of the social system was emphasized, often with very heavy penalties."

"This is frustrating." Carl stood and walked to a window to look out.

"Frustration is exactly it, and often, aggression is a consequence of frustration. Often—not always. It is a question for us why some people who are frustrated commit suicide, and others turn to homicide instead."

"Where do you suggest we start?"

"This man is fighting a terrible battle. From the notes, I would say he wants to be caught. Look for an average 'nice' man who has had a severe trauma in his childhood, maybe even had been molested or subjected to severe punishment for transgressions he didn't even understand."

"We have to do some real deep digging now."

"It won't be to hard to do for Paul, or maybe even Father McAllen, but what the hell am I going to do about Michael?" Joe complained. "And David, Jake, and Larry? Jake and Larry are pretty new to Helton."

"Let's dig as far as we can. If it takes some legwork, I'll get on it. The computer must have something we can get hold of."

"Well, I guess we better get into it." Joe sighed resignedly, knowing the amount of time and manpower this was going to consume.

Joe extended his hand to Dr. Reuger. "Thank you for all your help, Curt. You've been invaluable. I'd like to be able to bounce some ideas off you now and again, if I may. This case is one of the roughest I've had, and I'll need all the help I can get."

"Feel free to come at any time. Here." He took a notepad from his pocket and a pen from his desk. "I'll give you my home phone number. I'm very interested in this man. He needs help."

Carl snorted in disgust. "He needs to be beaten to a pulp."

"Mr. Forrester, I don't mean to sound unsympathetic to these women who have been killed, but this man is not an animal. He is a man who has suffered, and most likely is suffering, a great deal. Have you never committed an irrational act—one against all your principles, that you regretted?"

There was a heavy, dead silence.

"Yes," Carl said in a voice brittle with emotions he was holding firmly in check. "Maybe that's an even better reason to stop him. No matter what we suffer, we have no right to force the pain on others." Suddenly, Carl was silent. He had the first brief glimpse of his own redemption, and the brilliance of it was painful. "Come on, Joe. We've got a lot of work to do, and I'm already so tired I could sleep on the soft side of a board. Good-bye, Professor Reuger, and thanks again."

Curt Reuger nodded and watched Joe and Carl leave the room.

In the car, Carl concentrated on driving, and Joe sat with his head back against the seat and his eyes closed. For a long time, they didn't talk. Then Joe spoke.

"I've known Curt Reuger a long time. He's a hell of a nice person, and he's really brilliant."

"What's that supposed to lead up to?" Carl's voice was chipped and hard.

"Just that—that he's seen a whole lot. Nothing surprises him. He worked in social service when he was a whole lot younger—worked with abused children until he couldn't stand it anymore. Then he worked in criminal counseling for a while. Had a private practice after that, until he retired. Now he teaches."

"Doesn't want to quit, does he?"

"He's too compassionate to quit. He'd cure the mental ills of the world, if he could. And he's a friend. He and I have had a lot of talks, most of which I find pretty hard to follow, so he leads me by the hand. If I get my mind in a blue funk, he's the one to reach in and grab me by the scruff of the neck and shake me out of it."

"You wouldn't be telling me I need a shrink, would you, old friend?"

"Hell, no! There's a lot of difference between talking to a shrink and talking to a friend. He just looks at things in a different way from anyone else I've ever known. Take this killer, for instance."

"Yeah. He'd have us believe this man's pathetic and needs help. Did you hear those stories he told us? If this guy is on that kind of rampage, nothing short of a bullet in the brains is going to stop him."

Joe's voice was heavy with warning. "We don't take the law into our own hands—not this time."

"I guess we're both tired, Joe. I don't think I meant what I said. Like the old professor said, I'm frustrated."

"I know what you mean. Combine being frustrated with a good dose of being scared, and you'll get an idea of how I feel."

"We both need some sleep."

"Well, I know I won't be getting any for a while. You going to drop me off and go back to the motel for a while?"

"No, I think I want to get into the computer with you. If we manage to turn up a lead, you might need a little help."

"I'll send out for some food and coffee."

Carl turned his car into the parking lot, and after locking the doors, he and Joe walked toward the police station.

He sat very still, listening to the quiet voice that spoke to him like the echoing sound from a deep well. *I told you if you pray, you will free yourself from the clutches of wicked women. You must atone for your wickedness. You are wicked, you know.* The voice was cold and derisive, filled with contempt and a tone of ridicule. *You were never good enough. You always had to be shown your wicked ways. You need to wash the evil from you, and the only way you can do that is to wash yourself clean of their filth. To desire one of them, to lust after one of them, how contemptible and wicked can you be? If you do not do what needs to be done, you will never atone for your terrible, terrible wickedness.*

He groaned and bent forward, his hands clasping his head as if to crush it and thereby wipe out the voice. On his knees beside a narrow bed, he held his head and rocked his body to and fro, but the voice would not be denied. Against his back he felt the imaginary blows of the thick leather belt.

I must whip the truth into you. I must make you understand the black wickedness in which you seem to want to live. Always, you try to hide the wicked thoughts from me, but you can't. You wear your wickedness for all the world to see, and I must help you rid yourself of it.

Again the cruel lash of the belt fell on his back, and he tried to kneel obediently in the proper position. One had to be in the proper position if one wanted God to listen. The belt fell again, and he ducked his head and moaned softly. Then he drew his hands down and folded them before him.

Wicked! Wicked! How could you believe the Lord would listen to you? You are wicked, and they are wicked. The belt fell again, and again, and again.

Then, after a long while, all sound ceased and his huge body stopped rocking. He reached to a small, nearby table and lifted the Bible from it.

He read for a long time, holding the same rigid, immobile position. His eyes skimmed back and forth over the pages as if he were seeking a path to freedom.

He found what he had been searching for, and to his relief, the harsh, insistent voice ceased when he picked up a pencil and paper.

He wrote rapidly, folded the paper and put it in his pocket, then tenderly laid the Bible aside.

* CHAPTER 22 *

"Well, we know pretty much everything there is to know about Paul Carterson, and Father McAllen seems as clean as a whistle," Joe said, with resignation heavy in his voice.

"What about Michael Brodie?"

"From what I could pull up on the computer, he's had a few minor arrests. Came from a broken home. Father got killed somewhere in Texas a few years after the parents split up, and the mother remarried. A year after that, Michael left and never went back."

"So, if Dr. Reuger is right, we should still be suspicious of all of them—Paul and Father McAllen because they're clean, and Michael because he's not."

"Damn, are we lucky." Joe crumpled the empty styrofoam cup in his hand and tossed it in the wastebasket.

"You still hauling them in?"

"To answer some questions, yes."

"You'd better fill your psychologist in on what Dr. Reuger had to say. Then, he can carry the ball from there. I hope he comes up with answers, because I sure as hell don't have any."

They had eaten half-warm burgers from a nearby fast-food restaurant and had drunk some strong, bitter coffee. The food, combined with their physical exhaustion, left neither man in the best frame of mind.

They sat side by side before the computer at which they had been working for several hours.

"This time I'm going to be smart." Joe leaned back in his chair. "I'm going to have them brought in one at a time. I don't want another scene like that last one. Michael might kill Paul next time."

"Wise idea. If you don't need me to help with this, I think I'll go and grab some sleep."

Carl was about to open the door and leave when it was pushed open from outside. He had to jump back a couple of steps to get out of the way. Phil Greggory stood smiling in the doorway.

His suave, well-polished look made Carl feel more disheveled than he was. He felt the rough stubble of his beard and knew his clothes were dirty and rumpled from being in the woods.

Phil's eyes roamed over him. Carl clenched both his teeth and his fists.

"Hi, Phil," Joe said hastily. "Come on in. Carl and I have been pushing the computer for hours."

Phil moved past Carl with a disdainful look. "Obviously you were doing something all night. From what I heard, there has been another murder. Joe, we can't have you and your henchmen here pushing computer keys while we have a killer running around loose, now, can we?"

The voice dripped acid amusement. The district attorney found a great deal of satisfaction in the flush of Joe's face and the light of anger in his eyes.

"Now look, Phil," Joe said sharply, "we're doing all that can be done. We had to go to the computer for background information."

"Have you seen the morning paper?" Phil asked casually as he withdrew a folded copy from his coat pocket and tossed it on Joe's desk. "They're having a field day scaring the hell out of people and sort of slyly implying that my office isn't doing as much about it as it should be."

"News travels fast," Joe said coldly as he reached to take the paper and unfold it. He scanned it swiftly and cursed under his breath. Carl walked back across the room and took the paper from Joe's hand. The large headline struck him at once: DERANGED KILLER LOOSE IN HELTON. The story told of the third murder, obviously committed by the same person. The story also suggested, albeit subtly, that something must be done soon, or all of Helton would be forced to barricade themselves in their homes after dark. Carl tossed the paper back on the desk.

"This bothers you a whole lot, doesn't it, Phil? You shouldn't be too upset. They spelled your name right, and just think, once we find him and you try him, it could be the sensation that sweeps you into the governor's office."

"We need an arrest pretty damn quick, or we're going to have a lot of angry people on our backs!"

"Angry voters," Carl corrected.

"This some kind of a joke to you?" Phil said frigidly, then his eyes hardened. "Oh, I forgot. Murder isn't always that important to you, is it? You're a law unto yourself."

Joe saw that Carl meant to hit Phil and moved quickly in front of him. "Now, get this straight, Phil. I'm working on this case with everything I've got. This is my town, too. I want it safe. Carl's been a bigger help than you know, and I don't intend to lose him because you don't want him here. Get off my back. You do your job, and I'll do mine."

Joe, like Carl, knew Phil's need for the notoriety that would come from trying and winning a case like this one. When the media was finished with it, he would have enough political clout to write his own ticket out of a town that was too small to hold his ambition.

"Just what *are* you doing, Joe?" Phil asked as he removed his coat and tossed it across a chair. Before Joe could answer, Carl interrupted.

"Looks like you're going to be pretty busy for a while, Joe. I'm going to get moving. I'll call you later."

He didn't wait for a reply, but walked out and closed the door firmly before he heaved a ragged sigh. His hatred for Phil Greggory seemed to grow every time they crossed paths. Only loyalty to Joe and a subtle and tenuous tie to Beth kept him from going back to the motel, packing, and leaving.

He left the police station and found a phone booth. He could have used the phone at the station, but he didn't want the grapevine picking up his involvement with Beth until the two of them could decide if that was what it really was. The phone rang several times, then he heard Beth's mellow voice. "Helton Library, may I help you?"

"Beth, this is your friendly neighborhood cop."

"Carl. I'm glad you called. I've sure been hearing a lot of gossip. What happened last night?"

"Joe and I thought we might be in time to stop him, but we weren't."

"I heard. This is so terrible."

"Listen, I'd like to see you tonight. How about a six-slice pizza and a big slice of conversation?"

"I'll take both, thank you." He could hear her smile and felt the lift in his spirit.

"See you about eight?"

"Fine. Carl? Where are you going now?"

"I look like hell, and I feel like hell. I'm going back to the motel, take a shower, and crash for a while. Then I'll pick up the pizza and see you later."

Carl awoke to the sound of traffic and a semidark room. He stirred and groaned as he reached for his watch. It was seven-fifteen, and he had told Beth he'd see her at eight! He was sitting on the edge of the bed when the first realization hit him that something seemed drastically different. He took a deep breath, mentally searching for what it was. Then it came to him like a lightning bolt. Sleep! He had had several hours of uninterrupted, dreamless sleep. He found it so surprising that for several minutes he sat in profound amazement. Then he laughed—an exuberant sound in the empty room. Was he free? Had he somehow escaped the nightmares that had sapped both his mental and physical strength? Then another thought quickly followed. Was it because he was so exhausted he couldn't do anything else but sleep? He would need a few more nights to find the answer for sure, but still, it filled him with an elation he had not felt in a long, long time.

He grabbed the phone book from the drawer and looked up the pizza parlor closest to Beth's house, then called in the order, hoping Beth liked her pizza with mushrooms.

He found himself whistling as he dressed. Then he drove to the pizza parlor, picked up dinner, and headed for Beth's.

"I said, what are you doing, Joe?" Phil's insistent voice drew Joe's attention back to him.

"I told you, everything that can be done."

"I think you'd better explain that in more detail. I want to know exactly what progress you are making on this case. I have to answer to the public, you know, and I want some answers to give them." Phil walked to the comfortable chair Carl always favored and sank down into it.

"All right, I'll give you a rundown. But first, I want to make one thing clear. Carl doesn't need your rotten remarks every time you cross paths. Everyone else, including Carl, has been able to let go of the past—everybody but you. You're like a bulldog, hanging on to a bone. Let go, Phil—leave Carl alone. When I needed him, he came here as a friend, and by Christ, he's going to be treated as a friend." Joe sat down in his chair. "If you want a rundown, here it is." He went on to explain all they knew about the case, including the stone wall that stood between them and the killer.

"So, your friend at the college feels this man is insane." Again, there was amusement in Phil's voice. "Is this someone's way of protecting, say, a priest or a local artist?"

"Neither of us is going to be the judge. And we're not going to smear it in the papers any more than we have to, no matter how good it looks for the prosecuting attorney."

"You're somewhat like Carl, you know," Phil said smoothly. "Don't be the same kind of fool that he is. Joe, you'd better think carefully. The last time someone was murdered in this town, Carl was mixed up in it. He has a rather unorthodox way of doing things that might end him up behind bars and leave you without a badge."

"Is that a threat?"

"Take it as you like. Just be smart and ship your friend out of town if you don't want him spoiling things like he did before."

"That's what's eating at you, isn't it? The last time we had a murder, Carl took the edge off all your glory. You had no one to parade through the court or in front of the media."

Phil rose abruptly to his feet, but his retort died on his lips when the buzzer on Joe's desk broke into the conversation.

"Yeah?" Joe snapped as he depressed the button.

"They're here with Paul Carterson and his attorney."

"Send 'em in." Joe turned to look at Phil. "If you don't have anything more to add, how about letting me get on with my job."

"Just catch this guy, Joe," Phil said quietly. He turned and walked to the door, which was opened from the outside by Tom, who entered with two uniformed policemen and Paul Carterson between them, and a slight, distinguished-looking man—an attorney named Malcolm Reese.

Phil held out his hand to Reese, who shook it firmly. "Hi, Phil. It's been a while."

"How are you doing, Malcolm? I didn't know you were a counsel in this case."

"Just keeping my client from being steamrollered." Malcolm said pleasantly, hoping to irritate Joe, who refused to rise to the bait. "I'll see you at the club next week?"

"To be sure," Phil replied. "We'll probably have a great deal to talk about." He was chuckling softly to himself as he left.

Paul's face was livid with suppressed anger.

"Lieutenant Marks, I'm Malcolm Reese, Mr. Carterson's attorney. My client feels he is being somewhat harassed by you and your department."

"I'm afraid he's quite wrong, Mr. Reese. I have simply requested that he come in here and talk to me. He is a suspect in a murder case—a suspect, I might add, who has been somewhat uncooperative."

"He is here, Lieutenant Marks, and he has come to

answer those questions that are pertinent to the case. I am here to see that he is not put under duress or forced to say things that infringe on his rights."

"If he will sit down and talk to me, I'll try and make sure I don't 'infringe' on his rights."

Malcolm smiled benignly at Joe's anger and then turned to Paul and nodded slightly. He moved to stand by the window while Paul sat down in the chair across the desk from Joe.

"So, what is it you want from me?" he said defensively.

"Look, Paul, you'll be a whole lot further ahead if you try a little cooperation."

"You mean, confess to killing those women."

"Only if you did."

"I didn't!"

"Where were you last night?"

"Home."

"All night?"

"All night."

"Paul," Joe said quietly, "think about it."

"About what? I was home."

"Carl came out to talk to you. He says you weren't there."

Paul was still. "Look, I heard him knock. I even saw him go look over the wall to see if I was around. I was half drunk, and I didn't want to talk to him. Surely I have the right to pick who can come into my home."

"He'd have given you the beginnings of an alibi."

"I don't need an alibi, dammit! I'm not guilty of anything. If you brought me in here to confess, you can go to hell!"

"No, Paul, I didn't bring you in here to confess. I'd like to ask you some questions about your life."

"What?"

"I want you to agree to talk to our psychologist."

"Now what! Am I supposed to be crazy?!"

"No, I just need a little background. What have you got to lose—or to hide?"

"Nothing." Paul sucked in his breath. He looked toward Malcolm, whose face was puzzled.

"Why should my client agree to this?"

"Why shouldn't he?"

"Look, if it will get you off my back, I'll talk to anybody."

"All right. I'll give him a call, and arrange for you to see him this afternoon. A few questions, Paul—that's all."

"This murder has gotten everyone upset, Lieutenant Marks," Malcolm said. "Paul is innocent, and the innocent need not hide anything."

"Yeah?"

"But," Malcolm insisted, "this innocent man's attorney needs to ask a whole lot of questions, and needs to demand that he be with his client no matter who questions him—even a psychologist."

"To answer your questions," Joe grinned amiably, "I want to find out just what kind of a little boy your client was. I want to know about him from diapers to graduation."

"What?" Malcolm asked.

"I'll tell you about it sometime. Right now, I'd like to get Paul on his way. Oh, and Mr. Reese . . . go with him, please. I wouldn't want to step out of line."

"It is incumbent on me to advise my client . . ."

"By all means, advise him. If you can find one thing to object to, advise him."

"Lieutenant Marks," Malcolm smiled, "don't try anything devious with my client."

"He has nothing to be afraid of, if he's not guilty."

Malcolm nodded, motioned to Paul, and the two of them left. Joe sat back in his chair for a minute, then he reached for the phone. In a few minutes he had John Lawrence, the official police psychologist and a long-time friend, on the line. They spoke for several minutes, and when he hung up, Joe was satisfied. He sat back in his chair and waited for the arrival of the next person on his list.

"Joe! Is that you?" Sally called from the kitchen late that afternoon.

"Yeah, it's me. Why would you think it was anyone else?" Sally appeared in the kitchen doorway. "Who else," Joe demanded, "has a key to my front door?"

Sally laughed. "You just never know, fella. You deserted my bed last night. I think that's grounds for something."

He walked to her and lifted her from her feet in a bear

hug that took her breath. "It's grounds for finding it early tonight."

When he set her down, he kept his arms about her. "Honey, you look terrible."

"I know, and I probably look better than I feel."

"You need to eat and get some sleep. I've never seen you like this."

Joe moved to a comfortable chair and sagged into it. "It's this damn case. I get the feeling I'm no closer to finding this guy than I was after Martha was killed. Phil Greggory paid a neighborly little visit today."

"What's he want?"

"What everyone else in this town wants from me—the murderer. They've a right to that. It shakes a whole town, Sal, when someone can walk around and kill, and no one can stop him."

"Where's Carl?"

"He left a little early."

"Right after Phil came?"

"Yeah. I think it was either that or belt him, and I'm afraid if Carl gets mad enough to jump him, he's not going to end it with one punch. He'll wrap Phil Greggory in a knot, and that's all Phil needs to feed the papers. After that, people might start looking back, and I need Carl's help too much for that to happen. Besides, he's a friend who needs help."

"Why don't you give Carl a call and invite him to have dinner with us?"

"I think," Joe smiled, "that he's going to Beth's tonight."

"Oh, Joe, I hope it works out between those two."

"Well, that's up to them. What's for supper?"

"Just like a man. You're so romantic."

"Maybe that's because I want you to remember that Carl and Beth both have problems of their own. Put them together and it might not be so easy. Besides," he grinned, "I want you to keep all your romantic notions at home."

"Huh! As tired as you are, you'll eat and collapse."

"Oh yeah?"

"Yeah." Sally laughed as she rose—quick enough to keep Joe from reaching her. "C'mon, I'll feed you, then we'll see where it goes from there."

"I think I'll take a quick shower first. I feel like I've been dragged through a barnyard."

"Okay, shower and I'll rustle up the food."

"You wouldn't want to come and wash my back by any chance?"

"I might, at that," Sally said with a mischievous smile.

She went to Joe, who put his arm about her, and they walked up the stairs together. In the shower, she kneaded the tiredness from him.

His hands slid over her wet skin and drew her tight against him. She slid her arms about him and closed her eyes as their parted lips met. It was a long and sensuous kiss that warmed them both. Joe reached behind Sally and turned off the shower, then reached for the huge bath towels Sally kept close. He wrapped her in a towel, then stepped out of the shower. Hand and hand they walked to the bedroom. He went to the bed, and with a soft laugh, Sally tossed the towel aside and joined him.

Waves of pleasure flowed through him in widening circles as he thought of all she brought him each time she came to him. He tried to drown himself in the tenderness and strength of her mouth. He kissed her closed eyelids, and followed the shape of her face and her slender throat to the softness of her rounded breasts. He took into his mouth one nipple that grew erect with the touch of his tongue.

Very slowly his mouth moved down her body, drinking in the scent and the salt-sweet taste of her. Her luminous skin was alive beneath his touch, and her flesh trembled with expectant yielding.

All of her senses were drawn to one pulsing spot, and he knew, because her need matched his, that he could no longer control the heat of it.

Suddenly, fiercely, he thrust deep inside her, possessing the throbbing dark center until it contracted, poised on the same precipice upon which he stood. Then they leapt, pulsing wildly until she cried out his name and shuddered beneath him. "Oh, Joe . . . Joe."

Joe felt the exultation, the freedom, and the love in her giving that was always the turning point when he walked a dark road. She smiled up at him. Sally could untie all the knots, ease all the problems, with just the touch of her love. He always felt overwhelmed by her ability, every time she did the magic she did.

"I love you, Sal," he whispered as he buried his face against her throat. "God, I love you."

* CHAPTER 23 *

It was just after four-thirty when the library phone rang again.

"Helton Library, may I help you?" Beth said automatically.

"Beth, this is Todd. Look, I've made some reservations at a good restaurant, and I thought after dinner you might like to come over and see my new apartment—sort of give it your seal of approval."

"I'm afraid I have plans of my own tonight. I don't suppose it would ever occur to you to call me before you made yours?"

"You're wasting a good dinner just to curl up with a good book? Come on, Beth."

"This, I'm sure, is going to come as a very great shock to you, but I'm not curling up with a good book. I just have other plans. Todd, I'm afraid I'm very busy right now—I've got a lot of work to finish."

"I got the impression the other night that you weren't still so bitter about us."

"Bitter?" she laughed. "Don't flatter yourself. I'm not bitter, and I'm not the stupid little girl you used to charm so easily. The other night was nice, but nice isn't a future."

"Maybe I'll call you later."

"Don't—I'll be busy."

"Then I'll call you tomorrow."

"No, Todd," she said firmly.

"Don't get so uptight. Maybe I am rushing things a bit,

but I've missed you, Beth, and if I'm trying too hard, I'm sorry. I want you back, and I'm going to fight for you."

Beth was silent for a long moment. "I don't want to hear you talk like this, Todd. Whatever was between us is over."

"Not so easy—something is still there, Beth," he said softly. "I could feel it and so could you. I want a chance—just a chance."

Again the pause was long and the silence pregnant with emotions.

"Not tonight, Todd. I told you I have other plans."

"All right. So long for now, Beth."

At five o'clock the part-time workers appeared. Beth took her coat from the closet and walked quickly to the parking lot. It took her only ten minutes to get home.

Carl had told her he would be by around eight, which would give her plenty of time to shower and change. It surprised her somewhat to realize she was excited—more excited than she knew was wise. How long Carl Forrester would be around was debatable. Whatever he had in mind, it was sketchy, to say the least. It was too fragile a foundation to support any plans.

She showered and put on a pair of comfortable slacks and a loose silk blouse. Then she snapped on the TV, in time to get the six-thirty news. It was far from pleasant. She watched Joe expertly dodge reporters and then say that the police were doing all that could be done and expected to have an arrest soon. Then she watched Phillip Greggory, obviously filmed at a different time, and realized both his rapport with the media and his lack of support for Joe and the men who worked with him. She did not know him, but she found herself disliking him as she listened to his smooth voice.

When the news was finished, she became engrossed in a book and didn't hear Carl's car pull into the drive. When he knocked she rose quickly and opened the door. He held the square white box in his hand with a wide smile on his face.

"Hot pizza coming up. Do you have any cold beer here?"

"No, I'm afraid not."

"I anticipated that, so I brought some. It's downright uncivilized to eat good, hot pizza without a glass or two of very cold beer." He held the six-pack aloft in his other hand.

When Beth smiled and wrinkled her nose slightly, Carl looked at her in pretended amazement. "Now, don't tell me you don't like beer with your pizza. Woman, I have to introduce you to the finer things of life," he said as Beth closed the door.

"I didn't say I didn't like it. Frankly, I haven't drunk much beer since I was in college."

"Well, then, it's time we renew old habits."

"Set the pizza down on the coffee table. I'll go get some plates."

"Napkins!" he called after her. "In my neighborhood, pizza's a finger food."

Beth returned and placed two plates, napkins, and glasses on the coffee table beside the pizza. She sat on the edge of the couch close to Carl, placed a slice of pizza on a plate, and handed it and a napkin to him. He watched her intently while she was unaware and only smiled when she turned to hand the food to him. He had a sudden desire to hold her in his arms. The smile was a result of him knowing just how welcome that would be right at this moment.

She sat back with her pizza. "You look much better than I expected."

"I feel better—if it's possible to feel better after last night."

"The papers and the television have had a field day with Joe. I feel so sorry—I know how hard he's working."

"It's rough, but Joe can handle it. That's not the pressure I'm worried about."

"What other pressure is there?"

"Our D.A. would like to have his own field day."

"Phil Greggory?"

"You know him?"

"No, not really. I voted for him." She smiled devilishly. "He really is a suave gentleman."

"Yeah . . . suave," he repeated disgustedly.

"I take it you don't like him?"

"There's no love lost between us."

"Just because you're involved in this case? That's illogical. Joe needs help, and the two of you are good friends. Why shouldn't you come and help Joe if he asks?"

"It goes a little further back than that."

"Oh." She knew instantly what he was talking about.

"What's the 'oh' mean?"

"Nothing, just 'oh.'" She shrugged.

"Shall I qualify the 'oh' for you? It means our D.A. was part of my past."

"Yes, I guess that's what I meant."

"You shouldn't be touched by ugly things," he added quietly. His eyes held hers and she had to fight the urge to touch the harsh lines on his face and smooth them somehow. She wanted to erase what she saw in his eyes and tell him that somehow the world could be made all right again, but she was too frightened to do that. Touching him would renew her uncertainties. He was a dangerous man because one touch could ignite something that was much too volatile. She remembered their last touch and the heat of desire. She had wanted him.

Carl set the remains of a can of beer aside and wiped his hands and mouth on a napkin before he answered. "Maybe that was why I came, but I know how wrong that was. I thought I owed you some kind of explanation."

"You don't owe me anything."

"I think you might see things differently from most."

"And what makes you think I would?"

"You already have."

"I don't understand."

"Right after I came, you found out about the field day the news media had with me at one time. It didn't seem to stop you from being a friend. I can tell you that you're in a very small crowd."

"Well, I've never been partial to large crowds, anyway. And what I read I'm sure, especially after what I saw on TV tonight, was strictly biased."

"To tell you the truth, I never looked at one paper the whole time, or at TV. I was kind of numb."

"You were always happy in this town, weren't you, Carl?"

"Yeah, I guess I was. I came here pretty young, and the first friend I made was Joe. We sort of hit it off right away. Anyway," he leaned back against the couch and searched for a way to begin. Beth said nothing. "I kind of think Joe and I wanted to be cops from day one. So when we joined the police, we were on top of the world. We felt invincible.

Just before I made lieutenant we made a bust, a couple of brothers—really bad news. I had no idea just how bad. They were both as psychotic as you grow them. They made a big stir at the trial when they swore they'd get me, one way or the other. In the end they chose the other—the one way to hurt me the most."

"Your wife?" she asked. He was quiet, a dark look in his eyes as they swept over her. He seemed to be gathering himself together. "You don't have to tell me anything, Carl." She said the words very quietly, hoping he knew that, for a reason she couldn't name, she cared.

"I haven't talked about it to anyone."

"Maybe you should."

He looked at her steadily, and her eyes held his, then he rose and walked across the room to stand by the window. He took his cigarettes from his pocket, put one in his mouth and lit it, and exhaled slowly. Beth didn't speak.

"Sara," he said her name like a whisper. "Sara was like morning sunshine—all gold hair and tan skin and blue eyes that always looked for beauty. I gave her a speeding ticket, then I followed her home because I couldn't get those blue eyes out of my mind. Would you believe she asked me out first? She said the ticket I gave her would cost the balance of her paycheck, so I owed her dinner."

"I think I would have liked your Sara."

He looked at her again for a long moment. "Yeah, you would. You two would have understood each other. You're different in every way, and yet you're alike somehow."

"Is that why you looked at me so funny the first night we met?"

"You kind of rattled my cage that night. First night in town and I come face-to-face with a situation I couldn't handle, so I ran. I figured I wasn't going to be much help to Joe if I couldn't handle something like that."

"But, you managed."

"I didn't, you did."

"I did?"

"I was all prepared with shields and self-defense, and you just slapped me in the face with, I could go to hell and you didn't need me and my shadows. I think you got my full attention about then."

"So, maybe you decided to quit running from your shadows?"

"If I didn't quit running, at least I began to think."

"About what?"

"About all the reasons I was running. I was a cocky cop. I played loose with those two, even when I knew they were on the street again. So when they hit, I was caught like a rookie."

"And Sara was killed instead of you."

He was quiet so long she thought he didn't mean to answer. Then he did with one cold word. "Yes."

"It must have been a terrible, terrible thing, Carl, but you can't carry the blame for it around forever. There comes a time when grief has to end—when you have to put it and your guilt in the past."

"I know you're right. I've said the same things to myself a million times. Guilt is a hard thing to wash away."

"So are memories you refuse to let go of. If you want to hold on to them, you're never going to have anything but memories."

"You think it's because I want to!"

"Don't you?"

Silently, angrily, he stared out the window. He was so caught up in his thoughts he didn't notice the car parked at the curb across the street. Beth came and stood behind him.

"Don't you think you ought to admit the truth to yourself, Carl? You use your guilt as a whip to keep yourself from daring to love anyone else, to keep yourself from taking that risk."

"What are you saying, Beth?"

"I guess the same thing any other woman would say. I'm not going to be a stand-in for a dead woman. You can't just reach out when you're hurting and find someone to lean on. Before you grab something new, you have to let go of something old."

"You think that's what I've been doing, using you?"

"You said the same yourself. Listen to me, Carl, I'm not some girl fresh from school. I don't know what there could ever be between us, or even if either of us wants anything strong. I only know that I won't be a surrogate woman for your dreams. If you want us to go anywhere, you're going to have to let go of the past. I can't fight a ghost, and I sure am not going to live with one."

How could he tell her? There was so much more to the story. He couldn't do it, no more than he could find words to explain that he needed her. She would be certain it was a temporary need, and he wasn't too sure it wasn't.

He turned from the window and walked to her then, and sat down only inches away from her. She could see that the barriers were still there, and it made her wonder what it was he hadn't told her.

"You're right about a lot of things, I guess," he said. The tension in him made her reach out instinctively and touch his hand. He grasped hers when she did, and when their hands met, the contact was electrical. He looked down at the hand he held, concentrating on it as he spoke. "About the kind of hold I have on the past. But it's easy to say and not so easy to do. You shouldn't be touched by ugly things." He tightened his fingers about hers and drew her slightly toward him. "You're not only beautiful, Beth, you also have a deep sense of caring that's like a warm fire on a snowy day."

Their eyes held and the air about them seemed filled with the same current. She knew what he had said to her was only part of what was buried so deep he could not expose it. She felt a helpless ache for him for what he couldn't bring himself to say.

Gently, he laid a hand against her cheek. It rested there for a moment, then slid into her hair to the back of her head. He used no force, just held her like that while he memorized every feature, every line of her face.

Then slowly, their eyes still meshed, he drew her closer.

"I have to kiss you," he whispered raggedly. Within him it was suddenly a desperate need.

She lifted parted lips to his and he took them with a heated urgency that left little doubt of the burning need he felt. All her logic told her that no answers had been given and that this was not one either, but still, she could not withdraw from the magnetic pull of the slow, growing passion.

He could feel a hollowness slowly being filled, and he let the kiss deepen until he could hear a muffled moan purr from deep in her throat.

Beth was drowning in the heat of him. She had lost the empty feeling of loneliness while the kiss lingered.

Both were breathing deeply now. Beth's eyes were closed, but she could feel his hand caressing her back in slow, long strokes. Then they curved about her, slowly moving to cup her breasts.

His lips moved across her cheeks to touch her eyes, her nose, then returned to her mouth, open, hot, and hungry now. His hands were moving in slow circles over her breasts, and through the fine fabric of her blouse, she could feel the erotic sensation as her nipples grew taut and her body arched toward him, seeking.

His fingers moved to the buttons of her blouse, opening it. Then he bent his head to press a kiss to the hollow of her throat, and to the soft flesh above the line of her bra. Her eyes were closed now, and she lay back on the couch as his hands moved to free her from her clothes.

Both were inflamed, and surrendered completely to the wildfire that engulfed them.

The shrill ring of the phone jolted them back to mind-staggering reality. They jerked erect and sat for a moment, searching for some kind of control for their ragged breathing.

Beth fumbled to button her blouse as she rose from the couch.

"Jesus," Carl muttered. His body was sizzling and hot, and he was hard enough to explode. The frustration was almost overpowering. He could have ripped the intrusive phone from the wall.

Beth, too, was fighting shattering emotions. She buttoned her blouse with shaking hands, realizing she had gotten lost in something she never should have started. Her hand shook so badly she almost dropped the phone, and she had to clear her throat before she could answer.

"Hello?" She listened, then said, "Yes, Mr. Forrester is here. Just a minute."

She turned to face Carl, and he could read her eyes.

"Beth, don't . . ."

"It's for you," she interrupted. She had no control and she needed to find it. Carl rose and walked to her, then took the phone from her hand. He didn't want to talk to whoever was on the other end. He wanted—no, needed—to talk to Beth. He put the phone to his ear.

"Hello . . . yes. Couldn't that wait until tomorrow?" Again he paused. "All right, I'll be right there." He hung up and turned to look at Beth again. She had regained her outward composure, but inside she was still in turmoil.

"Beth, I've got to go down to Joe's office. Something has come up."

"It's all right." She said the words quietly.

"The hell it is. Dammit, I'm sorry."

"No, it's all right, Carl. Just . . ."

"I want to come back." It was a statement more than a question.

"No, Carl. No, not now. We both need time. You'd better go."

"Beth . . ."

"Just go." She was almost pleading, and Carl knew he could not argue with that. But there was no way he was going to let this go—not this time. He'd seen and tasted and felt something redeeming, and he meant to find out if it was all he thought it was. He left, and when the door closed behind him, Beth sagged down in a chair and inhaled deeply. She was frightened.

* CHAPTER 24 *

Todd hung up the phone and paced the floor of his apartment in total disbelief. He had had his own way most of his life, and his family had been wealthy enough that he had never wanted for anything. He had wanted Beth from the first minute he had seen her and, of course, had swept her off her feet.

But, even so, Beth had been special. He had basked in her adoration and self-sacrifice. She had built her world around him and he was quite satisfied with that, but never once had he sacrificed his freedom. He liked having a pretty and extremely intelligent wife, but he liked to have a stable of lush beauties on the side, as well.

He had never been more furious with himself in his life than when he had made the foolish move of taking that friend of Beth's to bed in their house, but he had been certain that Beth wouldn't be home for hours. He could still see her face when she had walked in on them in the midst of a wild, passionate encounter. She had simply frozen in the doorway, and by the time he had gotten free of the girl and grabbed a sheet to wrap around him, Beth's car was already leaving the drive.

It seemed a waste of Janet's hot nature not to complete what he had started, so he returned to the bedroom and coaxed her back to the bed, where they shared an afternoon of pleasure. Only after Janet had left did he try to find out where Beth had gone. He followed her to the hotel and used every ounce of charm he had, to no avail. Beth had decided to divorce him.

He found that without Beth, he had a kind of emptiness he had never experienced before. He realized he loved her, in his own way, and didn't want to lose her. She was the security he needed to balance the part of his life he couldn't control. She was logic and poise—symmetry amid the confusion. He wanted her with a desperation new to him—in fact, he needed her to preserve his rationality.

He had to admit that Beth was an exceptional hostess, and could add a great deal to his career ambitions. Besides all this, he remembered how he could always dominate her in bed. She was always passionate, and sometimes he took a little devious pleasure in demanding more and more from her, until he knew he was making her feel helpless and inadequate. And in her love for him, she had believed she was.

Now, however, he was pressed for time, annoyed by the fact that another man had walked into Beth's life. He wasn't going to let some hick cop come along and ruin his plans. He wanted Beth back, and he intended to have her.

He had had several drinks and watched the time tick away. He walked to the phone again, then changed his mind. Instead he pulled on his coat and drove to Beth's house. He knew she had a guest inside. He watched the house from his car across the street. Eventually, the guy would leave and Beth would be alone. Then he would take over. By ten-thirty he was becoming both cold and angry. He folded his arms across his chest and kept an eye on the dashboard clock. Beth was not a casual woman, to go from bed to bed. He had been the first man for her, and he knew she had never cheated while they were married.

Of course she could have changed, maybe she had slept with a lot of men since he was put out of her bed. But his self assurance sustained him. She could not have shared what she had had with him. All he needed was to get her back, and he would make her forget her small town cop.

Todd had almost dozed off again when he saw Beth's door open. It was ten-forty. Carl stood in the doorway, looking back into the room. A new rage struck Todd. It was obvious from the way that Carl looked at Beth that they had been very intimate.

As Carl's car pulled away, Todd decided against confronting Beth. Instead, he started his car and followed. Carl stopped at the police station, and again, Todd sat and waited. His anger had changed to cool calculation.

Just under an hour later, Todd followed Carl from the station to his motel. He watched Carl go inside. Then he cut his motor and got out of the car. He walked briskly and with determination to the front door and knocked.

Carl stood for a moment, completely surprised. He hadn't noticed anyone familiar parked outside. He slipped his gun out of its shoulder holster and held it down as inconspicuously as possible as he opened the door.

The men looked at each other for a moment in utter silence. Then Todd smiled sneeringly. "Carl Forrester." His voice was heavy with arrogance. "What are you planning to do with that small cannon—make Beth a widow?"

Carl knew this must be Todd and immediately hated him

in the same heartbeat. His first instinct was a Neanderthal urge to do just what Todd suggested. Instead, he smiled.

"So you're the jackass who let Beth get away. Why don't you come in and explain to me just how ignorant one man can be?"

Todd's face froze into lines of fury. He brushed past Carl, who closed the door and followed him into the room.

"You'd be smart to stay away from my wife. Beth and I are going to be getting back together, and it might prove pretty difficult for her if you get in the way."

Carl was on uncertain ground. He wasn't sure just where he did stand with Beth, or even where he wanted to stand. He knew what he would like to do with Todd, yet he wasn't too sure what Beth's reaction would be if she knew about this confrontation.

"Funny, Beth never told me she planned to remarry you. In fact, I hear it the other way. I hear she moved from wherever you were to Helton just to make a clean break. If you're under the impression I'm going to swallow your story, you're more of a fool than I thought. Whatever the truth is, I'll hear it from Beth."

"Why don't you just get the hell out of town? I've heard this town got rid of you once."

Carl had reached the end of both his patience and his tolerance of Todd. He reached out a hamlike hand and grabbed a handful of Todd's shirt, jerking him nearly from his feet. At the same time, he put the muzzle of the gun in front of Todd's eyes and watched his face go gray.

"You listen to me, little man," he said very softly between gritted teeth. "What you want means less than shit to me. Now, before you try my temper any further, I suggest you get your ass out of here before I jam this barrel up it and pull the trigger. I hope you understand this real clear, because if I catch you pushing Beth one inch, this will stop being a threat and become a fact. Are you listening?"

"Yes."

"Good, because if I thought you weren't, I'd have to make it a little clearer."

Carl shoved Todd away from him.

"You're a fool. Beth will be really interested in what kind of a bastard you are."

"And you can't wait to run and tell her," Carl taunted.

"You're a son of a bitch. Put the gun down, Wyatt Earp; this is not a gunfight at the OK Corral. It doesn't make you tough. You put that gun down and then we'll talk."

Carl was as mad at himself as he was at Todd. It was a juvenile thing to do, waving a gun at Todd. He smiled and laid the gun aside. "Insulting my mother doesn't make you much of a jock, either."

"You want to use brawn instead of brain?"

"What's that supposed to mean?"

"You've got a cop mentality. So you convince Beth to stay with you. What the hell do you have to offer her—a cop's pay, and nothing else. She'll have to work the rest of her life to help support you. Want to compare? I've been made vice-president of the Stafford Organization. One more step and I'll be the president. I can offer Beth a good life—a hell of a lot more than you can—and one where she won't have to be afraid her husband might get himself killed one day."

"My chances of getting killed on the street aren't any bigger than your chance of getting wiped out by some irate husband or boyfriend. At least Beth would know where I am and who I'm with."

"I take it you've talked a lot about me."

"Not really. I can read between the lines. You left her feeling like she was nothing. You think you can build on that?"

"Everybody has a skeleton or two in the closet. I bet I'd be safe in saying you had one or two rattling around in there yourself."

Much as this stung, Carl had no intention of letting Todd get to him. He disliked everything about him, but he had to admit the truths that had been thrown in his face. He had more problems than Beth had and a future that was vague at best.

Todd was quick to see he had struck some kind of vulnerable spot; he just wished maliciously that he knew what it was.

"Look, I think it's best you get the hell out of here before we do anything stupid, like breaking up the place." Carl spoke the velvet threat firmly. He wouldn't mind a bit punching Todd's face.

"I guess you're right."

The urge grew, and Carl had to turn his back to keep from jumping him. He heard Todd leave. He inhaled deeply, knowing it might always be his curse to be violent. He walked to the window and looked out. Todd's car was still there; he sat in it, watching. Then the motor roared to life and he drove away.

* CHAPTER 25 *

Father McAllen could hear music from somewhere deep within the house, and knew the person he sought, in more ways than one, must be locked away in the depths. He knocked again and waited. After another few minutes the knob turned and the door opened a few inches. The face that appeared was ravaged and scowled darkly, condemning his intrusion in silence for several minutes.

"What do you want?" The voice was raspy, as if it hadn't been used for some time.

"Michael, I'd like to talk to you."

"I ain't got nothing to say to you."

"I didn't ask you to say anything to me. I said I wanted to talk with you."

"If you've come here to put in a good word for that smart bastard Carterson, you can just haul yourself back to your car and get out of here."

"Michael, please, let me in. You need some help."

"I don't need nothing! I don't need meddlers prying in my business. All I want is to be left alone."

"I have something I have to tell you and it's important. Give me a few minutes."

Michael glared at him, but Father McAllen was not intimidated. Mingled with all the anger, he could see the doubt and a dark kind of pain. For a while he was sure that Michael had decided not to let him in, but then he turned from the door and disappeared inside, leaving it open. Father McAllen pushed it open wider and went inside.

It was a small, four-room bungalow, and Father McAllen had entered by way of the kitchen. It was obvious to him that no one had cleaned it for some time. Dishes were stacked in the sink, and rows of empty beer cans stood on the table. Michael carried one in his hand. He drank the last of it, crumpled the can in his fist, and tossed it toward a waste can that was already filled beyond capacity. It tumbled off and fell to the floor, but Michael ignored it.

"So, what do you want here, Father? If you're digging in the dirt for souls to save, don't bother—I don't need it. It's your artist friend who needs saving."

"Because that test might have proven Paul could be the father of Martha's baby doesn't necessarily make him guilty of her death."

"What makes you think he ain't?"

"What makes you think he is?"

"I'm tired of hearing the talk about it. I know what I think and I'm going to get that bastard if it's the last thing I do."

Michael's eyes burned with his rage, but if he thought his anger or his language was going to shock Father McAllen, he was mistaken. He had heard much worse and faced more kinds of anger than Michael could muster.

"I'm not here to be an advocate for Paul."

"Then, why are you here?"

"Because of Martha," he said quietly. He watched some of the anger wash away and a wave of pain rise in Michael's eyes. Then, the shields went up again.

"I don't need you or your church to tell me anything about Martha. What would you know or understand?"

"Martha and I were good friends, Michael. She came to me in that same friendship for counseling and support."

"That how you get your kicks, Mr. Holier-than-thou Priest—listening to her talk about us? Just how much did she say—enough to make you feel good?"

Father McAllen could feel the heat of his own anger rise and clung to its control mentally while he gritted his teeth to keep words he didn't want to say from spoiling whatever chance he might have to help Michael. He also realized that Michael lashed out at Martha only because, as the old song said, you always hurt the one you love the most.

"She said she loved you, Michael—that she really cared about your life and what you were capable of doing with it. She knew the terrible childhood you had and how hard things had been for you. I know what kind of man you are under that rather obnoxious exterior, just as I know what kind of a woman Martha was."

"Shit! You been wearing dresses and lighting candles most of your life. You're more woman than man. No balls. What do you know about any woman, much less Martha?"

"I became a priest when I was twenty-five; I've been a man a lot longer than that." Father McAllen was beginning to lose his fragile hold on his temper. He knew his violent temper was one of his failings, and he wanted, especially this time, to win out over it. "Look, Michael, we are pretty nearly in the same boat. We both look guilty, and we're both innocent. We need to help each other."

Michael's face twisted into a cold sneer. "I'm not so sure you're so damn innocent. You weren't the father of the baby, but maybe you slept with her. Maybe you had a little something that didn't include prayers."

Father McAllen was beginning to see the red haze before his eyes that heralded an explosion, but he hung on grimly. He wasn't going to let Michael drive him away when he knew he was a wounded soul that needed help.

"You're hitting out at Martha because you're hurt. But you're hurting her worse than anyone else can by saying such things about her. At the same time, you're hiding your grief behind a whole lot of self-pity. Well, nobody else has come to your pity party. If you don't know it, I'll tell you. The music's finished; the dancing's done, the party's over. Now, why don't you try to be the man Martha thought you were and start picking up the pieces? Why don't you defend yourself, instead of making yourself look guilty by hitting out at everybody else?"

"Oh, yeah," Michael snarled. "She cared so much she went out and got knocked up by that smart-assed painter. She really cared."

"She did care! I know what happened between her and Paul, and it didn't happen the way you think."

"That kind of thing only happens one way. She screwed the guy and got pregnant. What the hell does love have to do with that—especially loving me?"

"It was an accidental, one-time thing—a thing of need, not love, and it never happened again. She needed you, and you were too damn wound up in your own hurts to see it. Paul understood, but that doesn't mean she loved him."

"She didn't need him half as much as I needed her. Why the hell didn't she come to me? Why didn't she tell me about the baby? I would have taken care of them both."

"Maybe she tried and you didn't understand. Whatever it was, she came to me. We got only as far as the fact of her pregnancy and her love for you. There was a lot more she wanted to tell me—I knew it—but she never got the chance. She was killed before she could tell me any more. We all need someone sometime, Michael, and she knew you needed her. She just didn't want you to be hurt any more than you had been."

"What did she tell you about me?"

"Very little. Only that she wanted to bring you closer to the church. She felt confession and a release of some of the pain you've known might have helped."

"Me! Me, close to the church! Me, come to you? Hell, no. I've had my fill of being pushed by do-gooder churchgoers. My whole family were saint prayers. I had my nose rubbed in it long enough. Even Martha wouldn't stand a chance for that."

"You have to believe in something, Michael."

"I believe in me. Wherever your God is, he hasn't had time for me since I was a kid. I spent a lifetime dodging him so he wouldn't take any more from me than he already had. But he's got keen eyes. He always knew when I had something I really wanted just within reach, and he snatched it away. Even Martha—he even took Martha."

Father McAllen could hear the intensity of Michael's

pain. It seemed like a deep, dark well and Father McAllen stood on the edge. He wasn't too sure he could brave the blackness he felt. This kind of pain had to have grown from something so terrible that it could frighten Michael, and even frighten him.

"You can't blame Martha's death on God, Michael. It was a human hand that took her life. But you've got to stop living this ugliness."

"Don't preach to me! Don't tell me what I have to do or not do. I don't want your lies, and I don't want your vicious God!" Michael reached a hand to push Father McAllen away before he finished speaking. "He's a thief and a liar!" Michael lashed out with his fist, and Father McAllen lost what control was left. He blocked the blow expertly, gripped the front of Michael's shirt with both hands, and slammed him back against the wall with a force that made him grunt in surprise.

"Look, you drunken idiot. You're hurting and you're taking out your pain on the only one who can help you." Michael struggled, but Father McAllen held him in an unmerciful grip. He was too angry to let him off easy. "You won't believe this now, but maybe one day you'll wise up. Martha loved you, and she knew you needed help. You've got to remember what was good between you, and if you want to survive, you've got to get rid of this hate you're carrying around. If you don't then your whole life is one big waste, and Martha didn't want that. You know that, and for what it's worth to you, so do I. Now, are you going to be a fool and throw the rest of your life away, or are you going to turn into a man somewhere along the line?"

Michael's body shook. He pressed his head back against the wall, closed his eyes, and drew a ragged breath. Father McAllen could feel the strength and the fight flow from him. He was breathing roughly himself, and he was also realizing he'd again lost his battle. He released Michael and stepped back.

"Get out of here," Michael rasped. "Just get out." Father McAllen could hear his voice tremble at the breaking point.

"I'll go. But you know where to find me." He paused. "I understand, Michael—I really do. But Martha's gone, and you have a right to some peace."

He left Michael where he stood, sagged against the wall, his bleak face speaking volumes. His despair was clear to read. But he had also read a stubborn resolve and a seething emotion that frightened him. Michael would either explode one day or get hold of himself, but he saw a capability in him—a capability of murder.

Michael sank into a chair. He had not shed a tear since he was a little boy, but now tears washed down his face unheeded. In the quiet of the cottage the sound of his weeping went unheard.

Father McAllen gripped the steering wheel in both hands. He felt miserable; he had failed Michael, Martha, and himself, as well. He started his car and backed up, then pulled out on the highway and headed back to town.

His mind was so intent on all that had happened in the past few days that he didn't realize his foot was adding steady pressure to the gas pedal or that the speedometer was climbing. In fact, he didn't realize anything outside his thoughts until he heard the siren, looked into his rearview mirror, and saw the flashing red light of the police car.

"That's it," he muttered. "On top of everything else, this is all I need." He looked up toward the car ceiling. Well, this was one time prayer wasn't going to change the fact that the tall policeman was walking toward his car. He pressed the button that rolled down the window.

Roger Maxwell bent forward to rest his hand on the frame of the open window, then lowered his head to see who was driving. He was speaking as he bent forward.

"Where were you off to in such a hurry? Don't you know the speed limit is . . . Father McAllen!" He gulped the name in surprise.

"Hi, Roger, how are you doing?" Father McAllen smiled.

"Fine, Father, fine."

"How's Polly, and that son of yours?"

"They're fine, too, Father. Ah . . . look, Father, do you know we clocked you doing a little over seventy?"

"I imagine you're right. I'm afraid I had my mind on a handful of problems, and I forgot what I was doing."

"Yeah, well." He was upset at being the one who had

pulled Father McAllen over. He could just imagine what his wife was going to say if he gave him a ticket. He closed the little book he'd been prepared to write in. "Look, Father, I have to give you a warning. We've been watching this road pretty close for the last couple of weeks, so if you're going to rev it up, be careful here. I'm not always the one on duty."

"I appreciate that, and I'll be careful from now on. I don't usually go hot-rodding around. Why have you been watching this road?"

"It crosses Old Plank Road, where those girls who were murdered were found. Seems strange to me. This nut who's killing them always heads for pretty much the same place. He's whacko."

"He's sick, Roger," Father McAllen said quietly. "What are you looking for? Something in particular?"

"My partner and I are keeping a record of the license plates of people using Old Plank Road. If they're nosing around, we shoo them off, but we keep track of them in case Joe has any questions he'd like to ask."

"Sounds like a good idca. What have you run across?"

"Couple of kids necking." He shrugged. "A few nosy types who want to see where it happened. Sounds ghoulish, I know, but people are funny. They gather around at accidents, too—some kind of fascination with death."

"Maybe. Death is pretty hard to understand. Maybe it's some kind of relief or assurance of their life. They're glad they're alive."

"That's finding a lot of good in people, Father, but there's some that just enjoy somebody else's grief. It's kind of like they're gloating."

"Man's a pretty complicated entity. I guess we're a long way yet from understanding him."

"Yeah. This killer, he's got to be a psycho. I knew those girls, and they were pretty nice. What kind of a guy would want to do a thing like that?"

"A hurt, troubled person who doesn't know the difference between right and wrong. He's hitting out at more than just these girls."

"Well, I hope Joe can put a stop to him pretty quick. He's getting a lot of help from Carl Forrester."

"You know Carl?"

"I was a cadet at the academy when Carl got his gold shield. He's a damn good man."

"With a lot of problems of his own?" Father McAllen prodded.

"Well, he had a hard time a few years back, losing his wife and all. I never did believe he killed those two guys, like they said. He would have had to be crazy to do that. Anyway, he'll be a lot of help to Joe, and maybe they can lock up this nut before he terrorizes the whole town."

"I hope so, too."

Roger stood and watched Father McAllen pull away, then walked back to the cruiser and slid in behind the wheel.

"You didn't give our speedster a ticket?" Gregg Wilson, Roger's partner for three years, asked.

"Know who it was?"

"No."

"Father McAllen. I could no more give him a ticket than I could fly. When Polly had Nick, he's the one who stayed up all night with me when I thought we were going to lose them both. He came to the hospital almost every day after that while Nick was struggling to live, and he prayed for hours. I'm still not sure that wasn't what brought Nick through. I wouldn't give him a ticket—no way."

"You know, it's funny."

"What?"

"Well, remember the night before that Dexter girl was killed?"

"Yeah?"

"That car was out by Shaffer's old house."

"That's off Old Plank Road, too. He was most likely at Shaffer's doing something for the old lady."

"Yeah."

"Look, I know that we have to suspect everyone, even Father McAllen. But I just don't believe he could know anything about this. He's a fine man."

"I don't have any ideas about him, but we have to put his name and license on the list. I know if Joe thought we weren't doing our job, he'd have our asses in a sling."

"I guess so. Go ahead, put down the name and license,

but when I drop them off at Joe's office, I'll explain about Father McAllen."

"Good enough. At least we'll be off the hook, and he'll know we're doing our job."

"Well, let's pull this buggy back and see if any other spiders drive into the web."

He pulled the car back onto the road, made a U-turn, and backed into a packed dirt circle under the branches of a tree. The car then had easy access to the road but was completely out of view of any travelers along the road. They sat quietly and waited.

He prayed strenuously with an effort that made beads of perspiration pop out on his forehead. He had never prayed so hard in his life—not even when she had stood over him with that leather belt and let it fall again and again with such rhythmic blows that he began to conform his prayers to the chanted rhythm.

Few people were in the church, and each seemed caught in his own world. The church was so silent that it echoed with the light coughs, an occasional soft whisper, and the rustle of people moving restlessly.

His hands were clasped before him, and his eyes were closed as he strained mentally. He tried to escape that harsh sneering voice—escape into the prayers—but he couldn't. The voice was cold and filled with derision.

He had wanted to love her—had desperately wanted to love her since his world had been so suddenly emptied of love. But he felt, with a choked kind of fear, the black hatred begin to grow. If he hated her, he would have no one. Maybe he didn't deserve anyone, as she said. Maybe he had been wicked. Maybe all those things she said were true. But he didn't want them to be. It hurt too bad to know he was beyond the help of anyone's love.

He had stopped crying externally a long time ago, but he could still feel the drip of tears, like acid, as they ate through his spirit. Often it had wakened him in dreams, horrible beyond description. But even those were fading now, as he learned that he could kill her. He could wipe her words and that hard voice away. Of course, she came back, again and again. She came back in such wicked ways, tempting him and taunting him. But he knew her, and he swelled with the power of knowing he could kill her again and have that short time of freedom before she crept back into his mind.

She was back again now, her voice whispering in his ear. He smiled. He had the message for her in his pocket, and when he killed her, he'd make sure to leave his message so she would know.

It made his heart pump furiously, driving the blood to his head in pounding waves. But he ignored that, as he always did, and remained on his knees. The prayers, like wave after wave of disoriented thoughts, drifted in and out of his mind. The Act of Contrition mingled with the Hail Mary. The prayer of St. Francis blended in a disassociated jumble until the prayers were words—words that battered him.

After a few minutes he rose from his cramped kneeling position. He would find her soon. No matter how she tried to hide from him, he would find her. He would punish her for her cruelty and for the blows that had driven him to his knees.

He walked to the door, and as he left, he passed a woman on her way in. She smiled and he spoke as she passed. She was not the one. She was too old, and her clothes were colorless and demure. She was not the one. But she couldn't hide from him. He would know her when he saw her. He continued on his way, a smile lighting his handsome face. He would find her . . . and he would kill her.

* CHAPTER 26 *

"Jim Frasier's been pretty good about the articles he's run in the paper," Carl offered. "They seem supportive of you."

"Yeah, but I can't say the same for the TV people. They're beginning to make me look like an incompetent ass."

"You know how TV feeds on this stuff. It's good for their ratings. But the people in this town are pretty loyal to you. There's not going to be a witch hunt, no matter what the media says."

"I hope you're right."

"I am," Carl grinned. "I always am."

"Shit," Joe chuckled. "What are you doing for lunch?"

"I've got a date with a beautiful lady."

"Beth?"

"Nope. I called Mrs. Lowrey on my way here, and she's making some of that beef stew, with the thick gravy and vegetables, so I invited myself to lunch."

"Always the shrewd operator."

"Well, I invited her out to lunch, but she insisted I come over."

"So, after you argued a while, you let her convince you."

"I could almost smell the stew over the phone."

"And after what I assume will be a prolonged lunch?"

"I'll come right back—I promise, Dad."

"I want to take a ride back out to the murder scene."

"Something bothering you?"

"I don't know. I got an itch between my shoulder blades. It keeps telling me I'm looking this guy in the face and not seeing him."

"You, too? I've had it since this thing got started."

"Well, get some lunch. I have some phone calls to make, and I'm waiting on some more answers from the lab. We'll go out there this afternoon."

"Fine." Joe had already lifted the phone and was pushing buttons as Carl left the room.

When Carl turned down the street and drove toward Mrs. Lowrey's house, he was surprised to see another car parked in her drive. It looked familiar to him, but he couldn't remember where he'd seen it before. Automatically, he memorized the license number. It was a habit hard to break. He stored it in his memory and left it, to be recalled if he should ever need it.

He knocked and waited, and in a few minutes she appeared.

"Well, Carl, it's about time you got here."

He bent to kiss her cheek as she closed the door.

"I stopped by Joe's office on the way over."

"Why didn't you bring him with you?"

"He's knee-deep in work. Is the car out front your boarder's, or does it belong to another guest who appreciates your cooking as much as I do?"

"Both." She chuckled. "Come in the kitchen."

Carl let her walk ahead of him into the kitchen, and as he came through the doorway, David Mondale grinned at him from a seat at the table.

"You're right. I heard you in the hall. Ever since I moved here, I've been coming home for lunch as often as possible. I'm deeply devoted to good food, and Mrs. Lowrey makes the best."

Carl smiled and sat down across the table from David. "I don't know if you've been fully adopted yet, but I can tell you from experience that if you get the chance, grab it."

"Oh, I intend to. Mrs. Lowrey's been like a mother to me."

Carl watched Mrs. Lowrey's benevolent smile. "David has been a great help, so a little food is not much in return. He reminds me so much of you, Carl."

"Outside of my voracious appetite, just how could he remind you of me?"

"Oh, he's a hard worker, and kind, and . . ."

"Sounds like you've got another Prince Charming." Carl winked at David. "We have her buffaloed, so don't rock the boat."

David laughed. "I know which side my bread is buttered on."

"Oh, you two," Emma chided as she set a bowl of stew before each one. "Go ahead and eat."

"We'll wait for you. Get a bowl and come on," David said quickly. When she joined them at the table it seemed to close a circle, and for a while, they ate and conversed on random topics. It was David who first broached the subject of the murders.

"So, Carl, are you making any progress on these murders? It's an awful thing to have happen in a nice town like Helton."

"You're right," Emma agreed. "It's made people afraid to go out of their houses."

"What's worse is that we have a lot of suspicions and not very much proof."

"Not very much? Does that mean you have some clues?" David inquired. His smile faded to a frown of puzzlement.

"Well, there are a few things I really don't have the freedom to talk about. Joe's a good cop. One way or another, he'll catch this guy."

"What kind of a reason could a man have to kill such sweet, innocent girls?" Emma said, her voice sharp with anger. "He has to be deranged. No man in his right mind could find any reasoning in this kind of thing."

"Well, I'm glad you people were smart enough to take Father McAllen off your list. How anyone could think that he would do such a thing is beyond belief." David's voice was an echo of his relief.

Carl was quiet for a minute. He needed to keep David from upsetting Emma, but make him understand his position. "Look, David, I know how you and nearly all the rest of this town feel about Father McAllen. But we can't take any man who had a connection with these women off the list before we find out who's guilty."

Emma was aghast, and David's eyes reflected his disbelief. Carl felt as if he'd been caught in a crime. "In a murder case, everyone is a suspect until we can put our finger on the guilty one. Neither of you would want us to overlook a clue that might make a difference in finding him, would you? Father McAllen can provide a lot of insight into these girls, if nothing else, and we need every lead we can get."

"You have a lot of people who can give you more insight than they've given, and who stand a big chance of being guilty."

"Like who?" Carl said patiently.

"Paul Carterson, for one, or better yet, Michael Brodie. I felt kind of sorry for him at the police station, but he sure had a motive."

"To kill Paul maybe," Carl replied, "but I don't think he knew a thing about that baby, so that lets his motive fly out the window."

"Not so you'd notice it," David said, his anger evident.

"I don't understand," Carl prodded.

"And I don't either," Emma broke in. "David, if there's

something Carl should know, you should tell him. How can we expect him and Joe to put a stop to this terrible thing if we don't offer all the help we can?"

"You asked me if I noticed anything at Paul's the night of the party," David began hesitantly. "It was like there was an electrical current between Michael and Martha all evening. They kept as much distance between each other as they could, and a couple of times, Michael looked at her as if he could have hit her right there."

"As if they might have been fighting before they got to the party? Do you have any idea what they could have been fighting about?"

"No way to know for certain, but if it were up to me to guess, I'd say because Martha was going to dump him. I think she had had about enough of him and wanted out."

"And maybe that was because of Paul Carterson," Carl said thoughtfully, annoyed at his feeling that there was something else he should see.

"Could very well be. After all, if Paul Carterson was the father of her baby, they must have been pretty close once or twice."

"So, you think Michael is lying about knowing about the baby?"

"Not necessarily. Maybe he was just suspicious, and he had another fight with Martha later and lost his temper and smacked her around. One thing led to another, and he ended up killing her. Maybe he didn't even mean to."

"So why Leslie and Paula then?"

David shrugged. "Maybe they knew more than they said, and he got scared. I don't have all the answers, but I'd sure as heck suspect Michael Brodie before I'd suspect Father McAllen. Michael's nasty temper is probably why he destroyed the painting Paul was doing of Martha. It was really beautiful, and Michael probably saw there was a lot more in it than just paint and canvas, so he took a knife and worked it over."

"This is all supposition!" Emma inserted. She had listened in silence, but as always, she couldn't help being sympathetic to the one who seemed defenseless. Both Carl and David understood this and exchanged the look that irritated her. "Well, it is. No matter what you say about those two men, I don't believe they were responsible for what happened. And as far as Michael was concerned, well, I just don't think all these stories ring true."

"Mrs. Lowrey," David chuckled, "you wouldn't suspect the devil of committing a sin."

"No man is that evil," she said emphatically.

"Emma," Carl smiled to ease his words, "man can become a pretty twisted thing. Somewhere along the line his wires get crossed, and he shorts out mentally. In that case, there isn't much he couldn't be responsible for."

"But is he responsible then, Carl?" she asked gently.

"Maybe not, but I can't let him go on doing such things just because he can't stop."

"I wonder..." Emma began.

"Wonder what?" Carl responded quickly.

"Oh, nothing," Emma replied. But the idea had already formed in her mind. She intended to pay Michael Brodie a visit. She wanted to look in his eyes and see for herself.

"Well, listen." David rose to his feet. "Much as I hate to, I have to get back to work."

"You don't want any more stew?" Emma asked.

"Save it for later. You know me and midnight snacks."

"Good, I'll keep a bowl in the refrigerator."

"I'll be home late today. Practice is going to run a little longer than usual. Don't wait supper for me." He extended his hand to Carl. "I don't mean to condemn anybody, but it's against all I believe to think that Father McAllen could even consider doing such a thing. Why don't you talk to Michael again?"

"I'll do that." Carl smiled. David's handshake was firm, and Carl was again caught by his charm. When he left the kitchen, Carl could actually feel the vacancy he left behind.

Carl sat back down in his chair and grinned at Emma. "I wouldn't mind a second bowl, unless you're going to show favoritism to your boarder."

"Now, don't be funny, young man." She smiled as she rose and carried the bowl back to the stove, where she ladled it full again. "Of course," she set it before him and sat back down, "I really shouldn't treat you so well. From what I understand, your stomach shouldn't be in such good shape." Her eyes twinkled mischievously.

"Now are you and Sally playing mother hen again! What am I going to do with you two? Always comparing notes like I'm a six year old." Carl complained.

"Maybe you shouldn't act like one," Emma replied complacently, "besides you need looking after. Heaven help you if someone wasn't around to keep you on the straight and narrow."

"I've been doing a reasonable job for the last three years. Without you or Sally's help, I might add. Of course I'll admit I haven't eaten as well."

"I doubt if you've done such a good job. I know you, Carl."

"What's that supposed the mean?"

"It means you're not happy," she stated bluntly.

"Not many people have had as much happiness as I've had. I lost it, and I don't think it's replaceable. Maybe we all get doled out just so much in a lifetime, and I've had my share. I'm getting along fine, Emma."

"Carl, tell me the truth. When this is over..."

"If it's over."

"No, when it's over," she said stubbornly, "are you going to stay in Helton or go back to Cambridge?"

"To tell you the real honest to God's truth," he laughed, "I don't know."

"Good."

"Good?"

"You have some doubts. I was afraid you'd be a little more definite."

"You are a stubborn cuss, Emma, my love, and I'm getting out of here while I have my skin."

"If you don't talk to me," she said wickedly, "I'll just talk to Sally...and use my imagination."

"Which is overworked." He rose, "Like I said, I'm getting out of here while I still can."

Emma rose from the table and came to stand beside him. "I'm one of a whole pile of people in Helton who care a lot about what happens to you, Carl Forrester, and I don't want you to forget that. If I push, it's because I miss you, and I think you miss us and your town." She placed a slender hand on his arm. "You keep that in mind when this is all over and you decide whether to go back to Cambridge or stay here."

Carl bent and kissed her cheek. "I'll do that, and... thanks."

He drove back to Joe's office in a state of confusion, amplified by his inability to see beyond today and try to take a step away from the past.

Joe was waiting impatiently and had stepped around his desk before Carl was a few steps into the office. "Where the hell have you been? Two hours is more than I can spare you."

"I ran across David Mondale at Emma's. He boards there."

"Yeah, I know."

"Well, he was home for lunch and we had quite a conversation."

"Tell me on the way. I want to get out there and go over that place again. I don't want to miss anything, even if it's as small as a grain of sand."

"Your men have gone over it already."

"Humor me." Joe grinned. "C'mon, let's go see what we can find."

Joe drove, and Carl reported what David had said to him.

"So, he thinks Brodie knew about the baby. He sure was a good actor if he did. I think my professor friend told us our killer would wear a pretty good face. If Michael knew, it's sure a good motive."

"David thinks Michael ripped up that painting, too. Another sign—if you believe signs."

"You don't think he did?"

"Christ, I don't know, Joe. If he did, then it supports the theory that he killed her."

"Lord, Lord," Joe muttered softly under his breath. "We have to count on two things. That he's made a bad mistake somewhere, and that we don't make any."

Carl could only nod in agreement. They waved at the black-and-white car parked just off the dirt road that led to the wooded area.

Joe pulled his car to the side of the road, and he and Carl walked across the leaf-strewn ground. The bare branches of the trees were no barrier to the sunlight that brushed the carpet of dead russet leaves with a pale glow. They did not talk, and the only sound was the rustle of the leaves as they walked through them.

Some distance ahead they could see the area where Martha Dexter's body had been found. It was tied off with a band of yellow, ribbonlike cord that was strung between trees to form a large square. Beyond it, less than a hundred yards, was another section enclosed with the same yellow band. The ground moved downward in a steep curve, so they could not see the area beyond the second section, but they knew there was a third square. They stopped just outside the first one.

"You know, there is one strange thing," Carl said thoughtfully.

"What?"

"He put Martha in a shallow grave, but the others were found on the ground."

"Have you looked at the pictures?"

"Yeah."

"It was like he'd laid them out for a funeral."

"There's something . . ." Carl shrugged as if he were uncomfortable with an elusive thought.

"What?"

"Well, the rosary, the way he arranged them, the Bible quotes—he's telling us something."

"That he's a religious fanatic."

"Or just the opposite—that he's got something against religion."

"From what I see, Paul Carterson has no religious persuasion at all, except his art. We know where Father McAllen stands. Michael Brodie has a big chip on his shoulder against the whole world, and that includes the church—any church."

Carl released pent-up breath in a disgusted sigh. "Want to check these places out together, or split up?"

"Might be faster if we split up."

"Okay, you take this one, and I'll take the one over the hill, then we'll meet at the middle one."

"Good enough." Joe bent to go under the ribbon, and

Carl walked around the square, headed for the scene of the third murder.

Carl had no idea what he might be looking for. The department had gone over the area carefully. Still, there was the rosary he'd found earlier; it had been overlooked by the searchers. Like Joe, he had a gut feeling that there was something obvious that they still needed to search for.

When Carl reached the third sectioned-off area, he stood outside the yellow barrier and let his eyes scan the scene. He could see the flattened place where the body had lain; he remembered it well. He closed his mind to every thought except the discovery of something different or alien to its surroundings, but he couldn't see a thing. Only after he had looked the area over very carefully did he bend to get under the ribbon. He moved very slowly, not wanting to disturb anything that might lead him to the man who had used this pretty place in such a terrible way, but there was nothing to be found. He bent under the ribbon again and walked toward the center square. As he came up over the small grade, he could see Joe was already there.

"Find anything?" he asked as he came to stand beside Joe.

"Not a damn thing. How about you?"

"Nothing."

"Well, let's hope we're luckier here."

They didn't speak as they moved slowly about the small square, and after almost fifteen minutes, they were both prepared to give up the search.

"Looks like we ran out of luck again." Carl's voice was deliberately controlled.

"Yeah, looks that way. Well, it was just a hunch that didn't pay off. My men are good. They cleaned this place pretty thoroughly."

Carl waited for Joe beside the tree under which Paula's body had been found. He had both hands in his pockets and his shoulder braced against the tree while Joe finished moving about. Joe had to satisfy himself that no strings were left untied. Carl knew the feeling, so he said nothing until Joe stopped in the center of the square and turned to look at him.

"Well, that's that," Joe said disgustedly.

"We tried. Like you said, your boys are good."

"Don't console me; I'd rather have found something they missed. At least I'd have a lead."

Carl chuckled, and as he did he glanced down toward the roots of the tree. At first he thought it had just been his imagination, or the strong desire to find something. He stood very still and let his gaze move among the tangled roots. Joe could see where his eyes were directed, and he knelt down to look closer.

"What did you see?" Joe asked.

"I don't know. Something glittered like . . . look, there." He pointed to a narrow, grassy spot between two roots. Joe reached out a hand and gently threaded his fingers through the grass until they came across a small, round object. It was gold. As he lifted it, the sunlight caught it, and it sparkled momentarily.

"What is it?" Carl asked in a hopeful voice. Joe held the object on the flat of his palm and extended his hand so they could both look at it. It was a very tiny medal, the kind both men recognized—one that a Catholic child might be given at first communion.

"Another religious object—like the rosary."

"Someone lost it here, or left it on purpose. Like the notes."

Their eyes met over Joe's extended hand. In silence, they walked back to Joe's car.

* CHAPTER 27 *

The library had been exceptionally busy for a Friday and Beth was exhausted. She'd heard nothing from Carl and was annoyed that this bothered her. On top of her exhaustion and irritation, she had to shop for groceries on the way home and the checkout had seemed interminable. She hauled the four bags of groceries into the house one at a time, which added to her weariness, then spent half an hour putting them away.

She had left the library early—before four-thirty—and it was now past six. She wasn't really hungry, so she made a cup of tea and carried it with her to the living room. She snapped on the TV.

The news was on. The newscaster was discussing the third murder in Helton and suggesting that Joe was not capable of handling the case. This reflected on Carl, too, when the newscaster noted that a detective from Cambridge was here to help and didn't seem to be making much headway either.

A knock on her door made Beth jump, and when she opened it, Todd stood there.

"Todd?" She regained her composure quickly. "What's the matter—has the phone company gone out of business?"

"Sorry. I was really eager to see you. I called the library, but they said you had left early. Are you all right?"

"Certainly I'm all right."

"You look tired." He smiled warmly as if he could relieve any problems she had. "Tell you what. You kick back and relax. If you haven't started dinner already I'll cook, and you can just get yourself together for a comfortable evening."

"I don't think that's a very good idea, Todd."

He reached out to take her shoulders in both hands, and as he did, he moved around her. "Don't worry about a thing. You just relax. Old Todd is here. I'll mix you a drink and you can tell me about your day. I know just how you like your drinks." He moved across the room to her small bar. Beth was annoyed, but she closed the door and walked toward him. Todd looked innocent and charming, and from past experience, she knew he looked the most innocent when he was guilty of something.

"What's on your mind?"

"On my mind? Nothing. Why?" He chuckled and concentrated for a moment on the drink he was preparing them both. Then he carried hers to her. "I stopped by to talk to you last night," he said the words casually, "but you already had company."

"I told you I'd be busy."

"Yeah. When he left I went and had a little talk with

him." He said it as if he was amused, and Beth became very still, the anger rising so swiftly it threatened to choke her. She continued to look at him in utter disbelief, but he went on, unperturbed. "It was like facing Wyatt Earp in a shoot-out." She knew at once he was referring to Carl, and instead of the embarrassment he hoped she would show, her eyes clouded with anger.

"Have you taken to spying on me now? You don't have the right to do that, or don't you remember? And what are you talking about, Wyatt Earp and a shoot-out?"

"Well, he was making like a Texas Ranger, waving a gun under my nose and making threats about murder and mayhem."

Beth's anger was like a hard knot in the pit of her stomach. "If you hadn't been someplace you didn't belong, that wouldn't have happened. You just can't get the idea through your head that I can do as I please."

"You shouldn't make a fool of yourself. He's not exactly the kind you should be tangled with—or have you lowered your standards?"

Beth slammed her glass down on the coffee table and crossed the room to stand before Todd. She was angry enough now to be shaking. "I don't know where you get off thinking this is any of your business! It isn't, and I want you out of my affairs."

"Affairs is about right!"

"You condemn what I do? You weren't so tight with your own morals when we were married. It was anyone, anywhere. Don't walk in my house and preach to me! You don't have the slightest idea what you're talking about. You wouldn't know fidelity if you tripped and fell over it."

"I'll tell you what I do know."

"And just what is that?"

"I know all about your policeman friend. I've checked him out. Do you know he was tried for murdering two men? He damn near lost his badge for it. He was guilty as hell, and he couldn't take it, so he ran away to Cambridge."

"That's not your business either. If he had been guilty, he'd be in jail. You have no right to do this!"

"I'm worried about you. That man has an uncontrollable temper. You have no way of dealing with that. He waved a gun under my nose, and if you cross his path, he might do the same to you."

If Beth hadn't been so angry, she might have laughed at the thought of Carl waving a gun under her nose. But any amusement was gone at his next words.

"I'm afraid for you alone in this house, so you pack and I'll take you home with me. He wouldn't dare touch you there." Todd started toward the basement door. "Do you still keep your luggage in the basement? I'll get it, and you can pack. We'll be out of here in no time."

Beth was so furious she found it hard to breathe. Todd turned to face her, surprised when she didn't jump to obey what he thought was a very logical plan.

"Come on. That nut might come here at any time, and I want you safe with me before he gets a chance to do anything about it."

"Where do you get the unmitigated gall to go checking into Carl's past? You probably deserved having a gun pulled on you. I'm just surprised that some angry husband or boyfriend didn't do it a long time ago. As far as packing goes, I wouldn't stay one night with you if you were the last man on earth. If you even attempt to go down that basement after my luggage, I'll lock you in and call the exterminator!" Beth moved past him to the front door and threw it open. "Now, get the hell out of my sight. Do me the best favor you can do me—get out of my life and stay out of it!"

"Now, Beth, wait a minute. What I'm doing, I'm doing for your own good."

"Out!"

"Babe, please try to understand."

"I do—completely. Get out!"

Todd sighed as if she were an unreasonable child. He moved past her slowly and stepped outside. He turned to reprimand her again and tell her he would be ready to take care of her if she needed him, but the words never came. Beth slammed the door so hard between them that it rattled. She walked back into the living room, her eyes blazing and her face crimson with rage. She snatched the drink from the table and rushed to the kitchen to pour it down the sink.

"Knows just how I like it," she muttered as she set the

glass aside. "He's never known anything I like. Damn idiot!" She walked back into the living room. It was impossible to sit, so she paced. "Pack a suitcase and live with him! God! Checking out who comes and goes from my house!" The rage almost made her want to shriek. "My house! Fighting over me! They argue over me like I'm a piece of furniture or a prize of some sort. Ohh, I could kill them both!"

Her ranting and pacing was interrupted by the shrill ring of the phone. It was Carl! She knew it was! And she was too angry to hold a phone conversation. She reached out, took the phone from its cradle, and slammed it down as hard as she could, hoping perversely that the sharp crack hurt.

Carl jerked the phone from his ear and cursed before he gave it a surprised look.

"What's the matter?" Joe frowned at Carl's expression.

"She just slammed the receiver and damn near broke my eardrum. I have a feeling the lady is upset about something."

"Like what?"

"How would I know? She was fine last night. I think I better get over there and find out what's going on."

"Good luck." Joe chuckled as the door closed behind Carl.

Beth sat immobile when she heard the knock at her door. It must be Carl. She just could not bring herself to open the door for him. He knocked again. Forcing her voice under control, she called out sweetly, "Come in." She felt like a spider inviting a tasty fly to its web.

Carl walked in with a smile. "What's wrong with your phone? I tried to call, but I got disconnected. I thought you might want to go out to dinner, since it's Friday. We could . . ." He noticed her stony face and her brilliant, anger-filled eyes. "What's the matter, my nose on backwards?"

"No, but I would happily arrange for it to be."

"What's wrong, Beth?" he asked. He was prepared to be sympathetic, and she heard it. It was the straw that broke the camel's back.

"What's wrong, Beth?" she mimicked. "Am I everybody's baby? Is it the big policeman's job to be my keeper? Well, you're fired! I don't need a keeper, and I don't need someone to make my decisions for me!"

He gazed at her, somewhat in awe. Beth's anger startled him.

"Decisions? About going to a restaurant, for God's sake? We don't have to go anywhere—we could just eat at home."

"That's big of you."

"Now, dammit, what the hell's wrong with you? If you're fired up about something I've done, you could at least tell me what it is and let me defend myself."

"You're so much like him—funny I didn't notice it before. I guess it's a male attitude neither of you can control. You just have to be top honchos and give the orders."

"How would you like to back up a couple of steps and tell me what brought this on?"

She rose from her chair and walked to within inches of him. "Where do you get the nerve to start waving a gun at people and ordering them about?"

Carl smiled. Now he had a good idea of what had happened.

"You find it funny?"

"Kind of," he replied. "So, the little man was blabbing? I should have expected it. What did he do, run to mama? I can't picture you with him tied to your apron strings, Beth."

"Little man! You're like little boys fighting. Well, this is not an arena, and I'm not some kind of a prize for whoever is left standing!"

"Maybe if you just settle down I can tell you what really happened, instead of the crap he had obviously been handing you."

"You have the floor. Go ahead and explain."

"You're a tough jury, lady. Are you really ready to listen?"

"I'm listening."

"Well, first off, I'm sorry about what happened. Waving my gun under his nose was one of the dumbest things I've ever done, but the louse really deserved it."

"What happened?"

"He was running off at the mouth, and I'm afraid I lost my cool a little. The weasel was telling me to get lost—that you and he were getting back together. That's when I decided to run him off."

"Just like that?"

"Just like that. He was bragging that you and he were

going to take up where you left off. I kind of lost hold on the argument."

"Why?" she questioned quietly.

"Why? What do you mean, why?"

"Why should you be angry? You don't have any kind of claim, and you don't choose to make one, so why should it matter to you what he said?"

Her eyes held his, and the questions seemed to echo in the now very silent room. What she said was more truth than he had faced for a long time. Only this time, he found he didn't want to back away from it.

"All right, so it's confession you want. I care about you and what happens to you."

"You have an amazing way of showing it."

"You're something else—you know that!"

"Is that a compliment, by any chance?" She smiled for the first time since he'd come into the house.

"No, it's not a compliment." He scowled.

"Because I don't want somebody's good intentions making my decisions for me? I may not have all the answers for you—you don't have many yourself." She rose from the chair and walked to him. "Look, I don't know what this means to you, if it means anything at all, but I have no intention of making Todd a part of my life again. You and I are somewhere, Carl, but I don't know where. I'm telling you as honestly as possible how I feel. I guess the rest is up to you."

"I won't say that the news that you've finally cut yourself loose from him upsets me. If I'd known that last night, I would have punched his head in. I don't want you hurt, Beth, not by him or by me."

"There you go again." She tried to smile. "I'm not looking at the world through rose-colored glasses—not after Todd. And I'm not asking you for a happily-ever-after fairy tale."

"You're blind as a church mouse if you think I'm any kind of Prince Charming."

"Don't worry," she said adamantly. "I'm no Cinderella, either. But if I am in control of my life, I think you had a little to do with that. If you hadn't been around, I might have considered going back with Todd."

"I doubt that. Whether I was here or not, you were doing your own comparing and your own growing. You've just grown past him, that's all." He reached out a hand and brushed his fingers across her cheek. "So, where do we go from here, Beth?"

"Well, like you said, why don't we start back at square one? You can either take me out to dinner, or, if you're feeling very trusting, you can stay here and I'll whip up something. If you want, you could go for a bottle of wine. After dinner we could talk, maybe get to know each other a little better."

"Sounds good to me. I'll take the home-cooked meal. You just tell me what kind of wine you like, and I'll go get it."

"Oh, a good burgundy will do."

"Okay. Burgundy it is." Beth turned from him, but he caught her arm, and she raised her eyes to his again, questioningly. "Beth, you're damn special."

"Well, I'm glad to hear that note of appreciation. I thought you were going for wine."

"Are you sure you really want wine? I could get high on other things."

"Go get the wine. A little self-control is good for the system. I'll start dinner. I expect you back in twenty minutes."

"I'll make it ten."

She moved away from him to give him a light shove. "On your way. You're trying to weaken my resistance. I'm going to have you know I'm not so easy." Her voice was touched with humor, but beneath it the same old fears lingered. This was some kind of game. Carl played by his rules and she had to play by hers.

"Well, I am. If you put a little more effort into it, you'll find my resistance is not worth a dime."

"Nobody wants a pushover."

"Now she tells me."

"Go get the wine."

He shrugged into his coat and started for the door. "Ten minutes," he reminded, and was pleased with her laugh as he closed the door behind him.

Beth heard Carl's car pull out of the drive and walked into the kitchen slowly. Now that he was gone, she felt the uncertainty well in and weaken her resolve. She was the last person in the world to deliberately throw away any kind of emotional security. Now she was walking on a thread of a relationship with a foundation that was, to say the least, fragile. No promises, no commitments, no future, and no past—just today.

What bothered her the most were the dark secrets within Carl that had a death grip on him and she wondered which was going to prove stronger—the ghost of Sara Forrester, or the future she and Carl might be able to build. At that moment she was filled with a kind of despair. If Carl had not been able to let go of the past for all this time, how could she expect to reach in and change things?

Maybe it would be better to put an end to this tentative relationship before she got hurt, but she knew she couldn't. She had to find the answers—one way or the other.

Carl was as deep in thought as Beth as he drove toward town. Even though he had not actually lied to Beth, he was not as ready to commit himself as he had led her to believe. She was a woman of strong drives and deep sensuality, but he felt he was standing on the edge of an abyss—she on one side, and he on the other. He knew she was extending a hand to him, urging him to jump the distance between them, silently telling him that once he did he would be safe. All he needed to do was to take that final step, bridge that gap, and he would find what he needed. But he could not seem to draw his eyes from the yawning void below him. He was afraid to make that leap for fear their hands would miss, that his grip would slip, and he would fall into the unending depths.

He was being unfair to Beth, but he realized it was his own weakness that would not let him be fair. He needed her; he needed her belief in him, maybe because he had so little in himself. He needed her firm sense of self to help him recover his own self-esteem, and he needed just to know that she was there.

He bought the wine and headed back to Beth's house. When he arrived he knocked, and Beth let him in. He held up the two bottles of wine.

"I bought two, just in case."

"Just in case what?" she inquired with a laugh.

"Just in case you find my resistance too strong, and you're forced to ply me with wine."

"I thought you said your resistance wasn't worth a dime. I think it's mine you have in mind. You're about as hard to read as a Helton road map."

"You've got a suspicious mind." He followed her to the kitchen and set the two bottles down. "Something smells good."

"Well, help me fix a salad, and we'll have some dinner pretty quick."

* CHAPTER 28 *

Carl tipped the bottle and drained the last of the first bottle of wine into Beth's glass. He laughed lightly. "Well, it looks like we killed this one."

"You're sly. I think I drank two glasses to every one of yours."

He widened his eyes innocently. "Are you accusing me of trying to get you drunk? Me, an upstanding officer of the law? I'm devastated."

"I'll bet you are, but at the risk of destroying your little ploy, I must warn you that it will take more than one bottle of wine to do me in." She smiled amiably as she sipped the wine.

"You're a formidable lady, but," he grinned with obvious wicked intent, "I hope you remember I did bring another bottle."

"Umm, I can see I'm going to have to be very careful with you."

Carl relaxed back in his chair to drink the last of his glass of wine, then set the glass down and spoke very seriously. "Do you get the evening paper?"

"Sure, it's on the table inside the door. I always drop it there when I come in. Why, is there something special in it?"

"Special? No. I just thought I'd take off my shoes, get comfortable, and read the paper while you do the dishes and tidy up the kitchen."

"Oh you do, do you? Well, let me tell you the rules of this house. He who eats helps out with the dishes."

"I can't do that. I'm a dyed-in-the-wool chauvinist, or have you forgotten? Besides, do you know what would happen to my reputation as a tough cop if word were to get out that I'm doing dishes? Not to mention the fact that I'd get dishpan hands and probably not be able to draw my gun in case of emergency."

"I'd cry for you." She laughed as she rose and lifted her dish from the table. "But somehow, your little sob story just doesn't move me. C'mon. If you're a good boy, I'll save your dishpan hands. I'll wash, you dry."

He followed her, carrying his plate. He set the plate on the sink, and Beth tucked the large dishtowel into his belt.

"I was sure you'd draw the line at an apron. But if you want to know the truth, you're quite fetching in a dish towel."

Amid their aimless chatter over the dishes, both felt something slowly moving them beyond barriers and boundaries. Beth was a little breathless, as if she were treading on very fragile ground. Carl was just as insecure and somewhat disbelieving at what was developing, but more excited than he'd been in a long time. Beth was fun and relaxing, and this thought made Todd leap uninvited into his mind. Maybe he should have bounced Todd just a little harder. It would have given him immense satisfaction, but Carl wasn't too sure that wouldn't have swayed Beth toward Todd. The only thing he was certain of was that Todd could do nothing but harm Beth. That he was supplying protection without commitment was something he refused to recognize. Women's sympathies were easily aroused and as hard to stop as a jet plane, and Beth was vulnerable.

They finished the dishes, and Carl, with the second bottle of wine in hand, led the way into the now-dark living room. Beth snapped on a lamp in a far corner.

She brought two glasses with her and started back toward

Carl, who had set the bottle on the glass top of the coffee table. She could have sat beside him at the corner of the couch, but every instinct told her she might be stepping into a dangerous situation much too quickly. Instead, she sat on the floor close to his knee. Carl said nothing; he just reached for the bottle of wine, poured both glasses half full, and handed one to Beth.

"Well, here's to good food, good wine, and good company." He touched her glass with his.

"Thank you." She smiled up at him. Both sipped their wine, then set the glasses side by side on the table.

"Carl—this thing with Todd is over, and I'm grateful to you for being there, and for giving me back some, I don't know, self-esteem."

"Well, if I didn't get anything else out of coming back to Helton, at least there's one really bright point. I'm glad I was there. There are no buts, Beth." He had stepped back and both of them knew it. "And don't be grateful to me for something you would have done for yourself in time."

"You're sure of that?"

"You bet."

"Carl, what about you? What are you going to do?"

"Help Joe solve a murder, if I can."

"I didn't mean that. Not now—after."

"I know what you meant, but I don't know. Go on back to Cambridge, I guess."

"You can't stay here?"

"No, I don't think so."

"Why?"

"Because," he answered quietly, and his eyes held hers, "it just wouldn't be fair to you."

"I see." Her answer was just as quiet, but her eyes seemed like a brilliant flame. Abruptly, she got to her feet. "Damn you," her voice grated. "Who asked you to be fair!" She wanted to say so much more, but her thoughts refused to be verbalized. She turned from him and walked to the window. Clasping her arms about her, she listened to the silence behind her.

Carl set the glass he held on the table and walked across the room to stand behind her. What he could say was not what she wanted to hear, and what she wanted to hear was out of his reach. He brushed the tips of his fingers across her shoulder. "I'm sorry, Beth."

"Don't be," she replied without turning around. "No one asked you for sympathy, either. Whatever you're looking for, Carl, you're never going to find because you look everywhere except inside yourself, and that's where this cancer is eating at you."

"Beth, I . . ."

She turned around, and he was shaken to see tears in her eyes. "You'd better go, Carl, and I don't think you should come back."

There was no argument he could make, and the look in her eyes told him there was none that she would accept. A few minutes later she heard the door close softly.

She was numb for a long, quiet moment. Then, she sucked in her breath and released a choked sob. She sucked in her breath again, reaching for control.

She was fiercely and overwhelmingly alone, and she could feel Carl's absence like a huge void. She knew what she had done and said had been right for both of them, but it hurt so dreadfully. She couldn't remember anything that had left such a cold emptiness inside her.

Carl walked to his car with a measured tread, almost unaware. He got in, turned the key, and pulled the car out of the drive. Beth was right. Of course, she was right, and it was what he had to do, wasn't it? He didn't want the doubts to enter; he had no room for them. Through gritted teeth he cursed Joe, Phil, whoever the killer was, Sally, Helton, death, Sara, and finally, when he knew there was no truth in the others, he turned on himself. He was too scared to pull away the layers of guilt and anguish and expose the rawness beneath.

He drove aimlessly, too caught in his own thoughts to realize where he was going. Only when he realized he had turned down an old, familiar street did the reality hit him. He pulled to a stop in front of the house and sat looking at it for a while. Too well he remembered his last attempt, and yet he was already removing the key from his pocket.

It slid easily into the lock, and the door swung open.

There was enough moonlight for him to see by, but he didn't need it. He walked slowly to the bottom of the steps, then began to climb.

He paused only for a second at the bedroom door, then opened it. At first the ghosts were only a whisper, a sensation.

"Keep the good memories, Carl, and put away the bad ones until you can handle them." And the good memories were here.

He walked in slowly and sat down on the edge of the bed. He'd left his defenses outside, and now the first gentle touches of the sweeter memories came. Tears filled his eyes, and as they fell, sorrow washed away with them.

After Carl had gone, Beth paced the floor in misery. She had reached out to him, and he had pushed her away. His chains to the past were too strong for her to break. He was gone and she had closed the door between them. She knew there wasn't the kind of future there that she needed.

She had taken a leisurely bath, put on a nightgown and robe, and gone back into the living room to turn out the lights when she heard the sound of footsteps on her porch. Then someone was pounding on the door. Her heart stopped. Who would be knocking on her door at this time of night? All the terror that stalked Helton came to her mind. She didn't remember ever being so frightened. She walked to the door slowly.

"Who is it?"

"Beth?" It was Carl's voice, only different. She was really scared. Something must have happened. She opened the door and stepped back so Carl could enter. "Why did you come back here—now, tonight?"

"I was looking for something," he said quietly, as he took a step toward her. Again she backed away, afraid of what she only sensed. "I looked in all the corners and finally realized where I'd left it."

"It's crazy—you just . . ."

"I know—crazy that I was so blind that you had to send me away before I realized what I was giving up. Don't run, Beth," he said quietly. "I've stopped and I'd hate it if I couldn't stop you or find you again." The sound of his voice was so different that Beth still couldn't quite grasp the reason.

He took another step toward her and saw the first faint realization reach her. She blinked and still her eyes blurred. She found she couldn't talk because she was fighting a mixture of laughter and tears. Carl reached out and caught her to him.

"I thought . . ." her voice caught. "Oh, God, I . . ."

He crushed her to him. His mouth sought hers and he kissed her with all the need and passion that had been dammed up in him for so long. It was a hungry, wild, and heated kiss. She leaned into his body, her arms circling him, wanting as much as he.

"I need you, Beth," he whispered hoarsely, "I need you so bad."

She met him more than halfway, as she had wanted to do for so long. It seemed now that just to touch and to kiss would not be enough.

His hands found the belt to her robe and loosened it. He pushed it off her shoulders and let it fall. Feverishly, he moved his hands over her, trying to rid her of the nightgown. Suddenly, she was as desperate as he. In seconds his hands were hot on her bare flesh. She was panting full of heat that seemed to grow until she wanted to scream out her need for release.

No longer was it enough to touch, to kiss. The tide of passion was growing so fierce that neither could fight the need to let it lift and carry them.

Her hands now began to tug at his clothes. He helped her, tossing them aside. He groaned as he felt her hands move over him, singeing his flesh where they touched.

There was no time to find the perfect place; there was only need. He pulled her down to the softness of the carpet, wanting only to be embedded deep inside her, to feel her close about him and draw out the empty loneliness.

And it was that way. He could hear her cries as he possessed her fully and deeply. Their bodies glistened with sweat as a relentless force made them surge together over and over, until the sweet torment was at a peak. She wrapped her legs about him and moved with him to meet every thrust. The climax tore a cry from the depths of her; then his mouth took hers and he drank in the moans of her pleasure before he drowned in his own.

All was silent except for their panting. Long moments passed before either could reach for control.

"I didn't hurt you?" he whispered.

"No. I'm just shaking." She tried to laugh, but the sound caught in her throat. "Are you sure, Carl?"

"I've never been more sure. I was a fool, Beth, and I almost let you go." He kissed her gently, tasting her mouth as if for the first time. "It's a beginning. We need more than this and I guess it's time. You're like some kind of a healing power. I need you. I said that before, but it bears repeating. I guess I just didn't realize how badly I needed you." He felt a heavy constriction in his throat when Beth reached up, slid her hands into his hair, and drew his head down to hers. Her kiss was giving and cleansing; and when she ended it, he realized that possessing her once was never going to be enough. He had emptied himself of the blackness, and now he meant to fill himself with her until he overflowed.

Beth made no protest as he rose and drew her up beside him. They stood together in the semidark hall. He caressed her shoulders, letting his hands move over her as if they had to memorize her.

He smiled. "We'd be more comfortable in the bedroom?" he asked, waiting for her to let him know it was what she wanted.

"Yes, we would," she whispered. She watched the excitement and pleasure dance in his eyes.

He took her hand in his and pulled her close, lifting her from her feet as his arms circled her waist and drew her tight against him. She arched her back, pressing her body to his, conscious in a new and thrilling way of the difference of their bodies. Then he released her and took her hand, and they walked into the dimly lit bedroom.

They kissed again, exploring with mouths and fingertips the extent of this explosive thing that was sweeping them beyond control. He backed to the bed, drawing her with him, and they lay side by side. She was ready for him and he knew it, but he wanted to make the sweetness last as long as possible. He kissed, fondled and caressed her body, forcing the tension to grow until she tried to pull him to her to fill this boiling need. But he resisted until the stimulation of her hands, the pressure of her body, and her kisses told him that her urgency had become as unbearable as his.

He shifted his weight onto her, and suddenly he was inside, smooth and easy. One sensation after another rippled through her, drawing her upward to meet the force of his body. They were soaring in a storm of powerful sensation as they moved rhythmically together, transported beyond all but the feelings that flooded them and culminated in an explosion that was glorious and mind-draining.

When it was over he held her close, stroking her body with gentle hands. She closed her eyes and lay against him.

"I don't think I ever want to move again," she murmured, brushing her lips against his skin. "I thought it was good before, but this time was perfect."

"What we have here *is* perfect. I don't want to spoil it."

"How can you spoil it?"

"You deserve all the truth, Beth, and maybe I need to be able to say it."

"I know the facts as the newspaper reported them, but I want to hear, Carl." The last words were spoken quietly. "I don't want to be judge or jury. I just want . . ."

"What?"

"To be enough."

He smiled, kissed her, and drew her close to him.

* CHAPTER 29 *

Carl was slow to start his story, and Beth said nothing to disturb his thoughts. It was going to be hard to dredge up a past hurt he had spent three years running away from. But so much depended on this one thread that existed between them.

"Sara never wanted me to be a cop, from day one." He said this as if it were suddenly a new revelation to him. "She was always scared the phone would ring one day, and she'd get news she wouldn't be able to handle." Carl propped one elbow on the pillow and rested his head on his splayed fingers. His other hand lay on Beth's waist. "Sara used to love the beach, so we spent a lot of time there. We'd picnic, walk, or just lie around and get toasted. Lots of nights we built a fire and sat close, talking. That's where we were the night she died. That's where the Masone brothers decided to get their revenge. I'm usually pretty alert, but that night was kind of special. Sara had just told me she was carrying our child."

"Oh, Carl."

"Three months. We were celebrating and so damned happy. I'd drunk a little more than was good for me. I wasn't ready—not for what happened."

Beth waited in silence. There were no words to urge him on that would sound right.

"We'd spent the whole day at the beach, and we were lying beside the fire talking, making plans, just being together. I never heard the two of them come until they were on us. God, I don't think I'll ever forget the look in their eyes when they thought they had me helpless. They waved their guns around and made all kinds of threats. I was scared, and I don't think I'll ever forget that, either. I practically begged them to let Sara go, but they got nastier, said they were going to kill me, and taunted me with what they were going to do to Sara. I was going to jump them and Sara knew it. What happened next, happened fast. I started to move; they got edgy. Sara screamed and leaped between me and them. They shot, and the bullet slammed her into me. I could feel the blood on my hands, and from there on, I had very little control. I jumped the first of them, and got shot in the shoulder. I didn't even feel it. I must have hit him enough times because I broke his jaw and a couple of ribs. The other started to run, and I ran him down. I beat him, too. Then," his voice was a hollow echo, "I took their gun, and I shot both of them. I shot them the same way I'd shoot a rabid dog."

Beth sucked in her breath sharply. Carl sounded so cold and dead—he spoke of killing as if it were nothing.

"I'm sure you didn't mean..."

"I meant exactly what I did. They had deserved to die before that; but after what they did to Sara, I didn't care anymore."

"Carl..."

"Did I tell you it took almost twenty minutes for Sara to die? She died in my arms, crying over me and the baby that was dying with her. Someone must have heard the shots and called Joe. He came—too late to do Sara any good, and much too late to do me any good, either. I didn't really care anymore. I felt as if my world had exploded in front of my eyes and there was nothing left.

"The police had to take Sara out of my arms by force. I guess I was carrying on pretty bad, and I said a lot of things that were carried back to Phil, who had been trying to get my badge for years. He came to the hospital when I was conscious enough to talk, and he was madder than hell. It seems my buddy Joe and some of his men had closed ranks and were protecting my badge for me. They recreated a whole new scene. Phil didn't believe them. He put me on suspension, then had me arrested for murder. He meant to go all the way with it. He had a picture in his mind of what had really happened. He knew the gun wasn't mine, and the Masone boys were pretty battered. The trial was the Helton sensation of the day, and believe me, Phil threw everything at me, but I guess Joe had more friends than Phil did. They stood like a rock, and the jury came in with a not-guilty verdict. It might just as well have been guilty, because I've never been able to walk away from it. That's when the dreams started. They've never stopped since. Sara's there and it's the same." His voice was ragged. "Then I have to live through it again and again until I'm walking on a thin edge. I was responsible for the deaths of four people—two killers, the person I loved more than life itself, and a baby who never got to be born."

"You didn't kill your wife, Carl."

"Maybe my stubbornness was to blame. I wonder now if I could have done anything else with my life and been happy about it with Sara. But, no, I had to make her understand that I had to be a cop. If I'd used my head, maybe Sara would be alive today."

"No."

"No? Think about it, Beth."

"What if you were driving down the road, or if she were crossing a street? One can't fight fate. It could have happened some other way."

"Do you really believe that?"

"I certainly do."

"Maybe you're right, but you have to face the fact that I'm a cop who committed a deliberate and cold-blooded murder. And like I said, I'd do it again if I could. I've killed those vermin over and over again in my mind, only sometimes a little more slowly and painfully."

"Carl, you've been tried for it, and the jury knew what justice was when they let you go."

"They let me go, Beth, but don't you see, I couldn't let it go—and I couldn't get it to let go of me."

"You have to. Knowing your Sara from the things you've told me, I think that she wouldn't have wanted this—she wouldn't have wanted you to hurt like this. You're alive, Carl, and you have a life to live. I'm trying to understand. I don't suppose I'll ever know all you feel, but . . ."

"It's hard for anyone to understand. I guess Sally and Joe came the closest. Then . . . there was you."

"We could learn to understand together. I care about what happens to you, and I want you to be part of my life. You're not a quitter. You have been fighting this ever since you left Helton."

"You don't know what you're talking about."

"I have a feeling you've been having these dreams a long, long time." Her voice had grown quiet and she watched his face closely. His silence was an eloquent answer. Beth rose to her knees beside him. "I care," she said softly, "but I can't care alone. You've got to help me. You've just got to care enough to try. Wounds can't heal if you keep prodding them to stay open. Maybe it won't be easy, but if you want help, then let go and reach out. I'm here."

"I don't want to hurt you, Beth."

"What makes you think you will?"

"It could be a long, hard pull, and I'm not sure I'd be worth it. Because I need you so badly gives you no cause for helping me."

"Don't make judgments for me. I told you once, I make my own decisions."

"What if you're making a hell of a big mistake?"

"Then it's my mistake. I've made a few before, and life goes on. I guess it will go on again. I just happen to think it would be more fun if you were along."

Carl leaned forward and touched her lips with his—a quick and silencing kiss that lasted only a second.

"That's better," she murmured. The pressure of his hands grew firmer as he drew her back to him.

Her mouth was warm against his, and she invited the full intimacy of his kiss. When she felt his total immersion in it she drank him in, letting her tongue caress his and feeling him probe the deep recesses of her mouth. She became aware of many sensations at once—the heat of his body; the taste, smell, and feel of him. She allowed them all to surround and engulf her.

It was as if she were floating, weightless; her bones seemed to melt. Never had she been so vitally alive, with every sense awake to the pleasure of loving and giving.

He fitted her snugly against him while his hands caressed the curve of her back and the roundness of her hips, stimulating and arousing her need for even closer contact.

When he moved his lips from hers, he took her face between his hands and kissed her forehead, her eyes, and her cheeks before he returned to her mouth. She sighed, a soft moan of sheer pleasure as swirling heat sent electric sensations dancing along her nerves.

Breathing raggedly, she leaned back to look again into his eyes. "I think I'm in love with you, Carl."

"Does that scare you?"

"A little."

"I guess I've been carrying the shadows so long that maybe I'm a little afraid, too."

"You," she said gently, "are not afraid. You've been

alone, and I don't want you to be alone anymore. I'm ready to fight."

"You're ready to fight." He chuckled. She knew he was thinking about Todd. "It's just come to me that you've done a hell of a lot better with your ghosts than I have."

"It was easier. There wasn't this special thing between Todd and me like there was between Sara and you, or . . ."

"Or you and me?"

"I hope it grows into that. With Todd it was . . . well, it lacked substance. He was never really there for me. We only shared each other physically."

"He's a damn fool."

"He was a little boy who always wanted things his way, no matter what. He had a charm that could draw you close, but when you got there, it was like standing in quicksand." She bent toward him and kissed him. "With you it's like standing on solid rock."

He tightened his arms about her and pressed a kiss to the hollow of her throat. "Don't kid me. You were hurt, and I could kill him for that."

"But it really isn't the same. By contrast, what there was between Todd and me was so . . . so weak."

"Well, you're strong, lady," he said, "very strong. And I think we're going to try to put everything else where it belongs—outside of our lives. Let's just get a good hold on each other and forget everything else."

She didn't want to ask any more questions—not tonight. Everything was too new for them and much too delicate. Tomorrow, and maybe other tomorrows, would be time enough. "Yes," she replied softly, and wound herself into his arms to sleep.

Beth wakened abruptly and quietly looked at the iridescent figures on the clock. Four o'clock. She lay in the curve of Carl's body with one of his arms resting across her. It had never been better than it was between her and Carl. He was a considerate man, a special man, in many ways.

She slid quietly from the bed without disturbing him and pulled on a robe. Then she went to a chair near the window and curled into it to try to think. She remembered his stories of his nightmares and watched him. Now he slept quietly.

The thought that she had exorcised his demons excited her. She sat down beside him and watched him sleep, feeling warm with the remembrance of the night.

When Carl stirred, he threw his arm and bumped her, and she caught his hand, bolting him awake. He opened his eyes, alert immediately, surprised to find Beth sitting beside him and his hand held in hers.

"No nightmares?" she whispered.

His reality of this truth drew him completely awake. He shook his head in wonder. "No—no nightmares."

She squeezed his hand, and he caught her quick smile before he gave a tug and pulled her down on the bed beside him. She laughed softly as they tussled for a moment before she surrendered to his kiss, then curled against him again. They slept holding each other.

Carl opened his eyes to a brilliant morning. A deceptive sun, all light and no heat, brightened the room. The last thing he wanted to do was move, he felt so warm and comfortable. Beth lay curled against him, her head resting on his arm, her legs entwined with his, one arm across his middle. They must have been lying so for some time because his arm was asleep.

He tried to move gently to keep from disturbing her, but she stirred, and he instantly stilled. He wanted to hold her a while longer. He wanted to relive the unconditional passion they had shared, for he still found it hard to believe that Beth, so quiet and gentle, could explode in such wild abandonment. She gave everything of herself there was to give—every part of her.

Deep in his thoughts again, he didn't realize Beth was awake—and as deep in her thoughts as he. It took Beth a moment to realize Carl was awake. She smiled and ran her fingers lightly across his middle and down enough to get him to react. He chuckled softly.

"If you're proving a point, then you win. You're enough to raise the dead, and I'm far from dead."

She turned in the circle of his arms, and he winced as needle-sharp pain shot through his arm. She rose on an elbow quickly when an expression of pain crossed his face.

"What's wrong?"

"Nothing." He laughed. "My arm's asleep."

"Oh." She sat up and turned to face him. Carl folded his hands behind his head, and the appreciation danced warmly in his eyes as he let his gaze skim over the fullness of her naked breasts and the curve of her waist. She watched his face and felt suddenly warm, as if he had actually reached out and caressed her.

"So, what do you have planned for today?" she asked as she rested back on her elbow.

"I don't see anything wrong with what we're already doing."

"All day?" she said. "Not even you."

He pulled her into his arms, wrapping them about her and pulling her tight against him. "Try me. It's a challenge I'll try to rise to meet."

Squirming against him, she returned his laughter. "I can already feel you 'rising' to the occasion, but that's not what I had in mind."

"Yeah, well, against all my instincts, I'm afraid you're right. I have to go in to see Joe and find out what he's got."

"So, I'll see you later?" Beth said quietly.

"You can count on it. I'll call you and we can make some plans for tonight."

"I'll make some dinner if . . ."

"Nope. I'm taking you somewhere tonight. With all these gruesome problems going on, we haven't had much chance to have fun. It's about time."

"Great." She tried to move but his arms tightened. "Carl, we have to get up."

"Why?"

"Well, I've a hot shower in mind, and if you're real cooperative, you can wash my back."

"You have a way of making a point that's absolutely outstanding."

Carl released her slowly and watched her get up from the bed. He couldn't take his eyes off her, and she was well aware of his gaze. She walked to the door and turned to smile. "Coming?"

He kicked the covers aside and got up from the bed, but

waited, giving her a little time, then went to the bathroom. The door to the shower was already steamed, and he could see her outline through the door.

Beth let the warm water wash over her, and she smiled as she heard Carl moving about the bathroom. She wondered how it would be to share every day with him. It was a shaky thought, and she was scared for a moment. Her first marriage had been such a disaster that she felt insecurity flood her. That was the moment Carl slid the door open and stepped inside. They faced each other, and in one quick glance Carl knew and understood what she was thinking. He realized the damage Todd had done, and for a few brief seconds hated him with a very live passion.

"I thought you told me not to reach out with one hand and draw back with the other," he reminded her.

"Was I doing that?"

He rested his hands lightly on her shoulders and bent forward to touch her soft, wet mouth. "Don't, Beth—don't let go now. You're a hell of a lot stronger than that. Besides," he smiled tentatively as his hands moved down her arms to her waist, "I need you to hold my hand, remember."

She smiled up at him. Rivulets of water made her skin look like satin. "You want me to hold your hand right now?"

"Later." His voice was thick with emotions that made more words unnecessary. "For the moment, I need both hands." He slid them up her ribs and cupped her breasts as he bent to kiss her. A tremor surged inside her, and she moved into his arms. Her hands pressed against his chest, then slid up over his shoulders to circle his neck. Suddenly they were clinging and laughing, then kissing furiously again and again as passion surged between them. He reached to cup her buttocks and lift her. With her eyes closed she clung to him, circling him with her legs and feeling herself impaled on his rock-hard shaft. Strong hands moved her body up and down. She tossed her head back and allowed all sensations to be tasted. The climax was incredible. She cried out once, then became still in his arms. They stood so for a moment, letting the soothing water calm their trembling bodies.

Slowly he withdrew from her and let her feet touch the

floor. Gently he began to soap her body, starting at her shoulders and working his way down. Then, she did the same for him. They shut off the shower and reached for towels to dry each other.

"Hungry?" he asked as she pulled on her robe. "I'll make some coffee while you dress." With his arm about her waist, they walked back to the bedroom. At the door, he turned her into his arms. "You all right?"

"I've never been better. Carl, holding hands with you is quite an experience."

He laughed, bent to kiss her, then turned her around again. "Wait 'til we get to bigger and better things."

"Braggart." She walked into the bedroom, listening with pleasure to his laughter as he walked to the kitchen.

Carl had coffee made and was sipping a cup when she came in. He filled another cup and handed it to her.

"Umm, good."

"Of course." He grinned. "I supply the best of everything."

"You have a one-track mind."

"But it's such an exciting track."

"Go get dressed. I'll whip up some breakfast. Want your eggs over easy?"

"Any way. I'm hungry enough to eat sawdust."

"Well, I think I can do better than that." She began to move about the kitchen. Then, after a few minutes, she turned and saw him still standing in the doorway, watching her. She smiled. "So, get dressed. I don't want all my good food to get cold. Why are you still here?"

"Just trying to figure out how I got so damn lucky."

"You might not feel so lucky when you find out how temperamental this chef can be. Go get dressed."

He nodded, paused another minute, then left the doorway. Beth watched him walk away, and for a minute, she felt a touch of the old fear. Was she enough for Carl—and was she making another mistake trying to be?

She went back to breakfast preparations, deliberately pushing every thought from her mind other than the necessary procedure to cook the meal.

After a while, Carl came back into the room with a puzzled frown on his face.

"What's wrong?"

"I was just thinking about something you said."

"Me? What did I say that bothers you?"

"You said I had a one-track mind."

"Why should that bother you?" She pulled her lips to a half smile. "It's an obvious fact. I can vouch for it." She expected a smile or a flip remark, and got neither. "Carl?"

"I just wonder if that doesn't apply to this maniac that's running loose."

"I don't understand."

"Maybe I've followed everybody's example and put my suspicions where everyone else's are. Bad way for a cop to work."

"I still don't understand."

"I'm concentrating on men who just might not be guilty, while whoever is is getting a big laugh out of it."

"What are you going to do?"

"I think I'll go to Joe's office and use the computer."

"For what?"

"To look into somebody's past."

"Whose?"

"I don't know."

"If you don't know, how are you going to look?"

"Start with a list of names."

"And go through every one?"

"Yep, one at a time."

"Until you find what?"

"Again, I don't know."

"Sounds like a pretty weak lead."

"It's not a lead at all—just a hunch, I guess you'd call it. I have a feeling I've screwed up by overlooking someone who's right under my nose."

"Well, eat. The computer can wait a little longer."

They sat across the table from each other, but Carl's mind had seized upon an idea, and Beth could see he was engrossed in it.

"All right, get going." Beth shook her head as she rose to clear the dishes. "You don't even have to help with the dishes. I said you have a one-track mind, and now you've got it on something else."

He came up behind her as she stood at the sink and put his arms around her. Then he nuzzled her shoulder. "I'm sorry, Beth, it's just that . . ."

She turned to face him, the smile gone. "I know, and I want you to catch him as badly as you do. Go ahead and go, and I hope you find something."

"Thanks." His eyes smiled, even if he didn't.

"Don't thank me; it's a selfish move. I want your full attention when you're here."

"I'll leave the station early and change clothes. I'll pick you up about seven, and we can go out on the town. I'll make up for this, and believe me, you'll have my full attention." She nodded, and he kissed her lightly, his mind already on what he would be searching for.

Carl left Beth's house and was seated behind the wheel of his car before it struck him that he had just said to Beth what he had said to Sara so many times—"I'll make up for lost time, lost touches." He knew that never happened. As he drove toward the station, he tried to piece his feelings together. He didn't want to see in Beth's eyes what he had too often seen in Sara's—that terrible dread that one day he would leave and not come back. For the first time since Sara's death, he began to make himself promises.

* CHAPTER 30 *

"Morning." Carl closed the door and shoved his hands into his pockets.

Joe looked up from the papers on his desk. "Some morning—it's past ten-thirty."

"It's also Saturday. What's bugging you?"

"Ah," Joe said disgustedly as he pushed the papers aside. "A little frustration, that's all. What are you doing here today?" Joe rested his elbows on the desk and bent forward.

"I want to nose into people's pasts with your computers."

"I thought we did that once. Who are you looking for?"

"I don't know. I'll start with Jake Magee and Larry Jackson, then go on to David Mondale. We didn't look at them deeply or inclusively enough."

"What are you getting at?"

"Beth just told me I have a one-track mind. Maybe we're so cocksure the killer is one of our three suspects that we aren't looking where we should be. After we start with Magee, I'll add everyone that Martha or the other two had any kind of relationship with—even just a friendship."

"David has an alibi that's as good as gold. Mrs. Lowrey never told a lie in her life."

"So humor me. Let's dig up his past anyway and have a look. Can't do any harm to tie up all the loose ends. Suppose you get on the horn to Father McAllen, and I'll go see what the computer has to offer."

"Good enough." Joe was already reaching for the phone as Carl left the room.

Carl pulled a chair up close to the computer and began to chase letters across the keyboard, watching the screen intently. He had laid an open notebook and pen beside him and occasionally made a note. His frown grew deeper as he tried to find information on David Mondale. He threw questions at the computer from all directions and came up with the same answer every time. David had a perfect record for the two years he had lived in Helton, but as far as the computer was concerned, he didn't exist before then. Carl tried to remember what David had said. He had come from Bridgefield for the teaching job. He had lived with his aunt and uncle—what were their names? Robert and Caroline something—he'd have to find out again. Nobody had a blank for the first twenty-five or thirty years of his life. It was worth looking into.

Carl shut the computer down and leaned back in his chair just as Joe came in.

"So, what did you find out?" Carl turned to look at Joe, then filled him in.

Joe shook his head. "Father McAllen said he had good records and a reference from a priest friend in Bridgefield, so he hired him on that."

"Maybe it deserves a little more looking into." Carl stood and stretched. "I think I'm going to call on David Mondale and then shoot over and talk to Ellen. From what I hear, they were a pretty steady thing, and they went to Paul's party together."

When Carl left the station, he drove straight to Emma's. He had gotten out and started toward the house when he heard his name called from down the street. He turned to see David jogging toward him. When he stopped beside Carl, David was smiling and breathing heavily. He could have been an advertisement for jogging suits, Carl thought, irritated that David even looked good when he was sweating.

"Morning, Carl. Paying Mrs. Lowrey another visit? She'll be pleased. You're about all she talks about lately."

"Actually, I came over to see you."

"Me? What for?"

"Couple of questions."

"Shoot."

"You were born in Bridgefield?"

"Yep."

"Lived with your aunt and uncle after your parents died when you were five. What was their last name?"

"What's this got to do with what's going on here in Helton?"

"Tying up loose ends." Carl grinned. "From the blank file on you, you could have been born two years ago."

"My past is none of anybody's business. What are you doing poking into it, anyhow?"

"Got something to hide?" Carl asked mildly.

"No! But you don't have a right to poke into my affairs. Am I a suspect?"

"Not at this moment."

"What does that mean?"

"It means," Carl said firmly, "that in a murder, any thread you pick up can be the one that leads you to some answers. If you have nothing to hide, then you've got nothing to worry about."

"I don't have anything to be afraid of. You know damn well where I was when Martha was murdered."

"So, what is your aunt and uncle's last name?"

"Rossman." David's eyes were brilliant.

"Address?"

"It's four-oh-seven East Hartman," David replied. "Leave them alone—they're old, and they have nothing to do with this."

"Thanks. Is Emma home?"

"No, she's gone shopping."

"Oh, well, tell her I was around, and I'll try to get over to see her in a day or so."

"I'll do that."

Carl turned away from David and walked back to his car, but he could feel David's penetrating gaze follow him. He drove away, toward the next name on his list—Ellen Knight.

Ellen was striking. Taken separately, her features were not perfect. Her nose was a trifle too long, the eyes too deep-set, and the mouth much too full and wide. Yet assembled, she was beautiful. Her auburn hair was cut short and blunt and swung free, and she was athletically slim. Right now her eyes were full of both recognition and questions.

"Hello, Ellen. I don't know if you know who I am, but . . ."

"You're the detective who's helping Joe with these terrible murders."

"Right." He smiled his warmest smile. "Do you mind if I ask you a few questions?"

"I don't know how much help I can be, but come in. You can ask anything you like, and I'll do my best."

"Good enough." He was relieved to find one cooperative person. "Ellen, you were at that party Paul Carterson held before Martha's death, weren't you?"

"Yes, I was."

"What can you tell me about the situation between Martha and Paul?"

"Martha and Paul? There was no situation there. Paul is in love with Amy, and Martha was just as involved with Michael. There wasn't anything between Martha and Paul except a lot of gossip."

"You don't believe any of the gossip?"

"Definitely not. I know all four much too well. They were matched with the right people."

"And yet," Carl said gently, "I'm sure news travels fast

here. You must already know Martha was pregnant, and evidence shows Paul Carterson was the father."

Ellen nodded and for a moment, she was silent. Then she smiled. "I'll not say anything about it until I talk to Paul. I don't believe Paul would look at anyone but Amy."

"Just like you and David?"

"What?"

"A close couple, like you and David."

"David and I can't be considered a close couple. In fact Paul's party was the last time David and I were together."

"You had a fight?"

"No, we sort of just agreed to part. We're still friends, and I guess I'd date him, but it's not serious. It was better to work it this way while we could still be friends."

"Ellen, I'm afraid I have to have some more answers. I know this won't sound important to you, but trust me, it is."

"What do you want to know?"

"Why you broke off with David."

"I didn't actually break off. It's kind of hard to explain. David is really a nice person, and for a while, I was flattered that he wanted to go out with me. But I realized we were too different to get along. He's a perfectionist." She laughed. "And I'm kind of a slob. He wants everything right—you know, how you dress and act. He was kind of straitlaced, too. If I drank two drinks he got huffy, and if I danced with anyone but him he got mad. All these things were small, but they piled up. I just thought it was best to cut it off. He understood how unsuited we were, and we never argued over the split. I like David. We're still friends."

"How did David take it?"

"He said maybe it was for the best, too. David's really a wonderful person, and he's great with the kids at school. I guess it's just that he and I could never make it unless one of us changed a lot, and neither of us wanted to do that."

Carl had been making notes, and when she finished, he closed his notebook and replaced it in his pocket.

"Well, thanks, Ellen. I may be around to talk to you again. Is that all right?"

"Fine—any time."

Carl returned to Joe's office to find him getting ready to leave.

"Find anything new?" he inquired.

"Nope. Psychologist says if Paul had any traumatic experiences when he was a child, either he's a good poker player or it didn't leave any mental marks on him. Brodie's past is kind of on the ugly side, with a whole lot of problems with religion. It seems he had a couple of religious fanatics for parents, but he ran away from home when he was about thirteen. He was caught and put in one foster home after another, then he got too old for help. He fell through the cracks and got lost. Society treated him pretty crappy."

"What about Father McAllen?"

"I've got a whole lot of lines open and busy. We'll know all about him by tomorrow. What did you find out about David Mondale?"

"He got a little upset when I asked about his past. Still, he didn't give me much of a battle about supplying the names of his aunt and uncle."

"And Ellen?"

"Well, there are a few things to look into there. From what she tells me, she and David broke it off the night of Paul's party."

"How'd David take that?"

"Like a Boy Scout."

"That doesn't give us much to go on."

"Joe, I'd like you to put a hold on things until Monday."

"What for?"

"I'm going to take a ride up to Bridgefield and talk to David's relatives. I think it's important we know about him."

"He's still got Emma for an alibi. I don't think we can break that."

"I'll cross that bridge later. Right now, we need information."

"Okay, we'll let it hang until you get back, but make it fast."

"I'll be back by Monday morning."

"Carl."

"What?"

"If anything happens between now and then, I'm going

to haul those three in. I can't do anything less, or Phil is going to jump in with both feet."

"Well, I guess we better pray our killer takes the weekend off."

"Yeah—pray."

"I'll make it fast. I'm leaving right after I take a pretty lady to dinner."

"Sounds like you two are hitting it off."

"Well, we're takin' it a day at a time."

"Best news I've heard since this damn thing began."

"Joe, wipe that satisfied grin off your face. There's no cause for celebration."

"Yeah." Joe's grin grew broader. "Have a nice trip to Bridgefield."

Carl sighed disgustedly and left, ignoring the wide smile that now split Joe's face.

He drove to Beth's house, and when he turned down her street, he could see a car in her driveway. Now he smiled. He figured Todd was paying his last visit to Beth.

* CHAPTER 31 *

Amy pulled open the freezer compartment of her refrigerator, removed a carton of chocolate ice cream, and carried it and a spoon to the living room. On the way she passed a large hall mirror, and stopped and stared at the reflection that faced her. She looked tired because of the sleepless nights, and she wore the same sweat suit she had worn for three days. Her disheveled hair framed her face wildly. At that moment she hated herself, and hated Paul even more for having the ability to affect her like this.

She drifted on into the living room and threw herself down on the corner of the couch. She had been living on junk food. Candy wrappers and an empty bag of potato chips gave mute evidence to this.

Saturday morning cartoons filled the room with raucous sounds. She had them on because she desperately needed something to keep her from breaking down and crying. She had to laugh, or she would be lost in a well of black thoughts.

As she scooped out a spoonful of ice cream and put it in her mouth, a knock sounded at the door. At first she was going to ignore it; then she thought, what's the difference? She could get rid of whoever it was. She laughed to herself. One look at her should do it.

She rose and walked barefoot across the carpet to the door. When she opened it, Paul stood looking at her in open-mouthed amazement.

"Well, well." She chuckled mirthlessly. "If it isn't Helton's Romeo. Don't stand on ceremony, come on in." She turned and walked away, leaving Paul to follow her or not, whichever he chose.

Again she plunked herself down on the couch and drew her knees up until she sat cross-legged. She returned her attention to the ice cream and the television.

Paul closed the door and followed her into the living room, stunned again by the condition of the room itself. Amy had always been an immaculate housekeeper and very particular about herself. Now, it seemed, she just didn't care. The touch of guilt made him run his hand through his hair nervously and lick his dry lips before he started to speak.

"Amy, I want to talk to you," he began.

"Really?" she replied nonchalantly, not bothering to look in his direction. "Get a dish. You can have some ice cream. Sorry, no pretzels or chips left."

"I don't want any ice cream."

"Suit yourself." She shrugged, and took another bite of ice cream.

"Amy, what the hell's going on around here? You don't ever eat junk like this. The place is a mess . . . and cartoons, for God's sake. What are you trying to do?"

"What I do," she said casually, "is none of your business. If you don't like it here, shove off. Nobody's going to miss you."

Paul ignored this. "I went down to the track this morning. I thought I'd find you running. They told me you hadn't been there for three days."

"I thought it was time to break my routine. One has to get rid of old habits. I started with you and just got carried away."

"Amy, I want to explain . . ."

"Wait!" she interrupted deliberately. "This is where Wile E. Coyote almost catches the Road Runner. I'm learning a lot from that bugger. The next time a coyote tries to grab me, I'll just shout 'beep, beep' and take off."

Paul brushed a pile of magazines off the couch and sat down, but Amy refused to turn her attention to him. A commercial came on advertising Barbie dolls, and he began to lose his control as Amy professed avid interest.

"I could go out and buy you one of those," he said.

Her mouth was full of ice cream and her eyes remained on the TV. "If you want to be a smart ass you can leave right now. I don't recall inviting you to interrupt my program."

"Amy, for God's sake, stop this! Talk to me!"

"Why? What on earth could you have to say to me? Go out and bark at the moon somewhere else. At this point, I don't give a damn about you or what you want to talk about."

"Amy, you have every right to be angry."

"Thanks. I assure you, that makes me feel better," she said dryly.

"But you've tried and sentenced me without giving me a chance to say anything in defense."

"Defense!" She laughed. "I'd like to hear that. It would probably make a fine novel—maybe even get you a Pulitzer prize! If anyone deserves it for the best piece of fiction, you do."

"Will you just listen?" He was nearly shouting, although he knew this was not going to gain him any ground with Amy. "Look, Amy, I love you."

"Sure," she replied derisively. "Me, Martha, and God knows how many more. Artists have always had reputations as great lovers, and you're sure trying to live up to it." She finally turned to look at him, but her smile was chilling. "I'll bet I know." She snapped her fingers. "You came by for a testimonial for your next victim. I could tell her you're damn good in bed, but you leave a lot to be desired in other fields."

"Just hear me out," he said through gritted teeth.

"I'm listening."

"Yes, but you're not hearing."

"Paul, I've got things to do. I'm very busy, so if you'd just go, I'd be pleased."

"Busy doing what?" he demanded.

"Well, let me see. First I'm going to finish this ice cream. Then I'm going to watch Pee-wee Herman, and this afternoon there's a great fantasy on. Not as good as you can create, but pretty good. So, you can see, I have a full day. Why don't you shove off?"

"That's the easy way, isn't it? Just walk away as if we never meant anything to each other. It looks to me like it's going to be pretty easy for you, but it's not that easy for me."

"You say all this has been easy for me?" Now Amy's voice rose. "I stood up for you when everyone else had doubts. I lied for you! I told them you spent the night with me when Martha was killed. You're the one who walked away. You walked away from me the day you made Martha Dexter pregnant! You let me believe—God," she gasped, fighting tears, "I wanted to be the one to have your children. I told you that, and you swore there was nothing like that between you and Martha. That kind of lie is too much!"

"Amy . . ."

"No, Paul. Get out. I can't take this anymore. I can't look at you without seeing the two of you together. Please just go away."

"I also told you it was not the way you think it was."

"I need time to get myself together. I don't know right now just what I think. I'm mixed up and confused, and until I find my way, I don't want to see you again."

"You don't mean that! You're hurt, and you're angry, and I don't blame you. But for God's sake, Amy, don't throw both of our lives away like this. Whatever else you believe, I do love you, and I will go on loving you, no matter what. And whether you want to listen or not, I'm going to tell you how it was with Martha. I hadn't seen her since I got back to Helton. I was too involved with you and my painting. My whole life was just that—you and my painting. I met Martha on the street one day, and we patched up old differences. She wanted to be friends, and I could see she meant it. I saw her a few more times, and then I asked her to pose for the painting. There was never any more than that between us.

"After a while, I could see she was unhappy and I asked her why. Then she told me about Michael—how much she loved him, but how he was kind of a renegade. She was trying to change him, and she wanted me and Father McAllen to help. I guess Michael got pretty rough with her a few times, and she was really miserable. *She really loved him*. The night she came to me . . . well, I was alone and painting. You'd gone to that conference, remember? It was a stormy night, and I guess I had a drink or two. She had had a hell of a fight with Michael. She was crying and really upset so I told her to come in, and she had a drink. I don't know how it really happened. She was frightened and lonely, and I was feeling lonely, too. We had too many drinks, and one thing led to another. She regretted it, and so did I. We promised each other we'd never say anything about it to anyone, ever. Nothing ever happened again—neither of us wanted it to or even thought of it. Amy, it wasn't any kind of love; it was comfort. Can't you try to understand that? I never cheated on you again. I never wanted to. Amy, try and forgive it . . . and someday forget it."

"I'm sorry," Amy said quietly, "but right now, your words just aren't good enough. I need to be alone, and I need to figure out just what I do believe. Please go, Paul—please leave me alone."

Paul sighed. He couldn't reach her. He was scared that he would never be able to again, and the thought panicked him. He walked from the room and on outside, then closed the door behind him and stood on the porch. For a moment, he contemplated going back in and forcing her to listen. Then he heard the lock click sharply.

Amy stood with her hands pressed against the door for several minutes, then turned and walked into the living room. She picked up the ice cream and spoon and sat down on the couch. She was facing the TV again, but her eyes were blurred with the tears that ran down her cheeks. She didn't even realize she was crying until she reached to brush her hand across her eyes so she could clear away the blurriness. Her hand came away wet and she looked at it in shock. She was not going to cry; she was going to think logically. He was not worth crying over. She was determined. As if she were moving in slow motion, she set the ice cream on the floor. Then she drew her arms about herself, as if she were suddenly disintegrating into little pieces. The first ragged sob tore at her, followed by the next and the next. Then, she fell against the couch cushions and cried bitterly until she was left with dry, choking heaves and no more tears. It seemed she had to wash all kind of pictures and words from her mind before she could force new ones in.

She had supported Paul in every way, as a woman in love would support a man she thought innocent of what he was accused. She had faced all their questions with control, and justified all she'd done and said with the shield of Paul's love—his promise that he loved her and only her.

Carl knew she was lying. She had looked into his eyes and seen the disbelief dance there, but she'd lied anyway and dared him to call her a liar.

She had told them Paul had been with her all that night, but he hadn't. And through everything, Paul had never once told her where he had been. She had never doubted him, had never believed that Paul was able to kill anyone. But she was shaken by a thought she didn't want to face. Was he guilty?

She sat up and brushed the tears from her cheeks. She should go to Carl and tell him Paul had not been with her until nearly one in the morning. But what if Paul was not guilty? He would never be able to prove his innocence after that. No one would believe anything either of them said, and innocent or not, Paul would be labeled a murderer. She had to make a decision, and once she did, it had to be final, because it was a matter of life and death—both Paul's and hers.

Paul left Amy and drove aimlessly for a while. He didn't have any place to go. When he had been accused of murder he had felt a lot of terrible things, but nothing could compare with the aching void that Amy's distrust and pain had left behind. This was something he was not prepared to handle. Finally, he turned his car toward home. Maybe Amy would think about what he had said and call him. He pulled in the drive, parked, and made his way to the house. Once inside he threw his jacket across a chair and walked across the wide living room to the huge window, then slowly turned and faced the portrait of Amy. Every line, every stroke of color, was etched in his memory. He wondered if he'd really be able to paint like this again if Amy never returned to his life. He couldn't stand it! He couldn't stand here inactive and helpless! He had to do something. He grabbed up his jacket and left.

Michael had spent most of Friday night in a state of total oblivion, and on Saturday he awoke with a fuzzy mouth and a throbbing head. He staggered into the bathroom and did what he could to pull himself back together.

He returned to the living room and threw himself on the couch. He had never felt so lost in his life. The more he thought of Martha being pregnant with Paul Carterson's child, the angrier he got. It swelled within him like a huge tidal wave. The thought of Martha lying with Paul, making love to him, enraged him.

Pushing Paul from his mind only brought Father McAllen to the surface.

"Always the do-gooders," he muttered, "pushing and shoving, telling you they have all the answers." He stood up from the couch and began to pace like a caged animal. His whole body was taut. Like a rubber band drawn to its full extension, he was ready to snap, to rebound and send his destructive impulses flying.

"She loved you, Michael," he muttered, repeating Father McAllen's words. "How much did she tell that sanctimonious papist? What made him think he had the answers? Nobody had the answers for Michael Brodie, and especially not a priest!"

He stopped pacing near the doorway between the kitchen and living room. In a sudden and vicious display of the pent-up fury within him, he doubled his fist and struck the door frame again and again, until he could feel the blood on his knuckles. His whole arm throbbed with the ache of reaction. Then he leaned against the door panting and closed his eyes.

Worse than the vision of Paul and Martha together was that of Martha and this priest. He could see their heads bent together, laughing and talking about him. Well, no priest was going to tell him how to live his life. He had walked away from that a long time ago. Even though Martha had tried to draw him back, it was useless. Now she was dead, and there would be no more questions about it. He hated the fact that when Martha found herself in trouble, she had turned to that priest instead of to him. What had he said? That 'it was an accident—a one-time thing of need, not of love.' Michael didn't understand the difference. She had still slept with Paul and had still gotten pregnant with his child. What the hell did Paul Carterson understand that he wouldn't have? Michael made a soft groaning sound, as if the battering thoughts were too much for him to stand.

Again Father McAllen's words pounded in his head. "You have to believe in something, Michael. You've got to stop living this ugliness." What did a priest know about ugliness, with his quiet church and candlelight? Michael could tell him enough about ugliness to shatter his equilibrium. He could tell him—but what was the use? He would still hear the same platitudes, the same chant of dogma that meant nothing to him anymore.

He walked to the door and opened it to stand in the doorway, letting the crisp, cool air help sweep some of the tangled cobwebs from his mind.

He looked at his watch. It was nearly four. He knew he had drunk most of the night, but hadn't realized he had slept almost all day.

It would be dark soon, and he would have to face that same barren loneliness again. The thought of it made him sick, and he fought the wave of nausea that struck him so often.

With deliberate steps he walked back into the house to get his jacket and helmet. Then he pulled the door closed behind him, half ran down the steps, and straddled his cycle. It roared to life, and he rode away from the house and its memories.

* * *

Patric sighed and leaned back in his chair. He squeezed the bridge of his nose between thumb and forefinger and closed his eyes. He was tired, and he was frustrated more with himself than anyone else. For Martha's sake he had wanted to reach Michael somehow. It was a terrible thing that three young lives had been snuffed out. Three girls with promising futures had died so brutally, but Michael was killing himself.

He wondered about God's ways. Maybe, somehow, Martha had paid for the mistake she'd made. There was always some form of retribution that struck when anyone broke away from God's plan for life. He inhaled deeply and was about to stand up when the phone on his desk rang. He muttered what he hoped would be a beneficial prayer as he heard the phone being picked up by his young assistant, Father James, in the next room.

It was after ten o'clock and Patric was hungry for his usual late night snack; but he knew from the brief conversation he overhead that the call was for him, even though Father James was trying to put the caller off.

He walked to the door of the outer office.

"I'll take it, James," he called out.

Father James pressed his lips together in exasperation. It seemed to him the people of this town truly didn't believe Father McAllen needed to eat or sleep. Look at the time! Ten o'clock. They called him at any hour, and Father McAllen always took the calls, even when he was close to exhaustion.

Father McAllen walked back into his office and picked up his phone as he sat back down in his chair.

"Hello?" He listened intently for a minute or so. "Well, yes, I know about how he feels." He listened again, the frown marks growing deeper between his eyes. "It's pretty late. How about if I come over first thing in the morning and . . . What? Yes, I'm sure it's important. I talked to him not too long ago."

"All right, listen, I'll slip into the kitchen and grab a quick bite. You hang on to him if you have to tie him up. I'll tell Father James to take over for me. I'll be there to meet you in just over an hour, all right?" He hung up the phone and walked to the door.

"Don't you think some of these people could bring their

troubles to you at a decent hour and give you a minute or so to call your own? You're exhausted."

"My help's needed," Father McAllen said quietly. "It's the one sheep gone astray. I'll leave you here to take care of the other ninety-nine. What would the Lord say if we let the lion eat the lamb because we were too tired to go and see to its care?"

"You're right, as usual," Father James grinned, "but there are times when I'll bet the shepherd would like to use his staff like a club and do a little pounding on both lamb and lion."

"Don't tempt me. Violence is just under the surface with us all. I almost lost control with a lamb yesterday, and I don't intend to do that again. I'll be back soon."

"I'll bet." Father James laughed. Father McAllen responded to his laugh with a wry smile, waved a jaunty salute, and left Father James pressing his lips together and shaking his head.

* CHAPTER 32 *

Todd pulled up in Beth's driveway and walked to the front door.

Beth heard the car pull up. Certain it was Carl, she didn't take the time to look, but ran to the door and pulled it open.

"You're late. What . . . ?"

"You look all pretty and excited. How about inviting me in?"

"What are you doing here?"

"I have to talk to you, Beth. I deserve at least a chance to apologize." He managed his best abused-little-boy look. "Let me come in and try to explain why I got so upset."

"I don't think so, Todd." Beth's voice was firmer than he had ever heard it before. "There's no future for us. I've already made my plans and they don't include you."

"But they include Carl Forrester?"

"That's none of your business, but yes, they do."

Todd knew whatever was growing between Beth and Carl couldn't be too stable yet. He had to destroy it and he had to have Beth back in the place he'd always had her. In the palm of his hand. He couldn't recognize defeat when he saw it in her eyes. He had manipulated her too many times before.

"Please, Beth . . . give me five minutes, and I'll go.

I'm going to be leaving Helton. Can't we have one last drink and a friendly good-bye?"

"One drink. Then you leave."

"Absolutely."

Beth held the door open and Todd walked past her. She followed him to the living room.

"Scotch, as usual?" she said warily.

"You remember just about everything, don't you?"

"Yes—the good and the bad," she replied as she walked to the bar and prepared his drink. She took it to him.

"Aren't you going to have one?"

"I'm going out to dinner. I'll have one then."

"Forrester?"

"Yes," she said so firmly that he was startled. Where was the insecure and self-deprecating Beth he knew so well? He took a different tack.

"Beth, I've tried to warn you about him. You don't know what people in this town say. There's a lot of gossip."

"I never was one to listen to gossip, as you remember. If I had, I would have been wiser about you."

"Beth, a man can change. I have. I know what a mistake I made losing you. I just wanted a chance to make up for it."

"I'm over you, Todd. I'm over being your shadow and your handmaid. All I want is to say as friendly a good-bye as possible and have you get out of my life—this time, for good."

Todd set his drink down and came to Beth, surprised that she didn't back away from him. She held her ground. He reached out to draw her into his arms, but she pushed his hands away. "Look, Todd, I'd suggest you leave while I'm still in control of my temper . . . and before Carl gets here."

"You cared for me once. You loved me once, and there has to still be something there—some of the old passion. I know there is."

This time he pulled her against him. She braced her hands between them, but before she could say anything to stop him, another voice intruded.

"Little man, you sure push your luck, don't you?"

Both spun around to face the doorway and to see Carl leaning against the door frame, his arms folded before him and a smile on his face that never reached his eyes—eyes that happily promised imminent murder.

"What the hell are you doing here?" Todd snarled.

"Carl . . ." Beth began.

"Beth, I think you'd better move away from him. He needs a little lesson on being stubborn . . . and damn stupid."

"Carl, don't! It's not important!" Beth turned to Todd. "Just go, Todd."

"Not unless you come with me."

"Now, that's downright funny." Carl laughed. "Beth's not going anywhere with you, now or ever. Do you want to leave peacefully, or do as the man said—make my day?"

"Look, you damn murderer!" Todd shouted as he started for Carl. "No woman in her right mind would let you close! You're a killer! For all we know, you could be the one killing all these girls. Once a killer always a killer. You . . ." The last words came in a gurgled squawk as Carl leapt from what looked like a relaxed position. Todd never quite knew what had struck. The fist that connected with his chin was like a sledgehammer, and the hand that gripped his arm and twisted it in a quick move was like iron. He yelped again in surprise and pain as Carl held his arm twisted behind his back and propelled him through the still-open door and across the steps. Then he was pushed forcefully and landed at the bottom of the porch step.

Carl grinned amiably and dusted his hands, then pointed a finger at Todd. His voice was low, but carried very well. "If I find you here again, little man, the arm will be broken and so will a couple of other bones."

"You'll pay for this, Forrester. I'm not finished with you yet." Carl chuckled, but his smile faded as Todd continued, "And not with her, either. She'll regret this!"

Carl stepped down one step. "Don't think of putting a hand on Beth or you won't have one left."

"What are you going to do, tough cop, kill me? You're good at that, aren't you? I'll get even—you can count on it." He turned and made his way to his car and Carl was frozen by an old, familiar fear. He'd heard those threats before, and ignoring them had cost Sara's life. It would never happen like that again—not even if he had to do something very final to Todd.

Carl walked into the house, his smile intact when he entered the living room.

"Are you going to start pounding on your chest like Tarzan now?" Beth was doing her best to contain her laughter, but the sparkle in her eyes was evidence enough for Carl.

"Now, Beth, the little man had it coming and you know it. Would you rather still be fighting him off?"

"Why do you keep calling him little man? Todd's over six feet tall."

"It's his mentality, my sweet. It's about as big as an acorn. Sometimes you have to crack the shell of a nut to let in a little sunshine. He won't bother you anymore."

Beth came to Carl and looped her arms about his neck. "You're something else, you know that?"

"I thought I said that to you once."

"So you did. Well," she raised one hand to draw his head down to hers, "maybe we're something else."

Carl enjoyed the kiss. He took a great deal of pleasure in wrapping his arms about her and holding her close. When the kiss broke, both were smiling.

"How'd you like to run away with me for a day or so?"

"Run away? Where?"

"I have to go to Bridgefield, and I won't be able to get back until Monday."

"I have to work Monday."

"Get a replacement for one day. C'mon, Beth, let's get out of here and take a drive. We can find a nice motel, and who knows, I might just let you take advantage of me."

"Big of you," she said suspiciously. "Is this cop work?"

"Well, truthfully, yes." He grinned. "But it will only take a little while. We can have some getaway time, and we both need that. What do you say?"

"All right. I'll toss some things in an overnight bag and

make a couple of phone calls. Make yourself a drink and I'll be right with you."

Beth went into the bedroom and Carl walked to the bar, feeling better than he'd felt in years. He started to pour a drink when someone knocked on the front door. He was pretty sure Beth hadn't heard it, so, drink in hand, he walked over and opened the door. It was Eve Pierce.

Eve absorbed Carl's casual appearance with one quick gulp of understanding and her smile was quick and warm. "Hello, Carl Forrester. I'm pleased to see you again. We haven't seen each other since that night in the restaurant. I don't know if you remember."

"Eve Pierce." Carl's smile was more appreciation of her warmth. "You're Beth's best friend. Come on in."

"Where's Beth?" Eve asked as she passed him. Carl closed the door and followed her.

"In the bedroom. She'll be out in a minute. We're going out, so she's changing." He had no intention of telling her they were going away for the weekend. Beth's tolerance might not stretch that far. "Can I get you something?"

"No, thank you." Eve was watching Carl closely, feeling a great deal of satisfaction in what she saw. He was a solid, earthy man—just what Beth needed. "I just stopped by to see how Beth was doing. Someone told me her ex-husband is moving to Helton. He's caused her enough grief, so I wanted to make sure she knew and that she was all right."

"She knows," Carl replied. He sipped his drink, watching her over the rim.

"He's been here?"

"Recently."

"Am I to understand there's been a confrontation?" Eve's lips twitched in a smile and her eyes sparkled wickedly.

Carl's smile broadened. "Let's just say that he's not likely to be causing her much trouble."

"That's good news." Eve studied him carefully. "Beth is a special kind of person. I'd hate to see her jump from the frying pan to the fire."

"She's not jumping anywhere. Beth can take all the time she needs and make her own decisions. Nobody's rushing her, or making any decisions for her. Don't you thinks it's best that everyone give her a little breathing room?''

''Meaning, even her friends?'' Eve actually laughed. She was beginning to like Carl even more. ''I get your point. But I'm too much of a friend not to keep my eyes open, even if I keep my mouth shut.''

Carl was about to reply when the bedroom door opened, and Beth came out, carrying the overnight case in her hand. For a minute she stood motionless; the damning evidence in her hand spoke eloquently about what was happening. She did her best to smile, but the smile was weak.

''Hi, Eve. This is a surprise.''

''I just stopped by to check up on you. I've been chatting with Carl, but I really have to get going.'' She reached out and took hold of Beth's arm, then bent to kiss her cheek. Her voice was quiet but firm. ''You're a very special person, Beth, and you deserve happiness more than anyone I know. I'm as close as the phone if you want to talk. If you don't I want you to know that I wish you the best, and that I think you're making one of the best moves you ever made.''

Beth couldn't find words, and Eve didn't wait for any. She walked to the door, then paused to look at Carl.

''I wonder if you know how lucky you are? I hope so; I wouldn't want to see anyone get hurt.''

Carl raised his glass to her. ''I know.''

Eve smiled in satisfaction, then left. Beth regained her composure quickly and set her overnight case down in the doorway. ''I think I'll take that drink now.''

Carl didn't answer, just turned to the bar and made her one. Beth sipped the drink thoughtfully.

''Did Eve's visit bother you?''

''What do you mean?''

''I know this little town. Does she talk a lot?''

''Eve! God, no! She's the kind of friend everyone should have.'' Now Beth laughed. ''Since that night in the restaurant, she's been matchmaking us.''

''Smart woman,'' Carl said agreeably.

''I guess she and Sally have seen me at my lowest. I suppose, being the kind of friends they are, they don't want to see me like that again.''

Carl went to her, took the drink from her hand, and set it aside. Then he took her in his arms. "Beth, outside of finding out that I want to be with you all the time and that I want to make love to you until I'm half blind, I want to be your friend, too. I want you to talk to me, tell me what you feel when you feel it. I don't want any kind of silent walls that might grow into something bigger. We ought to start, whatever this thing is, off with an open communication system."

"What are you asking me, Carl?"

"I guess it's if you're having second thoughts or if you have some reservations."

"No."

"Not even after your friend's visit?"

"No, not even then."

"Good. Let's get out of here before someone decides to call or make another visit."

He picked up her small suitcase, and she retrieved her coat from the closet. After she'd carefully checked windows and doors, she locked the front door after them, and they walked to Carl's car.

"We have to stop by my motel room so I can pick up a few things. It will only take a minute."

They drove for a couple of minutes in silence, then Carl laughed.

"What's funny?"

"Well, if everything had gone as it was planned a month ago, I would be fishing off the Florida Keys right now instead of starting off a weekend with a beautiful girl. How lucky can a guy get?"

When Carl pulled up in front of the door to his room, he asked Beth if she wanted to wait in the car or come in.

"I'll come in. I'd like to see the bear's den."

"It'll be a mess. I'm a genuine slob. Sara used to say . . ." He stopped abruptly and Beth's eyes sparkled with annoyance.

"Stop being afraid to say her name in front of me! I don't want you to forget her, and I don't want you to be afraid to say things about her. I don't want to fight a ghost you keep in the closet. If you're afraid to talk about her, then pretty soon I'll be afraid, too, and we can't build anything on that."

Carl unlocked the door without saying any more. Beth felt a chill as if she had cursed in church.

They stepped inside, and Carl pushed the door closed. Beth gasped as he gripped her arm and swung her around into his arms. He smiled down into her eyes.

"You make Ghostbusters look like Swiss cheese. I'm trying not to make it hard for you."

"Hard?" She lightened her voice and the smile returned to her eyes. "You're not hard—you're a round-heeled push-over with a heart of gold."

"Pushover, am I?" He scowled. "You have some proof of that?"

She squirmed her body against his and reached with both hands to pull his head down to her. The kiss was effective enough to make him reach out and lock the door behind them. The soft laughter and slow undressing followed them all the way to the bed. Two hours later they left the motel and started to drive toward Bridgefield.

* CHAPTER 33 *

Bridgefield was nearly two hundred miles away, but Carl was sure they would make it in about three or three and a half hours. Of course, neither of them had eaten, so they stopped at a place about halfway to Bridgefield. There was time to talk and Carl used it to find out all about Beth's background. Beth, wise enough not to let him get away with just talking about her, pulled a lot of stories about his life from him, including a few anecdotes about him and Joe as boys that were very funny.

"You weren't always a good boy." She chuckled.

"I'm still not," he said, laughing. "Good boys don't have as much fun as I'm having."

They left the restaurant and drove the balance of the way

to Bridgefield. The town was a good deal larger than Helton, and its bright lights met them around eleven o'clock. Carl had no trouble finding the motel and checked in, tossing the one key in Beth's lap when he got back in the car.

"I think this guy expected me to register as Mr. and Mrs. John Smith. I'm pretty sure he was upset when I showed identification. He was all apologies and wanted to make sure my 'wife' didn't need anything."

Beth shook her head at Carl's obvious enjoyment. "You're incorrigible."

"Just proving he shouldn't jump to conclusions."

"What's the next step?" she asked. Carl's eyes glittered wickedly. "I mean," Beth added, "what's the next step in finding David's relatives?"

"David has already given me the address. I'll just check it against the phone book for a number."

"I hope this proves that David is just what he appears."

"I do, too, but it's funny that he got so upset about my asking their last name. I don't think he expected me to go see them personally—maybe just make a phone call."

"Why didn't you just call?"

"Because I like to look into people's eyes when I talk to them. There's a language other than verbal that can give a lot of answers."

"I suppose you're right."

"I saw a nice little place for drinks as we pulled in. Want to go have one?"

"Sounds fine."

They dropped their suitcases in the room and strolled slowly the short distance to a bar connected to the motel. When they were seated, Beth ordered a rum and Coke, and Carl a cold draft.

"Carl, are you really suspicious of David?"

"It's not suspicion, exactly. I wouldn't doubt Emma Lowrey for the world. If she says he was there at ten-thirty, then he was. I just have a feeling he knows a lot more than he's saying, and he's too defensive, both of himself and of Father McAllen."

"He's defending Father McAllen? From what?"

"Who knows. He's a one-man admiration society, and

when you cast a shadow on the priest, David gets his hackles up."

"Maybe it's just that, admiration."

"I suppose. Father McAllen seems to be admired by a whole lot of people. But whether I like it or not, he has no alibi, and he's still considered a suspect."

"I'm not going to try to argue you out of anything. You're the cop, not me."

"Does that bother you, Beth?"

"Am I acting as if it does?"

"Now who's evasive?"

She took a sip of her drink, giving the question its first serious thought. "I don't know if I can answer that, Carl. I've not had any reasons to be frightened of the idea, and besides, I don't want you making any decision because of my uncertainties."

"The only problem is, I don't think I'd do another job as well. I'm a good cop, Beth."

"I don't doubt that for a minute. Why are you trying so hard to convince me?"

"I don't have an answer to that, either. You think I'm whistling in the dark?"

"Maybe a little, but then we're all a little afraid at one time or another. You've got a lot of reasons."

He leaned back in his chair and watched her closely for a minute. Then he picked up his drink and touched his glass to hers. "Thanks for coming with me." The words were said quietly and filled with promise. Beth smiled.

"I think it's getting late, Carl," she said softly. "Don't you think it's time we walked back?"

He nodded, stood, and tossed some bills on the table. Outside, Beth slipped her hand in his and they walked back to the motel room, not needing any more words between them.

The dark car cruised slowly, which was all right in Helton's red-light district. Many cars cruised slowly here, driven by people looking for the same physical outlets and unrealized dreams and unattainable goals vitalized by frustrations and the inability to cope with their problems.

The driver had his attention riveted on the auburn-haired

girl who walked down the street with swaying hips and laughing lips, stopping occasionally to talk to one or two people, dodging reaching hands and laughing with the sheer joy of being young and alive and having the fun that made her hard-working days worth the effort.

Barbara Winslow was twenty, vibrantly pretty, and out, for the first time in several weeks, to celebrate.

She was not exactly promiscuous, but she wasn't one to deny herself any chance for fun. She was not selling or giving away any part of herself; she was just out to have a good time. She was to meet friends soon, and they would laugh and dance the balance of the night away.

He followed her slowly, his mind twisting and writhing in fury at her and his thoughts on words etched in his mind.

Only wisdom from the Lord can save a man from the flattery of prostitutes. These girls have flouted the laws of God. The men who enter them are doomed. None of these men will ever be the same again.

Of course she would make her mouth so pink and lush; she was a whore, wasn't she? Look at the way she walked, swaying her hips, inviting men to look . . . maybe to touch. How dare she defile the town he was trying to protect? She was just like all the others—wicked from the day of her birth. Her body was wicked. Look at how short her dress was, revealing her long, slim legs. Look at the way she teased and taunted men. She was beautiful . . . beautiful.

He knew it would happen. As soon as he saw her, he knew she was the reason he was punished. Her kind brought the dull pounding in his head and the shrill voice that tormented him. His shoulders hunched as he felt the blows and heard the voice commanding him to remove the blot of evil that had tempted him. He must not be tempted anymore. He could not stand the punishment. He could not let it go on any longer.

He pushed the accelerator down, and as Barbara reached a street crossing, he pulled to the curb.

For a moment she looked alarmed, then recognition brightened her eyes, and she walked to the car as the window slid down.

"Hello. What are you doing down here?"

"Out on a little Good Samaritan trip. What about you?"

"Well, I was supposed to meet some friends at Charlie's. We're going to celebrate my birthday with a few drinks and a little dancing."

"Do you think your friends could spare you for an hour or so?"

"Sure, why?"

"I need a little help."

"Doing what?"

"Well." He chuckled and his eyes glittered appreciatively. "I guess I'll level with you. The one who needs the help is me." His voice lowered with obvious suggestion.

"I . . ." She tried to disguise her shock and obvious interest. Her eyes grew bright with the intriguing thought of where he meant this to lead. She felt the glow of excitement—a new and different excitement.

"I've seen you at St. Catherine's, but . . . well, I thought you . . . I mean, I just never . . ."

"Everybody needs someone sometime. Right now I need someone to talk to, to be with. Can you understand?"

She heard a sympathetic plea that did not exist in the mind of the man who smiled so warmly at her.

"Where?"

"I thought we might take a ride—sort of find a nice quiet place where we could talk."

"My car is parked a little way from here. Maybe it would be better—for you, I mean—if I were to follow you. That way, none of the pious people of Helton need to know we've . . . talked."

"You're a sweet, understanding girl, Barbara." He reached to lay his hand over hers on the window frame. She felt an electric shiver go through her. This was, without a doubt, the most unusual thing she had ever done.

"Pull down to the corner," she said. "I have a little red hatchback. I'll come up behind you, and you can lead from there."

He nodded and smiled a grateful, rather boyish smile. But the smile faded as she walked away. He pulled his car to the corner she had suggested. In a few minutes, her car was behind him. The smile was murderously contemptuous as he pulled away, and she followed.

Joe had left the office right after Carl. Sally wasn't home when he got there, so he went to the refrigerator and took out a plate with some cold chicken on it and a bottle of beer. He carried them into the living room with him and snapped on the TV. Then he relaxed in his favorite chair and watched the tail end of a western that finally led into a news special. He groaned when he found that the sensational murders in the small town of Helton were the subject. By the time Phil Greggory's smirking face appeared, Joe had had enough. He got to his feet and switched to a musical. Anything was better than watching Phil Greggory gloat. He was in a less than contented frame of mind when Sally arrived home.

"Hi, honey. I'm glad to see you home so early. You're supposed to have Saturday off, remember?"

"I know." Joe kissed her and took the packages from her hands. "Groceries?"

"No, why? Are you still hungry?"

"I cleaned up the leftover chicken and had a beer."

"So, does that mean you're still hungry or not?"

"At the moment, no," he said, "but by the time you shower and change to a pretty dress, I'll be set to take you out. On our budget, we can afford a movie and a pizza. How does that sound?"

"What's wrong, Joe?"

"Wrong? Nothing, why?"

"Because you're like a stick of dynamite with a short fuse."

"Yeah, well, maybe you're right. I guess I need to put some space between me and the tangle of these murders."

"Where's Carl? Maybe he and Beth would like to take in that movie with us."

"Carl's out of town."

"Where did he go?"

"Bridgefield."

"Why Bridgefield?"

"He's checking out David Mondale's aunt and uncle." Joe explained what he and Carl had been doing. "So Carl thought it might just be a good idea if he went up and made sure any loose ends that might be trailing will be tied up.''

''Carl doesn't really suspect David, does he? Do you, Joe?''

''There's just no possible way David could be the one who killed Martha. He was with Emma at the time. But Carl thinks David knows something or is protecting someone.''

''I wouldn't want to be the one to cross-examine Emma. So Carl's in Bridgefield,'' Sally said thoughtfully.

''Yeah, said he'd be back by Monday. He should be; there's not much to check into. It's only a visit to David's family and a few questions.''

''Did he go alone?''

''Well, of course he went alone. Who . . . ?'' Joe stopped and thought that one over while Sally grinned.

''I'd like to think so,'' she said.

''So, find out.'' Joe returned her smile.

Sally dialed Beth's number. ''What time is it?'' she asked as she listened to the phone ring. ''No answer.''

''Let it ring a while—it's only six-thirty.''

Sally waited. ''Ten rings. That's official.'' She laughed.

''She could be out to supper with someone we don't even know.''

''Wanna bet?''

''Nope. When have I ever won one with you?'' Joe laughed, and gave her a little shove. ''Go take a shower.''

Sally watched Joe carefully all evening. He squirmed through a movie he couldn't have cared less about and worried through pizza and drinks later. By the time they came home, Joe was exhausted.

They went to bed, and as she drifted into sleep, she felt Joe's arm come about her. She didn't move, knowing all he needed was to hold her. Several hours later, she came awake slowly. The red digits on the clock told her it was three-thirty, and she realized Joe's side of the bed was empty.

She sat up. The room was just as empty as the bed. Kicking the covers aside, she got out of bed, left the bedroom, and walked down the hall to the moonlit living room.

Joe stood by the large front window, holding the curtain

aside with one hand and dangling a half-forgotten cigarette in the other.

"Joe?"

He turned to look at her. "What are you doing up?"

"What about you?" she countered. "You shouldn't let this get to you so hard."

"It's not that. I don't know why, but I've got this damn feeling."

"Like what?"

"Like I should be doing something—like something rotten is happening right at this moment, and I'm helpless."

"Joe, come on to bed. You need some sleep. Worrying yourself sick isn't going to help anyone."

He put his arm around her waist and they walked back to the bedroom together. "I guess you're right. This thing is getting to me. I just wish I knew what all our suspects are doing right now."

At the same hour, Father McAllen opened the rectory door, careful not to make any noise. He closed it just as softly behind him. He needed no light, because he knew just where every piece of furniture was placed.

He walked out of the reception hall into his private study. There he sagged into a chair, bent forward, and clasped his hands—almost as if he were praying. He seemed totally exhausted.

When the light came on suddenly, he was startled. He looked up to see Father James in the doorway.

He looked relieved. "Oh, it's you. I thought we had intruders. Are you all right?" He had just noticed that Father McAllen's clothes were disheveled and his jacket had a small rent in the sleeve.

"I'm all right, James. I'm just fine—tired is all. Go back to bed. I'm going to bed myself. It's been a terrible night."

"Where were you?"

Father McAllen was silent a moment. "It was personal, James," he said quietly. "Go on to bed."

He nodded and reluctantly turned away. "Turn off the light," he added.

Father James snapped the light off, leaving Father McAllen in the dark and in an oppressive silence.

Michael Brodie's house was dark, and silence hung over it. The bright moonlight chased shadows into the corners, and the chilling wind forced its way into a slightly open window, causing the curtains to billow in the bedroom. The bed was empty, as was the entire house. No lights had been lit, proving that no one had been in the house for many hours, since long before the sun had set. The breeze bent the trees to brush against the house, and the sound whispered through it with ghostlike murmurs. Then all was silent again.

Paul slammed the door of his car, then staggered to his door. He leaned against it, blindly digging in his pocket for his elusive keys. He finally found them, fumbled to unlock the door, then entered, leaving the door slightly open behind him.

He staggered to the couch and collapsed unconscious. His shoes had left muddy tracks across the floor, and the white moonlight danced through the large windows, turning them to clumps of black. But Paul saw neither the mud nor the moonlight. He was deep in the black oblivion of sleep.

* CHAPTER 34 *

Carl woke to the sound of the shower running. He sat up on the edge of the bed for a minute, drawing his thoughts together.

Beth was humming softly and he smiled to himself, admitting the sound made him feel better than he had in a long, long time.

He slid the drawer open on the bedside table and removed the phone book to search for a listing, but it wasn't there. Obviously, the Rossmans didn't encourage callers.

Well, encouragement or not, he meant to see and talk to them as soon as possible. He replaced the phone book and stood up from the bed at the same moment Beth came out of the bathroom with both her hair and body wrapped in towels.

"Umm, and you said I looked fetching in a dish towel. You don't have any idea what fetching is."

"I left the shower running—I thought you'd want to get a move on this morning. It's already past ten. By the way, did you find a phone number?"

"No, it's unlisted, I guess," he said, but instead of moving to the bathroom, he stopped beside her. Beth moved into his embrace freely, and he pressed a kiss on her bare shoulder, inhaling deeply. "You smell good and you're warm."

"I told you you were easy." Her responding laugh was throaty and sensual. "But you'll have to try playing a little hard to get, or we'll never get going." She playfully pushed his away a little.

"Beth?"

"What?"

"I'd like you to stay here. This is sort of an official visit, and there could be a problem if I took you along. It won't take me long."

"Carl, you could have just left me in Helton."

"You have to be joking," he said. "I don't really want to let you out of my sight at all. That suggestion was out of the question."

"Then, when you get back, we'll have to get right home and report to Joe?"

"Today's Sunday."

"What does that mean?"

"Sunday is a day of rest," he explained.

"There is no rest for you. You have work to do, so get a move on."

He eyed her speculatively. "No chance of breakfast in bed, huh?"

"Nope. Go shower. Now that you're talking about breakfast, that reminds me, I'm hungry. Do you think the Rossmans might be in church now?"

"That's likely. Let's have our breakfast, and then I'll run out to their place about noon."

"And hope they don't decide to go out to dinner after church."

"It's a chance I'll have to take." Carl shrugged.

He left her to dress, while he made quick work of a shower and shave. In the motel's small dining room where they had breakfast, Carl asked directions, then set out for what he hoped were some answers.

The Rossman house sat on a tree-shaded street in what looked like a reasonably well-to-do area of Bridgefield. It was a two-story frame home with a large front porch covered on two sides by latticework filled with climbing vines. The grass was neatly cut and the shrubs carefully pruned. All in all, it looked to Carl like a typical middle-class home.

Carl walked up on the porch and knocked. The house was silent. He knocked again and waited for a full three or four minutes.

"Looks like Beth was right," he muttered. "Maybe I'll just have to hang around town until they get back from dinner."

But before he could leave, the door opened and Carl turned quickly to smile at the woman who appeared in the doorway.

"Mrs. Rossman?"

"Yes." Her voice was reserved, almost cold. Her face was not quite beautiful—it was somewhat large—but she had absolutely perfect features; great blue eyes, a Grecian nose, and a full pink mouth. She had a mass of chestnut hair like polished satin piled atop her head. She was a large woman with heavy limbs, buttocks, and breasts; but she gave an impression of immaculate cleanliness, and the sweet scent of talcum came to him. But Carl's interest was piqued by her face. Unlined and smooth, without a wrinkle, it was totally devoid of expression, and he wondered if she ever took the chance of wrinkling her skin by laughing or smiling.

"My name is Carl Forrester. I'm an acquaintance of your nephew, David Mondale."

If possible, her face grew more closed. "David?" she repeated. "I'm afraid he no longer lives here. He left this house several years ago." She stopped talking, subtly making the point that she was not giving any information, nor did she desire any. Carl thought it was time for a little pressure. He reached for his wallet and flashed the gold detective shield.

"I'm afraid I'll have to ask you a few more questions about David, Mrs. Rossman. May I come in?"

He had finally shocked her into some degree of comprehension. She stepped back, and he saw her glance past him to scan the street for watchful eyes. Carl smiled to himself. Obviously, she was one who worried about what the neighbors thought. He stored that thought and followed her into the house.

He was led into a living room filled with enough bric-a-brac, porcelain figurines, and odds and ends of all sorts to make an antique dealer grow ecstatic.

"Is your husband at home, Mrs. Rossman?" he inquired. "I would like to talk with both of you. I need some information about your nephew."

"Hardly my nephew," she said, her voice frigid again. "He is the son of my husband's sister. She was a wild and immoral woman. My husband and I took him in when his parents died, and a good thing it was, too. He was as rough and unmannerly as they were. It took a great deal of discipline on my part to get his feet back on the straight and narrow."

While they talked, Carl looked about the room. There were hundreds of crucifixes, religious symbols, and statues, and candles illuminated some of the icons and pictures. Carl felt stifled, as if his breath were being crushed in his chest.

"I see. So David was a difficult child?"

"Wild, unruly, disobedient," she said, smiling thinly, "but hardly difficult. I would not tolerate that. He learned to be quite disciplined before he left our house."

"You did say your husband was home?"

"Yes, but I hardly think it necessary to talk to him. David's training was left up to me. Generosity made my husband take David in. He knew I would see to the child's development."

"Well, I should like to speak to your husband as well, if you don't mind," Carl said firmly enough to make her understand he was not going to back down. Her mouth grew thin with controlled anger, but she rose and walked to the bottom of the stairs.

"Robert, do come down here. Someone needs to speak to us." She did not call again, but returned to her chair as if she were sure her husband would never ignore her first and only call.

In a few minutes a man appeared in the living room doorway. He was a tall, slender man, so fine-boned he could have been called dainty. His beautiful and tranquil face was crowned by a thick mass of white, wavy hair, and he had the clearest, bluest eyes Carl had ever seen. He was fascinated by their strange color, but gazing into them, he was struck with the most overpowering sense of evil he had ever felt in his life.

"Did you call me, Caroline?"

"Yes, dear. A detective is here. He wants to talk to us about David." She did not turn to look at her husband, and the man in the doorway did not move. The two seemed united against Carl.

"What do you want to know?" The man's voice was as delicate as he was.

"How long ago did David leave here?"

"Over six years ago."

"He came here when he was five or six?" Carl asked.

"Yes," Caroline answered. No emotion touched the ivory features. "His parents were killed in an accident. We knew our duty."

"He was a nice little boy," Robert said in his gentle voice. With one white hand, he absently rubbed his arm. "Such a pretty boy, with lovely eyes and skin like his mother's—soft . . ." Suddenly, he became aware of Carl's penetrating, all-knowing gaze. He licked his lips, walked to a chair, and sat down.

"Was David good in school? Did he have a lot of friends? Was he ever in trouble?" Carl asked.

"In trouble?" Caroline protested. "David was never in trouble. He was an excellent student and he made friends very easily. He was good! Good! You must understand; I took my duty very seriously. I am a firm believer in what the Bible teaches us. Spare the rod and spoil the child. He had better be good or else. Why, by the time he was seven he was an altar boy in our church. Even when he was grown he listened to me and never chased the wild girls. He understood that I did everything for his good. No, David was never bad. Even though it often caused me a great deal of pain, I would resort to corporal punishment. But David understood, you see. He knew that it hurt me more than it did him. I had to prepare him, make him understand what was right, and give him the strength to face the seduction of the evil in the world."

"Oh, yes. You must understand," Robert said in an almost plaintive voice. Beside him on a stand was a tall, slender wooden carving. It was smooth and gleamed with a polished finish. Robert slid his fingertips up and down its length. He licked his lips again as he continued. "It hurt me to witness the welts on his soft, soft skin. I would hold him afterward and soothe his little body. He was a beautiful child . . . so beautiful, but he had to learn to behave, to appreciate all we were doing for him."

"I see," Carl said.

"Of course, you know he studied hard and was often sickly, but Robert and I took good care of him—especially Robert. He would devote whole evenings to reading to him at his bedside."

Carl ran his finger around his collar to loosen it. He was badly shaken. Though he had not a shred of evidence, he could feel the current of insanity that underlay the quiet words. He wanted out of this house, and he was a grown man capable of ıunning. David must have lived in sheer terror.

Carl stood. He had heard enough, but Caroline finished the episode with pride-filled words that almost made Carl groan with the thought of what David's hell must have been like.

"I chose David's path; I made him good. I groomed him and made him ready. When he left here, he went to the seminary to be a priest. It's not my fault that he chose to leave it. Those foolish men didn't recognize what he was. But I couldn't let him come home—not unless he came as a priest. So I told him to leave. We couldn't shelter him anymore after he failed us."

Carl could not bear it any longer. There was a cold rage in him. He said his thanks quickly, dodging Robert's extended hand and Caroline's cold, emotionless eyes.

Outside, Carl turned to look at the house. It was no longer a nice, middle-class home. It was a possessed house. A ghastly darkness lived there, and it had seeped into the mind of a six-year-old boy and drained away his life. He felt a surge of relief and inhaled the fresh, clean air as if he hadn't breathed from the moment he stepped into that house.

When he turned the key in the lock at the motel, Beth stood up from the bed. She had been watching TV. She smiled. "Well, that didn't take too long. What did . . . Carl? What's wrong?"

But Carl didn't answer. Instead, he took her in his arms, breathing in the pure scent of her. He kissed her so deeply that Beth could only cling to him. His need for her was so strong, she found it impossible not to respond.

Later, when they lay together on the bed, Carl tried to explain what he had found. He tried to assume the requisite policeman's detachment, but his voice broke when he described the coldness of the woman, the sensual pleasure the man took in recalling the child's tortured body.

"Oh, Carl, that poor boy."

"I wonder if he is just a poor boy any longer. I wonder if he's not something much worse now."

"Carl, does this make David the killer?"

"No, it doesn't. Michael Brodie's background is just as bad. It just tells me a little bit about how he ticks. You seem to forget that Emma can prove where David was."

"Then I don't understand this."

"This what?"

"The purpose . . . what you thought you'd find."

"A key, maybe. If David is protecting someone, maybe this is why."

"You mean, Father McAllen knew!"

"Could be. Maybe that's why David was protecting him all the time—sort of a true father image. If he thought Patric McAllen was in danger . . . if he had reason to believe . . ."

"God," Beth breathed. "What will you do if you find out . . ."

"I'll arrest Father McAllen."

It had been past one when Carl had left the Rossman home. By three o'clock he had found the church David had attended when he was a boy. Conversation with the priest led to the name of the seminary, and by four o'clock, Beth and Carl were again on the highway.

After another two-hour drive, they were ushered into the office at the seminary. The priest who sat across the desk was a scholarly looking man with receding sandy hair, green eyes that crinkled in laugh lines at the corners, and a wide, generous mouth. He was tall, very slender, and yet rather athletic-looking.

"I'm Carl Forrester, Father Dempsey." Carl flipped his badge. "This is Beth Raleigh. We need a few questions answered about David Mondale. I believe he studied here for a while?"

"Yes, David was here for a while—a short while."

"What was your impression, Father?"

"Impression? You mean, what did I think of David? He was intelligent and, it seemed, quite intense about his desire to be a priest."

"A little too intense, maybe?" Carl asked.

"Why are you here asking questions about David? Is there some problem? Is he in trouble?"

"What makes you think he would be in any kind of trouble? Is that what you expected when you sent him away—when you decided he couldn't be a priest?" Carl was fishing for a reaction and he got it. Father Dempsey leaned back in his chair and sighed.

"David had some problems. He was too meticulous, if you can understand that. There was no tolerance in him for any part of humanity. He could not bend, nor did he show any sign of compassion for his fellowman—all qualities a good priest must have. We felt—well, we felt David did not really have a vocation. But we did not toss him away. We simply told him to go home and take time to think and to decide if he really felt he had chosen the right path."

"And she threw him out because he had failed her," Carl muttered.

"What?"

"Nothing, Father." Carl stood and shook the priest's hand. "Thank you. You've been very helpful."

"I'll walk you out."

The three walked to the seminary office's front door.

"Mr. Forrester, David was a troubled boy when he was here. He was subject to terrible dreams and fits of depression, followed by bouts of euphoria. We felt he needed professional care for a while. Then suddenly, he seemed to change, but it was not a change of the inner man, if you understand. It was as if . . ."

"As if he had suddenly assumed a mask and no one was allowed to look behind it."

"Exactly. I hate to think we failed him, but neither he nor his family would hear of professional help."

"You didn't fail him, Father. You had the right idea. Life failed him, and it happened many years before you ever met him."

"Can I ask you why you came here, Mr. Forrester?"

"I'm investigating a multiple murder in Helton. Three girls are dead and the killer is on a psychotic rampage."

"And you think it's David!?"

"I can't prove that, but at least now he steps up beside the other three to the rank of suspect."

"How terrible. I cannot believe David guilty of that. He was sensitive and sometimes difficult to understand . . . but murder?"

"Maybe he was too sensitive, but he'd have to have the hide of an elephant to have grown up in the evil household of his aunt and uncle without being damaged."

Father Dempsey gave Carl and Beth a keen and compassionate look. It was one that understood all the unspoken words behind Carl's spoken ones. Then it faded into a sadness. Again he held out his hand to Carl. "If I can be of any help . . . to anyone involved in this, please let me know."

"I'll do that."

"Mr. Forrester?"

"Yes."

"David is not, in truth, responsible, if what you say is so. Maybe you can catch an illness from a diseased soul just as you can catch it from a diseased body . . . It's a killing disease."

"I wish I had read Freud, Father, but I don't have time to try and analyze the reasons behind this. I have to put a stop to it. There are those much more capable than I to care for the mentality of whoever is doing this. I just have to catch him."

"Good luck, Mr. Forrester," Father Dempsey smiled, "and Freud not withstanding, I think you understand compassion."

Beth smiled too. "And I agree with you, Father. Finding a compassionate policeman is very rare . . . And I've never read Freud either."

"Good luck to you both."

Father Dempsey watched Beth and Carl get into their car and drive away. Then he walked back inside with a feeling of sadness he couldn't explain.

It was getting close to dinnertime when Beth and Carl got back to the motel. Both felt drained and somehow contaminated by the villainous things they had unearthed.

"Are you hungry? We can go somewhere."

Beth was silent for a long time, then closed her eyes for a moment, inhaled deeply and then turned to look at Carl. Her eyes were moist with tears.

"Would you understand if I told you I wanted you to take me in your arms and make love to me? That I have to feel alive. Oh, Carl, it's as if we've dug into an old grave. I've never felt such things before. I need you to make me feel life again."

There was no need for words, even later, when he made love to her gently and carefully, erasing the ugliness. They lay quietly together for a long time, neither of them spoke. It was Beth who broke the silence.

"Carl, do you think about having children now?"

He was quiet and Beth waited. He was less sure of her than of himself. Finally, he spoke. "Yeah. I've thought about it a time or two."

"I . . . neither of us have used anything. Did you think I had?"

"To tell you the truth, I wanted you so bad I never thought. I guess I was stupid. I'm sorry."

She turned in his arms and looked up at him. "Sorry because you don't want to, or what?"

"Sorry because I didn't ask," he replied. A new and very exciting thought had come to him: having a child with Beth. "It's not because this thing with David hit you so hard?"

"No, it's because . . . when you made love to me I really felt—I wanted it to happen."

He hugged her and laughed. "Bless you, Beth. I never thought I'd ever feel as whole again." He tipped her chin up so he could hold her eyes with his and make sure she knew. "I love you, Beth Raleigh—I love you."

"Carl," was all she could whisper before his lips touched hers.

It was very late when they went out to eat, then returned to Carl's room.

Carl dreamed that night, for the first time in several nights, but somehow the dreams had lost some of their sharpness. He found whispers of the good moments mixed with the nightmares.

He awoke without the sense of violence that had always clung to his dreams. Beth slept soundly. He experienced a kind of joy in holding her he had thought he would never feel again. He closed his eyes and pulled her tight against him.

* CHAPTER 35 *

Paul groaned and cracked his eyes open to a narrow squint. The sunlight was full in his face and the pain of its brilliance ricocheted through his head, which felt as if it were going to explode. He closed his eyes quickly and tried to find the answers to several questions. The first was how had he wound up sprawled on his couch, and then, what had happened to Saturday night?

He rolled over, letting his legs fall to the floor. Now he was on his knees, his torso resting on the couch. He was contemplating the distance between where he was and the bathroom, concluding that it was at least ten miles.

He forced himself to stand up, then, using pieces of furniture and wavering walls, he made his way to the bathroom where he was sick.

He reached blindly for the shower knobs and turned them on. He stripped, moving cautiously, for his head was threatening to fall off.

Under the shower he stood with his eyes closed and tried to piece together the previous night. He remembered a couple of bars, driving . . . and a girl—someone with an infectious laugh and auburn hair who reminded him of Amy. But that was all that he could grasp through the fog in his mind.

He felt slightly more civilized after he showered and dressed in clean jeans and a cotton shirt. He walked on tentative feet to the kitchen and, being careful not to make excessive noise, put a pot of strong coffee on to brew. When it finished perking, he poured a cup and, holding it between two shaky hands, he sipped. He carried it with him back into the living room and slowly finished it.

"Damn fool," he muttered, condemning himself for spending the night with a girl he scarcely remembered, trying to wash Amy out of his mind. "It will never work, and you're sure as hell not going to give up this easy."

Amy had been hurt by his deception, he knew that, but she wouldn't hurt that much if there wasn't still something vital there. He would keep trying until Amy found some way to forgive him for his stupid mistake.

He set the empty cup aside, lay back on the couch cushions, and closed his eyes again, resting his arm across his eyes. He couldn't recall feeling as miserable any time in his life as he did now.

After a few more minutes of contemplating his discomfort, he decided that something to eat might help his stomach settle. He stood on legs that felt rubbery and walked to the kitchen. There was very little in the refrigerator. A package of lunch meat and a quart of milk seemed his best bet. He took out the meat and opened it. The slimy feel and the green tinge around the edges, combined with the odor, almost undid him. He walked to the garbage can, quickly threw it in, and covered it. His stomach flipped for a minute, then he regained control. At least he could have a glass of milk. His only other choices were water, which would only make him drunk again, or orange juice, which would most certainly be the last straw for his queasy stomach. He took out the quart of milk, pinched it open and smelled to make sure. The scent of spoiled milk made his stomach roil, and he gagged as he poured it down the sink. By now he was sweating and gritting his teeth to regain control.

He swung open a cupboard door and saw a jar of peanut butter and half of a package of buns. He set the jar of peanut butter in front of him, and as soon as he picked up the package of buns, he knew they were stale. By now he was in a state of utter desperation. He tore one bun in two and spread the peanut butter on it. Then he grabbed up a paper towel and returned to the living room.

Gingerly he sat down on the couch and put the sandwich on the paper towel and set it in front of him on the coffee table.

He rested his elbows on his knees, hanging his hands limply between his legs, and contemplated what it was going to cost him physically to take a bite of the concoction sitting before him on the coffee table.

He reached out a shaky hand and raised the sandwich to his lips, then took a bite and combined the crunch of the stale bread with the peanut butter that promptly adhered to the roof of his mouth.

It was at that moment the door swung open and Amy walked in.

It was a picture Amy wasn't prepared for, and Paul was prepared even less. He couldn't even speak at first because of the thick glob of peanut butter that was obstinately refusing to go down.

"I'm sorry to interrupt your lunch," she said in a controlled voice that he was sure could have been chipped with an ice pick.

"Lunch," he gurgled. "What time is it?" came out a

muffled garble. He looked at his watch. Twelve-fifty! God, he'd slept the day away!

"I've just come for the things I left here," Amy continued as she moved into the room. "I won't disturb you, and I'll be gone in a few minutes." She paused as she grew close enough to understand what the situation was. Paul could have groaned as he saw the malicious gleam in her eyes.

"My, my, Paul, are you sick? You poor thing." Her eyes caught the sandwich. "And only a peanut butter sandwich for lunch. No matter what I think of your ratty ways, I can't go and leave you hungry. I'll make you something."

"No," he began, finally working most of the peanut butter free from the roof of his mouth.

"No bother," Amy said brightly as she walked across the hardwood floor with footsteps that sounded like cannons in his head. "A little music, and I'll whip up something in a flash." She stopped by the stereo, chose a tape, and slipped it in the stereo. By this time, Paul was standing and moving toward her. The blast of heavy rock hit him like a wall, and he staggered from it. His head was beating furiously, and the one bite of sandwich was not settling too well.

Amy was already moving into the kitchen, banging cupboards and rattling pans. Paul wasn't sure which noise was going to finish him off, so he started for Amy first.

She had put a frying pan on the stove none too gently and was cracking eggs into a bowl. Just as he reached the kitchen door, Amy lifted the bowl and held it toward him.

"How do you want them?" she smiled sweetly.

One look at the raw eggs floating in the bowl brought a muffled curse from Paul. He turned and moved as fast as legs without muscles would carry him into the living room again, Amy's soft laugh following him. He got to the stereo and literally stripped the tape out. His agony was so bad that he slipped his finger behind the ribbon of tape and pulled it loose.

"Hey! You owe me a new tape. That was mine, you know!" She ignored his dark and somewhat menacing scowl as he moved toward her.

"Now that you're here, you can listen to reason," he muttered.

"I didn't come to battle it out with you, chum. I left a few of my things behind, and since I don't want any of your ladies playing with my toys, I've come to collect them."

She tried to sweep past him, but he caught her arm, swung her around, and just about threw her down on the couch.

"There are two of you moving around, and I can only handle one of you at a time, so sit down!"

She bounced up as rapidly as she had sat down. "The hell I will," she snapped. "From what I can see today, I just don't think you're big enough to make me."

"Amy, stay here for a while. At least talk to me . . . and at least try to understand what I've been trying to explain to you."

"All I want to do is get my things and get out of here. I need to get on with my life."

"So do I, and I can't do it until you have enough sense to listen to me."

"It doesn't take a lot of sense to listen to you. It just takes a lot of gullibility to believe you."

"Boy, when you get down you don't let up, do you?" he said. "Give me a break, Amy—or are you too damn stubborn to admit you should back off a little bit."

"Why should I back off? One step back by me and you charge in and make a fool out of me again."

"What happened would never happen again!"

"So you say."

"Yes, so I say."

"What am I supposed to do, fall into your arms after that little profession of fidelity?"

"I don't expect that. I just don't want you to break our relationship completely. We could give it another try."

"I don't know if I could."

"How can you say something like that after all we've meant to each other?" he protested. "Can you just throw it all away that easy?"

"It wasn't easy! It hurt like hell!"

"If you didn't love me it wouldn't hurt, and you can't just turn love off and on like a faucet."

"Like you did with Martha?"

"That wasn't love, and one mistake shouldn't condemn someone forever. You can't throw our love away like this!"

"Paul, I can't just forget it, not like that. It's not that easy. I told you I needed time, and I do. I also told you I would think about it. That's all I can say. I can't make promises I might not be able to keep."

"I won't let you go, Amy," he said. "I'll be with you every move you make, and that's a promise I really intend to keep."

"Then, we'll just have to wait and see where it goes, won't we?"

"I guess. Just so you know. You can't be any more demolished by this thing than I am. I lied because I was scared as hell that I'd lose you. Well, I'm paying for the lie, but I still don't want to lose you."

"I just can't make a commitment again—not until I get myself together. I can only say I'll think about it."

"While you're at it, think about more than the lie. Think about all the other days and nights we had that were more than special. Think about that, too."

"I will." She started to turn away, then paused and turned back to him. "Paul?"

"What?"

"I want something from you."

"What?"

"My painting."

"Your painting! You have to be kidding!"

"I want it."

"No."

"Why? It's mine."

"How the hell do you figure that? It's my work."

"It's me!"

"It's mine! And you damn well can't have it."

"Why not? What do you want with it?"

"I want you to want it." He smiled for the first time. "And I want you to come and get it. I also want to have some part of you here." He walked to her slowly.

"What did you do with Martha's portrait?"

"I destroyed it," he admitted.

"And if another woman comes into your life, will you do the same to mine?"

"I destroyed it because you were everything that filled

my life, and she had no part of it. She was a way to hurt us, and I didn't want it around anymore."

Amy felt his presence, and knew she wasn't strong enough to fight the physical attraction she felt for him. He was a potent force, and she had to have more time to regain her ground before she exposed herself to his magnetic pull.

She turned away, but Paul reached out and gripped her wrist, turning her about and pulling her into his arms. He kissed her with a frantic passion that did more to make her angry than seduce her. The slap that followed it made his head explode into pinpoints of lights.

"You can run if you want to," he said, "but you can't run from the truth, and the truth is, you still love me, too."

"Is that confidence I hear?"

"A little. I don't think you're a liar, and my memory goes back to a lot of nights when you told me you loved me, plus a whole lot of other interesting things."

"You don't fight fair."

"I fight to win, which means to get you back, I'll even fight dirty if I have to."

Amy's eyes held his, and she recognized a part of Paul she had always known—pure, iron-hard devotion to what he thought was right. It began to make Amy give the situation a second thought.

"All right," she said softly. "Good luck. Give it your best shot." She turned and left the house while Paul fumbled with the meaning behind the words.

He walked to a large, wood-framed mirror that hung on the wall, suddenly feeling less sick and more confident. He studied himself; he even looked a little better.

His reflection smiled back at him, assuring him the best fight since Adam had begun the battle with Eve.

Amy drove home more confused than she'd ever been. She had expected Paul to be out, as he usually was on Sunday mornings. He was a creature of habit, and on Sunday mornings he took his sketchbook and made hundreds of sketches. It was more to commune with himself than anything else. Paul had always told her it was the breath of air he needed to be able to get back to painting.

Finding Paul at the mill had thrown her off stride, and her

defenses had to be quickly erected before he got behind them and destroyed them completely.

In the privacy of her thoughts, she had to admit that Paul had the same effect on her as if she had touched a hot electric wire. Much as she fought, the truth was, he had shaken her resolve completely.

She remembered the look in Paul's eyes when she had faced him with the truth and the look now, when he had promised her he wasn't going to let go of what they had so easily. She smiled. Maybe she didn't want it to be over either. She would see what tomorrow would bring.

He knelt in the quiet church, and the relaxed look of his body told of his self-satisfaction. His thoughts and the upward curve of his handsome mouth would have confirmed this.

He had to do what he knew was the rule. He had rid the world of an evil. He also had silenced the voice that tore at him. Maybe this time it would end; maybe this time he would not hear that sugar-coated voice and feel the slice of leather across his back. Maybe he had killed her, once and for all, and found some peace. He remembered, he heard, and he knew he was doing what was right. The blackness swirled about him like a heavy mist. He remembered.

The room was oppressively warm, yet all the windows were closed. Candles of all sizes sputtered in the thick air. Shadows danced on the walls in the flickering light, creating grotesque shapes that were metaphors for the fear and pain that filled the room.

It was small and very austere—only a narrow cot and one dresser. Above the cot hung a huge gold crucifix. Another gleamed in the candlelight above the dresser. There was no clutter—no toys or games, no sign of the boy who lived here at all. He knelt beside the bed, his thin, bony knees filled with pain, for he had been kneeling so for almost two hours.

He was just over six years old, thin and large-eyed. His gaunt face was streaked with tears, and his hands were folded before him.

He was trying desperately to do as the towering form over

him demanded, but his mind seemed filled with an unbelievable darkness. He could not grasp one lucid thought.

The form that towered over him seemed to him immense and overpowering. She was a woman, strong of arm—an arm that now raised a heavy leather strap and brought it down upon the boy's bare back while she intoned his guilt in a deep, singsong voice. His mind could not grasp all her meaning. He had tried to be obedient and pray for his evil soul. Yet he didn't know what he was guilty of, and he wasn't too sure the entity she forced him to pray to existed, or if he did, whether he cared at all.

"You are a wicked, wicked boy. Did you think I wouldn't know? Did you think you could keep a secret from me?"

The strap fell again. He winced but didn't answer. He had learned this discipline a long time ago. Any answer would immediately be construed as argument, and would only bring more punishment.

"I must teach you not to be so evil, never to have lustful thoughts. You must learn to be pure if you are going to be His servant. You are going to be a priest, so you must learn that girls are wicked and will lead you astray."

The strap fell again and again, then finally ceased. The blows stopped, but the voice echoed in the deep well where his mind had gone to hide.

"Now, let me hear your confession. Tell me how evil and filthy you are."

He struggled for the words, sensing from past experience what he might have done wrong and hoping it was the right answer.

"I walked home from school with Cassie," he said in a broken whisper.

"Evil boy . . . wicked boy."

"We were sitting on the front steps talking, and she was showing me the game she brought to school."

"You are filthy . . . wicked."

"I won't talk to anyone on my way home again—I won't."

"Of course you won't. You know you will be punished if you do, don't you?"

"Yes."

"But you needn't worry. I will make you good. I will

wash away your evil. In time, I will make you obedient. Now you may go to bed, but you will have no supper—not until you learn to be obedient."

He crawled into the bed and curled into a ball. The worst of all things was to come yet.

The huge female left. Then came the quiet, stealthy one—the one with the delicate voice and soft hands. The one who stroked his flesh and talked in a whisper that made his darkening soul shriek in terror. Then the hands and the softness would hurt him, and he would finally be able to cry.

Only in the wee hours of the morning did he sneak from the bed and grasp the only book he had. He leafed through the book until he found the passage he had read over and over—the only passage that ever brought him any kind of peace in his torment-filled world.

He read it now with cold satisfaction. She had taught him to believe in these words, and now he had finally found the ones to which he could turn for a shield between himself and the pain—between himself and punishment.

He read it three times, and only then could he find the peace to face the next day . . . and the next night. The words were like a lullaby. He could almost sing himself to sleep with them.

Leviticus 24

Also, all murderers must be executed. The penalty for injuring anyone is to be injured in exactly the same way: fracture for fracture, eye for eye, tooth for tooth. Whatever anyone does to another shall be done to him.

The face he lifted to the altar was lit with the candle glow. It was handsome, and set with a look of contentment. He was an instrument, a protector, and he had done both deeds well. This was one moment of peace . . . one moment.

Scott Andrews tipped his hat to the back of his head, leaned back against the car seat, and sighed. He hated night duty, but he didn't complain. Murder was something he had been trained to handle, although he had never before been involved in such a case. But now his small town had been visited by a killer, and he had to use everything he had learned to get the man.

As if their minds had silently been working on the same thoughts, his partner Tyler said, "I can't see why that guy keeps coming back here."

"Yeah. But at least he can't get into this strip of woods again. There are only two roads in, and he'll never get past Brady."

"I'm going to stretch my legs," Tyler said.

"It's sure a pretty night for this time of year. The moon's so bright you can see like day." Scott opened the car door and stood looking skyward. "Maybe I'll stick to the radio, and you can walk the road a ways, then we'll change off."

"Good enough."

Scott leaned against the car, folding his arms to keep the chill out. He was tired of just sitting. Besides, they had to cruise the road off and on, and taking turns walking would be a little easier on the legs. He was too tall to sit cramped like that for long.

No more than fifteen minutes later his partner came running toward him. At first he wasn't alarmed, then he realized Tyler wasn't jogging, he was in a real hurry.

When Tyler reached Scott's side, he was panting. "Get on the horn, Scott."

"What's wrong?"

"I sure as hell don't know how he did it, but that son of a bitch got past us."

"What the hell are you talking about?"

"There's a little red car down there. It's sitting right in that first clump of trees."

"So?"

"So, there's a girl inside."

"Is she . . . ?"

"I didn't disturb anything, I just checked her. She's dead. Her face is battered, and she's sitting behind the wheel. How the hell did he get her and that car in here? I don't understand."

Scott was already radioing back to the station. While they waited, both men studied the area. Whoever the killer was, he had made a fool of them and killed successfully again. Anger was beginning to grow like a thick black cloud.

Joe groaned awake at the shrill sound of the phone. It was four o'clock in the morning. His heart thudded heavily as he reached for it, and long before he said hello, he knew that there had been another death. He dreaded the voice on the other end of the line.

"Joe?"

"Yeah."

"Briggs. You better get down here. He's got another one."

"Same place?"

"Yeah, and don't ask me how. Andrews, Tyler, and Brady were there, and they're the best. That guy knows this place like the back of his hand. How he got in and out nobody knows, but he left another body."

"Who is she?"

"We don't know yet."

"I'll be right down." Joe hung up and got out of bed.

"Joe?" Sally said sleepily.

"Go to sleep, Sal. I'll be back in a while."

Sally sat up. She didn't speak—she just read Joe's face and knew. "Oh, Joe . . . who?"

"I don't know, babe," Joe said wearily. "I don't know—but I'm getting scared now, too. Go back to sleep." Joe bent and kissed her, and left her wide awake and worried.

* CHAPTER 36 *

Joe watched the body bag being put in the ambulance and felt the same futile fury. He held a piece of paper in his hand that he had read at least fifty times in the past hour or so. He tore his eye from the body and looked again at the note.

Proverbs 29

For you closed your eyes to the facts, and did not choose to reverence and trust the Lord, and you turned your back on me, spurning my advice. That is why you must eat the bitter fruit of having your own way and experience the terrors of the pathway you have chosen. For you turned away from me . . . to death. Your own complacency will kill you. Fools!

The one you called from a distance is not any wiser than you. He stumbles in circles and does not see the right path. None of you can recognize the hand of God and the necessity for its touch.

Joe scowled at the paper. The demented mind that wrote this was beyond his understanding.

"Joe?"

"Yeah?"

"We're just about finished here."

"You've checked the place carefully?"

"Yes. We've dusted the car for prints."

"Did you trace her tire tracks in here?"

"Yeah, we found a few of hers. We also found a blurred set that wasn't hers. We're having a cast made now."

"Did you get an ID?"

"Yeah, Brady knew her. Her name's Barbara Winslow. Brady's going to go tell the family. I guess they reported her missing late Saturday night. You know how scared people are. We had to get past the twenty-four-hour missing-person wait before we could do anything, but they found her, so that's that."

"That's that," Joe repeated. "And a girl is dead because I've been pussyfooting around. Well, I'm done playing games."

"What are you going to do?"

"I'm going to yank in all three suspects and hang on to them as long as I can, until one of them slips."

Joe put the note in his pocket and drove back to the station, where he put out the word to pick up the suspects and bring them in. Then he reached for the phone and dialed Carl's motel. After the phone rang at least twenty times, he gave up and dialed Beth's house, with the same result. He called and told Sally he wouldn't be home for hours.

He dialed Carl's motel back and left a message, urgently requesting a return call. Joe walked across his office to pour himself a cup of coffee. He stood and looked out the window at the gray dawn. It promised to be a very long day.

Although Carl and Beth woke very early, it was nearly noon before they reached Helton.

"Come over to my place, Carl. I'll whip us up a little lunch before you go back to work."

"Sounds good to me. I'll call Joe from your house."

They were inside the door only a minute or two when the phone rang. Since Beth had carried her overnight case to her bedroom, Carl answered.

"Carl? It's about time you got back." Carl could hear the frustration in Joe's voice.

"I've got some news for you, Joe, but I'm not sure just how it ties in."

"Well, I have some pretty strong news for you, too," Joe replied.

"What's the matter? You sound like hell."

"I feel worse. I should have picked those three up a long time ago. This might not have happened."

Carl felt a jolt in the pit of his stomach, as if he were on a roller coaster. "It happened again."

"Yeah—a girl named Barbara Winslow. Her body was found pretty near the same spot, note included. This time he says you're a stupid bungler."

"By name?"

"No, he just casually mentioned the 'one I called from a distance.'"

"I'll be right over."

Beth came out of the bedroom just as Carl hung up. "What's the matter, Carl?"

"Our man's done it again. It's as if he thinks he has divine protection and can't get caught. He left a note again, and he actually thumbed his nose at us." He picked his coat up from where he had tossed it when he answered the phone. "I'm going over. I have to fill Joe in on David and have him at least picked up and asked a few questions."

"What about Mrs. Lowrey?"

"I don't know. I'll go see her again this afternoon and see if I can pick that alibi apart any way."

"Want a sandwich before you go?"

"No, I'll grab something later. I don't know how long this day will be, but I'd like to see you later."

"Come over."

"It might be late."

"I don't turn into a pumpkin at midnight."

He shrugged into his coat, then went to Beth. He grabbed her and dramatically swept her back over his arm to kiss her. She was laughing and breathless when he stood her erect again.

"Rudolph Valentino has nothing on that." He chuckled. "I'll see you later."

"I wish you luck, Carl. You've got to stop him."

When Carl walked into the office, Joe looked up, grim-faced. "I've yanked those three in," he said, "and I'm going to question them until I break their stories into pieces and get some answers."

"Joe, you may be making a mistake. I want to fill you in on what I found out in Bridgefield."

"So shoot." Joe leaned back in his chair. "I want to put a stop to all of this as fast as I can."

"I saw David's aunt and uncle—the Rossmans. Two of about the ugliest pieces of humanity I've run across. If David was tossed into that den of perverted fanaticism at six I hate to think of what happened to him. They both look like child abusers to me and the aunt is a cold piece of fish capable of anything."

"That doesn't make him guilty of anything. A lot of people had bad childhoods—Brodie, for one. It's a toss-up as to whose was worse."

"I know it doesn't make Mondale guilty, but he fits Reuger's profile for the murderer, and at least it makes him another suspect."

"With an unbreakable alibi."

"Yeah," Carl said morosely, "but only for the first

murder, and I still have a twitch in the back of my neck about that. I'm going to see Mrs. Lowrey again and see if there are any holes in that alibi."

"You really think he did it?"

"I can't be sure of anything. Joe, can you figure a way he could have gotten into those woods without one of our boys seeing him? There are only those two dirt roads up to the highway, and they were being watched pretty close."

"I have a whole gang walking those woods right now, looking for some other way in that we don't know about."

"You know we used to run those woods as kids. It seems there's something we should remember, but I sure as hell don't know what."

"Me either. But I'll find out if I have to take those woods apart, tree by tree. I don't like the idea of the freedom the killer has to walk in under the noses of three of my best boys. That is a challenge he's going to get answered."

"I'd like to talk to Paul, Michael, and Father McAllen before I go and see Emma."

"They haven't been questioned yet, so feel free. I'd like to start something moving here."

"Maybe you shouldn't pick up David until we get these three stories straight."

"Why not? A suspect in hand is worth three in the bush."

"If he is off his rocker, he'll just clam up and wait us out. We have no evidence. Let me talk to the other three and see Emma first."

"All right, Carl, but don't take too long. I wouldn't want him to hit again while I'm sitting here sucking my thumb."

"It'll be quick. I'll go see Paul first."

"Fine."

"Oh, I forgot to tell you." Carl turned at the door. "Our friend David studied for the priesthood for a while. Give your professor another call. See if it ties together."

"I'll do that." Joe was again reaching for the phone when Carl left.

Carl had Paul taken to a small room for questioning. He was there when Paul was brought in. His face was pale and his mouth pulled to a taut line. He was also very scared, and Carl wondered why, if he was not guilty of anything.

"Paul, sit down."

Paul sat without a word, clenching his hands before him. "Look, Carl, if you want to ask me where I was Saturday night, you can forget it. I don't have any answers. I was drunk as a skunk—so totally wiped out that I don't remember a damn thing."

"Pretty poor alibi. Why'd you tie one on?"

"You've got a lot of nerve asking me that. You come along and tear up everything good in my life, then watch Amy walk out on me, and you have the gall to ask me why!"

"If you had told Amy the truth at the beginning, she might not have walked."

Paul's shoulders sagged and his hands grew even more tightly clenched. Carl was reasonably sure it was to keep control of himself.

"If she loves you, Paul, she'll get over the hurt. She might find you're in trouble and come running."

"Sure, I'll believe that. Carl, I didn't do any of this. I may have been out of it the other night, but surely when I woke up at home I would have had some evidence on me or around me. I got drunk, but I sure as hell didn't kill anyone."

"Paul, you've been around here most of your life. Maybe you can answer a question."

"What?"

"When we were kids, Joe and I, we used to play in the woods. I keep feeling I've forgotten something. Have there been any changes around those woods in the past few years?"

Paul looked puzzled for a minute, as if he were searching his memory. "Well, I remember when they laid the new highway, so that would be about the time they cut the dirt roads in. They needed a roundabout. Those are the only two roads I know. I guess the third road would be whatever's left of the old highway. It was a one-laner, and most likely it's all overgrown by now."

Paul's description brought the memory of the remnants of the old road back to Carl. He realized he or Joe should have thought of it sooner.

"I think Joe will be springing you as soon as we trace your movements on Saturday night. I'm sure if you got as drunk as you say you did, someone saw you."

"This is one time I hope the whole town saw me."

"Okay, Paul. I'm sorry we have to keep you, but Joe is checking everything out." Carl pressed a button under the table, and the door opened almost at once for the uniformed policeman to return Paul to his cell.

When they were gone, another policeman poked his head in the door.

"I guess I'll take Michael Brodie next, and after that, Father McAllen," Carl told him.

Michael came in, and Carl was struck at once by the almost subdued look about him. He came in slowly and sat opposite Carl. There seemed to be less belligerence in his eyes. Carl was sure something had softened the edges, and he wanted to know what.

Michael seemed much younger than he had when the obvious chip had been on his shoulder. He had been an enraged man battling the unfair world. Now, he seemed to have changed.

"Michael, are you okay?"

"I'm fine."

"There's been another killing," Carl said quietly, expecting an explosive reaction. He was disappointed.

"I know; I heard. But I had nothing to do with it. This is one time I can prove where I was."

"And just where were you?" Carl countered. The answer he got was the last one he expected.

"I got a visit from Father McAllen on Friday. He said a couple of things that hurt. Then I got this phone call from a friend of his, Emma Lowrey."

"Who?" Carl was startled enough to let his chair drop back with a thud.

"Emma Lowrey. She wanted to come and see me, but I told her to get lost." Michael smiled a taut, straight-lipped smile. "But she came anyhow. I gave her all kinds of hard words, and she threw them right back at me. She said she knew I wasn't guilty, and she wasn't going to let me wallow around in self-pity like a pig in a pen—which is what she called my house. I couldn't believe her. She started cleaning and talking and—damn, you won't believe this, but the next thing I knew I was helping her and talking as much as she was."

"Oh, I believe it." Carl laughed, "I know her well. So what happened?"

"She left and said if there was anything I wanted to say, or if the hurting got too much, I could just come see her."

Michael bent forward and rested his arms on the table. His face was still filled with surprise at what had happened. "I told her to go to hell. She laughed and said she not only had no intention of that, but in her words, she had hold of the seat of my pants and she wasn't going to let me either. That broad is really something, you know?"

"Yeah, I do. But this doesn't tell me what happened Saturday night or where you were."

"Saturday night was a bad night. I guess I got caught up in a lot of old memories. I went out and rode around for a while, stopped at a couple of places and had a drink, and I swear I don't know why myself, but I wound up on Mrs. Lowrey's porch knocking on her door. She didn't even act surprised, just told me to come on in. So we got to talking, and one thing sort of led to another, and I was spilling my guts to this old lady who reminded me of . . ."

"Your mother."

"Hell, no, my mother was a bitch. Dropped me when I was about thirteen. She reminded me—You ain't gonna like this."

"Try me."

"She reminded me of this old madam I knew. She had a rough hand, a hard mouth, and a heart like Texas."

"Christ, Emma would just love to be told she reminded you of an old whore." Carl was containing his laughter with a great deal of effort.

"Emma? She a friend of yours?"

"Very close."

"Then, for God's sake, don't tell her I said that."

"How long were you at her house?"

"After Father McAllen left, I spent the night on her couch."

"Father McAllen! Was he there?"

Michael sighed and nodded. "He came over sometime around eleven or so, after she called him."

"And he was there with you two the rest of the night?"

"Until about four or five. I had been home only about three or four hours when the cops came beating on my door and dragged me in."

"You know, Michael." Carl grinned. "This is about the best thing I've heard since I got here."

"You sound about as cuckoo as she does. Why should it make you feel good that you just lost your best suspect?"

"Best suspects," Carl corrected, "and I just couldn't feel better about it."

"Now I know you're nuts. Does this broad only associate with people as crazy as she is?"

"Hopefully. I'd like to think I'm as crazy as she is. You'll be out of here pretty quick."

"You're springing me!"

"Yep. What are you going to do?"

Michael looked sheepish for a minute, then replaced his rigid mask, as if he were still afraid Carl would see beyond the face he presented to the world. "I guess I kinda owe her a debt, so I was going to go back over to her place. It needs a whole lotta work. It ain't that she's anything special, but I don't want to owe anybody. I pay back favors. I don't take nothing for nothing."

"Sure," Carl said solemnly. "I'm sure Emma could use a little help. You might even consider moving in and boarding with her while you work on the place."

"Yeah . . . well, maybe you're right. It would be more convenient for me."

"Right."

"I wouldn't have to be running back and forth."

"Right."

"Somebody oughta be there to see she don't get into any trouble."

Michael's brow was furrowed in a frown he hoped would convince Carl he wasn't being softhearted. Carl extended his hand to Michael as he stood up.

"Take good care of her, Michael—she's a real special person."

"Yeah . . . I'll do that."

Again Carl pressed the button, and Michael was temporarily returned to his cell. Carl went back to Joe's office.

"I'm on my way over to Emma's right now. I'll talk to her again. If there is a flaw, I've got to find it or we'll be starting all over again. Are you going to keep Paul?"

"I have some people checking around the bars. If someone can ID him near the time of the murder, I'll release him."

"Good. I'll see Emma, then I'll be right back. If there's anything out of sync with David's alibi, we'll pick him up. We can at least ask questions."

"Get on your horse. I want this thing over before it drives me to drink."

Carl waved and was gone. As he walked out of the police station, he came face-to-face with Amy Realton.

"Amy. What are you doing here?"

"I heard Paul had been arrested."

"Does that concern you now? I thought maybe you'd come around to supply him with another alibi."

Amy flushed, knowing Carl knew of her past lie to protect Paul.

"If I told you he was with me . . ."

"I wouldn't believe it any more now than I did before. But don't be so scared, Amy. I think Paul will be free pretty soon—if that means anything to you."

"I didn't want it to. After I found out about Martha I was hurt, and I guess I had to hit back."

"But you never took back your lie."

"No, I . . ."

"I guess maybe that proves something, doesn't it?"

"Carl, he's not guilty. No matter what happened between him and Martha, Paul just couldn't commit murder. And one murder after another? No, Paul could never do that."

"Yes, I know."

"You know? How?"

"I can't talk about it. Later, when everything's settled, I'll explain. Right now, I think there's someone you want to see more than you want to talk to me."

"Is he all right?"

"After he sees you, I have a feeling he'll be fine."

"If he'll see me now."

"Don't be a fool. If you back away now, it might cause a rift that can grow. Go on in and see him."

Slowly Amy walked into the station and requested to see Paul. She was led down a long hall to a locked door. Beyond it were several cells. Paul stood in one, his back to the door and his arms folded on the windowsill as he looked outside.

At the click of the lock, he broke from his reverie and looked around. He stood paralyzed as his eyes met Amy across the room. They stood so for several minutes. Neither was sure who had moved first, but suddenly they were in each other's arms, she whispering his name and he kissing her over and over again.

* CHAPTER 37 *

As Carl drove toward Emma's house he remembered, in a quick flash, the day he had been there and shared lunch with her and David.

He remembered David's overprotective attitude toward his mentor Father McAllen and his knowledge of the slashed portrait at Paul's party. It occurred now to Carl that David had had no way of knowing about the portrait's being sliced. He'd never told him about it, yet David had asked about it. The only way he could have known is if he had been the one to cut it.

Carl pulled to a stop in front of Emma's house and took the steps rapidly, but before he could knock, the door was opened and Emma's smiling face appeared.

"Well, it's about time you got back to visit me. I called Joe—did he tell you?"

"No, I guess he has his hands full and forgot. Was there something you wanted?"

"He told me you had gone out of town looking for some evidence." Carl could see the sparkle of mischief in her eyes and groaned mentally. Emma was, as always, one jump ahead of him.

"You're a busybody," he said, laughing, "and I'm not obligated to tell you anything at all."

"Have you had any lunch?"

"You trying to corrupt me? Bribery won't get you anywhere."

"Are you corruptible? I can give you a fresh-baked-ham sandwich and top it with a piece of apple pie à la mode."

"What a black heart you've got."

"Just a fair exchange," she said. "I've got something to tell you."

"I'll bet it's about Michael Brodie."

"How did you know?"

"I just talked to him at the jail."

"Jail! Why was he there?"

"There was another girl killed. Joe picked him up."

"When was she killed?"

"Saturday night."

"That boy's innocent. He was here on my couch all Saturday night."

"I know."

"He told you?"

"Not the details. But his being here is alibi enough. Joe will be letting him go."

"Carl, that boy has had a hard time, and Martha was the only good thing in his life. I can't blame him for being angry with the world—not after what I know about him now."

"You going to tell me what he said to you?"

"No," she answered with a softer smile. "He's on the path to being straightened out, and I'm not going to set up any roadblocks."

"He kind of thinks you're a cross between Queen Elizabeth and Catherine the Great."

"He said I was like one of them?" Emma chuckled, pleased as punch.

"Well, he didn't exactly name them, but he said you were like a very important lady he once knew who had a heart the size of Texas," Carl answered diplomatically.

"I must remember to save him some pie."

"Now I'm second fiddle."

"So stick around town, handsome, and maybe you'll still be in the running."

"I'm seriously thinking about doing just that."

Her eyes snapped to his, and he could see the excitement blossom. "Are you really, Carl? That's the best news I've ever heard. Do Helton and I have a certain Beth Raleigh to thank for this?"

"If the offer of pie still stands, I might just be coerced into telling you."

"That little story might get you two pieces."

Carl had followed her into the house as they talked, removing his coat and laying it across a chair. Then he followed Emma into the kitchen and slid into his favorite chair—at Emma's kitchen table.

"Carl?" Emma was at the sink board slicing pie, her back to him. "I'm glad you don't believe that Michael had anything to do with all this. I feel kind of sorry for him. But I feel happy too. At least he's starting to get a grip on himself. I'd like to help him."

"I'm sure you will, Emma. In fact," he laughed lightly, "I don't think poor Michael has one chance in Hades to do anything else but straighten up." He accepted the pie she placed before him. "He'll be trotting around here just like all stray puppies and kittens do, because you always have a plate of food for strays," Carl continued. "But I guess I feel pretty good about it too."

Emma sat down opposite him, and he concentrated on the pie to keep from meeting her gaze.

"So, Carl," she said gently, "why don't you tell me what's on your mind."

"Do I look worried or something?"

"No, you look like you're chewing on a bone."

"What's that supposed to mean?"

"Something's bothering you. Do I have an answer?"

"Maybe." He put down his fork. "Emma, you listen to me and don't say one word until I'm done, agreed?"

"But, why . . . ?"

"Not one word. I need a promise. Just listen to me and answer my questions. I'll do all the explaining after I get some answers."

"All right."

"When did David come here to board?"

"David?" She was surprised. "Why do . . ."

"No questions. I have your promise. Now, when did he come here to board?"

"Two and a half years ago this past August."

"Did he just walk up on your porch and ask you if you took in boarders?"

"Good heavens, no. Father McAllen brought him over."

"Did he ever talk to you about his past?"

"No."

"Did he ever talk to you about himself at all?"

"No, not really. He seemed . . ." She became thoughtful. "In fact, come to think about it, he never wanted to talk about himself. He said he was an orphan, and talking about it only depressed him."

"Did he discuss religion with you?"

"Yes, we used to have great conversations. I told him many times he should have been a priest. He is very devout, you know."

"Yes, I know. Did he talk about girls much? I mean, a kid his age and handsome as he is, he probably dated like crazy and had girls calling him all the time."

"No, he never got any phone calls here." She frowned. "Come to think of it, he never got any calls ever."

"The night Martha was killed, you said he was here at the time of the murder."

"Precisely. Ten-thirty. I remember looking at the clock when he came in from jogging."

"Emma, is there any way you could be mistaken about the time?"

"If I hadn't just glanced at the clock I might be. But David had bumped his watch against something, and it had stopped, so he asked me what time it was when he was fiddling with it. Anyway, I looked at the clock, and it was ten-thirty-two."

"You're absolutely certain?"

"Yes."

"Now, I want you to think back to that night, very carefully. Then I want you to tell me every move you made and everything you did, up to the moment David asked you what time it was."

"All right. I went shopping early in the afternoon, came back, and put the groceries away. Then I made a roast for supper. It was just a little past five when David came home. We ate dinner, then he helped me with the dishes. He went to his room for a while, then came back down around eight." Her brow furrowed. "He was dressed in slacks and a sweater. He was just putting on a jacket, and said he was going out for a little while. He was gone about an hour, and then he came back. He chatted with me until about nine-thirty, then said he was going jogging for a while. He was so sweet. He turned on the TV and made sure I was comfortable on the couch. Then he went out. I was watching a TV show, and I must have dozed off. He was shaking me awake and laughing. Said he'd make tea if I wanted a cup. He had already shut the TV off."

Carl had become very alert, and as she went on, he smiled and leaned back in his chair. "So you had tea, and while he was at the table, he claimed his watch had stopped and asked you the time while he set it."

"Right. That's the entire evening. Now, if your questions are over, I have one of my own."

"You ask, and I'll explain. Then I have an important request."

"You suspect David, don't you?"

"Emma." He tried to say it as gently as he possibly could. "It's not suspicion any longer. I'm sure. I just couldn't prove it because he seemed to have been here at the time of the murder. But now I know how he pulled that off."

"It can't be David—it just can't. He's a fine, hardworking, devout boy. How could I be that wrong? I don't believe it. He was here at ten-thirty, and that girl was killed after eleven."

"No, dear, he wasn't here at ten-thirty."

"But, I saw the time!"

"You saw the time that he set. He made you comfortable and you fell asleep. He came back from killing that girl and found you asleep, so he set the clocks back to produce the perfect alibi. When you went to bed he must have changed the clocks again."

"Oh, Carl, that's impossible to believe."

"I believe it. I only wish I could prove it."

"What was the request?"

"I want you to let me in David's room. I need to look around. I might just be lucky enough to find something."

"I don't know."

"Emma, I don't have a search warrant. It's illegal. But I need to know if he made a mistake and left evidence where I could get my hands on it."

She sighed and stood up, took a key from a hook on the wall, and put it in her pocket. Without a word, she led the way up the stairs to David's room. She put the key in the lock and swung the door open.

"I've not been in here since David came. He cleans his own room, and I've always believed in privacy, so I left him alone."

Carl walked into the room, and Emma followed somewhat reluctantly. Both stood in open-mouthed surprise at the sight that met them. The room was neat and very clean, bare of all but the essentials. But what drew their attention was the extra-large gold crucifix on the wall with the small prayer bench before it. Around the crucifix were newspaper clippings—not only from Helton, but from other sources. All had pictures of the murdered girls and stories to go with them. They were pinned at random in a circle all around it.

"Oh, God," Emma whispered. There was no way to deny the truth now. Carl felt sick, and he felt scared. This was something, but it still wasn't proof enough. Keeping stories and pictures about a murder could be construed as strange, but not evidence of guilt.

He took hold of Emma's hand and drew her gently from the room, reaching for the knob to pull the door shut. They went downstairs again, and Carl made Emma sit down while he made her some tea.

"Does this mean he's guilty, Carl?" she whispered.

"It means he's a very sick man, Emma. He needs to be stopped. I have sympathy for the boy all those tragic things happened to, but I've got to stop the man before he does any more harm than he's already done."

"I suppose."

"I want you to come with me now, Emma."

"Where?"

"If David comes home tonight and doesn't find you here, he might not be upset. But as shaken as you are, he's going to read your face like a book. He might harm you, and I couldn't have that. I want to take you over to Beth's. You can stay with her until this is over."

"Tell me." Emma tried to smile. "Is there any reason I should be going to Beth's? I believe I know Sally better."

"Yeah," Carl said quietly. "I want the two most important women in my life to be together where I know they're both safe."

"Oh, Carl, I'm so glad."

"So am I." He took her arm. "Come on, Emma. I'm sure you and Beth are going to want to talk, so let's get you out of here."

"You bet Beth and I will talk. There's a lot of Carl Forrester I can fill in for her."

"Don't get carried away. I want the girl to marry me, not get scared off."

"Marry?"

"I just thought of that now, so keep your mouth shut. I'd really like to ask her first."

Emma's eyes brimmed with happy moisture. "So, you've finally put your ghosts to rest. Well, I couldn't be happier."

"Let's go. We need to get things rolling."

"I would like to talk to Father McAllen first."

"I'll call and see if Joe's sent him home. If he has, I'll run you over. I'd like to apologize to him, anyway." Carl went to the phone, and was quickly assured that Father McAllen had been released from custody.

"Come on, Emma. I'll take you over to the rectory, then to Beth's."

At the rectory, they were met by Father James and Father McAllen.

"Emma," Father McAllen said gently, quickly observing her pale face and shaking hands. "Are you all right?"

"No, I am not all right. Carl and I need to talk to you. I think what we have to say will be upsetting, so we would like to do it in private."

"Would you mind, James?" Father McAllen requested politely.

"Of course not," Father James replied.

Father McAllen sat down beside Emma on the soft leather couch. "Emma, what's wrong? You look as if you've had a terrible shock."

"I have, and I don't think I can explain everything. Carl can do that better than I."

"Carl, does this have something to do with my very sudden release from jail today?"

"I'm sorry about all the accusations and the inconvenience. We have a job to do, and Joe and I are trying to do it the best way possible."

"I'm sure you are. Joe was rather close-mouthed about the whole thing. I guess this means you've found the guilty one. I hope it wasn't Paul or Michael."

"We're reasonably sure, but we don't have proof."

"Sure of what?"

Carl took a deep breath. "That it was David Mondale."

"David! Don't be ridiculous—David wouldn't hurt a fly. What in God's name makes you suspect him? Besides," he turned to look at Emma, "I thought he was home with you at the time of Martha's murder."

"Let me explain," Carl went on.

"Please do. I'm sure you're on the wrong track. David just couldn't do a thing like this."

"Let me ask you first. You hired David to teach and to coach at your school. What credentials did he have?"

"His degree and a letter of recommendation from a very dear friend of mine—Father Martin from Bridgefield. I didn't think he needed anything else."

"Father, these murders have a highly religious overtone. It's as if the killer were either a religious fanatic, or hated the church with a passion. Now I'm asking you to think about that, then think about David's attitude."

"Well, after the past few days, I can sure eliminate Michael for you."

The day was growing short, and Carl was worried about the night. David could kill again, and unless Carl could either catch him or find a way to break him, he could never prove anything.

"What about David?"

"Well, it's true he attends mass every day, but that's hoped for in every parishioner."

"Let me tell you what Ellen has told us, and what we've just found in his room." As Carl told him the details, Father McAllen's face grew a little tighter. "Now, let me tell you what Professor Reuger at the college told us and some facts about David's background, which you don't seem to know." Carl went on to explain what he and Beth had encountered and the professor's interpretation. "On top of everything else, I don't think Paul and Michael would be throwing quotes from the Bible at us, but David might. There's another point I'd like to make. David has an inordinate admiration of you. I feel, and I may be wrong, that somehow, mentally, he switches places with you. He saw these women as some kind of an evil force, and when they came in contact with you they came in contact with him, too."

Father McAllen felt the pain of David's darkened soul like a knife in his heart. He blamed himself for not being able to see a need such as this.

"You couldn't have stopped him, Father. The damage was done to David when he was very young. By the time he got to you, he was beyond repair."

"I'd like to be with you when you go for him. He will need me then," Father McAllen said miserably.

"I can't arrest him until I can prove he murdered those girls. Everything I have is so tenuous that a good attorney could get my case against him thrown out. I've got to get a handle on him—something I can make stick."

"What are you going to do?"

"Right now, I'm going to take Emma over to Beth Raleigh's. I don't feel she's safe in that house. Then I'll go on over to Joe's office, and bat it back and forth with him to see if we can work out a way to handle this."

"I'd like to go with you. I'll stay with you until this is over."

"Father . . ."

"Carl, please. I have a responsibility here, too—maybe even more than you do. I'm not official." He smiled weakly. "I'm sure you can pull some strings downtown."

"Yeah, I guess I can. This might not be very pretty. If we catch him, you might see a David different from the man you know."

"A few years back I was pastor at the mental institution in Hillsville. I don't think you'll scare me off, Carl. Besides, David is alone and afraid. Maybe I can give him the first taste of what the church should be."

"If it's not too late."

"It's never too late."

Carl surrendered in the face of Father McAllen's grim determination. "Okay, I'll clear it. You might be helpful. He might resist us, and you just might be able to reach him."

"I hope."

"Then let's get going. Joe needs to be filled in, and I want to get Emma to safety."

"Like you say, maybe I can talk to him."

"All right." Carl turned a sympathetic gaze to Emma, whose eyes were filled with tears. "Are you ready, Emma?"

Emma nodded slowly, but her eyes were on Father McAllen. "Why?" she whispered. "Why a sweet boy like David? How could this happen?"

Father McAllen came to Emma's side and knelt before her. "Emma, we don't understand—maybe we never will. But this is a tragedy of evil, and we can only pray the Lord will balance it."

"I suppose you are right." She stood, and the three left the rectory and drove to Beth's.

When Carl left Beth, she decided to go to the market and then to stop by the library to make sure everything had run smoothly while she was gone.

She shopped carefully, planning a very special night. She and Carl had come together with an explosive suddenness, and tonight they needed to talk and make plans.

She parked her car in the library lot and went inside. She was caught up in conversation longer than she planned to be, and because it was late fall, it was already growing dark when she left.

She walked around the building to the semidark parking lot, removed her car key from her purse, and inserted it in the lock. But before she could unlock the door, a sharp footfall behind her made her turn around.

Beth wasn't at home when Carl, Emma, and Father McAllen arrived there.

"Where could she have gone? We just got home."

"The store, maybe," Father McAllen offered.

"Yeah, she might." Carl didn't want to leave, yet it was important that he and Father McAllen get Emma somewhere safe. He took out his notebook and scribbled a note telling Beth to meet him at Sally's as soon as she came home. He stuck it in the door so Beth couldn't miss it. He left reluctantly, feeling he should search for her, instead. "I'm getting paranoid," he said.

"Well, you're not alone," Father McAllen replied. "Let's get Emma over to Sally's. You can call Beth from there."

"Good idea." He was quiet all the way to Sally's, hoping that Beth was there, or had at least called.

But she wasn't. Sally controlled her impulse to ask a million questions. She welcomed Emma and urged the men to leave. Carl called Beth and grew more nervous when the phone rang for several minutes. When they were alone, Emma turned to Sally.

"Come, let's sit down. I have a lot to tell you, Sally, and none of it is pleasant."

When Carl and Father McAllen returned to Joe's office, Carl was annoyed to find Phil Greggory there. Phil's look at Father McAllen was, to say the least, insulting.

"Do you personally escort your suspects to Joe's office to be interrogated, or is this some special treatment of one Catholic by another?" Phil said to Carl.

"I'm afraid, Phil, old boy, that Father McAllen is no longer a suspect. You owe him an apology. If you'd care to say anything else insulting, I'd be happy to be a witness in a slander suit." Carl's voice was quiet, cool, and taunting. Phil knew when to back down.

"So he's cleared. Just how did you pull that off?"

"By finding the one who's guilty," Carl said innocently. "Isn't that what Joe's running this office for? The newspapers will be more than happy with him."

Phil's attitude changed abruptly. News coverage was what he wanted. "Who did it?"

"We can't jeopardize the case yet," Joe inserted. "When we get the loose ends tied up, the report will be on your desk, about the same time I release the news to the papers. I'll be sure to remember to have them spell your name right—at least, I hope I will."

"I should be doing that!"

"Not this time. We don't have anything to give you yet. Once the arrest is made, we'll let you know. Right now, any premature news will scare our killer off," Carl stated firmly. "So, for once, you'll have to keep your mouth shut. Then, when you do talk, it will have to be to congratulate Joe on a job well done. Practice a while. I'm sure you can do it if you try."

Phil's face was livid with helpless anger. "When this is over, I want you out of this town."

"Ah, Phil," Carl said, exultantly, "I'm afraid that's another bitter little pill you're going to have to swallow. You see, Joe's offered me my old job, and I've decided to come back to Helton and take it."

"I'll kill you in the papers," Phil stated.

"After the people of Helton read all the praise I'm going to give him for helping to solve this case," Joe said, "I don't think you'll be able to do him any harm. Not again, Phil—never again."

Phil looked from Joe to Carl and realized he was facing a united wall. He slammed out of the office.

* CHAPTER 38 *

Joe was hesitant to discuss much in front of Father McAllen, until Carl made it clear just how much help he might be.

"I've had some feedback on Paul," Joe said. "He made enough of a splash Saturday night that a whole lot of people remember him. He left his trail in a dozen bars over the evening."

"Then that ties it. We have our guy. Now, how do we prove it, and how do we stop him?" Carl asked.

Before Joe could answer, the door opened and Briggs stuck his head inside.

"We got a report from those boys in the woods. Someone did drive in on the old road. It was so covered over it took a long time to find. We also have a cast of the car tires. We found one good print of that and one footprint nearby. All we have to do is match 'em to the car and the driver."

"Does that give us enough to pick him up on?" Carl asked quickly.

"No. Anybody could have driven in and parked there. When we were kids, we did a lot of parking in those woods, too. It doesn't put him at the scene of the crime."

"Dammit! What do we have to do—catch him standing over a body, for God's sake?" Carl snapped a look at Father McAllen. "Sorry."

"Don't worry about it. I'm as frustrated as you, and probably just as scared. Besides, I've said and heard worse." Dismal amusement twitched Father McAllen's lips.

"Can we set him up somehow?" Carl asked thoughtfully.

"You talking entrapment?" Joe asked dryly. "The law's getting hard to deal with on that method."

"Well, let's go over and match that cast to his car, anyway, and the footprint, too. If we don't do anything else, we might scare the hell out of him," Carl responded irritably.

"I wish it were possible to do that," Father McAllen said.

"Do what?" Carl asked.

"Scare the hell out of someone. I'd make a crusade of it."

Joe looked at his watch. "It's after six; I'd better call Sal. Then we can go on over. David should have gotten back to Emma's by now."

"Since she's always there to cook his meals, he might get spooked when he finds she's gone. He's not working on all cylinders."

"Joe, find out if Sal has heard anything from Beth."

"What's bothering you, Carl?"

"I don't know. Maybe it's just nerves. I'd like to know she's there."

"Okay."

Joe dialed and Sally answered, but he shook his head at Carl, who watched him with a worried frown. Where the hell was Beth? Some instinctive thing drew his nerves taut. Father McAllen interrupted his thoughts.

"You will give me a chance to talk to him?" Father McAllen was quick to ask.

"I'm not going to guarantee that, Father. There's no telling what he might do. I'm not going to take the chance he might just go off like a rocket," Joe replied.

"Let's take it easy," Carl suggested. "Maybe if the three of us just sort of drop in and talk to him, we might catch him off guard enough that Father McAllen can get to him."

"Carl, if something goes wrong, Phil will have a field day. My head's on the block, too."

"David and I have been very close," Father McAllen offered. "As Carl says, part of this may have involved his feelings toward me. I might be able to keep him calm and talk to him. I don't want to see him hurt any more than he's already been."

"I can't take that chance. I'm sorry, but we go, and we

take a black-and-white backup. We'll check the tire and the footprints. If either one of them matches—well, we'll try to take him easy and peaceful, but we won't jeopardize another life."

Father McAllen felt helpless as Joe called for a black-and-white escort and a man to bring the cast material. He followed Joe and Carl out reluctantly.

David felt as if he were moving in a world of hazy contentment. He had been thinking about Ellen all day. Now he knew why the pain and the prodding ugly voice had come back. He had failed, and the voice behind the wielded belt wouldn't forgive him. How could he be free if he didn't fulfill his destiny; if he didn't do as the voice commanded?

He had fallen in love with Ellen, and that was wrong—he knew now it was wrong. He was forbidden love; the voice assured him of that. He had a vocation, a dedication to God, and Ellen had drawn him from the path.

He had desired her, had wanted to be with her more than he wanted to be obedient to the voice that controlled his life. But now he knew he was wrong. She had been a bad influence; she had been evil in wanting him to be with her. He remembered with revulsion the scent of her perfume and the feel of her in his arms.

He had tried to lead her away from the evil, but she had insisted in making herself look like a whore, with her short dresses and her painted lips. But it was all right now. The voice assured him that once he had punished Ellen, everything would be all right. He could redeem himself, and the pain would go away. He would be assured again by the voice that he was acceptable.

He stopped his car in Emma's drive and unlocked the front door, feeling a tingle of surprise that it was locked and Emma wasn't home.

He stood in the hallway and tried to understand why he felt uncomfortable with the fact that the scent of food didn't come to him and that Emma hadn't greeted him at the door, as she should have.

He took the stairs two at a time and reached his bedroom—his sanctuary. He unlocked the door, stepped in, and closed it behind him. He walked across the room and knelt before the crucifix. He folded his hands before him and waited for the voice to come, as it always did. He had to be assured he was right—and he was. He felt the first blow, heard the taunting voice telling him of his unworthiness—unless he could rid his town of the evil that walked in it. After all, one day he would be their spiritual leader. He must do what needed to be done.

He finished his devotion and went to his beloved book to find the words he would leave this time. He wrote the message and put it in his pocket. Now he was ready for his drive to Ellen's house.

Ellen Knight arrived home from work a little earlier than usual. She was tired and not quite hungry enough for dinner, so she took a warm shower and slipped on a pair of comfortable old jeans and a sweatshirt.

She carried a drink into the living room and curled up on the couch with a book she had been reading for the past week. After a while, she had to reach behind her and snap on a light.

She was so involved in the story, she was taken by surprise when she heard the knock on the door. She was even more surprised when she saw David.

There was no doubt about it. David Mondale was one of the handsomest men in Helton. He had the tanned beach-lover's body, and his blond hair and blue eyes were striking. He smiled now—the smile of a billboard model. Ellen had been more than fond of him, and his presence was magnetic. He was the kind of man most girls dream about but seldom run across. Still, their relationship had been shaky, and she had broken it off once. He made her feel off balance and insecure.

"David, what are you doing here?"

"I just wanted to talk to you."

"Don't you think it's a little late for talk?"

"I hope you don't mean that. I've been giving our relationship a whole lot of thought, and I realize how wrong I was."

"I don't see much use in us discussing who was right or wrong."

"I'm sorry about how it ended between us. I hate to have to finish like that. I thought we could at least part friends."

"What do you have in mind?"

"Well, since you're dressed so charmingly in jeans, and I must say you look terrific, how about that pizza place out on the highway just before you get to Parma Woods?"

"I know the place. Andy's Pizza Palace."

"Yeah, that's the one. Why don't we have a pizza and just talk?"

Ellen was fascinated with what looked like an extreme change in David. She could see interest and enthusiasm in his eyes, where before, she had seen a kind of cold contempt.

"You've changed a lot," she murmured, then grew quiet as if it were a thought she hadn't meant to verbalize. David's face grew contrite, and he ducked his head. He looked up at her again with eyes that seemed sad.

"I lost you. That made a whole lot of difference in my life. Maybe I got a good look at what I should have done. I'm sorry it ended between us the way it did. Really, I'm sorry it ended at all. I'd like to have a chance to at least make up for some of the problems I caused. A pizza and a drink isn't a whole lot to ask, is it . . . for old times' sake?"

He was persuasive and charming, and Ellen could feel herself wavering.

"I don't know. I'd have to change and . . ."

"No. You've never looked better. Snug jeans were meant for a girl as trim and pretty as you are." His grin was catching and brought a responsive smile from her.

"David, I want you to understand. I . . ."

"I know," he interrupted gently. "This needn't mean anything except casual conversation. I understand that. I can just hope that by the time this evening is over, you will feel differently."

Ellen hesitated. She wanted to go, and yet some instinct she would never understand made her decision for her.

"No. I don't think I can—not tonight. Call me sometime next week."

"Ellen, please . . ."

"No, really. I just don't want to go out tonight."

"You're not still angry?"

"I never was angry."

He was hesitant, but surprised her again by showing no sign of anger. "All right, I'll call you, okay?"

"Yes, all right." She felt distinct relief when she finally closed the door between them. She walked to the window and drew the curtain aside to watch him walk away.

Ellen had always considered herself lucky to have found her nice little apartment. It was in a quiet part of town, directly across the street from the library.

When David appeared on the sidewalk in front of her apartment, his attention seemed to be concentrated on the library. Ellen followed his gaze and saw Beth Raleigh come out and walk around the building. A few minutes later she saw David cross the street and go down the alley between the library and the building next to it. She was unaware that Beth and David knew each other so she thought little of it. She dropped the curtain and returned to her book.

"There's no sign of him here," Joe stated. "Either he hasn't come home yet, or he's come and gone." They stood before Emma's house.

"Yeah, but gone where?" Carl added.

"Don't anybody walk on that drive until you check for tire prints," Joe shouted. The four blue-clad officers moved around the edge of the drive, one of them carrying the white plaster cast of the tire treads from the murder scene. They moved slowly, inch by inch, until one of them called out.

"Over here, there's about six or seven inches of track."

They moved to his side, and all hovered near as the officer carrying the cast knelt down to lay it beside the track on the drive. There was no doubt that they were a perfect match.

"What's the next step, Joe?" Father McAllen asked. He was a little breathless at the confirmation that David was indeed the one they were after.

"Maybe you can tell me why he isn't home. Does he have a lot of things to do after school?"

"He has football practice, but even that should be over by now. He should have been home by this time."

"We've got to go into the house and check to see if there's any sign of his having been here . . . or why he decided to leave," Carl said.

"I don't have a search warrant," Joe said quickly. "I can't do a thing about that."

"Well, I can," Father McAllen said firmly.

"Father, you can't break that door down," Joe protested.

"I don't need to." He grinned. "I have a key."

"A key! How'd you get a key?"

"Emma used to let me use her living room for meetings before the new school was built. After that, I tried to give it back and she told me to keep it. She said I might need it again. I guess this falls in thc category of need."

"It sure does," Carl agreed. Reluctantly, Joe followed them back up on the porch and stood while Father McAllen unlocked the door.

Father McAllen was the first to recognize the briefcase David always carried back and forth to school. It sat just inside the front door.

"He's been here and gone," he said. He was filled with foreboding. "The only thing is, how long has he been gone? And where did hc go?"

"You mean," Joe added softly, "just whom has he chosen for his next victim?"

"There's no way to tell," Father McAllen said.

"No—no way," Joe replied. "Let me make a couple of phone calls from here."

"To whom?" Carl looked at Joe sharply.

"If he has some suspicion, he might try to hit either at one of us, or at someone connected to him."

"Like Ellen Knight," Carl said quickly.

"Ellen!" Joe said quickly. "I'd forgotten about her. She was pretty close to him."

"Close enough that I thought they might get serious one day," Father McAllen replied. "But I can see now that would have been an impossibility."

"It's impossible, all right. He doesn't mean their relationship to be anything but fatal. We've got to get to her. Ellen is David's next intended victim. I would stake my life on it," Carl said.

"Then, let's get the hell over there. Maybe we can stop him before he gets to her," Joe replied.

Joe drove and Father McAllen sat in the back, amazed that the car kept to the road at all. Carl would have laughed if he hadn't been so scared that even with all the speed they had, they might not make it in time.

They pushed the button on the elevator in the lobby. "What floor is she on?" Carl asked.

"The third," Father McAllen said quickly.

They didn't speak again until the elevator door opened. They rushed to Ellen's door to knock and wait in the hope they had moved in time. They breathed a sigh of relief when Ellen opened the door. She was taken completely by surprise.

"Father McAllen! What . . . ?"

"Has David Mondale called you?" Joe asked quickly.

"No, he didn't call me. He . . ."

"Great," Joe said in relief. "If he does, find out exactly where he is. Oh, can we come in for a minute?"

"Well, of course, you're welcome to come in, but I'm sure David won't be calling me again. He's already been here. What's wrong?"

"Been here?" Father McAllen said blankly.

"Yes, he wanted me to go out with him, but I just didn't feel like going."

"Well, Ellen," Carl said gently, "you might just have saved your life."

Ellen's face grew pale. "You mean . . . David?"

"Is sick, Ellen—sick," Father McAllen said.

"He's killed all those girls? God, I can't believe it. Martha, Paula, Leslie? It's . . . oh my God!"

"What?" Carl grated the question, but one look at Ellen's white face, and again his instincts rose.

"I watched him when he left here. He stood on the sidewalk for a while, just looking across the street at the library."

Carl's heart began to pound and he could feel his hands begin to sweat. "The library?"

"Yes. I watched Beth come out and walk around to the back." Her eyes rose to Carl's. "David followed her."

"Jesus." Carl could hardly breathe. A wave of well-remembered blackness rolled over him like a tidal wave. "Beth! The son of a bitch has Beth!"

"We don't know. Let's get to the parking lot," Joe said quickly. He had seen the same look in Carl's eyes once before, and the thought terrified him.

They rushed from her apartment, leaving Ellen, distraught, behind them. Disregarding the elevator, they raced down the stairs, taking two to three at a time. Carl crossed the street at a dead run, ignoring the blasting horns and screeching brakes.

He reached the car first. His heart was pounding and his breath coming in ragged gasps. He wanted to scream out his fury and cry at the same time. Beth's car sat before him . . . unoccupied.

The old terror burned in him. Could it happen again? Could he see the death of someone he loved again? No! He couldn't! Again the fear coursed through his blood, blinded his eyes, and left him shaking. The urge to kill rose up until it was a bitter taste in his mouth.

Joe walked over to take a quick look inside the car, but nobody doubted it was empty. Father McAllen stood close to Carl, knowing he was in the grip of something that was rapidly getting out of control.

Joe turned to look at Carl. He, too, could see something building—something he had seen before. "We know where they are. Let's go."

Carl started to move away, and Joe and Father McAllen had to run to keep up with him. "Carl . . ."

"This is no time for words," Carl said in a voice much too quiet to please either of them. They exchanged a look that shared the same worry.

But Carl couldn't be reached by looks or words. Only one thought dominated his mind—Beth, and his need to find her. For this moment he held the rage at bay. But if Beth had been hurt . . . .

* CHAPTER 39 *

Joe was calling for help as they drove. He replaced the mike, very aware of Carl's stony silence. He knew where Carl's mind was, and it scared him.

Carl seethed like a volcano. The old guilts prodded him with barbs of steel. He had been the reason Sara had died, and now he had walked into another woman's life and maybe cost hers. He loved Beth so much it hurt. In defense, the anger began to create a shield. If David had hurt Beth, then he didn't deserve to live. He needed to be killed, like a rabid animal. The thoughts churned. He could feel Father McAllen's eyes on him and Joe's worried glances, just as he could feel the gun he wore.

"He's sure to go to the same place, isn't he?" Father McAllen asked.

"There's no doubt," Joe answered.

Carl was silent.

"God, what pushed him over the edge?" Joe asked half to himself.

"Well, from what little bit of psychology I've had and what you tell me Professor Reuger thinks, I'd say that when David found himself falling in love with Ellen, that was when he went over the edge. In the state of confusion his mind must be in, he couldn't acknowledge loving someone—or, perhaps, having someone love him, as I'm sure Ellen was trying to do. If he felt some distorted religious responsibility, he twisted it to fit his insanity. His having been in the seminary, then working with me, somehow allowed his fantasy to go on existing," Father McAllen explained.

"You mean he kills because he feels he has a right to?"

Carl's voice sounded dead. "As if he's the final judge and jury?"

"That's pretty much it," Father McAllen replied reluctantly, "and it's one of the reasons I feel I might be the one to reach him."

"And if you break his little balloon, Father?" Carl said. "I don't think you'd be very safe. He'd turn on you. I'm afraid the only thing we can do is try to corner him and take him—no matter what."

"You mean if you have to kill him," Father McAllen protested. "That should be our last move!"

"And if it means another life, what do you want us to do—wait until he kills her, then try and talk to him?" Carl said angrily. "After what he's done, he doesn't deserve so much gentle-handed consideration. And if he hurts Beth . . ."

"He's not an animal!"

"He's not?" Carl said grimly. "You go and tell that to the families of the girls he killed. Tell them he needs gentle, loving care. Somehow, I think you'll get an argument, and don't even try to tell it to me."

"Carl, I didn't mean to sound unsympathetic to them. God knows they've suffered, but he's suffered, too."

"My heart bleeds for him," Carl said quietly. "What he needs is to be put out of circulation before he can do any more harm. If we can't wipe him out because it's not civilized, we should lock him in a room and throw away the key."

"Carl," Joe said in a quiet voice filled with warning, "whatever we do here, we do for everyone's good—including David's. Let's not make a mistake that's going to cost a hell of a lot more than it's worth."

A silence fell that was filled with meaning for both Father McAllen and Carl. For Father McAllen it held the recognition of the simmering violence in Carl.

Carl's silence was filled with the realization that David could die before his eyes and he would have little pity. He wanted David to suffer. A side of him he thought had erupted as the result of one personal tragedy was growing dominant again. For the first time, he looked his capacity for violence in the face and saw it stripped bare. He didn't like what he saw, but he knew he had a very fragile hold on it.

Joe remained silent. He didn't want to reopen any old wounds for Carl, but he knew if Carl couldn't harness his brutal side, it was going to lead to the kind of confrontation that had been his ruin before. With a twinge of worry, Joe felt that this might be the circumstance where Carl would have to prove just how far he had come since Sara died.

Beth struggled with the fear that was beginning to blossom within her. She could hardly keep her eyes from the glitter of the silver blade of the knife that lay across David's lap as she drove. She had never tasted such terror in her life.

David's voice was gentle, as if he were explaining something difficult to a child. "You see, I have so much I must explain to you. You must understand why I have to do this."

The quiver of fear bubbled into real terror as the impact of his casual revelation of intent struck her. But Beth was a courageous woman, not given easily to panic. She would not let him see how truly frightened she was. Her mind began to search wildly for some avenue of escape. They had driven down a road that hardly seemed to be there. The car was parked now and moonlight cast an eerie, pale, white-blue glow about them. There was no way to protect herself in the car, so she knew she would have to get out of it to have a chance. She thought of Carl, and unwanted tears filled her eyes, but she wanted him so badly she couldn't break now. She was afraid as much for Carl as for herself.

She knew what she might face, but she would fight to the end. David was the one who knew this road; David was the one who had been here before; and David was the one who had killed. There was no doubt in her mind of the mentality she was dealing with. She was scared, but she knew if she gave way to her panic, she might not see tomorrow.

"David," she said calmly, "I know you feel as if I have done something wrong. If you're angry with me, why don't you explain to me what you feel I've done? Maybe I can change—if it would make you happy."

David was taken off guard. He had expected her to realize he was the guardian. He had expected her to be afraid, to cry, and to beg him for mercy, as all the others had done. He had expected to have to explain why he could not spare her, but he had not expected this.

"But you must understand. You must," he insisted.

"I don't."

"You are evil; you are a trap." His voice was disbelieving.

"Have I trapped you, David?" she asked softly.

"No! No! You couldn't trap me. I can see the evil, you know." His voice now was almost childish. "I've been called. I had a vocation, and you tried to turn me from it. She told me about you; she told me you were trying to stop me. She warned me."

"Who told you about me?"

If she could keep him talking, keep his mind off her movements, maybe she could find a way. She steeled herself to try.

David's mind struggled in a panic. She had no business to ask about . . . he didn't know who. He couldn't name the voice; that would be like insulting God. The voice was the messenger of God. He wasn't allowed to question it. He would be punished terribly if he did. His hands would be pressed against the hot stove. He would feel the clammy, probing hands stroke and fondle his body, and worst of all, he would feel the stinging cut of the leather strap across his bare back. No! No! He couldn't name the voice. He could only obey it blindly and perfectly. He could only destroy what the voice said was evil. He turned to look at Beth.

"You just refuse to understand," he complained. "I'm not to blame for those who need punishment."

"Who is to blame?" She could feel the perspiration on her brow and the clammy wetness on her hands.

"You are," he said, surprised that she didn't realize this. "You're like the others—like Ellen. She made me desire her; that was wrong. She made me want her more than I wanted to listen to the voice, and that was wrong. I wanted to kiss her and to see her naked. I wanted to make her body belong to me, and it was wrong! Wrong! So I had to kill her. But she wouldn't go away, and I had to kill her again and again. The voice told me how bad I was, and that I was going to be punished again if I didn't kill you. You see, you're to blame." He reached out to touch her arm.

Charlie's voice was so urgent on the radio that Brady was surprised. He picked up the mike quickly.

"What the hell's going on, Charlie?"

"Our killer's grabbed a girl. He's got her down in the woods, or at least Joe thinks so."

"How'd he get in? No one passed me."

Charlie explained about the old highway. "Joe, Carl, and the priest are going down the old road, quiet and no lights. They want you to do the same here. Joe wants to close in on him carefully, so if he hasn't hurt her, maybe we can drop him before he does."

"Who is it, Charlie?"

"David Mondale."

"David! Jesus! I don't believe it."

"Well, it's true. Joe wouldn't be hot on his heels if it wasn't. You better move slow and easy, and if you spot him, better play it cool until Joe gets a chance to move in."

"That guy's been teaching my kids! Training my boy in football!"

"He's as nutty as a fruitcake and as deadly as a rattlesnake, so move easy. I'm going to get Andrews and Tyler on the move."

Brady agreed and broke the communication, but his jaw was clenched in a scowl, and his eyes were intent as he slipped his car in gear and moved slowly and quietly down the dirt road.

Joe moved down the highway at a frustrating snail's pace. It was a difficult thing to find the road, which was overgrown and had been forgotten for years.

"Dammit, it's got to be right here."

"It is," Carl agreed. "It has to be." He held a flashlight on the berm of the road, watching for the telltale cutoff. "There! There it is, Joe! Douse those lights."

Joe snapped the lights off and turned in to what looked like brush and overgrowth. Unsure of where he was going, he moved slowly. They had no idea at what moment they were going to overtake David, and they didn't want to precipitate any action on his part. Foot by foot they moved forward. Then they saw the outline of a car about fifty feet ahead of them. Joe stopped his car. No sound came from the one ahead of them, and their hearts were in their mouths as they soundlessly slid out. They drew their guns and began to inch forward.

No sound came from the car ahead of them. Not a twig snapped underfoot, and they held their breaths as they moved close enough to make the car out clearly.

Carl's heart was pounding. He was the only one who was certain now that they just might be too late—that maybe the car ahead of them held the body of another victim. The ancient rage began to fill him. If Beth were dead, he thought, nothing would stop him from running David down. Carl's mouth was dry, his hands shook, and the violence bubbled inside him. Beth was everything to him. He couldn't lose her! He couldn't. What would be left? Ashes and emptiness. He'd never be able to face it again.

If Carl was anxious and nervous, Joe was even worse. He saw Carl remove his gun from its holster. He heard the hammer being clicked back, and he felt the same fear hit him. This was the first moment he wished Carl weren't here at all. If he were to make one misstep, if he were to kill, even someone as demented as David was, then there would be no place for Carl to run to avoid Phil's revenge.

Father McAllen had never been involved in anything like this before. He prayed, silently and fervently, and he wasn't sure for whom he prayed the hardest. Beth was uppermost in his mind. The terror of her situation took his breath away. To him the car looked ominously silent. They moved to within a few feet of it before Joe silently held his hand up. They all remained motionless, then Carl and Father McAllen moved to Joe's side.

"I can't tell if they're inside," Joe whispered. "I'd sure as hell like to know if she's all right before I move in."

"You think the boys are pretty close?" Carl asked.

"They should be."

"Then there's only one way to find out," Carl whispered. Before Joe could protest, Carl crept toward the car.

Carl reached the back of the car without incident, which worried him even more. He made a decision quickly and moved to the passenger side of the car first. He had to see Beth, to know she was alive. If he could surprise them, he might just be lucky enough to get her to safety.

He was crouched low as he came around the back of the car, then his breath caught in his throat. The inside of the car was dark and he couldn't see anything.

He cursed under his breath and slowly stood erect, assuring himself he was right. No one was in the car at all. He turned and motioned to Joe and Father McAllen, who moved toward him a little more rapidly. Fear and a certainty that what they were to view would be terrible made them move more quickly.

When the two stopped by Carl, they could see the car was empty. There was no sound from the woods around them. Joe bent his head close to Carl.

"Where the hell do you think he's dragged her off to?"

"Got to be where we found the others," Carl responded quickly. "There's no sense in being quiet anymore. We've got to move fast. I had some hope when we thought they were in the car, but now I'm not so sure. Let's cover some ground."

* CHAPTER 40 *

Beth felt each breath would be her last. She had opened a door in David's mind, and he seemed lost to all but that. She knew the distance between her and any kind of help was too great for even a scream to be heard. She had to get out of the car. It was the only chance.

When David had touched her arm she had felt a live terror such as she never had felt before. She wanted to scream and fling herself from the car, but she was clever enough to know she wouldn't make it. He hadn't tried to harm her, not yet. He seemed to feel he had to convince her of his reasons before he could finish what he had started to do.

"If you had only changed your ways, I might not have had to do this, but it's too late for you. I'm afraid I must be very firm with you."

Her hand had reached the doorknob, and she gently pressed down, feeling the door on the verge of opening. She moved her foot nearer the door and braced her body in preparation. She knew she would only have one chance; if she failed, there would never be another.

David appeared to be listening, his head tipped slightly to the side. Then his body gave a slight jerk, as if he had been struck. She had the eerie feeling that some presence existed in the car outside of her and David. It was a strong, threatening presence, and she could actually taste a kind of agony. It was the moment she needed, for David did not seem to be aware of her at the moment.

She shoved the door with all her strength and rolled away from David, falling from the car so hard it nearly struck the breath from her. Quickly, she was on her feet and running. She had only gone a few feet when she was grabbed from behind. A hand closed over her mouth and an arm that felt like iron lifted her from her feet as if she were a rag doll.

She thrashed wildly, all bravery gone in the face of self-protection, but she might have been a child, for all the effect it had. He said nothing more, but instead of returning to the car as she thought he would, he dragged her deeper into the woods.

He was cutting off her air by holding his hand over her nose and mouth at the same time. She could feel herself growing dizzy, and star-studded blackness swirled before her eyes. Her body was growing weaker and the thrashing less and less as he continued to drag her on and on.

She wanted to cry, and couldn't even find the strength for that. For a moment, the blackness claimed her, and David carried her to the spot that he had so carefully chosen such a long time before. Here he dropped her to the ground and the solid meeting of ground and body brought her almost to the surface of consciousness.

She blinked her eyes open to find herself braced against a tree and David kneeling before her, his face inches from hers.

Pale moonlight washed down through the branches of leafless trees and reflected in the madness in his eyes. Gone was the laughing, handsome man. In his place was a huge presence that wore the grotesque mask of insanity.

"Do not scream." The voice was hoarse and full of threat. "If you do, you will not have time to ask forgiveness, or to pray."

"Oh, God," she whimpered as she pressed back against the rough bark of the tree. "Please, David—please let me go."

"But I told you." He laughed a boy's laugh. "I can't do that. She knows you're here, and she knows I must punish you. I have to."

"No," Beth sobbed. "Please, no. David, I never hurt you. I always liked you."

She had said the wrong thing at the wrong time. David's body gave the same slight, traumatic jerk, and he choked out a sound that could have been mistaken as a cry of pain.

"But I'm not allowed to be loved. No one will love me if I become part of something evil. I must keep myself pure if I am to be guardian and protector. Now, you must confess your sins to me."

"No, David—don't," she sobbed.

"You are not obedient." His voice was chiding, as if he were teasing a child. "Not like the others. It took so little time with them, but they knew how evil they were, and they confessed. You must learn to be obedient." The voice grew gentle. The blow came from nowhere as his open hand caught her across the cheek, slamming her head back against the tree and stunning her.

She began to cry.

"The others cried, too—especially Martha. She begged and cried about her baby, but the baby would have been evil, too, so you see why I had to destroy them both. She would have corrupted it with her loose morals and vulgar ways. In the end, she confessed her sins, as you will." He struck her again, and she could taste the blood in her mouth.

"The others were stronger than you. They fought. Why don't you . . ." He didn't finish the words as she kicked out wildly, catching him in the stomach. He fell backwards, but escape was not so easy. She was dizzy and weak, and as she tried to roll away, he caught her and dragged her upright against him. His huge hand was about her throat, cutting off her air. The trees spun about her, and she began to sag against him.

David was prepared to squeeze the final breath of life from her when a familiar voice almost paralyzed him.

Carl, Joe, and Father McAllen moved quickly now, their eyes beginning to get used to the surroundings, and it was only a few minutes after they found the car that they saw the huge form ahead of them half-carrying, half-dragging Beth.

"Good God, the way he has hold of her, he could break her neck before we get to them," Joe whispered.

"You're right, he could," Father McAllen affirmed. "He has immense strength."

"He can be strong as an ox, but he can't stop a bullet," Carl supplied in a voice that made Joe go cold.

"You don't have a clear shot. What if you miss him and hit her?" Joe said angrily.

"We've got to get her away from him," Father McAllen whispered, "and I'm the only one who can do that."

"How do you figure that?" Carl protested.

"Because I play some kind of part in his mind. I'll be stumbling in the dark, but it's better than trying to shoot him and making a mistake."

"Get her a little away from him, and I won't make a mistake."

"Carl!" Joe had reached the end of his rope. He knew it was because Carl was scared for Beth's safety, and that he was seeing Sara in Beth's place, but he couldn't let him do it. "If there's any shooting to be done, I'll do it."

"Still protecting my backside?"

"You'd be fed to the wolves this time and nobody would be able to do anything about it."

"He's dropping her and kneeling down beside her. Let me get closer," Father McAllen said quickly. "If I can get him to leave her side for an instant, you two move in."

"What if he's armed by more than his strength?" Joe asked. "He might just kill you, too."

"There's less chance of that than there is that he would kill one of you. Look, when I get his attention, maybe one of you can circle around to the others. Everyone has flashlights. If I get his attention from her, hit him with all your lights. It will confuse him."

"You hope," Carl snapped. He started toward the two forms with a low, primitive growl from deep in his throat. He'd seen David hit Beth.

Joe gave Carl a push. "You get around behind him and see if you can find Brady or Andrews and Tyler. When Father McAllen gets his attention, hit the lights."

"Joe . . ."

"Carl, this is my job. I asked for your help, but in this case, you follow my orders, or I'll have you dragged back to the car and kept out of this."

Carl was quiet for a minute. Then he smiled grimly as he realized Joe meant exactly what he was saying.

"Okay, buddy, okay." He gave Joe a pat on the shoulder, then, despite his size, he was gone as silently as a ghost.

"You sound scared for him, Joe."

"I am," was all the reply Joe would give. "Okay, it's up to you. If you can, talk him out of there. But, Father, if he goes wild—if he tries to finish her—one of us is going to kill him, and at that point, I don't care which one it is. Is that understood?"

Father McAllen nodded and stood up, even though his knees were shaking and his stomach felt sick. He took a step or two toward David and Beth. He was an open target now as he moved into the small clearing.

"David, I've been trying to find you."

His voice was gentle, smooth as velvet, and it echoed from a distance into Beth's consciousness. She had felt David's hands tighten, had realized with finality that she was going to die here. Her fists had been doubled and she was fighting with her last breath when she heard the voice and felt the pressure about her throat ease until she could draw a gasping, ragged breath.

Carl had reached Brady's side and passed along Joe's orders—flashlights and no guns unless Father McAllen failed to get Beth away from him.

"That bastard's crazy, Carl," Brady said in an awed voice.

"Yes, he is." Carl's voice was calm, deadly calm. "He's completely crazy, and he'll snuff out her life as easy as look at her. So when Father McAllen gets a step or two closer, I want all your lights on them."

"Okay. Whatever you say. But I think Joe's making a mistake. That guy has already killed four. He's sure not going to hesitate to get Father, either, if he gets in his way."

"Maybe Father McAllen can crawl inside his head and get him to let Beth go. Right now, she's all that's important." Carl moved so he would be standing some distance away from the others. His plans didn't include their interference. He held his gun with his arm pressed close to his side. He knew he would do what he had to do. The old familiar rage was pounding in his head. He had let killers loose before, and they had killed Sara. He wasn't going to let it happen again. Beth and Sara blurred in his mind, and all he was left with was the need to stop Beth from being hurt—no matter what the cost. He owed it to Sara and to Beth to keep the past from being repeated. Blood throbbed through his veins and the hand that held the gun shook with the fierceness of his grip.

David's attention snapped from Beth to the voice that had called to him. Father McAllen took another step or two toward him. David let her slide down until she was kneeling at his feet. At first he seemed puzzled, then his smile turned almost beautiful.

"Father McAllen," he said in a pleasant, almost conversational voice. "You've come to help me."

"Yes, David, I've come to help you."

"I knew you would understand. You must have felt their

evil, too. Every time they came to you and touched you, you must have felt it as I did."

"I understand you, David," Father McAllen said quietly as he took another step or two. "And I've come to take care of everything." Father McAllen was praying David would not grasp the double meaning.

David stared at Father McAllen who could feel the sweat pop out on his brow. David stood motionless, and Father McAllen realized it was as if he were listening. There was a puzzled look on his face. At that moment, four high-intensity flashlights illuminated the scene.

Everything seemed frozen in time. Father McAllen stood immobile, watching with a pain deep within, while David still stood attentively engrossed in something only he heard.

Father McAllen took another small step or two toward David and froze again as David's eyes focused on him.

"Don't come over here." David's voice was eerie, with a singsong quality. "She'll contaminate you, too. I'm here to make sure none of them can do that. I've done my job well. She'll be pleased. She'll care for me. If I do what I must do, she'll care for me."

"Who's he talking about?" Joe whispered to Carl, as he came to Carl's side and knelt beside him again. He felt the need to be as close to Carl as possible.

"His aunt, I'd say," Carl said coldly. "I wish she were at his feet now. I'd walk away and let him do whatever he pleased. She's the one who deserves it, believe me."

The uncomfortable sensation that spread through the watching men grew in intensity as Father McAllen again took another step. "David, I want to help you, but first you must give the girl to me. Then we will talk, you and I, and we'll find the way."

"No!" David cried. He reached down and dragged Beth up beside him. "I have done my job well before; I can do it without your help. You go back, go away from here."

Father McAllen was frightened at the increase in David's instability. He didn't want to push him over the edge into an abyss that might cost Beth her life.

Carl and Joe motioned to the men with them and they drew the circle a little tighter.

But the move was one too many. David saw the lights waver with motion and knew there were others. He turned a snarling, rage-filled face to Father McAllen at the same time he reached into his pocket. At first none of them realized what he was doing, or envisioned that he might have a weapon. The past deaths had all been by strangulation. Then a blade clicked, and the light glistened along its silver edge as David grasped Beth by the head and placed the knife at her throat.

Father McAllen was paralyzed. If he even breathed too hard, David might pull the knife across Beth's throat and end her life before their eyes.

"No! David, please," Father McAllen begged. "No one is going to do anything. Don't hurt her."

"You don't really understand either, do you? All the things I've done for you, and you don't understand yet." David's voice was full of disbelief. "I thought you would know, but maybe you are not good either. Maybe you have allowed them to do as they have."

"David . . ."

"No, you go away! You betrayed me, and you would have me betray my destiny, wouldn't you? You go away, and make your friends go away, too." The voice had now become plaintive, like a child's. "I should have known it would not be easy to be what I must be, but I will succeed. Take your friends away." He made a threatening move with the knife that caused Father McAllen to suck in his breath and all the other watchers to hold theirs. "Go!" David cried, and his voice was enough to make Father McAllen back away into the shadows.

Beth had regained full consciousness and was fighting the terror that held her with all the strength she could muster. She could feel the cold chill of the blade against her throat, and the hand that held her seemed to have superhuman strength. She had never prayed so hard in her life or felt so desperate. She knew now that others were here, that help was near, but it might just as well have been a million miles away.

Carl, too, was reaching the end of his precarious hold on his self-control. He motioned to the men around him. "Turn off your lights, all at once—now," he ordered. Then he moved away from them and as close as he could get to David.

It suddenly went very dark and only moonlight caught David's tall, broad-shouldered form.

He knew he was just a shadowed form to David, and that's what he counted on. He moved to keep distance between him, Joe, and the others now. He was closer than anyone else. That also was what he had bargained on. A kind of quiet concentration held him.

"David." He said the words in a voice raised a few octaves—one that sounded masculine, with a brush of feminine texture. "David, boy, don't you recognize me? It's Uncle Robert, son. I've come to tell you that we're very displeased with you."

David gave a soft, whimpering sound, and Beth could feel something shudder through him. "No, no, no," he whispered. Only Beth heard the agony in his voice and felt his huge body shake. The knife moved away from her throat an inch or so.

"David," Carl said the name again like a sweet caress. "David, come here to me, boy. Come here, or I will be forced to be angry."

There was a gasping sob from David, and the knife lowered a little more.

Father McAllen felt a wave of nausea wash through him as he envisioned what David must have known and suffered to make him so crushed and vulnerable.

"Please, no," David whimpered pitifully, and even Joe, who had seen terrible things in his years of police work, felt the misery.

Carl could only keep his mind on Beth and pray he could carry this thing far enough to get her free.

"You have to come, David—you can't get away. You have to come here," Carl demanded in the falsetto voice.

"I've been good. I've tried to be a good boy," David whispered. "Don't hurt me. Don't do that to me again. You hurt me. Don't do that to me again, please, you hurt me."

"Aunt Caroline wants to see you, David, boy. She wants you now."

Beth felt David's hold loosen, but she was too frightened to move. She could feel his breath on her cheek, and the knife was still before her, about waist-high.

"Aunt Caroline . . . no, please." David was crying like a hurt little boy. "You were there every time, you saw, you knew. I've always done what you wanted. You can't hurt me again."

Beth moved slightly as his arm relaxed. Then she inched a step away. But David didn't seem to know she was there at all. He was shaking so badly now that the knife thudded softly to the leaf-strewn ground.

The moon chose that moment to appear full and bright from behind a bank of gray-white clouds. It was bright enough to lighten the entire area about them.

Beth took another step away at the same time that Father McAllen took a step toward her.

But the clouds moved and the moon's glow made Carl, who had been standing in shadow, suddenly illuminated.

David stood frozen as the broken pieces of his mind tried to pull together the fragments of reality. He staggered at the first surge. This was not the person he thought it had been. Then the entire curtain of fantasy was torn in two. He had failed, and the truth of his failure came with the recognition of the man he faced. Carl stood less than ten feet from him, his gun hanging in his hand.

All past hatreds, all the pain and agony, every moment of lost childhood bubbled up in a terror that was the culmination of it all. He was thrown back in time and stood helpless, a vulnerable and hurt little boy again.

Carl knew what he was going to do. His heart began to pound furiously. He wanted to kill David. He had lost the part of him that he had searched for for so long. But Beth's attention was on Carl, too, and slowly he raised the gun. Holding it steady with both hands, he took careful aim at David. At this range, he could hardly miss.

"No," Joe yelled, angry at himself for letting Carl put so

much distance between them. He could never reach Carl in time to keep him from pulling the trigger. "Carl . . ."

"Stay there, Joe," Carl said in an icy calmness that made Beth choke back a sob, "or I'll blow his head off."

David was confused, lost in a morass of insanity. It was Beth's cry of anguish that rent the air.

"No, Carl. Please, no!"

Carl's eyes moved to her for a second. He gritted his teeth and returned his intent gaze to David, who took one step toward him. Beth moved another step away from David, as if she were hoping to draw Carl's attention to her. David seemed now to be completely lost. He was the hurt child again. He was lost and alone in the dark world. The gun remained steady.

"Get out of the way, Beth."

"No. Oh, Carl, please. If you do this, what will be left for us?" She had never been so frightened. Tears blurred her eyes. She felt the heavy constriction in her throat. Her love for Carl was too deep, and she knew he had a fragile hold. If he killed David—the thought was beyond reason.

"He would have killed you! Just like . . ." Carl snarled.

She could feel Carl's anguish, and she knew he was being overwhelmed by the past. She had to stop him somehow before he was so lost in the past that he repeated it.

"I'm not Sara, and I won't let you do this. I love you, Carl. Don't destroy us."

Her voice echoed in his mind and reached into a black place to rip and tear until a ray of light entered. For the first time, he let his gaze move from David to Beth. "He would have killed you; he deserves to die."

"Not by your hand. I won't let you!"

David had sunk to his knees and begun to weep softly, like a child lost in the night. It would be so easy. All Carl had to do was take one step aside and pull the trigger. Joe had frozen, as had the others. Carl was too close, and they were too far from him. The gun could be used long before they could reach Carl. Joe could hear the love in Beth's voice and prayed as he had never prayed before that it was enough to draw Carl back from the edge.

Beth knew she could not reach him in time to stop him.

"Let us have a chance." He could hear the tears thick in her voice. His eyes struggled from David to her. In the white of the moonlight he could see her clearly. He felt the harsh wall of bitter anger beginning to crumble.

"I love you, Carl, and I won't let you destroy yourself. I care too much to let you face that hell again. When you kill him you kill us as well. What would we have left?"

Father McAllen had now come to stand beside David, who was still weeping quietly. It seemed he had been drained of thought.

"Will you remember, Carl," Beth asked softly, "how much I love you? Don't do this. For us, don't do this."

The gun trembled, then slowly lowered. After a minute it fell to the ground. With a soft cry, Beth ran to Carl and he gathered her into his arms, crushing her against him and whispering her name over and over against her hair.

Joe felt as if he hadn't been able to breathe for the last few minutes, but now it was over. Father McAllen was leading the childlike David away, and Carl and Beth stood locked in an embrace.

* EPILOGUE *

The shock of David Mondale's capture and subsequent commitment to an institution, accompanied by the release of the news that he had been responsible for the deaths of the four girls, reverberated through the town like ripples of a tidal wave. People whispered together first in deep shock, then in even deeper relief.

Michael Brodie found Emma to be a source of strength at a time when he felt as if his world was shattered. She shared silent moments, quiet meals, and helped him put together the pieces of his life. What emerged from the sullen, bitter person was a young man who faced the future with the first sign of promise.

Paul and Amy talked openly, not wanting any secrets to exist between them any longer. Paul was delighted that the tragedies seemed now to be drawing them closer together.

For Carl and Beth, it was also a time of drawing close together. Carl had made the choice, and was grateful to Beth for making him see what he would have lost. Todd had left town as abruptly as he had come.

Carl had faced the past, and Beth had insisted on facing it with him. They had returned to Carl's old home to find that the ghosts had been neatly swept away. He decided to put the house up for sale. They stood silently at Sara's grave, and that night, they made love with a renewed tenderness. Later, Carl talked for a long time, as if washing himself clean. Soon even the cobwebs of his mind were slowly dropping away. Carl found it almost impossible to believe.

Ten days after the conclusion of the case the entire group met for dinner. The restaurant was nearly empty except for the one table filled with people celebrating.

Father McAllen stood up and lifted his glass of wine, and the table grew silent. "Here's to beginnings," he said.

Carl smiled and raised his glass to touch Beth's lightly, and Eve, who sat next to Beth, couldn't have been more pleased.

Joe and Sally tapped their glasses together, too.

Emma, who sat at the foot of the oblong table, opposite Father McAllen and next to Michael, stood, raised her glass, and took a sip.

"Don't you think it's about time we had a few answers from you, Carl Forrester?"

"Why, Emma," Carl asked innocently, "to what do you need answers? You've always led me to believe you already had all of them."

There was laughter around the table. "Now, don't you get smart with me. It's been over a week since this terrible thing ended. Everybody here at this table is your friend, and everybody wants to know if you're going to stay with us."

"I'd say, after your confrontation with Phil, that Carl ought to stay just to go on making his life miserable." Paul laughed.

"Did you see his face when he found out everything? He had had such hopes that he could break Carl. He really wanted to do a lot of digging into the past at the same time," Joe added. Carl and Beth exchanged glances. Paul didn't know how close to breaking Carl had been.

"Joe, that was horrible," Sally said quickly. "He had no business trying to put Carl through that."

"It was the best thing that could have happened. Phil has finally gotten it through his head that he's not going to get any good headlines out of trying to railroad Carl."

"I guess it kind of surprised him when Father McAllen came to Carl's defense." Amy smiled. "He was furious, and his face grew a lovely shade of puce when the judge became annoyed at his charges and congratulated Joe on bringing an end to this nightmare."

"But all this doesn't give any of us the answers we want," Emma insisted. "Joe, have you offered Carl his job back?"

"With open arms, Emma, but he's as close-mouthed as a clam."

"So, Carl, give us some answers," Emma demanded.

"Speaking of answers, Michael." Carl dodged the question nimbly. "I'm really glad you could make it tonight."

Michael grinned. "You know this old broad. Do you think I had a chance in hell of saying no?" Everyone laughed. "Besides, I owe everyone some kind of thanks." His eyes caught Carl's. "I wouldn't have missed it," he added quietly.

"You've been a godsend to me, and I told him you all wanted him here. Michael is a changed man. He's gotten out of that self-pity routine and has started to look around to see who's in the world besides himself. I have a feeling he'll be fine," Emma stated.

"Now that everyone is talking about the future," Paul grinned as he reached to take Amy's hand, "Amy and I would like to take a minute to invite you all to our wedding—in two months, with Father McAllen officiating at St. Catherine's."

There was laughter and congratulations.

"Which," Emma added shrewdly, "brings us back to Carl and plans he hasn't talked about."

Carl stood and took his glass of wine in his hand. Everyone around the table grew expectantly silent. "I haven't talked over any of my plans with anyone because I wasn't sure just what Phil was going to get away with. I want to tell you all—my friends—that I'm grateful for your friendships. When we walked out of that courtroom today, I don't think I have ever felt such a sense of belonging in my life. I guess I knew then what I wanted to do. If Joe wants to give me a job, I'm coming home."

Joe laughed and raised his glass. "The job is yours, my friend. It's been waiting for you for three years."

"Thanks," Carl said quietly. Then he reached down and took Beth's hand and drew her up to stand beside him. She was surprised, but smiled and stood with him.

"I have put away a lot of things in the past. I thought I couldn't do it, and I was right." Beth's smile wavered and the table grew silent again. "I certainly couldn't have done that if I hadn't had someone like Beth to help."

He bent to kiss her lightly. Then they all stood to touch glasses and toast, as Father McAllen had said, to beginnings.